FATHER of mine

FATHER of mine

MIKE FLORIO

ALSO BY MIKE FLORIO

Playmakers
(PublicAffairs, 2022)

On Our Way Home
(coming late 2023)

30 America Avenue
(coming 2024)

Paperback: 979-8-9879440-1-1

Ebook: 979-8-9879440-0-4

TO BUTCH AND ALEX

One

NOVEMBER 22, 1963

JOHNNY MESAGNE

I NEVER SHOULD have had kids. I got one. Some guys who got none will add "that I know of," like they're trying to be funny, but sort of bragging. I would know if I had any other kids. I never, ever let my guard or my pants down for someone I didn't know. Every girl I ever slept with I saw again at some point in the next nine months. If any of them ever had a baby, I would have known.

One was still too many for me. I was a bad father. I just wasn't made for that life. For sleeping when everyone else sleeps, working when everyone else works. She tried to make me fit that way. I went with it for a long time. Longer than I should have. I'm not sure why I ever did.

Really, why did I even try? I didn't need to get married in order to have regular company. I did pretty well for myself. Handsome, in a hoodlum sort of way. Like Maria always said, I had high cheekbones and low scars. Just good-looking enough to get them interested. Just dangerous enough to get them a lot more than that. I looked like the evil twin of Elvis Presley, at a time when it was very good to look even a little bit like the King.

I guess I loved Maria, best as I ever understood the word. Maybe

I didn't understand it at all. Maybe I still don't. Love. I wasn't faithful. But we had a kid. That's what tied us together. Whether I loved her or not, I had an obligation to provide for him, and for her.

And I did. I absolutely did. The way it matters. He had what he needed. He grew up normal, or as normal as he could. Even after she found Jenkins, I still made sure that boy had enough. I didn't blame her for getting married again. I didn't blame her for letting my son take Jenkins's name. I was the one who couldn't live that way. I wasn't going to tell Maria she couldn't have a real life. I thought maybe she'd have more kids. It would have been good for Junior to have a brother or sister, even if them other kids wasn't mine.

I left home the night they shot Kennedy. Maria didn't seem to care that somebody killed the President. I got mad at her about it. She was confused why it bothered me so much. She said the guys in our thing hated him for trying to shut it all down. But his brother was the one who was making it harder for us. I never bought that they had Kennedy killed to get his brother to leave us alone. Why not just kill the brother?

Maria was making dinner. Sauce bubbling in one pot, pasta boiling in the other. My day was just getting started. That's the way it was. Work most of the night, sleep most of the day. I don't know whether Kennedy getting shot in the head made her think I would at some point get shot in the head, too. I know she always worried. She worried too damn much. I was the one who stood to get shot in the head or someplace else, and I wasn't half as worried as she was. I wasn't worried because I had no choice. That was the life. Someone once said it's the life we've chosen. I don't remember doing no choosing. If anything, that life chooses us. Draws us in like one of them giant round magnets they hook to a crane.

So she gets a little riled up, I get a little riled up. Next thing you know, she's throwing a big spoon at me, splattering cooked tomatoes all over one of my best white shirts. She goes in the bedroom and starts smoking cigarettes, one after another. Junior had to know what was going on. The house was too small, with two bedrooms right off the kitchen. He always did his homework on Friday nights so it would be done and he could enjoy the weekend. That was the kind of discipline I never had, and never will. And the kid was only ten.

She stayed in our room. She'd rip through two or three packs, like no one knew what she was doing. As if the smell didn't make its way to the rest of the house. I decided then and there to go, but my stuff was all in the bedroom.

I went down to the basement. I tried hard to not make noise. The old staircase creaked and groaned with every step. I found a different shirt down there. It smelled a little like the hamper. But it didn't have tomato sauce all over it, so that made it better than what I was wearing. I pulled off the dirty one and put the clean one on.

As I buttoned up the front, I saw the metal racks across from the washer. There were boxes and coffee cans and jars. I hadn't really noticed them in months, maybe a lot longer than that. I started looking through some of the stuff. I opened one of the boxes. It was full of old books. That strong smell of mildew made me close it up. Then I peeled a plastic lid from a round metal container. It had dozens of marbles inside. I put my hand in there. They were cool, almost cold. I liked how that felt.

I looked up and saw a shoe box on the top shelf. I recognized it. I pulled it down and lifted the lid. I felt my face get a little brighter. If I wasn't in such a bad mood, I probably would have smiled.

My birth certificate was on top of the stack. It showed a crease from where it had been folded in half at one point. It was flat and open. John Michael Mesagne. September 1, 1933. Seven pounds, seven ounces. Underneath it was the Western Union that said my father got killed in World War II. I was ten when we found out, same age as my son was on the night I was getting ready to go away. It actually made me feel a little better about what I was planning to do. I wouldn't be dead like my old man was, just not living at home. I still felt bad about it.

Not bad enough to change my mind about moving out of that house on Poplar Avenue.

I kept flipping through the box. Old gray photos, with white strips on the edges. Cufflinks I never wore, not even once. A watch with a battery that died the day after I got it. A report card from high school, before I dropped out. When I saw them grades, I remembered why I did. The paperwork showing the phony heart murmur that kept me from going to Korea, thank God. A tiny pair of baby shoes. It looked like they once was white, or close to it.

Something was jammed tight inside one of the shoes. I picked it up and looked at it. I had no idea where it come from or how I got it. I stuck it in my pocket. I put the lid back on the shoe box. I put the box back on the top shelf.

As I went up the steps, I started coming up with a story about the thing in my pocket.

Two

BOBBY MARRONI SAT in the front seat of a green Vega they'd picked up at the regular place. Paul made sure a car was always ready for something like this. And it was always a real piece of shit. Bobby tried not to move around. On that cheap vinyl, he knew it would have sounded just like he was shitting in his pants. He could have used the laugh. But Vinny was already too mad at him to think anything he did was funny at that point.

"How the fuck did you forget the silencers?" Vinny said it again, like the answer was going to be different the second time.

Bobby's hand shook a little bit as he pushed at the line of hair he combed every morning across the place where it wouldn't grow any more, which at that point was pretty much all over the top of his head. He'd been working with Vinny for a long time, but the guy still scared the hell out of him. He scared the hell out of everyone he knew. Bobby thought Vinny liked it that way. Bobby knew Paul did.

"What was I supposed to do?" Bobby said. "The phone rang. I answered it. He said go right now. We went right now."

"Well, you had time to grab the silencers, because he's still in there," Vinny said. He gestured with his chin. His nose was missing a chunk at the tip. Cancer or something. He didn't seem to be bothered by it, unless somebody pointed it out. Bobby only ever made that mistake twice. Once while sober.

Bobby blurted out the first thing he thought of.

"Do you see him?"

"I see the car that brung him." Vinny said each word slowly, making the point that it was a stupid question.

Bobby knew he should have just kept his mouth shut.

"Are we sure this is what we're supposed to be doing?"

Vinny's eyes narrowed. The bags under them looked like they were about to bust open. Nothing good ever came after he made that look.

"Don't you think it's a little too late for that?" Vinny said. "Besides, you took the call. Remember? It happened right before you didn't grab the silencers. I always thought them dogs was fucking with your head. I sure hope they ain't fucking with your ears, too."

"Them dogs is fine." It came out stronger than Bobby wanted it to. He dialed it back a little. "And I know what he said. I just wonder whether this is the right thing to do."

"You had your chance to speak up. You're the one who set the thing up that went to shit in Ohio today. You should have said something then. You didn't."

"I didn't know what to say. I didn't know who to say it to."

"You was smart then," Vinny said. "You're being stupid now."

"Maybe I was stupid then and I'm being smart now."

"How long you been in this, Bobby?"

He started to try to do the math before he realized Vinny wasn't looking for an actual answer.

"I don't make those decisions," Vinny said. "You don't make those decisions. Somebody else makes those decisions. We do what we're told, when we're told, how we're told. And we don't ask no questions."

Bobby again should have just kept his mouth shut. But they didn't take out one of their own very often. Even then, it had to be a pretty big deal. And while Bobby still didn't know what went on in Ohio, this didn't seem big enough. Which started to make him a little nervous that the bar for getting yourself whacked by your own crew had been lowered. So he kept going, without thinking about what he was saying.

"I just don't understand this. I thought—"

"We don't think," Vinny said before Bobby could finish whatever his thought was going to be. "We just do. What the fuck's gotten into you all of a sudden?"

Bobby nodded. He made himself smile, like he'd finally figured it all out. He kept himself from messing with his combover. If Bobby was aware of his own nervous habit, Vinny knew about it, too. Bobby tried to think of something to say that would show he got the point.

"Do unto others before it gets done unto you," Bobby said. "I know how it goes." He should have stopped there, but he couldn't help himself. "I'm just tryin' to figure out why—"

"Stop it." The words came out like a snake hissing. "We don't try to figure out why. That's the point. It's not even something that enters your brain. This is like 'Simon Says.' Remember that one? We follow every single order we get. No exceptions."

Bobby understood it. He did. And Vinny was right. Up until that point, Bobby had gone along with the plan. But Bobby was on one hell of a roll. He decided to get technical about a game he hadn't played since he was a kid.

"Even in 'Simon Says,' you don't follow every single order you get," Bobby said.

That one did it.

"Every single order we get starts with Simon-fucking-says!" Vinny yelled.

Bobby looked outside the car to see if anyone heard Vinny. Vinny noticed, and quieted down.

"Don't be cute," Vinny said. "If you want to do this thing, you do this thing. Bobby, for Christ's sake, if I would have known you was going to pick tonight of all the possible fucking nights to start wondering why we do what we do and not just do it, I would have done it myself."

Bobby went back to thinking about why this was happening, a move against one of their own guys. Paul had said not to get rid of this one, to leave him right there on the sidewalk. That made it even stranger. Especially after how this mess had gotten started in the first place.

Shooting their guy right in front of the house where he used to live. There's a big difference between disappearing for good and having a family member find you there. Bobby thought of what his mother or his wife would do if something like that happened to him. He couldn't decide which one would be the first to spit on his corpse.

Bobby's eyes shifted toward the house as his mind continued to wander. The front door began to swing open.

"Vinny, look," Bobby said, sticking a quivering finger that way. "There he is."

Vinny squinted. Bobby always told him he needed glasses. Vinny was too stubborn to go get them.

"Way too much about this has already been fucked up," Vinny said. "If you fuck this one up any more, you'll be laying there right next to him."

At least my mother and my wife wouldn't be in a race to spit on my corpse, Bobby thought.

Three

SEPTEMBER 12, 1973

LESLIE FITZPATRICK

I PARKED ON Tomlinson Avenue, close to the intersection. There wasn't much room at the end of the curb. Luckily, the little Volkswagen Paul bought me would fit just about anywhere. I put the key in the handle on the outside and twisted it. He'd told me time and time again to always lock the door. And I always did.

He also told me to always check beneath the car for a bomb before getting in. I never did that. I wouldn't know what to look for. I don't know why he even thought I would. I don't know why he thought anyone would put a bomb under my car.

I walked toward the giant green hill that popped up out of nothing. A huge Indian burial mound. They named the entire town after that thing. I thought about it every time I saw it. Once every year on the exact same day, starting back in 1953 and still going two decades later. *Moundsville.* Who thought that name would be a good idea? It was definitely something only a man could come up with.

I turned right, onto 10th Street. As I walked toward the prison, I took out my chewing gum and put it in a tissue. I tucked the tissue into my purse.

I looked at the houses and the stores and the normal life

happening in a place that was anything but normal. Paul called it the world's largest collection of live cowboys and dead Indians. Everywhere else, it was just like anyplace else.

My father, my real one, was serving a life sentence for what the lawyers called felony murder. Basically, he was in the wrong place doing the wrong thing at the wrong time, when someone got killed by someone else. The law didn't care who did the actual killing, so Francis diFrancesco would be living behind bars in Moundsville until the day he stopped living.

I crossed Jefferson Avenue and turned left. The place looked like an old castle, except most of it was long and low and covered nearly all of three blocks. The only entrance was right in the middle. I never could get used to the sight of it, like it had been dropped out of the sky from some other time, or maybe even from some other planet. No, I never got used to seeing it there, even if the people who lived and worked around the place never seemed to give it a second thought.

The closer I got to the shack outside the door, the faster I walked. My heels clicked against the concrete. I moved as quickly as I could without running. The sooner I got inside, the sooner it would start. The sooner it would start, the sooner it would finish.

There were two guards in the small wooden hut. They tried to flirt. They always did. I gave them a polite smile, same as usual. It was easier that way. If it would get me inside a little faster, so be it.

After the shack, I walked to the front door. I could feel their eyes on me as I walked away. I wanted to turn around and give them the finger.

The wind was blowing my hair over the back of my jacket. I was glad I remembered to grab it. It was colder than I'd expected it to be. Fall was here. Winter was on the way. In more ways than one, I guess.

The guard standing outside the main door ran his eyes over me like they were connected to a metal detector. I knew not to react to him.

Yes, I've been here before, I told him. No, it hasn't been very recent. Yes, I know the rules. No, I don't have any contraband. Yes, I understand the risks of meeting face to face with a convicted murderer who is serving a life sentence without the possibility of parole.

I held my breath before I walked inside. It didn't help. That smell was inside my nose and mouth again. I didn't know what it was. I didn't want to think about it. All I wanted was to get it over with.

Another guard led me to the room where they'd bring my father to meet me. This one was younger. He looked familiar. There was more flirting. I dealt with it, even if I had the urge to ask why he thought I'd come to this godforsaken place in search of a man. But I still just wanted to keep things going. So I fluttered my eyelashes a little. I flashed a smile. I told him who I was visiting. It seemed like he was pitying me for a second or two, but then he slipped right back into flirting. He said he'd be a holler away if I needed anything. I thanked him. I said I'd be fine.

I really wanted to give him the finger, too.

I sat down. The table looked like it came from a school lunchroom, something they could fold up and roll against the wall. Other people were meeting with prisoners at some of the other tables. The inmates didn't wear uniforms. I always thought that was strange.

I tried not to look at anyone else. I didn't have a book or anything to read. I sat there, staring at my hands. Then I heard him from the doorway, talking to a guard with that deep voice of his. It always scared me a little bit during the years he lived with us, before he got himself in trouble.

I watched him walk my way. His ankles were chained together and his wrists were connected to a thick belt around his waist. When he looked at me, I made myself smile at him. He didn't smile back. I was sort of glad he didn't.

"Took you long enough to come back." He said the words before he even sat down.

"I've been busy," I said, still forcing my lips into a smile. His attitude confused me, because he knew I only ever visited him once a year.

"Busy." He twisted his mouth around the way he always did when he was just starting to get upset.

I saw a pink mark on his face. It looked like a scab had just been there. His hair was cut so short I couldn't tell whether he'd lost much more of it since last year.

"What made you not busy today?" he asked.

"It's your birthday. I always visit you on your birthday."

"Birthday, Christmas, Thanksgiving, every other day. They're all the same. You think they're baking me a cake in here?"

"I would have brought you a cake if I could."

"What I want I ain't ever getting," he said. Then he looked at me. He squinted one of his eyes as he did. "You're getting older. You ever going to bring a baby in here with you?"

"A baby?"

"Never mind. This ain't no place for no baby. Plus, I don't want you having no baby with the guy you'd be having it with."

"I thought you two were friends."

"We been over this, Leslie."

"He always says you were friends."

"He's right. We were friends."

"Is it because I'm with him?"

"That don't help. But there's way more to that one."

"He's never said anything to me about any of that."

"Of course he hasn't, Leslie. If he did, there's a chance you'd climb right out of his second bed."

I looked down so I wouldn't start crying. "And you wonder why I don't come more often."

"Sorry I got a problem with being inside here when he ain't."

"Why would he be in here instead of you?"

"I never said instead. I guess he's just luckier than me."

"What's luck have to do with any of it?" I said.

"It has everything to do with it. In that life, you live long enough to end up in here or dead. In here, you're already dead while you're waiting to die."

"It's your birthday. I just wanted to see you on your birthday."

"For who, you or me? You checked the box. Your conscience is clear until next September."

"Do you think this is easy for me?"

"You think it's easy for me? When this is over, you're walking through that door. I'm only ever leaving this place in a sack."

"I've never done anything to not leave."

Then he smiled, but it wasn't a happy one. He'd lost at least two teeth since the last time I saw him. "You're still part of it. I never dreamed you'd be part of it."

"I'm not part of it."

"Oh bullshit, Leslie. You're living off it. You get the best of both worlds. And once a year you get to see the worst of mine."

My bottom lip started to shake. I don't think he noticed. "I'm sorry you feel that way."

"You're not sorry. You're just saying it now so you won't spend much time thinking about it later."

"I should go. I wanted to cheer you up a little. I didn't want to make things worse."

"Don't worry. You can't make things worse." He stopped for a second, looking at me. Then he exhaled. I could feel his breath on the edge of my face. It smelled the same as the rest of the place. "I guess this is where I'm supposed to say I appreciate you trying to make things better. And to forget about what a miserable bastard I am. And to think long and hard about the choices you're making. If we do this next year, I'll be forty-seven. You'll be twenty-eight. It's too late for me. It ain't too late for you. But it's getting there."

He stopped talking and got up. He walked toward the guard without looking back at me.

I waited until he was gone. I hurried out of the room and out of the prison. Fresh air never tasted as good as it did whenever I left that place.

I walked past the guard at the main door. He tried to say something. I just kept going. I made my way through the shack. The guards there tried to flirt again. I didn't smile. I didn't even look at them. I just went as fast as I could back to the car. I unlocked the door. I got inside. I remembered Paul's stupid advice about checking for a bomb.

When I put the key in the ignition and turned it, part of me was hoping there was one.

Four

NOVEMBER 22, 1963

J.J. MESAGNE

I SAT AT the cheap metal desk in my bedroom. The door was closed, but I could tell something was going on between my parents. Their voices were sharp, not raised. They were trying to be quiet for my benefit. They didn't realize that whenever they argued, I could hear just enough to make me scared but not nearly enough to put my mind at ease. To let me know it was something stupid that maybe would go away as fast as it had bubbled up.

Trying to figure out what it was wouldn't make it any better. I'd learned at times like that to just stay put. I'd listen as closely as I could. I'd never say anything.

I was getting a little older. I was starting to think about the possibility of swinging the door open and asking them to knock it off. I kept asking myself why I shouldn't. I lived there, too. They'd say children should be seen and not heard. That children shouldn't speak unless spoken to. Those were always stupid rules to me, probably made up by people who just didn't want to have to deal with their kids.

I heard my mother slam the door to the bedroom next to mine. Within a few minutes, the smell of cigarettes came through the metal vent on the wall. She never smoked anywhere else in the house. The house wasn't big enough for it to matter.

I focused on my homework. I heard someone go downstairs. The creaking was loud enough to make me think it was my father. I was curious, but curiosity never got me to do anything I shouldn't. At least not back then. I kept working, listening, and waiting.

I didn't hear anything for a while. The sound of feet on the wooden stairs started again. I gripped my pencil, like I was bracing myself for whatever was coming next. Like the half-used yellow stick would be my weapon to fight off whatever it was. My head jerked when the knob turned and the door opened.

"Hey, J.J.," he said to me.

I nodded. His right hand was moving around in the pocket of his pants.

"Need any help with your homework?"

I started to get a little nervous, because he'd never offered to help me with my homework before.

"I'm almost finished," I told him. I was going to leave it at that, but something made me come out and say it. "What were you two fighting about?"

"We weren't fighting," he said in a low voice. He looked at the wall separating the two bedrooms. I could tell he was wondering how thick or thin it really was. "Parents don't always agree about everything. We were just not agreeing about something."

"You don't agree about something almost every day."

"Well, that happens when people are together all the time."

I didn't remind him that they weren't together all the time. That they had maybe forty-five minutes with each other every night. He'd wake up, he'd eat dinner, they'd fight about something or other, and then he'd be gone.

"Are you going to work soon?" I asked.

He nodded. "I am. I wanted to talk to you for a minute before I left."

Another first. I got a little more nervous.

"You'll be a man soon," he said. "You may not feel that way, but it's true. And your mother will need you to act like a man."

"Why does she need me to act like a man when you're here?"

"Well, I may not always be around."

My nerves were becoming more like confusion. "Where are you going to be?"

"It's not good for your mother to always be disagreeing with me about something. She may be better off if I go away for a little bit."

"Where would you go? Like to a different town?"

"I'll still be around. You'll still see me."

"I don't really see you now."

"Well, you'll see me on weekends." When he said it, his face looked like he had just come up with some great idea. "Every weekend. We'll do something every weekend. Go to the movies, watch football. You like football, right?"

I nodded at him, because I didn't know what else to do. Nothing I said or did was going to change wherever this thing was going.

"Then that's what we'll do. You may see me even more than you do now. You and Mom will be fine here during the week. We'll get together on weekends. It'll be great."

What was I supposed to say to that—"Sure, Dad, it'll be real swell"? I just kept nodding instead. His hand was still in his pocket. He finally pulled it out. He had something that looked like a watch.

"Look at this. It's been in our family for a long time. A really long time. My father gave it to me. His father gave it to him. His father gave it to him."

"Whose father bought it?"

"That's a good question," he said. "I don't know. All I know is that I've been carrying this around for years—"

"I've never seen it before."

"It's not polite to interrupt a grown-up, J.J. Anyways, I've been carrying this around for years. And now it's time for me to give it to you."

I held out my hand. I assumed that's what he wanted me to do.

I didn't know what I wanted to do other than to figure out exactly where this was going. I had a pretty good idea, even though it gave me a very bad feeling.

His hand reached toward mine. He dropped a brass circle into my palm. Yes, it looked like a watch.

"I already have a watch," I said. "I got it for my last birthday."

"It's not a watch. It's a compass. Do you know what a compass is?"

"I think so." I saw four letters. N, E, S, and W. There were markings between them. A needle floated and bounced over it all.

"It always points north," he said.

"But it's pointing to the S."

"You turn it until the needle lines up with the N. Then you always know where you are."

"It looks like it only tells me where I'm going, not where I am."

"Look, I was never much of a Boy Scout," he said. "The point is the men in this family hand this thing down from one generation to the next. And now I'm giving it to you. Someday you can give it to your own son."

I looked at the thing, still not quite sure what use it was. A clock told the time. To me this didn't really tell anything. I was so busy thinking about it that I didn't really think about what I said next.

"Should I give it to my own son the day I leave home, too?"

He seemed stunned by the question. He looked at the wall again. He acted like he heard something from the other bedroom. I didn't hear anything. I think he was just looking for a reason to end the conversation, so that he could make his escape.

"I should go," he said, acting all of a sudden like someone who had never lived in the house where the three of us had lived for as long as I could remember. I still didn't know what he wanted from me, so I just nodded. He nodded back.

He turned away.

He left.

He made good on his promise to come around on weekends, at

first. Then he'd miss one. Eventually, he'd miss two in a row. Once Mom met my stepdad, my father stopped coming around at all. By then, I'd hit puberty and everything that went along with it. I was still serious about school, more than I ever let my friends know. I didn't want any of them making fun of me for being a bookworm. It was simple to me. I focused on the work we did. I did that work the best I could.

I never had any bigger plan, like being a lawyer or a doctor or anything other than whatever it is I would become. I probably should have. Would it have mattered? One way or the other, I would have gotten myself into the same mess. Or this mess would have gotten me into it.

That sounds a little better. Because if that's true, it means none of this was actually my fault.

It's nice sometimes to think about it that way.

Five

BOBBY GOT OUT of the car after Vinny climbed to his feet. Vinny wobbled a little as he stood. He always wore big black shoes. They were too big for his body. The rest of the crew called him Bozo behind his back. No one would ever call him that to his face, not even Paul.

The man who had emerged from the house noticed them. His head spun toward the movements.

"Who's there?" he said. Vinny kept moving without saying a word, his black clown shoes flopping on the asphalt. Bobby stayed several steps behind Vinny, bracing for the sound of gunfire.

"We need to talk," Vinny said as he got closer.

Bobby hadn't pulled out his weapon. He didn't want to shoot a colleague unless he had no other choice.

"Talk?" the other man said. "What do we need to talk about?"

"Come with us," Vinny said. "Then we'll talk."

Bobby rubbed a hand against his face. He could feel the sweat trickling down from the bottom of his combover. Vinny had said nothing about bringing the guy with them. Bobby glanced back at the car. He doubted anyone would even fit in the backseat. He wondered whether what he'd been saying had made Vinny think twice about taking out one of their own guys.

"We can talk right here," the man said to Vinny. "No one's around to hear us."

Vinny kept going. He got behind the car that was parked in front of the house. The two men stood maybe fifteen feet apart, twenty at the most. Vinny stopped; Bobby watched. Vinny said nothing.

Things got quiet, still. It seemed to Bobby that too much time was passing for three men to be standing there, out in the open. Bobby could feel his heartbeat thumping against the top of his collar. He decided to say something.

As he opened his mouth, Vinny spoke instead. "Well, they're about to hear something they don't hear too often."

Before Bobby could tell himself that was a weird thing for Vinny to say, it started. First a flash and then the crack, loud and clear. Vinny lunged toward the man. There was another flash, another crack. The second one sounded even louder than the first. Light filled an upstairs window of the house behind Bobby.

"Let's go!" Bobby said.

Vinny ignored Bobby, or maybe Vinny didn't hear him. Vinny got closer to where the guy had been standing. Then came one more flash and one more crack.

Bobby yelled Vinny's name. Bobby cringed after the word escaped his mouth. He looked around to see if anyone had heard him. *Why not just ask him to shoot me?* Bobby thought. He rushed back into the car and started the engine. He hoped that would get Vinny's attention.

More lights came on. Curtains moved. Dark shadows gathered behind them. The houses seemed to squeeze together. Someone was bound to see Vinny. Usually, they'd wear hats pulled down and jacket lapels turned up, in order to hide their faces. That night they didn't have the time to grab any of that stuff. Bobby pulled the transmission into gear and wished those giant clown shoes could carry his boss back to the Vega faster than they were.

Vinny opened the door. He plunged into the seat, cursing as he landed. He was mad, madder than before. Bobby didn't care. He just wanted to get out of there. He jammed the accelerator before Vinny was able to close the door. The little car jerked away, tossing Vinny back against the seat. That pissed him off even more.

"What the fuck are you doing?" Vinny said.

"I think people was looking out their windows."

Vinny reached over to pull the door shut, cursing some more. "It was dark. No one saw us. Where was you, anyway? This was a two-man job, Bobby. What if he had a gun?"

"You acted like he didn't." Bobby drove as fast as he could, trying not to careen into any of the parked cars on the street that led back to the main road.

"I thought I had backup," Vinny said.

"Why did you wait so long to do it?"

Vinny didn't answer. That made Bobby think maybe he was right. Maybe Vinny really wasn't sure whether it was right to do what they'd all of a sudden been doing to guys from their own crew, orders or no orders.

"Why did you say you wanted to bring him with us? Why didn't you just start shooting?"

"I don't know," Vinny said. "Maybe I wouldn't have said that if someone hadn't been talking crazy."

"I was just talking."

"You was talking too much. You threw me off."

Bobby wanted to throw up. He shouldn't have said another word, but he couldn't help it at that point. "Don't blame this on me," Bobby said, with a hair too much attitude.

"I'll blame this on whoever I choose," Vinny said. "Especially if I want to blame it on someone who works for me."

Bobby tried to focus on driving the car. He wondered whether it would be the last time he ever drove any car at all. He thought about how for his last time behind the wheel it would be a piece of shit Vega and not a Cadillac or a Corvette.

"What the fuck are you smiling about?" Vinny said.

"I'm not smiling."

"The hell you ain't. I'm telling you, them dogs is fucking with your head. They're making you soft."

Bobby noticed Vinny had something in his hand. It gave Bobby an opening.

"What you got there?"

Vinny held it up. Bobby glanced over as he drove. It looked like a pocket watch.

"He had this in his hand," Vinny said.

"I didn't think you took no souvenirs."

"I don't. I just saw it. I grabbed it. I think he was holding it the whole time."

"So he had a pocket watch. People still have pocket watches, right?"

Vinny started fiddling around with it.

"This ain't no watch," Vinny said. "It's a compass. Why the fuck would he have a compass in his hand?"

Six

MARCH 14, 1973

JIMMY DACEY

I WOKE UP the morning after the funeral. I tried to tell myself it was all a dream. Then I looked to the empty side of the bed. It was real. She was gone.

I didn't know what to do with myself. I wished I hadn't retired. Then I remembered how they'd nudged me out. After more than forty-five years of crunching numbers with flawless precision, I had made a few mistakes. Rounding errors, basically. But that was all they needed. The next thing I knew they were shoving a slab of rubber chicken in my mouth, clamping a gold watch onto my wrist, and plunging a sharp blade deep into my spine.

At first, it was OK. It gave us a chance to reconnect. She wasn't quite sure what to do with me in the house every day. I sat around reading poetry. I spent so many years trying to hide it, thinking it wasn't manly. I could read the verses quickly. I read them repeatedly. I memorized a lot of them, without really trying. I liked the rhythm of it all. It soothed me.

Over the years, I had learned many new words. After a while, I started to speak differently than everyone else, more proper and exact. People thought I was from a big city, or something. I wasn't trying to show off. But the clients liked it. It made me seem smarter than I was. It made them think I was a better accountant. It would have been stupid for me to not take advantage of that.

When the mistakes started, it wasn't anything egregious. I really do believe they were ready to move me along. Sometimes, having an older man around is a reminder to all the younger men that, someday, they'll get old, too. If they're fortunate, they will. But they're far too young to think of it that way.

I was fine with being at home, until she got sick. Those were some of the most difficult and challenging weeks of my life. It's hard to take care of someone you love when they're fading. It's even harder to have no help. Our daughter lives in Pennsylvania. She has her husband and children to worry about. We had some family in town, but no one who could drop everything to take care of an old woman who was dying of breast cancer that had already spread to her bones.

I couldn't sit around the house and keep reading poetry, not after she was gone. The place felt too empty. Too haunted. I suppose I wanted to sell it. I never got around to doing it.

I'd known about Johnny Mesagne for a long time. Pretty much since he was born. Before that, technically. I knew he ran with those criminals. Mobsters or gangsters or whatever they call themselves. He had taken over that bar about six years ago, in '67. I'd heard he technically wasn't with Paul Verbania's people anymore, but that he still sort of was. I didn't understand how any of it worked. I never really wanted to. But when I woke up the morning after the funeral, I had to go somewhere. It was either the library or a bar.

I'd like to say I flipped a coin, but I didn't. I wanted to go to a bar. To his bar. I wanted something different from what I'd been doing all those years. I only had so much time left. I decided I was going to enjoy myself. I liked that it felt just a little dangerous. I had no idea.

I put on a suit and a tie. That's how I'd been going out in public for most of my life. I was comfortable that way. It made me feel less conscious of the words I used, of how I tried to enunciate each of them properly. I liked how it sounded to talk correctly. I never judged those who didn't. I just wanted to do it the right way, if only because it's what I preferred.

I covered my jacket with a trench coat. I eased my second best fedora onto my head, gently so it wouldn't knock my hair out of place. I didn't care that it was white, as long as it was still there. I got in my car. Not the one I keep in the garage, the other one. I drove into town. I parked around the corner from Johnny Mesagne's bar.

I walked inside. I took off my hat. He nodded to me. Even though I had never spoken to him directly, he knew who I was. He poured a beer without me asking for it. When I seemed surprised, he said he assumed I wasn't there for a cup of coffee. That made me laugh. It felt good to laugh again. I liked the beer. It was cold and rich and it gradually made me begin to forget.

I sat there at the bar. He went about his business, taking bets from others who showed up and answering the phone whenever it rang. It rang a lot. I looked around the place. It was nothing special to see. A long bar running along one side of the room, and four wooden tables on the other. The walls needed to be repainted. The furniture needed to be refinished. But I liked it there. I felt comfortable. The beer probably helped.

I'm not sure how many I had that first day. Technically one, because he kept filling up the glass from the tap behind the bar before I could finish it. I had a nice little buzz. He eventually had someone get him a sandwich. He got one for me, too. I didn't even ask him to. I didn't know why he was being so nice to me. Maybe he knew my wife had just died. Maybe he respected what I'd done for a living. Maybe he treated every stranger that way. Regardless, I found a new friend that day. I didn't realize I was looking for one.

Seven

SEPTEMBER 17, 1973

LESLIE FITZPATRICK

I STOOD AT the door. I could see the street from the lowest of the three rectangular windows. When I was young and the house belonged to my grandmother, I thought they looked like dominoes lined up on steps, like one was waiting to fall and knock the other two over.

Paul was late. I was used to it. He never wanted to be kept waiting, but he never thought twice about making someone else wait.

I saw the Cadillac rolling in from the right. Vinny in the front, Paul in the back. Same as ever. Vinny always smelled like soup. I wondered if his house smelled the same way. I don't think he had a wife. I decided early on the less I knew about him, the better. He didn't seem to like me. He didn't seem to like anyone. I used to try to make small talk with him, but he never did much more than grunt.

I wondered if Paul would walk to the door and knock. The first year or two, he always did. Then it got a little more spotty. Recently, he just expected me to notice the car and come out. At some point, I figured the routine would become Vinny blowing the horn for me.

When the back door to the Cadillac didn't open, I walked out and locked up behind me. The air was cool and clean. I breathed it in before I'd be stuck inhaling Vinny's beef and barley, blended with

Paul's tobacco. Those cigars stank to high heaven even when he was just chewing on the end of them.

I walked along the concrete path toward the driveway. I noticed my reflection in one of the Volkswagen's windows. I was starting to look older. Not old, but older.

You ever going to bring a baby in here with you?

I hurried toward the Cadillac. Vinny got out of the front seat and opened the door directly behind the steering wheel. I saw those ridiculous shoes. Were his feet really that big? I was just fine never knowing the answer to that question. I nodded at Vinny. I'd stopped smiling at him long ago, after I realized he was never going to smile back. I was holding my breath as I passed by him, but I still picked up a little of his aroma.

"What took you so long?" Paul was gnawing on a cigar. The end of it was wet and chewed up. And he wondered why I made him brush his teeth and his gums and his tongue before I'd let him try to kiss me.

"I came right out," I said. "You were late."

"Vinny's never late. Your clocks must be fast."

My shoulders slammed against the seat as the car moved out. Paul definitely hadn't made Vinny a full-time chauffeur for his driving skills.

"Where are we eating tonight?" I said.

"Same place as usual. Why?"

"It's so close by. Why didn't you just have me meet you there?"

"I felt like picking you up tonight."

"I thought maybe we'd go somewhere else."

The cigar drooped from his lips. His eyebrows moved up toward the place where his hairline had once been. "Seriously?"

"It just thought it would be nice to go somewhere else for a change. I haven't been to Ernie's Esquire in a long time."

"You can go tomorrow."

"That's not what I mean. We should go."

"Sure. You want I should have my wife join us?"

Vinny made a sound. I think it was a laugh.

"I just was thinking that maybe we can—"

"That's your first problem. Thinking. Thinking leads to ideas, and not many of them are good ones, at least not for me." He looked at the back of Vinny's head and turned toward me. His voice got low. "This can wait until later."

"That's the problem," I said in a normal voice. "Everything waits until later. And later turns into six years. And then later will be six more."

"Maybe we should just take you back to your place. If it's that time of the month or something, maybe you should just lay down."

I hated when he played that card. Anytime I said something he didn't like, he acted like I was having my period.

"Can't we just enjoy a nice evening?" he said. "I had a long day today."

I was going to wait. I decided not to.

"Whatever happened with you and my dad?"

I think I felt the car jerk a little bit after I said that. Paul looked again at the back of Vinny's head.

He kept talking to me in a low voice, as if Vinny couldn't hear every word. "Where's this coming from?"

"I went to see him the other day. It was his birthday. I thought the two of you were friends."

"What did he say to make you think we weren't?"

"He said if he told me what happened between you and him, I'd leave you."

"What else did he say?"

"That's it. He also wanted to know when I was going to show up with a baby."

"Is there a new store in town that sells them?"

That sound came from Vinny again. It was the most I'd heard from him in months.

"I'm just telling you what he said. You asked me what he said."

"Your dad's a good man," Paul said, moving the cigar around in his mouth like he always did when he didn't like where a conversation was going. "He got caught up in some bad stuff. I tried to help him. There wasn't much I could do. That fucking guy pulled the trigger. Geno was his name. No one expected Geno to pull the trigger. They all ended up in a jackpot."

"Were you there?"

He shook his head. "Me? No. I just heard about it, that's all. Like I said, I tried to help him. I did. It was just a bad deal. They thought they had a good plan, and they did. But someone had to be a hero, and Geno had to be a tough guy and that was that. We ended up losing four men that day. Two at the scene, and then your dad and that other one. Him and your dad got pinched, went to court, got life. I tried to help him. I tried to help both of them."

"How hard did you try?"

"Hard enough. Christ, Leslie. I'm sure we been over this at some point in the last six years."

"I guess so," I said. "I just feel like there's more to the story."

"There's more to every story."

"So you're saying I'm right?"

"I'm just saying there's details that matter, and there's details that don't. You know everything that matters. I don't know why you keep going to see him every year. Seems to me like he just wants to fill your head with ideas."

"I've got enough ideas on my own."

"And that's why I said you're better off not thinking. So let's stop thinking and just have a nice dinner."

The car stopped moving as he finished. We were at the restaurant. Vinny parked right next to the door in the back, the one that Paul and only Paul ever used. I think he owned the place. I never asked. He acted like he did. Then again, he acted like he owned everything and everyone. I can't say I didn't know that before I started up with him.

Still, there really was something more about him and my father. I knew Paul's reactions well enough to know that. But I also knew there was probably no way I was ever going to find out. Whatever it was, it wasn't going to change the way I'd been feeling.

Eight

SEPTEMBER 18, 1973

J.J. JENKINS

I NEVER EXPECTED to go back into that store, not even as a customer. I'd worked there from my sixteenth birthday until the night before I left for college. The owner tried to talk me out of going away. He said I could become the assistant manager when Rich Simpson retired. I told him Rich was only thirty-seven. He said maybe Rich would die soon. I didn't know whether to laugh at that.

I'd gone to Case Western Reserve in Cleveland. They wanted me more than I wanted them. They were persistent. They kept offering scholarships, shaving off more and more of the price tag until I agreed to go. I still didn't want to. My mother pushed me into it.

I struggled in college. I always felt a step behind everyone else. That first year, I heard some of the other students had used the same textbooks in high school. It was overwhelming, and knowing that plenty of others had gotten a head start didn't help. It also didn't help that I was eighteen and liked to do the things most normal eighteen-year-olds liked to do. I never thought I was all that handsome, but I knew how to talk to girls. How to say the right things. How to seem confident, even when I wasn't. I rarely lacked for companionship. That was the only thing about college I enjoyed.

I didn't enjoy the report cards. I went from being a straight-A student in high school to getting all Cs and a B in my first semester at Case Western. The second semester was the same, without the B. I went back to Wheeling for the summer. After two husbands, my mom was still living alone. I cut grass by day so I'd have enough money to chase skirts by night. I spent plenty of time with two of my high school friends who hadn't gone to college. Tony worked at a gas station. Willie worked at a record store. I felt bad about not having a clear plan for my life until I'd spend time with them. They were existing day to day, with not even a thought as to what the future might hold.

I hoped the second year of college would get a little easier. It didn't. I ended up on academic probation after the first semester. I didn't tell my mother about that. In the second semester, my grades didn't get any better. I was basically down to my last chance in the fall of my third year. I tried to hint around to her that things weren't going well. She didn't want to hear it. After the first week of classes, I knew it wasn't going to last. I decided not to wait for it to happen. I packed up my stuff. I went home on September tenth. It was a Monday.

My mother had a fit. College was my ticket out, she said. I didn't know where she thought I was going to go, even with an engineering degree. I probably would have ended up in Wheeling anyway, working at a coal mine or in a steel mill with something not much better than working by the hour.

She told me I had to get a job, that mowing lawns wouldn't be good enough, especially because the grass stopped growing in October. So I went back to Foodland to meet with Mr. Gleason, hoping to get my old job back until I figured out whatever I would do next.

He had aged a lot in two years. More gray hair. Maybe even more Brylcreem. He always had spots on his face that he'd missed with his razor. I almost asked him at one point if he shaved with his eyes closed.

I was sitting at one of the tables in the break room. It was otherwise empty. He came up to me, carrying a clipboard. He still carried around a pencil that was full of toothmarks.

"I had a feeling you'd be back," he said. I don't think he was trying to gloat, but it felt like he was, at least a little bit. I'd have to take it if I wanted the job. Besides, he was right. I was back.

"We all can't be what we want to be," I said. "I remember you telling me you wanted to drive race cars."

He was too impressed that I remembered what he'd told me to realize I was sticking it to him. "Real life gets in the way of things," he said with an exaggerated nod of his head. It was the same way he'd said it when he told me about the life he'd abandoned because he had a wife and a kid and needed a job more than a dream.

"Well, real life brought me back here," I said.

"Is this just a short-term thing while you regroup? I know a little about that school you went to. It's hard there. Are you going to start looking for an easier college and then leave in a few months?"

"I'm not going back to college," I said. It was the truth. It also allowed me to avoid saying I didn't plan to bag groceries and stock shelves any longer than I had to.

The most accurate truth was that Tony and Willie had been getting a little work on the side for Bobby Marroni. I remembered the name. He used to pick up my dad once in a while, back when he lived with us. Whatever my dad was doing, Bobby was doing it with him. They never told me exactly what my dad did back then. I assumed they didn't want me to know, in order to keep me away from it. Like it was in my blood, or something. I had heard enough of an argument one night to hear my mother say she was worried about that.

If they had just told me, if I'd known all about it, maybe I wouldn't have been so curious. Instead, it was mysterious to me. That made it more interesting. I had always wanted to know more. I'd never found out.

My father started running a bar when I was maybe fourteen. I remember Mom being relieved when she told my stepdad about that at dinner one night. I wanted to know why she was relieved. But the topic changed right away, because my stepdad never wanted to talk about my dad. I couldn't really blame him for that.

I'd tried plenty of times to get her to tell me more when it was just my mom and me, but she wouldn't. I guess it was her plan for keeping me away from that world. I wish she'd had a different one. It's not her fault. Maybe it was inevitable. Maybe it really is in my blood.

So now I had a chance to work a real job, and to maybe poke around at what Tony and Willie were doing in order to find out a little bit more about what my dad used to do, and about why he stopped doing it. If he actually had stopped doing it. It really was a mystery to me. The time had come to try to solve it.

"I don't have a regular spot on the schedule now," Mr. Gleason said. "I'd have to fit you in whatever gaps there might be."

"That's fine," I said.

"And I can't pay anything more than what you were making before."

"That's fine." It's not as if two years of college should have entitled me to more than minimum wage at a grocery store. Besides, it wasn't like I had to pay rent.

"How old are you now?"

"I'm twenty."

"That's old enough to be thinking about your career. That career could be here. I told you that before. If you work like you did before, there's no reason why it couldn't be."

"That's fine." I said it again, but that time it was a lie. This job would be temporary for me, until I found something else. That process of possibly finding something else would begin with finding out more about what Tony and Willie were doing for Bobby Marroni.

Mr. Gleason stood up. I did the same. He offered his right hand. I extended my own. After he released his grip, he looked at the spot where I was missing a pinky. If he'd forgotten that I was one finger short of a full set, his memory had been refreshed.

I ignored it. I was used to the reaction. And I was far more focused on my plan to go home and give Tony a call.

Nine

SEPTEMBER 19, 1973

JOHNNY MESAGNE

I TOOK OVER that bar after I got out of Paul's crew. No one knows how I pulled it off. Sometimes even I'm not sure. I kept all of that to myself. It was part of the deal.

It was also part of the deal that I'd take a different job. Paul needed a bookie. Sure, I was still working for him. But I wasn't actually working with him no more. It was a big difference. At least it was for me.

I learned how to take the bets, how to keep the records. How to count the money. When to let Vinny know someone wasn't paying. One call to Vinny, and whoever it was would be paying. It's the biggest reason why I rarely had to call him.

The bar wasn't much to look at. I didn't have much for sale. Beer on tap. Glass bottles of Coca-Cola. I kept a bottle of whiskey stashed for special occasions. I sent out for food. I always had a box of Slim Jims behind the bar. Redneck pepperoni, I called it. A little protein to get me through the busier days.

Guys hung out there and bet on whatever was going on. Horse races, baseball, basketball, even hockey. And football. Without question, football. There was something going on in sports almost every single day of the year. Which meant I worked almost every single day of the year.

I had to kick sixty percent up to Paul. That was the arrangement. All of his bookies in town did it. It was the cost of running the business. It bought the muscle to make sure debts got paid. It was protection against anyone else messing around with me. Not that anyone would. Paul had Wheeling under his thumb. He ran other towns around there, too. But Wheeling was his home base. No one was messing with him. Which meant no one was messing with me.

Football season had started. The accountant had been coming around for a few months. I liked him. He talked good, sounded smart. Always dressed up. Not in a flashy way. Classy. White hair, always in place. No wrinkled or rumpled suits or coats. Always wore a tie. I didn't have no father figures. I guess he sort of became one, without me realizing it.

I gave him free beer. I didn't do that with nobody else. I guess it was a trade-off for his company. Even on the slow days, he showed up and sat there at the bar. We talked about things. A lot of things. Pretty soon, you start running out of things to talk about.

So, yeah, I started telling him a little about what I used to do with Paul. I wasn't bragging. I wasn't proud of robbing trucks and selling drugs and starting fires and sending people to Ohio. I guess it made me feel a little better to open up. Sure, he could have gone to the cops. I knew he wouldn't. He was lonely. He liked having a friend. I did, too.

He was starting to poke around about how I got out. I can't blame him. Who wouldn't be curious? But there was no way I was going to tell him.

"I still can't believe he let you out," Jimmy said as he finished his second beer of the day. "I've always heard he can be a real son of a bitch."

"You heard right," I said. "But he made an exception for me. And it don't hurt that I still earn."

"Thanks to me, you earn."

"We love it when people bet. We love it more when they lose. We love it the most when they keep trying. Besides, you class up the joint."

He looked around. It was just me and him. "It's not so bad," he said.

"It stinks like flat beer and stale cigarettes," I said. "It needs paint and polish. And the jukebox ain't worked in three years. Other than that, it's fine."

"People don't go to a place like this for what it looks like inside," Jimmy said. "They go for what it feels like inside."

"Well, it looks like shit. Hopefully it feels a lot better than that."

"How does it feel to not do what you used to do?" He was fishing around a little, maybe getting ready to ask more of a straight question.

"It feels good. It feels safer. I was getting too old for that stuff."

"What are you, forty?"

"Good guess. I turned forty earlier this month."

"What day?"

"The first."

"I would have bought you a present."

"You did."

"Did I?"

"You bet heavy on the Patriots getting the points against Buffalo."

"Well, I had a feeling about the Patriots."

"Shows what you know about football," I said. "They've never been worth a shit."

"Since you've been doing this job, or ever?"

"Ever, I think. At least since I've been doing this."

He took a drink. I could feel the question coming. I didn't want to tell him I couldn't talk about it. I needed to figure out how to steer him away from it. I made the first move.

"How's your daughter?" I said.

He gave me the same look he made the other times I asked him about her. His eyes got droopy. His mouth got flat. I didn't want to make him sad. I just wanted to get him talking about something else, and that was the first thing I thought of.

"I probably won't see her before Thanksgiving," he said. "I'll drive up there, if she invites me. Maybe spend the night."

"Why wouldn't she invite you?"

"I've gotten to the point where I don't assume anything when it comes to her."

I nodded, relieved I got him away from where he was going but not proud about how I done it. And then he turned it around on me.

"How about you?" he said. "How's your boy?"

My boy. Oh boy. I wanted to think of what to say before I said it, mainly because I didn't want to come off as a bad father. Mainly because I knew I was.

"I don't talk to him too much. He's still in college. That place in Cleveland. He had to be real smart to get in. He didn't get none of that from me. I been giving Maria money the past few years to pay for it. She really wanted him to go."

"What did you want?"

"I wanted whatever she wanted. Mainly, she wanted to be sure he wouldn't end up like me."

"He could do a lot worse," Jimmy said.

"He also could do a lot better. Especially with what I used to do. Besides, the Italians are all about blending in, you know? Go to college, get a job, buy a house and a car, find a wife, have some kids, work until you retire and then—"

"And then hang out in a bar every day, dressed like you're on your way to church," Jimmy said. He took one more drink before standing up. "Do you ever wonder why I do this every day, why I put on a clean shirt and a tie and a suit, even though I don't work anymore?"

"I guess I never really thought about it."

"We'll all end up wearing a suit in the coffin. I figured I might as well be as comfortable as I can in one now."

He lifted his fedora from the bar and slipped it onto his head. He ran his hand along the edge, pointed at me, and smiled. Same as he always did whenever he left.

"I'm off to the doctor's office. I'll be back this afternoon."

"Everything OK?"

"Just getting the levels checked," Jimmy said. He tugged on the lapels of his jacket. "I won't be wearing this thing anywhere but here for a while."

He walked to the door. It looked like he had a little bit of a limp in his left leg. I hadn't noticed it before.

"If you get buried with a closed casket, do they still put you in a suit?" I asked.

"I don't know," he said, "and I don't plan on finding out."

I was getting curious about something. I didn't want to wait until he came back.

"Help me understand this," I said. "All those years of doing people's taxes, living clean, never coming around a place like this. And now you spend all your time hanging around a hoodlum like me. Why would you do that?"

"Maybe I finally decided to give the road less traveled a try."

"Road less traveled, huh? That sounds familiar."

"It's from a poem. By Robert Frost."

"A poem?" I started laughing, probably enough to make him think I was making fun of him. "Of all the guys that have ever come in this place, I guarantee you none of them knew no poems. Unless they started with, 'There once was a man from Nantucket.'"

He smiled at me. He didn't seem mad. His teeth were straight and clean, but I could tell they weren't dentures. An old man like that, still with all of his teeth and all of them still white and bright.

"Actually," he said, "I grew up on Nantucket."

Ten

LESLIE FITZPATRICK

I GOT TO the Laconia Building on Market Street maybe ten minutes early. I still knew how to get to his office. Dr. Ronald McCoy. Thick, bright red hair. I remembered thinking how lucky he was that Ronald McDonald wasn't around when he was a kid.

I tried to think of the last time I'd been there. It was at least a couple of years. The thing he helped me with wasn't legal at the time. By 1973 it was. That didn't make me feel any better about what I had done. But Paul had insisted.

The doctor had checked me out after it was finished to make sure everything was fine. He'd said it was. I told him I never wanted to think or talk about it again.

I talked to as few people as possible on the way from my house to downtown. It wasn't easy in a small city like that. People spoke to me. I kept it simple. Just enough so my mother wouldn't get a call about her daughter being rude or stuck up.

I sat on that white paper they use to cover the cushion of the table. There was a chart on the wall of an eyeball sliced down the middle. I wondered why they put pictures like that in doctor's offices. It can't put the patients at ease.

I wasn't at ease that morning. He walked in after I'd sat there for a half hour, maybe longer. He was friendly. I guess that's probably the most important thing a doctor can be.

"Miss Fitzpatrick." He said it like he didn't know me, like he didn't remember. He opened a folder. I could tell as he looked at the paper inside that it was coming back to him.

"It looks like it's been a while. March third, two years ago. You're looking quite well. How have you been feeling?"

"I feel fine, body-wise. I've got other issues. But don't we all?"

He smiled. It's funny how a stupid little thing like that can make you feel better. "We can make some of those other issues better, if they're bad enough. The body isn't healthy unless the mind is healthy."

"I came because I haven't had, you know, a checkup since the last time. And I was curious about something."

He didn't say anything. So I kept going.

"That thing from before. Some of my friends said that it can keep you from getting pregnant again."

"It's possible, if the procedure isn't done properly." He looked at the file again. "The last time you were here, everything looked in order to me. Are you having trouble conceiving?"

"Well, no. I haven't exactly tried. I just wanted to know if it would be a problem if I do."

"There's no way to know for sure until you try. I don't see any reason to think it would be a problem, based on my last examination. There still could be other issues. I could do another exam now, if you want. It probably wouldn't hurt to do a Pap smear."

"Now what's that for again?"

"It checks for cervical cancer. It's rare, but it happens. And it's always better to catch these things early."

"I remember enough about the last time to make me not really want to do it again. But if you think it makes sense."

"If you want to know whether I recommend it, I'll tell you that I do. I know it can be a little uncomfortable. But it won't last long, and it sounds as if it will give you peace of mind, in maybe a few different ways."

He gave me a gown. He pulled a curtain across half of the room. I changed as quietly as I could. I could hear him getting the table ready. I remembered those stirrups. I started to regret agreeing to the examination, but he recommended it. I didn't trust many people in my life. If I was going to trust anyone, I probably should trust him.

I didn't say anything until it was over. He didn't, either. I got up and went back behind the curtain to change.

"Everything looks fine," he said from the other side. "I'll send the sample off for testing, and we'll call you in a couple of weeks with the results. As far as I can tell, you should have no issues conceiving, when you're ready. Are you engaged to be married?"

"Am I what?"

"I'm just trying to estimate when you might be interested in conceiving. I can give you a prescription for birth control pills. They're safer than they used to be. You can use them until you're ready."

"I—well, I'm not really planning on getting married any time soon. So maybe I should do that."

After I had changed, he gave me a small piece of paper for a one-month supply, plus eleven refills. I took it. I thanked him, and I left.

I never got the pills.

Eleven

AFTER MY FATHER went to prison, my mother divorced him. She got married again. My stepfather's family was weird about accepting her, about accepting both of us. Like we were the ones who broke the law, or something. All of them were that way, except for my stepfather's cousin Maria. She treated my mother like a big sister. She treated me like a little sister.

Maria knew what it was like to be divorced from someone in that line of work, even though her ex-husband wasn't in prison. My life would have been a lot easier if he had been. But that's a different story altogether.

It's a story I don't think Maria ever knew about. If she did, she wouldn't have been nearly as nice to me as she was.

We met once every week or two for lunch. She picked Elby's this time. I drove there after leaving the doctor's office.

Maria was smoking another cigarette. The ashtray had maybe six butts inside. I hadn't had one yet. I liked to wait until after I ate.

She was fretting about her son. He'd left college.

"Maybe he'll go back," I said to Maria.

"I don't think he's going back," she said. "And there's nothing I can do to make him."

"Maybe he'll decide to do it on his own. Kids do that sometimes. They just need a little time."

"This has been coming. I could sense it, you know? He was struggling. He tried to keep it from me. I found his grades. He wasn't doing too good."

"So what will he do?"

"He's supposedly going back to work at Foodland," she said. "He told me he was going to talk to the manager today. I'll believe it when I see the paycheck."

"That's it? He goes to college for two years and then he's back to bagging groceries?" I probably shouldn't have been so blunt.

"I hope that's all it is."

"What do you mean?"

She dropped her chin and raised her eyebrows, like I should have already known the answer. I got it right away.

"You don't want him ending up like . . . ."

Maria tapped on her nose with the bottom of the filter on her cigarette.

"Have you talked to Johnny?" I said. "There's no way he'll want him getting involved in any of that."

"Johnny is all about Johnny," she said. "He'll say he can't do anything about it, that the boy is twenty and he has to find his own way. The truth is he doesn't care, especially not after J.J. took Frank's name."

I leaned closer to Maria. I tried to speak a little more softly, just in case.

"Maybe I can say something to Paul."

"You told me he doesn't like to talk business."

"This isn't really about business. It's about keeping someone out of the business."

She looked at me in a way she hadn't in a long time.

"I should hate you," she said. "You're gorgeous and you're sweet and you ended up on the arm of the most powerful man this side of Pittsburgh. And you're young. You bitch."

"Not that young."

"Twenty-seven is young. Especially when the one saying it is pushing forty."

The waitress brought our food. We stopped talking while she was putting the plates in front of us. Maria waited until she was gone to start again.

"So what would you say to Paul?" Maria said. "If you say anything, I mean."

"That you don't want J.J. getting involved in any of that. That you don't want him turning out like his father."

"Or turning out like Paul," Maria said. "But you should probably leave that part out."

"Paul would understand," I said. "I mean, I think he would." I took a bite of the sandwich and chewed it in the right corner of my mouth.

"How long have you been with him?" she said.

"Six years, I think. Maybe six and a half. The money got my attention at first because I was young."

"Still are young."

"Was young. When these guys get away from all that stuff they do, whatever they do—they're different, you know? Paul can be sweet. I know that sounds weird, but it's true."

"Johnny was never that way. Sweet? Johnny? No way. He was a lot of things, but never sweet."

"Maybe you met him too young. Maybe he's sweet now."

Maria blew smoke out her nose. "I doubt it."

"Do you ever think about getting back together with him? You're single. He's single. Maybe he's different now."

"Maybe he's not."

"Maybe he's better now that his life is easier."

"Maybe he's worse."

I took another bite. I chewed on the left side of my mouth. Someone told me that changing sides helps prevent wrinkles. I didn't know if it was true, but it couldn't hurt.

"Did you ever think about having more kids?" I asked her.

"I wanted to with Johnny, but he got himself fixed without telling me."

"He did?"

"Told me after he left. I guess he thought it would make me feel better about him leaving."

"I never knew he did that."

"Why would you?"

I changed the subject. "Does J.J. have a girlfriend?"

"Not that I've noticed. He was always popular that way. And he was never bashful."

"Well, maybe he'll meet someone and settle down. How old is he now?"

"Twenty," she said. "Can you believe that? My little baby is twenty?"

"Now *that's* young."

"Not much younger than twenty-seven."

I took another bite. I forgot to chew it with the other side of my mouth.

Twelve

SEPTEMBER 19, 1973

J.J. JENKINS

TONY WAS AT work. I called Willie instead. I didn't want to get him in trouble for saying too much. I also didn't want Tony to think I went to Willie because I thought Willie would talk.

He did.

He said they were making a few pickups for Bobby. Getting money from people who made weekly payments. Willie didn't know where the money came from. They probably kept him in the dark on purpose, for his own good and for theirs. Tony probably would know. I decided I would try to find out from him, at the right time.

Willie said they had to make a pickup the next night. He offered to swing by and get me on the way, said we could go get some beers after they were done. I told him he probably should run it by Tony first. Willie said he didn't think Tony would care, especially since Bobby used to work for my dad. I acted like I knew a lot more about that than I did. At this point, Tony and Willie probably knew a lot more about it than me.

At seven o'clock the next night, I sat on the top step of the front porch of our house on Poplar Avenue, waiting. My mom hadn't given me the third degree about going out that night. She was still happy

I'd gotten my old job back at Foodland. She'd started on the wine and 7-Up. She usually didn't get drunk from it, but she drank enough to stop worrying about every little thing. I was probably in the clear, at least for the rest of the night.

I heard Willie's car before I saw it. Big brown Camaro. It sounded like he'd taken off the muffler. It was moving faster than it should have been in a neighborhood that size. I looked at the sidewalks to make sure no kids were playing near the street. My car was parked in front of the house, a Plymouth I'd bought with the money I made at the grocery store. That Camaro nearly caved in a fender as Willie slammed on the brakes.

I pushed myself up and jogged down to meet them. I hadn't heard anything more since talking to Willie, so I assumed they still planned to take me wherever they were going.

Tony got out and popped the back seat, so I could climb in.

"You come home from school and you don't call me?" he said. "I guess I know where I rate."

"I tried to call you yesterday. You were working."

"So you just got home yesterday?"

It had been more than a week. I hadn't felt like answering their questions about why I'd left college. I wanted to at least figure out something else before dealing with my friends.

The Camaro lurched away, back end roaring again.

"This is a lot of car," I said to Willie.

"Girls like it," he said.

Tony turned his head toward Willie and laughed. Tony's mustache had a piece of something in it that looked like pie crust. It wasn't the first time I'd noticed food there.

"How many girls you had in this thing?" Tony said.

Willie paused to do the math.

"C'mon, Willie," Tony said, "it don't take too long to count to zero."

"Your mother was in the back seat last night," Willie said, "so that's at least one."

"Where are we going?" I said to them.

"Place in South Wheeling," Tony said. "Easy work."

"So you just pick up money?"

"That's it. Like I said, easy work."

"Why doesn't Bobby just do it himself?"

"I don't know," Tony said. "I never asked. And he never said."

"How many times have you done it?"

"Maybe a dozen," Tony said. "I think it's how they break people in. Throw us a bone. We show we can handle it. Then it goes from there."

"So where does it go from there?" I said.

"I don't know," Tony said. "It hasn't gone there yet."

"You guys are boring," Willie said. "Let's talk about something else."

"What do you want to talk about?" Tony said. "Batman?"

"Fuck Batman," Willie said. "He don't have no powers. He's just rich enough to buy all that stuff."

Tony shook his head at Willie. "So are you back for good or just a little bit?" Tony asked me.

"For now," I said.

"So for just a little bit?"

"It's for now. I'm trying to figure it all out."

"Tony said it wouldn't be long before you was back," Willie said.

"I never said it like that," Tony replied.

"You said, 'Willie, it won't be long before J.J. is back.' That's what you said."

"It's OK," I said. "You were right. I'm back."

"I missed you," Willie said, looking at me in the rearview mirror.

"I missed you too," I said to him.

Tony chimed in. "Ain't that sweet. We all missed each other."

I could see the side of Willie's face. He seemed genuinely confused.

"But you and me been here the whole time," he said to Tony.

Tony shook his head and scratched at his mustache. The piece of pie crust fell out.

Willie got excited all of a sudden. "Hey, what's that thing you call what we do, Tony?"

"What do you mean?"

"That name. Starlighting, or something."

"Moonlighting," Tony said. "We're moonlighting."

"I love that word," Willie said, laughing like something was tickling his belly. "Sometimes we moonlight when it ain't even dark out. Hey, J.J., you can moonlight with us, too. Even when it ain't dark out."

I looked out the window. It was starting to get dark. It was about to get a lot darker.

Thirteen

JOHNNY MESAGNE

I WAS PUTTING the last of the beer glasses back on the shelf when the phone started ringing. I looked up at the clock. The night's baseball games had started. Most of the regulars knew I'd be leaving soon. Usually, I'd get calls for the West Coast games after I got back to the apartment.

It was five blocks away. I'd made that walk sober. I'd made that walk drunk. Every time I made that walk, I'd ask myself how many more times I'd make it. I can't remember when I started doing that.

My bar wasn't great, but it was a lot better than my apartment. A woman hadn't been there on a regular basis in a long time, and it showed. Not that I didn't get around. When I did, I'd try to always spend time at their place. Once they saw mine, they didn't argue much about that.

Two of the guys was still sitting at tables, one of them at each. Smoking, drinking beer, counting the money they'd won or lost. Doing anything but going home. Some of them would've stayed there all night if I didn't shut down and leave. Except for Jimmy Dacey. He came every day, but he never stayed past five o'clock. He said he liked the feeling of driving home at quitting time, that it was the closest he would ever get to the days when he had someone to drive home to.

I walked over to the phone. The ringing was a lot louder when the place was mostly empty. I grabbed a pencil and pad on the way, since I thought I'd be taking down a bet. I wish I had been. I said what I always say when picking up a call.

"Go ahead."

"Get your ass over to Bobby's. Now."

The cigarette in my mouth fell on the floor. I stepped on it before it could burn the tile.

"Paul? What the hell is going on?"

"Your kid is over there."

"My kid? He's at college."

"Some guy from Bobby's crew got shot. And one of them skinny-ass potheads in South Wheeling is dead. The one who sells down there. Your kid was right there when it happened."

"I'm telling you. My kid's at college. In Cleveland."

"Well, maybe Maria had twins and never told you, because some kid who looks just like your kid is over at Bobby's with two other guys. I'm about to tell him to take them all to Ohio."

I felt like everything I'd eaten that week was about to end up in the back of my pants. Not that I seen the kid all that often or knew too much about what he was doing. I guess I knew even less than I thought. But he was still my kid. Maria's kid, too. If something happened to him, Maria would kill me.

"I'll go over there," I said. "I'll straighten it all out."

"It's too late to straighten anything out. Somebody's got to clean up the mess."

The other two guys in the bar was looking at me. They could tell something not normal was going on.

"I don't understand what happened. Whatever it was, whatever it is. I'll work it out."

"Somebody needs to work it out. And you don't want me to be the one to do it."

"Just give me a chance to try."

Paul got quiet. I waited and listened. I could tell from the sounds of cars going by that he was at a payphone somewhere. He never made calls from his house or his place. He'd have Vinny drive him all over town looking for different phones to use.

"I only called because your kid's there," Paul said. "If they don't tell me your kid's there, end of story. To Ohio they all go. You know I don't have time to fuck around with this shit."

"I know. I appreciate that. I do. Just let me go over there. I'll talk to Bobby. And I'll figure out what happened."

Paul paused again.

"I told you I don't need this shit. You know me good enough to know that. I got one guy gone and another guy clipped and who knows what kind of mess we'll have over this? Shit like this is what puts people away for good. I know this ain't your thing no more, but I don't know what the fuck your kid is doing in the middle of it."

"I don't know either. I promise you I'll find out. I'll get it all straightened out."

"I know you will. Because you know what'll happen if you don't." Then he hung up.

I slammed the phone back onto the wall. I shouted a few curse words, more than a few times. It scared the other guys. They got their stuff together and started to leave.

"It's fine," I said to them. "I'm fine. You're fine. But I need to go. I got something to do."

"Everything OK?" one of them said. He was nervous, almost too nervous to even ask.

"I don't know. All I know is I got to go."

I kept cursing as I packed up the cash, stashed it in the back, turned off the lights, and started out.

I had to walk back to my apartment to get the car. That night, I didn't ask myself how many more times I'd make that walk. Maybe I should have.

Fourteen

SEPTEMBER 19, 1973

LESLIE FITZPATRICK

I WENT TO my mother's house every Wednesday night for dinner, the same house where I grew up. That's the night my stepfather always went bowling. It was the best time for us to talk about things he didn't need to hear about.

I loved him. I did. He'd officially made me his daughter after marrying my mother. I didn't hesitate to take his name. Once my real father got life and my mother told me what he'd done to deserve it, I decided to embrace a new father and everything that went along with it. It didn't hurt to get rid of "diFrancesco." I was in the second grade when it happened. The sooner the other kids stopped connecting me to a guy who went to prison for killing someone, the better.

I smelled the jasmine candles as I pushed the side door to the house open. Mixed with whatever she was cooking. Probably veal. She loved to cook veal, even after she found out what veal is. I counted in my head the five steps up to the kitchen.

"You're early," she said without turning from the pans on the burners.

I walked over to kiss her on the cheek. "You'd rather I be late?"

"It's almost done. If I knew you'd be early, it would be done already."

"It's OK that it's not done. Unless you want me to leave and come back."

She turned around. "You're leaving already? You just walked in."

"You said I was early."

"You are."

"So I said I could leave and come back. You know, at the right time."

"But why would you do that? You're already here."

I dropped it. I walked over to the cabinet that had the dishes inside and opened the door.

"The table's set," my mother said. "You know I always set the table before I start cooking the meal."

I wasn't sure I actually knew that, but I went along with it. "What can I do to help, then?"

"You can open a bottle of wine. There's one in the dining room, next to where Charlie keeps his whiskey."

"Do you have a corkscrew?"

She laughed at that. "Corkscrew? You should know by now that we only buy the finest twist-top wine around here."

After we finished eating, my mom picked up a pack of cigarettes from the table, right next to her plate. She always smoked Pall Malls. She always had them close by. She took them everywhere except the bathroom. When I was ten, I started sneaking one at a time whenever she went to pee. Showing up at a friend's house with five or ten cigarettes to pass around became a pretty good way to get them to forget my real father had killed someone.

"You look like you're about to tell me something," she said to me as I stared at the red pack.

"There's a look for that?"

"There's a look for everything. If you live long enough, you'll learn them all."

"So what do I look like I'm about to tell you?" I reached for the pack and took a cigarette.

"You know I don't like you smoking."

"If I'll be breathing yours, I may as well smoke my own." I popped open her lighter and lit the end. I took a long drag. "So what do I look like I'm about to say? I'm curious."

"Something's bothering you. Something's nagging at you. I've sensed it since you got here. You're having doubts about something."

"I'm always having doubts about something."

"So what is it this time? Is it him? Are you finally thinking about leaving him?"

"I guess I'm always thinking about leaving him."

"You know, he's older than me."

"I know. You tell me that every Wednesday."

"It's true every Wednesday."

"You think it's easy to walk away from someone after six years? Especially someone like him?"

"That's why you shouldn't have gotten mixed up with him in the first place."

"You tell me that every Wednesday, too," I said, taking a longer drag than the first one.

"I'll say this, it feels more serious this time. More urgent. Urgent? Yeah, urgent."

"I've just been thinking a lot lately. I went to see him last week."

"I figured you see him more often than that."

"Not Paul," I said. "*Him*."

Her cigarette dropped onto the tablecloth. She scooped it up and almost put the burning end in her mouth. "Why would you do that?"

"It was his birthday. I felt bad for him."

"Don't." Her voice had a tone I didn't hear during many of our Wednesday night dinners. "He ruined four lives." She started counting with the fingers on her free hand. "Mine, yours, his, and that poor bastard they killed. Thank God the guy they killed didn't have a family."

"He didn't do it on purpose. You told me yourself he didn't hurt anyone. He was just there when it happened."

"He shouldn't have been there. He got what he deserved. I didn't know how deep he was in all of it. I knew he was involved with those bums. Just like you're involved with his partner now."

"They were partners?"

"Sort of. He never talked much about it. They all worked together. Partners, colleagues, whatever. They were in the same line of work."

"Then where was Paul that night?"

"Your father never told me that. Besides, I didn't care. Your father got arrested. Your father went to prison. Paul sent me some money at first, before I met Charlie."

"He did?"

"I don't know if Paul felt guilty or what. I don't know. I don't care. They all can go straight to hell. Instead of getting real jobs, they had to be tough guys and crooks."

"It's all they ever knew. That's what Paul told me."

"That's bullshit. They like roughing people up. They like stealing. It excites them. Your father told me that, one night after he came home drunk. Sticking it to someone else. Getting something for nothing." She mashed that cigarette into an ashtray and got another one. "It's all fun until someone gets killed and someone else gets sent away for the rest of their life."

"Paul doesn't seem like he thinks it's fun. It's just his job."

"It's his job now that he's in charge. They loved that action for years, him and your father." She didn't say anything for a little while. She looked at me. Her face got a little softer as she smoked some more. She took another drink of wine. I did, too.

"So what did he say?" she said.

"Not much. He never does. He doesn't look good."

"How could he in that hellhole? I haven't been there in at least ten years. I'll never go back."

"I said the same thing after I left. But I'll probably go back next year."

"I probably won't."

"He said something else," I said. "Something I sort of keep hearing in my head."

"He told you where he hid all the money?"

"He told me I'm getting older. He asked if I'm ever going to bring a baby with me."

"That's no place for a baby."

"He said that, too. I just keep hearing what he said."

"Well, I'm suddenly starting to like this conversation."

"I can't have a baby. Not with Paul."

"All the more reason to finally get rid of him. Then I can quit telling you every Wednesday that he's older than me."

"You act like it's easy. At this point, I think I have to wait for him to leave me."

"Well, if you're thinking about having a baby, you don't have very long to wait."

"I'd still have to meet someone else."

"You'd better not wait too long for that, either. You're not going to be that pretty forever."

"Thanks for the reminder."

"I'm just telling you the truth. Besides, he has a wife. He could have had kids of his own. He didn't. Why can't you just tell him you want to have a family?"

"He'd tell me I already have a family."

"I really don't think it's as hard as you do. You can figure out a way to make him want to leave you, if you really want to."

I started thinking about what she was trying to tell me. I finished the cigarette. I lit another one. We sat there for a while, smoking Pall Malls and drinking cheap wine. She just watched me, letting me come up with a plan.

"You're smart," she eventually said. "Smarter than you think. Think of why he started up with you in the first place. If that stops, he'll find someone else. Fast."

I knew what she was saying. I was glad she wasn't saying it more clearly. I also knew it wouldn't be easy. Not with him. Nothing was ever easy with him.

Fifteen

SEPTEMBER 19, 1973

J.J. JENKINS

I UNDERSTOOD WHY Willie couldn't drive that Camaro right after I ended up behind its steering wheel. Even a little bit of pressure on the pedals triggered a strong and immediate response. Of course, it wasn't any easier to operate the car with Willie in the backseat, a bullet in his shoulder.

I still don't understand what had happened or how it all went down. We showed up at the address in South Wheeling. It was on a street that ran along the river. Nothing special about it. Basic houses, basic street, basic neighborhood. I got the impression they'd been there before. I guess I was wrong about that.

I'd followed Tony and Willie to the porch. Tony knocked hard on the frame. I got a weird feeling when a skinny guy in a white sleeveless T-shirt pulled the door against the chain lock and acted like he was confused. He kept saying, "Where's Bobby?" and that he only gives the money to Bobby and we should go get Bobby. Tony tried to tell the guy we were there instead of Bobby, and Bobby wouldn't be happy if we went back without Bobby's money.

I told them we should just leave, but Tony was always a hothead. He kicked that door open. The skinny guy in the T-shirt ended up

60

on the floor. All of a sudden he had a gun. It looked like a bazooka in between those bony arms. Tony tried to reason with him until someone upstairs started yelling down. That made things just crazy enough for Tony to think he could make a move for the gun. When he did, the guy pulled the trigger. It caught Willie in the arm. Blood splashed against my face. I thought the bullet hit me at first. When I realized what happened, I threw up all over the wall.

As I was bent over puking, Tony took out his own gun from the back of his jeans and started pulling the trigger. It sounded like firecrackers going off inside a football helmet. I saw the skinny guy's chest torn open. That white T-shirt was soaked in blood and whatever else that was making its way out from his insides. I threw up again.

It was all a blur after that. Tony tried to snap Willie and me out of whatever haze we were in. He made us run to the car. He pretty much threw Willie in the back and climbed in there with him, trying to stop the bleeding. Tony took off his shirt and wrapped it around the top of Willie's shoulder and pulled it tight. Tony yelled at me to drive. I did, but I had no idea where I was going. He told me to go to Bobby's place, like I knew where that was.

I figured it was somewhere near town, so I went in that direction. I asked Tony for something more specific. He got mad at me that I didn't know. How was I supposed to know? Just because Bobby Marroni used to work for my dad, I should know everything about him?

Tony gave me the address once he realized that if he didn't, we'd never get there. I didn't recognize it at first, but when he said it was in East Wheeling, I knew where to go. I saw a spot on the street down from wherever we were going. I ended up putting the right front wheel of the Camaro up on the curb. I didn't bother pulling it back off.

Tony dragged Willie out of the back seat. He was getting delirious, singing his words instead of saying them. We both helped walk him to the corner of 18th and Wood. I looked up and saw big letters painted by hand over the main door. It said Doggie Do-Rights.

"Are we in the right place?" I said to Tony.

"Just ring the bell," he said.

I pushed my finger into the round button. I could hear dogs barking. I tried to look inside. It was dark. I could see enough to tell it looked like a store. Or maybe it used to be one. A bakery or something. There was nothing in the case that ran along the spot near the back wall. I noticed an old cash register on top of the counter.

Someone was coming. I could see the shape. It was a big guy. It wasn't Bobby, unless he'd gained a lot of weight. The lights came on fast, those bright fluorescent ones that buzz. It got really bright. My eyes blinked over and over again. The door swung open.

"What the fuck is this?" the guy said, his eyes going back and forth over the three of us.

"Tommy, something happened tonight," Tony said.

"Where's your shirt?" he said to Tony.

"I had to use it to help stop the bleeding." Tony pointed to Willie's shoulder. "See? He got shot."

"Who shot him?"

"I shot the sheriff." Willie sang the words, sounding like he was drunk.

"The skinny guy in that house in South Wheeling," Tony said.

"Fuck a mother. Let's get in the back and figure out what the hell this is."

The big guy named Tommy led the way. Tony helped Willie through the outer room. I thought about turning around and leaving. I had nothing to do with any of this. I was just along for the ride.

But I didn't leave. Sometimes I wish I had. Sometimes I'm glad I didn't. Regardless, I felt myself getting deeper into whatever it was with each step I took toward the back.

The dogs kept barking. They were behind the counter, along the wall that led to another door. As we got closer, I saw eight cages, with dogs in five of them.

Tommy yelled for the dogs to shut up. Four did. A tiny black-and-white one kept squawking.

"You too, Gnocchi," Tommy said. "*Basta!*" Tommy kept going, with Tony and Willie just behind him.

I looked at the dogs, each of them wagging their tails back and forth. The one called Gnocchi looked at me. I put my hand toward his cage as I walked past it. He sniffed my fingers. His stub of a tail shook even more.

"Let's go," Tommy said, speaking directly to me for the first time.

I nodded as respectfully as I could, even though I had no idea who this guy was or how he fit into whatever operation I was getting my first look at. I was confused. I was scared. I was also a little intrigued.

I was the last one into the back room. It stunk of cigarette smoke and dog food, maybe dog crap, too. There was a white cloud. Light from a bulb that hung over an old kitchen table made it all glow. I think there was a little pot in the air.

Three guys were sitting around the table. Beer bottles were all over the top of it. There were playing cards in scattered piles. It looked like they were in the middle of a hand, probably poker.

One of them stood up, a guy with one of those hairdos you usually see on old men who try to hide their bald heads.

"What the fuck is this all about?"

"They say something happened, Bobby."

"Something's going to happen if someone doesn't tell me what happened right now," Bobby said. He took it all in, looking at everyone. His eyes stopped on me. "Who the fuck is this? He's not with us."

"I'm J.J. Jenkins," I said.

"J.J. Jenkins? I don't know no J.J Jenkins."

I held up my hand with the missing pinky. "How about J.J. Mesagne?"

I wondered right away whether I should have said that.

Sixteen

SEPTEMBER 19, 1973

LESLIE FITZPATRICK

I COULDN'T GET comfortable on the plastic sheet that covered the couch in my mother's living room. I wrapped my body in an afghan my grandmother had made years ago, swaddling myself like the baby I kept thinking about having. I fell asleep on the couch, thanks to the wine. I heard my mother clearing the table and washing dishes while I fell asleep. I felt about twenty years younger. I liked that feeling.

I stirred a little when my mother came in and turned on the TV. She talked her way through the options. I could hear her flipping the pages of the *TV Guide.* I fell back to sleep.

I woke up as *Maude* was ending. My eyes opened during the theme for *Hawaii Five-O.* I asked my mother why she watched that show. She started talking about things she'd like to do to Jack Lord. I pulled the afghan over my head and squealed at one particular phrase I'd never heard my mother say before.

"Sorry," she said, "it's the wine talking."

"You only had two glasses."

"I guess some glasses are more talkative than others."

I watched bits of the show. Jack Lord or not, I didn't get it. I eased my way out of the afghan and straightened my clothes. I told my mother I'd wait for my stepfather to get home. She said she'd rather have some time to herself to think about Jack Lord.

I'd parked the Beetle on the street. I walked through the darkness. The orange paint glowed a little bit in the light from the porch of my mother's house. I unlocked the door. I laughed a little when I remembered I was always supposed to check for a bomb.

I drove back to my grandmother's house. I'd been living there for seven years, ever since she died. Paul wanted me to move into an apartment closer to town and rent the house to someone else. I wanted to stay where I was.

I parked under the carport. I locked the car and went inside. I turned on a lamp in the outer room and dropped onto the couch. It felt good to be sitting on something that wasn't covered in plastic.

I sat there for a while, thinking about the things my mother had said. Thinking about the things I had said. Thinking about the things I needed to do to get to where I wanted to be.

I got up to check the mail. The box was on the wall just outside the front door. I picked up the small stack and brought it to the kitchen table. I turned on the light and sat down.

There was another postcard offering membership in the Columbia Record Club. Eleven albums for one penny, and enough fine print to keep you paying full price for album after album after album for months to come. There was an envelope from the National Audubon Society. It was addressed to the neighbor across the street. At the bottom was a white envelope with handwriting in smeared pencil marks.

The letter was addressed to me, but it used my old last name. The return address was in Moundsville. After all those years, I still recognized my father's handwriting. I opened the envelope and read what was inside.

Seventeen

BOBBY'S HEAD SNAPPED when he saw the hand that was missing a finger.

"What the fuck are you doing here?" Bobby said to J.J.

"Tony and Willie are my friends."

"You might want to rethink that," Bobby said.

He then turned to Tony, demanding an explanation for what had happened.

Tony told Bobby the story, his mustache becoming more and more soaked in sweat. Bobby's face went purple after Tony said he'd shot and killed Reggie Smith.

"Are you sure he's dead?" Bobby asked through gritted teeth.

"Three shots to the chest," Tony said. "He wasn't moving."

Bobby told the three of them to sit on stools along the wall in the back room of the dog shop.

Tony reminded Bobby that Willie had been shot, too.

Bobby told Tommy to call the doctor they had lined up for situations like this. One of the best things about certain types of gambling debts was that they provided free and unlimited services that sometimes came in handy.

"Take him back to the storage room," Bobby said to Tony. "There's a desk. Clear it off and lay him on it until the doctor gets here."

Bobby watched Tommy as he called the doctor. When Tommy finished, Bobby went to the phone and dialed the number for Paul's place.

Vinny answered. He hung up when he heard Bobby's voice. He expected that. Bobby knew Vinny would take Paul to a payphone, and that Paul would call from there. Bobby never understood why they didn't care if he talked business on his own phone. He never asked for an explanation.

Bobby waited for the phone to ring. Tommy was back at the table, sitting with two others.

"Are we still playing cards or what?" Tommy said.

"I'm waiting for Paul to call."

"Paul? Why did you call him?"

"Haven't you been paying any fucking attention to what's been going on?"

The phone rang. Bobby scooped up the receiver.

"This better be important," Paul said.

"We had a little problem tonight."

"A little problem or a problem?"

"A problem," Bobby said. "A big problem, I guess. That kid Reggie Smith, the skinny one, he freaked out when I sent some guys to collect. I guess he threw a baseball at one of them. I guess they threw a baseball back at him."

"You guess or you know?"

"I know what they told me."

"Who got hit with a baseball?"

"Reggie Smith. He got hit pretty hard."

"You already said he got hit. Who else?"

"Willie Silvestri."

"Who the fuck is that?"

"Guy I been using for some odd jobs. I been trying to break some new guys in. You told me I should, you know, delicate."

"It's delegate. And, yeah, I did. But you need people you can trust."

"You didn't say that."

"It goes without saying, Bobby. Do you need me to wipe your ass, too?"

"I'm sorry, Paul. I don't know what happened. I'm just trying to figure out what to do."

"What did they do about the thing?"

"They left it there."

"They left it there? After doing that in his own house? Why didn't they just go turn themselves in, too?"

"Do you want me to tell them to do that?"

Paul didn't say anything. Bobby could hear Paul breathing through the line.

"Look," Paul said, "I know shit like this don't happen very often. But when it does, we've got to make decisions, fast. These new guys of yours, how attached to them are you?"

"I don't know. They ain't been working for me for too long."

"Maybe they need to make a trip to Ohio."

"Ohio? For one mistake?"

"It's a big mistake. This is as big of a mistake as they can make. This wasn't no special circumstance. We wasn't sending no message. The thing needed to be taken the fuck out of there and that place needed to be cleaned up. If it gets tracked back to them, then they get tracked back to us."

"So what do I do?"

"How many of your guys are there?" Paul said.

"Three. Tommy, Phil, and Rico."

"Send Tommy and Phil to get the thing. And tell Rico to take the other two to Ohio."

Bobby was getting ready to hang up. He stopped.

"There's one more thing," he said. "I almost forgot."

"It better be good."

"Those two guys. They had a friend with them."

"Three of them? Well, shit, I guess Rico can handle that, too."

"That's not it. Their friend is Johnny Mesagne's kid."

Paul went silent again. Bobby heard more breathing.

"Don't do nothing. Someone will be coming over."

The line went dead. Bobby hung up the phone. He looked around the room. He started to wonder whether everyone would end up in Ohio that night.

Eighteen

LESLIE FITZPATRICK

I READ THAT letter three straight times. The guards look at every piece of mail that goes in and out of the prison. I knew he had to be careful about what he said and how he said it. But I knew exactly what he was saying. I got a little more upset every time I read it.

I didn't have any booze in the house. I wished I did. I found a pack of cigarettes in my purse. It had about ten inside. I smoked all of them. I was still feeling agitated, nervous, confused. I looked all over the place for another pack. I found a drawer in the kitchen where Paul had left a few cigars. I looked at them. I took one. I cut the end off with a knife. I lit it.

It tasted awful, but it was all I had. I knew not to inhale. I smoked it while I read the letter again. And again. I don't know why my father decided to tell me what he wouldn't tell me when I was at the prison. I was glad he finally did. It was time to get out of the thing with Paul, even if I wasn't sure I'd be able to pull it off. In my mind, it was over then and there. I was moving on. All I had left to do was get him to decide to move on without knowing I'd already made that decision.

I sat at the kitchen table, smoking that cigar. I quit about halfway through. I pressed it out in an ashtray, ran it under the water in the sink, and threw it in the trash.

I went back to the couch and sat there. I kept telling myself what I needed to do. I'd act cold and disinterested. I couldn't do anything too obvious, like quit going around his place or stop eating dinner with him whenever he wanted to take me out. But I'd turn down any advances he made.

I'd tell him I was having lady issues. That always worked whenever it was true. I'd make it work whenever it wasn't. I'd probably have to go through with it once in a while. I'd make sure he didn't enjoy it. He'd get bored with me at some point. He'd find someone else. I'd be in the clear.

It wasn't a horrible plan. It was the only plan I had. I tried to convince myself I could pull it off. Like I told my mother, it wouldn't be easy. Like I told my mother, nothing was ever easy with him.

It was my own fault for getting involved with him. I didn't know any better. I was only twenty-one. I didn't know then what I knew after reading that letter. But that letter made it clear I needed to be very careful. I'd known for a long time what he was capable of doing to other people. I never stopped to consider whether he could be capable of doing it to me. Now, I knew he was.

He'd expect me to show up at his place the next day. I would do it. I had no choice. But I'd already made a much bigger choice that night. I was determined to make sure it worked out the way I wanted it to. I needed it to.

I hadn't been to church in a long time. I hadn't prayed in a long time, either.

When I went to bed that night, I prayed until I finally fell asleep.

Nineteen

SEPTEMBER 19, 1973

J.J. JENKINS

I WALKED BEHIND him, but not close enough to take a backhand if he decided to spin around and give me one. Not that he ever had. Then again, he moved out when I was ten. In the ten years since then, I'd never seen him as mad as he was that night.

Down the street from Bobby's place I saw the car. A 1963 Oldsmobile, with a Holiday Red paint job. He'd brought it home just a few weeks before leaving for good. "Holiday Red," he said back then, proud smile on his face after paying cash for it. "It feels like a holiday every time you get in it."

I thought there was maybe a chance to take some of the steam out of the situation. So when I saw the car, I said, "Look at that. Still Holiday Red."

It didn't work. He unlocked the door and waited for me to get in.

JOHNNY MESAGNE

I DIDN'T KNOW what to say to the kid. I was mad. But what was I supposed to do? He's a grown man. I couldn't believe how different he looked. I decided to do whatever his mother would want me to do, because before long she would demand to know what I did. The sooner I could put those two things together, the sooner I could get back to my own life.

I decided to come off like an asshole at first. "What the fuck was you doing with those two hoodlums?" I said.

"They picked me up. They didn't say where they were going."

"Why was they picking you up? Why wasn't you in that expensive school in Cleveland?"

"It's not for me."

"So you just walked away?"

"I guess I learned that from you," he said.

That one shut me up for a little bit.

J.J. JENKINS

HE WAS MAD. I couldn't really blame him. I didn't plan to get him in the middle of things. I didn't even think he was still involved in that life. He started lecturing me on how it's not about his past but my future. How if I keep doing what I did that night, I wouldn't have a future.

But I hadn't done anything. I went along for the ride, that's it. He didn't want to hear that. Or he didn't want to believe me. I couldn't tell. Regardless, he wasn't listening to me. And he was telling me they would have gotten rid of all of us if I wasn't his kid. Of course, if I wasn't his kid, I wouldn't have been interested in tagging along. I didn't tell him that part.

Maybe I could have ended all of it right then and there, if I'd just asked him to explain to me what he used to do. I didn't know how to do it. Or maybe I just didn't have the nerve.

JOHNNY MESAGNE

MARIA HAD BEEN worried he'd end up following the same path as me. So I told him I didn't want him messing around with anything like that. But, as I was saying it, I knew I didn't really care. Is that wrong? I already admitted I was a bad father. Why would I try to talk a grown man into doing something other than he wants to do? I couldn't explain it that way to Maria or to him, but that's how I felt. I can't help how I felt.

It didn't make it no easier that he took that other guy's name. I figure he had a bunch of reasons to do that. I probably was behind more than a few of them. It didn't change how it hit me when I heard he'd stopped using my name. It seemed like he turned his back on me. That's when I turned my back on him, even if I didn't know that's what I was doing.

I really didn't want to turn back around now. Sure, I didn't need to have his mother up my ass. Beyond dealing with her, I didn't want to deal with him. As far as I knew, there was a stranger in my car. A stranger who if he wasn't missing a pinky might have already been pushing up daisies in Ohio, right next to his stupid-ass friends.

J.J. JENKINS

HE WAS TRYING to scare me, talking over and over again about how if I wasn't his kid, they would have gotten rid of the three of us. Why? What did we do? That guy pulled a gun on us for no reason. Sure, Tony probably shouldn't have tried to take it away from him, but how did we cause the problem? Far as I could tell, Bobby should have known the guy was a little paranoid, or whatever. He shouldn't have sent people the guy didn't really know to make the pickup.

My father gave me a speech about staying out of that life. I'm not sure he really meant it. I figure he heard it enough from my mother over the years that he felt like he had to say it. Not that he actually wanted me to get mixed up with those guys. I just got the feeling that, deep down, he didn't care that I had.

Why should he? We were mostly connected by a name, and that wasn't even there anymore. We were two different people. We both knew it.

JOHNNY MESAGNE

MY BIGGEST CONCERN was that Paul would now think I owed him something, since he let my kid off the hook. I never asked him to, but I didn't dare say that to him. Paul would have called my bluff, would have told Vinny to take him to Ohio with the others. Paul would have forced me to ask him not to do it, and then it would have been even worse.

I didn't know what Paul would want from me. When you owe something to someone in this life, you never know. You just wait for them to ask. Even after I got my kid and my ex-wife straightened out, I'd be waiting for Paul to ask. Of course, Paul never asked. He told.

I drove the kid back to the house. I took him inside. Maria was surprised to see me, and not in a good way. She turned white like milk. I knew why. She'd been worried for years that the kid would end up like me. So here he is, dropped out of college and back in town, and who brings him home late at night but his dad, the former gangster?

J.J. JENKINS

RIGHT AWAY, IT felt like the old days. Tension and turmoil. The only thing missing was me sitting at the desk in my bedroom. This time, they told me to go out on the porch and close the door behind me. Mom gave me a look. I knew it meant I should stay close by, just in case. Was she afraid that he'd do something to her or that she'd do something to him? I smelled the Riunite in the air. I figured she was just about three sheets to the wind.

I sat on the top of the steps, same place I was before Willie rolled the Camaro down the street to pick me up. It was just a few hours earlier, but it seemed like a lot longer than that. I knew things had taken a turn.

I had no idea how big of a turn they had taken.

Twenty

BOBBY MARRONI SAT on the other side of the big wooden desk, waiting for Paul to say something else. Bobby hated that desk. Paul saw *The Godfather* one time and decided he needed a desk just like Brando's. It didn't make any sense to Bobby. The rest of the office looked cheap in comparison. The paint was cracked on the walls, the chairs were made of plastic. He had two bare bulbs hanging on wires and three curled strips stuck to the ceiling and dangling down with dead flies all over them.

Paul started in again on Bobby about making a bad decision to trust two guys who didn't know how to handle a tough situation, and who were dumb enough to take someone else with them without asking. It didn't matter that it was Johnny Mesagne's kid. Paul said that only made things worse, bringing the boy of a guy from the crew without permission.

Bobby didn't understand that one, but he wasn't there to ask questions. He was there to get grilled in the cockeyed code they used, because Paul was always worried about bugs.

"So they got that guy to the place?" Paul said.

"Yeah," Bobby said. "He made it on time."

"How big of a mess did he leave behind?"

"The other guy cleaned it all up. I guess he was smart enough to know someone would be back for the thing. He also was smart enough not to call no one about it."

"Do those other two know how close they come to the same ending?"

"One does. The other one is out of commission for now."

"Did the rabbit come to take care of him?"

"Like clockwork. That rabbit will do whatever we want, whenever we ask."

"What did you think about their friend?"

"Whose friend?"

"Whose friend do you think?"

"Oh, him. He's young. Wet behind the years."

"It's wet behind the ears," Paul said. "And so are you, Bobby. More than I thought."

"He wasn't supposed to be there. I didn't know he was going to be there. The others picked him up."

"We been over that. They should've known not to do that."

"They didn't know."

"You're missing the point, Bobby. They should've been told not to do it. By you."

"How was I supposed to know they would do that?"

Paul looked over at Vinny, who was standing a few feet away like a big, dumb statue, like he always did when someone was meeting with Paul. All that was missing was the pigeon shit. Vinny shrugged and made a face that said it all: *What do you expect? He's a dumbass.* Paul turned back to Bobby.

"How did he handle himself?"

"Who?"

"The friend. The kid. Did he piss in his pants? Did he mumble and stutter?"

"None of that," Bobby said. "He spoke when he was spoke to. He explained what happened. He knew everyone was pissed off. And his dad was more pissed off than anybody. Come to think of it, the kid never got rattled at all. He should have been. At that age, I know I would have been." Bobby was straying from the code, but he didn't know how else to say it.

Paul twisted his mouth and scratched his thumbnail against the tip of his nose. "Does he seem like his old man?"

"Not really," Bobby said. "Doesn't look much like him. Johnny's got that black hair, I guess not as black as it used to be. The kid has brown hair. Curly. Almost like an Afro. And he seemed smart, but not like an egghead. Talks good. He has, I don't know, confidence in his voice."

Paul looked at his watch and jumped out of his seat. "Shit. I'm late to meet Sally. Vinny, get the car. You, follow me."

Bobby did what he was told. He heard Paul fart as he walked ahead of Bobby. He held his breath through the cloud.

"Bring the kid in," Paul said.

Bobby exhaled. "Which kid?"

Paul stopped and turned around. "Which kid do you think?" Then he turned back around and kept going.

Bobby heard that sound again. He went back to holding his breath.

"I want to see if he's like his old man. Maybe we can find something for him to do."

Bobby emptied his lungs again. "I don't think Johnny will like that."

"Oh, Johnny Mesagne will fucking hate it," Paul said, laughing all the way to and through the front door.

Twenty-one

SEPTEMBER 20, 1973

J.J. JENKINS

MR. GLEASON CALLED the house just after eight o'clock on Thursday morning. He wanted me to take a shift that started at two. I figured it was a test to see how serious I was about going back. My mother answered the phone and got me out of bed to talk to him. I snapped out of it as best I could. I told him I'd be there.

I went back toward the bedroom. I told her to get me up at one. She asked whether that would give me enough time. The store was only like five minutes away, ten at the most. She said she'd wake me up at twelve, that it was better to be early than late. At that point, I didn't care. I just wanted to go back to sleep, especially after everything that happened the night before.

She started banging on my door at noon, like she said she would. If she hadn't been cooking up some bacon and eggs for me, I would have complained. I showered. I ate. I got myself ready to go. She said Mr. Gleason would be impressed if I got there extra early, even if it meant I'd sit in the break room reading the newspaper while waiting to punch in. She gave me hers, except for the page with the crossword puzzle.

I went to my room and finished getting dressed after I ate. I checked the time on the fake Rolex she'd given me when I graduated high school. It was on the desk in my bedroom, next to the compass.

That damn compass. A family heirloom or whatever. For years it had been a reminder of a life I wanted to forget. That compass all of a sudden seemed different. Not better or worse. Just different.

I picked it up. The needle always pointed to the north. From where I stood, that meant directly to the front door, like it always had. I thought about taking it with me. I put it back on the desk.

I told my mother goodbye. I walked out to the porch and down the steps. The Plymouth was parked on the street in front of the house. A Mustang rolled toward me. It was blue. I had a weird feeling that it would be stopping at the house, and indeed it did.

The door opened. I saw that head with the goofy hairstyle. I felt queasy.

"Where you headed?" Bobby said to me.

"I got a job. I'm going to work."

"Not today."

"Excuse me?"

"You're not going to work today," Bobby said.

"Well, where am I going?"

"Someone wants to talk to you."

"I talked to my dad last night. He drove me home."

"Not him."

"There's nobody else to talk to."

"Yeah," Bobby said, "there is."

I didn't understand why Bobby Marroni would be showing up at my house. I couldn't figure out who wanted to talk to me. Maybe I should have. Maybe I just didn't want to.

He was trying to put my mind at ease, I think. At one point he said if anything was going to happen, it would have happened last night. That was supposed to make me feel better. It sure didn't.

That's when it hit me. Paul wanted to see me. I felt scared. I also felt a little, I don't know, honored. The boss wanted to see me. The big boss. The guy my dad used to work for. I looked back up at the porch to see if my mother was paying attention to any of this. I didn't see her.

"How long do you think it'll take?" I said.

"Long as it takes," Bobby said.

"And he told you to come get me?"

"You ain't half as dumb as you look."

"Does my dad know about this?" I said.

"Your dad don't matter. This is about you and Paul."

"What if I don't go?"

"Do you really want me to tell him you said you ain't coming?" Bobby said. "Is that what you want?"

"I guess I don't. How long will this take?"

"Ain't we been over this? It takes whatever it takes. You really don't know how this works, do you? Whether it's five minutes or five hours or five days don't matter to me. I'm not asking him. And he's not telling me."

"How long do you *think* it will take?"

"If you talk to him like you're talking right now to me, it'll take a lot longer than it needs to take."

I didn't know what to do. I'd just gotten my job back. If I didn't show up, I probably wouldn't keep it. I thought about going back inside and calling Mr. Gleason and telling him I'd gotten sick, but then I would have had to deal with my mother.

So I knew what would happen. I'd be late. He'd call the house. My mother would say I left an hour ago. Then she'd look out front and see the Plymouth and lose her damn mind. I decided right then I'd rather deal with that later than refuse a direct request from Paul Verbania now.

"You'll bring me back here when it's done?" I said to Bobby.

"You'll be brought back. You seem nervous."

"Should I not be?"

"I told you, if they was doing something to Johnny Mesagne's kid, they would've done it already."

I had a bright idea, one that sounded better in my head before I said it. "If he wants to talk to me, I can go back inside and call him."

"He didn't tell me to come tell you to call him. He told me to come get you."

I didn't know what to do. I had no choice. I figured I could find another job, if Mr. Gleason wouldn't give me another chance.

"OK," I said to Bobby. "I'll go. But I don't like it."

"Good," he said, "because I don't like it, neither."

Twenty-two

SEPTEMBER 20, 1973

JOHNNY MESAGNE

EVEN FROM BEHIND the bar, I could hear that rumbling from outside. I knew what it was, right away.

"Paul's here," I said, to nobody in particular.

Jimmy sat at the bar, working on a beer and reading the racing form. It was early. No one else was there.

"Were you expecting him?" he said.

"Not really, but I guess I sort of was."

"There you go making all kinds of sense again," Jimmy said.

I had a wet towel in my hands. I dropped it into the sink and asked Jimmy to keep an eye on the place.

He looked around at the empty room as I walked away. "I think I can handle it."

What he said didn't register as a joke, because I was thinking about Paul. I didn't know exactly what he wanted. He wouldn't be there if he didn't want something. And it wasn't a coincidence he was showing up the morning after all that shit went down in South Wheeling.

I opened the door and saw the Cadillac parked in front of the place. Vinny in the front and Paul in the back. I knew I was supposed to climb into the empty seat behind Vinny.

"How's business this week?" Paul said after I got inside the car.

"Been good, now that the NFL is back. They're betting on the NFL more than ever."

"It's just a matter of time before pro football takes over. Looks too good on TV. And that Monday night thing they're doing now, it'll all get more and more popular. You wait and see."

"More money for us, I guess. As long as the Steelers don't keep playing like they did last year. I don't care how much we move the line, everyone around here keeps taking them. And they keep covering the spread."

"It all evens out in the end," Paul said. "The key is the handle. The more we handle, the more we make, even if we have a down week or two."

"They made the number too easy against Detroit."

"Everybody makes the number too easy against Detroit."

"I guess we'll see what happens when the Steelers play Cleveland this week."

Paul had a cigar in his mouth. He got quiet for a little bit and rolled it around in his teeth. I knew what was coming.

"Crazy times last night," he said.

"Crazier than anything I would have expected. Did they get everything taken care of?"

"Far as I know. Sometimes I wonder whether I get told the whole story. I guess it ain't a problem unless I find out otherwise. I just can't believe your kid was part of that. I figured your kid would steer clear."

"So did I."

"Didn't you tell him to?"

I didn't know what to say to that. I rubbed my hands on my slacks. I decided to be straight with Paul, not because I wanted to but because he was smart enough to figure out if I was selling him a bill of goods.

"I tried," I said to him, "but only because Maria has spent the kid's whole life thinking that's exactly where he'd end up."

"What happened to college?"

"I guess it didn't work out."

"I thought he was smart."

"He is. Way smarter than me. I don't know why it didn't work out, to be honest."

"I hope you'll be honest with me."

"I always am, Paul." As far as I could remember, that was true.

"So what do you want him to do?"

"Well, if he gets in, he gets in," I said. "But if he gets in, he's on his own."

Paul seemed surprised by that. I wondered right away whether I should have told him something else.

"You really don't care if he gets in?"

"Maria does. But what can I do? He's twenty years old. He can vote, he can drink, he can smoke, he can join the army if he wants to. I ain't been running his life for ten years. Why would I start now?"

Paul rolled that cigar around some more. He was thinking. Usually when he was thinking, I didn't like what he was thinking about.

"Well, this is interesting," he said.

I looked at Vinny to see if he reacted to what had just been said. He didn't. He pretty much never did.

"What's interesting?" I said.

"I was planning to tell you I want to meet with the kid. Maybe I can find some stuff for him to do, if that's what he wants to do. Why else would he be coming around?"

"He was with his friends last night, that's all."

"But he knew what his friends was into."

"I guess so," I said. "Regardless, I ain't standing in his way. As long as I can tell Maria I told him to stay away, whatever he does is his business."

"Well, I was going to ask if you'd let me put him to work, you know, to even things out for last night's mess."

I didn't know what else to say, so I went along with it. "I guess you already got the answer," I told him.

"I guess I do. Well, I'll let you get back to work. Maybe the Browns won't shit the bed on Sunday."

He was telling me we were done talking. I opened the door and started to get out. Then I turned back before closing it. I wanted to be clear about everything.

"So will this square us for last night? Me letting you talk to him?"

"How would it square us?"

"I just told you I ain't going to stand in the way."

"But you just said you weren't going to stand in the way anyway."

As I tried to think of something else to say, Vinny hit the gas and the Cadillac rolled away from me.

I stood there thinking about what had just happened.

Twenty-three

SEPTEMBER 20, 1973

LESLIE FITZPATRICK

I WOKE UP. It was getting close to noon. I thought about my plan again. It still made sense, even in the light of day. I got ready and went to Paul's place. I didn't have a key, but the front door was never locked during the afternoon. For as much as he worried about someone sticking a bomb under his car or my car or any car, he didn't worry about anyone walking right into his place. I guess he knew no one would ever be dumb enough to come after him out in the open like that.

I drove the Volkswagen. I made the trip slowly, trying to avoid being there for as long as I could. I still didn't want to show up too late, or maybe he'd start getting curious. That was the last thing I needed.

Just like I thought, the knob twisted and the door opened. I went in and looked around. No one was there. I lit a cigarette. I was there, like he would have expected me to be. Whenever someone else showed up, and someone else eventually would, they'd see me. I relaxed a little bit.

I turned on the TV in the main room and flipped through the channels. I put it on a soap opera. I started another cigarette. I thought some more about my plan. It made me nervous. I needed something other than the television to distract me. I turned on the pinball machine, stuck a quarter inside, and started playing.

It was a nice escape, even if only for a little while.

J.J. JENKINS

BOBBY DROVE ME into town. He didn't say anything on the way. I didn't say anything, either. I sat there wondering what was going to happen when we got to wherever he was taking me.

He parked the Mustang and got out. I got out, too, before he had to tell me to. I followed him. It was a building I'd seen before. I'd never been inside. I didn't know what it was. As Bobby got closer, I figured that was the place where I'd be meeting with Paul.

He went in first and held the door open for me. It was dark. I could see a pool table and a bar. A TV was on. I heard something else, a pinball machine. A woman was playing it.

The game said "Yukon" on the glass. It had a picture of a man falling from a horse. Someone else was in the picture, too, looking like maybe he had shot the other one. I thought about what had happened at the house in South Wheeling with Willie and Tony and the skinny guy on the floor. I started feeling dizzy.

"You're still messing with that thing?" Bobby said to her.

"Hush," she said. "I'm finally getting good at this."

I watched her play. I couldn't see her face. She was wearing jeans that were as tight as they could be without popping. She was moving her hips while she played the game. I tried to make myself look away. It wasn't easy.

When I did, Bobby was staring at me.

"You OK, kid?"

"I'm fine," I said.

LESLIE FITZPATRICK

I KEPT PLAYING that pinball machine. I don't know how many quarters I'd put into it. I took a bunch of them from the cash register behind the bar, so they were all ending up in the same place, anyway. It was helping me kill the time. It was helping me not think about everything I'd been thinking about.

When the door opened, I thought it was Vinny and Paul. I knew right away it wasn't, since whoever it was wasn't bringing with them the smell of soup or cigars. I glanced over and saw Bobby with that ridiculous hair of his. He said something. I told him to be quiet. I was actually having fun, standing there with a fresh cigarette in my mouth that I hadn't gotten around to lighting.

He asked me if Paul was in the back. It distracted me enough that the ball fell past the flippers and the game was over. I cursed. I turned to Bobby.

"I said, 'Be quiet.'"

Then I noticed the other person who was with Bobby. I squinted a little bit. I thought I recognized him, but I wasn't sure.

"J.J.?" I said. "Is that you?"

J.J. JENKINS

WHEN SHE TURNED around, I realized who it was. She knew it was me. I felt nervous all of a sudden. I felt bad about what I'd been thinking while I was trying not to look at the back of her jeans.

"Hi Leslie," I said. "It's been a while."

She looked at Bobby. She pulled a cigarette from her mouth. I hadn't noticed it wasn't burning.

"What's he doing here?" she asked. She had green eyes. They looked like they were glowing. I turned away. I felt even more nervous.

"He wanted to see him. Is he back there or not?"

"He isn't," she said. "I don't know where he is."

"Well, I thought he would be here."

"I don't know what to tell you," she said. I could feel those green eyes on me, even though I was staring down at the floor.

"He tells me to go get him, and then he's not here?" Bobby said.

"If you got something else to do, go ahead," she said. "I'll take it from here."

I kept my mouth shut. I could tell Bobby didn't know what to do.

"I should stay until he gets back. He told me to go get him."

"You went to get him," she said. "You did your job. If he needs a ride home when they're done, I can give him one."

I didn't like the sound of that, mainly because I sort of did like the sound of it.

"You won't take off or nothing?" Bobby said to me. "If I go, you'll stay?"

I looked up from the floor at him. "I'm already here. Last thing I'll do now is leave."

LESLIE FITZPATRICK

BOBBY FINALLY LEFT. I stood there looking at J.J. I couldn't remember when I'd last seen him. He had changed. I had no idea. He didn't look like his dad. That was good. And it wasn't. Then I remembered I had a cigarette in my mouth.

"Well?" I said to him.

"Well what?" he said. He didn't want to look at me. I thought it was kind of cute.

"Do you have a light?"

"I don't smoke," he said.

I rolled my eyes a little bit. "There are matches behind you, on the bar."

He turned around and noticed the small book of matches with a silver cover. He picked it up and handed it to me.

"Here you go," he said.

"How old are you?" I said.

She grabbed my wrist. "Twenty. I'll be twenty-one in January."

"Well, twenty-year-old-step-cousin-who'll-be-twenty-one-in-January, when a lady asks you if you have a light, she's asking you to light her cigarette."

I held out the matches and waited.

J.J. JENKINS

I DIDN'T KNOW what she wanted me to do, but I was starting to figure it out. I put out my left palm, the one that had all five fingers connected to it. She dropped the matchbook. I watched her hand. She left it there, just a little bit longer than she needed to.

"Do you know what comes next?" she said.

I swallowed hard. I looked at the matches. I fumbled to open them up, no longer worrying about hiding my hand that was missing a pinky. I don't know why I cared. She already knew about that.

I popped it open. I tore out one of the thin paper matches. I struck it against the brown strip at the bottom. It sparked bright white and then turned orange. She grabbed my wrist and pulled it toward her face. She moved her lips so that the end of the cigarette dipped down into the fire. After the cigarette was burning, she let go of me. She made her mouth into a circle and blew out the match.

"See," she said, "that wasn't very hard."

I swallowed hard again and waited for whatever she was going to say next.

Twenty-four

MARIA TOOK THE page from the newspaper with the crossword puzzle to the kitchen table and started working on it. She never finished the whole thing. But she always checked the next day to see the answers to the ones she didn't know.

She tried not to think about what happened last night. She hadn't seen Johnny in a while. She didn't realize until she saw him that she hadn't really missed seeing him. He used to make her knees weak. Now, he only made her stomach turn.

But there he was, walking through her front door with J.J. right behind him. Two peas in a piss-poor pod. She'd gone from wishing they would spend more time together to praying they'd never, ever cross paths.

Neither one would tell her the whole story. She tried with Johnny after he brought J.J. home. She tried with J.J. after Johnny left. All she got out of them was that there had been some sort of an accident, and that Johnny had helped straighten it all out. It was like they sat down somewhere and practiced what they'd tell her.

A real swell father-son picnic that must have been, she thought.

She knew Paul was in the middle of it, somewhere. Johnny didn't deny it. He just said he took care of it. She told him she wanted the boy to steer clear of the life Johnny had led, and of the life he was still leading.

He got out, but he's not really out, she thought. *He's still working for Paul.* He was a worthless bastard in her eyes, no matter how much money or power he had. She'd never understand why or how Johnny ended up with a job as one of Paul's bookies, but nothing more. She didn't want to know. Life's a lot easier when you know what you don't want to know. She had lived by that motto for longer than she could remember.

Her biggest concern was keeping J.J. away from it. She spent a dozen years worrying about Johnny ending up dead or in prison. She didn't want to spend the next twenty or thirty worrying about the same thing happening to her son. It was her own fault for letting a hoodlum knock her up when she was too young to understand what it all really meant.

She focused on the page from the newspaper. It had a fresh puzzle on one column and the answer to yesterday's game on the other. She checked that one before trying the new one. She slipped into a nice little groove, like she pretty much always did. When she hit a road-block, she lit up a cigarette. She used to only ever smoke in the bed-room. Once J.J. left for college, she realized it was easier to just smoke in the kitchen. She could sit there and do things. All she could really do in the bedroom was read paperback books she'd buy at the grocery store for forty-nine cents each.

She'd managed to get J.J. to leave for work by one o'clock. He was supposed to start working an hour later. At about fifteen minutes after two, the phone rang. The moment it started, a funny feeling spread across her stomach.

It was Mickey Gleason, the manager from Foodland. He said J.J. was late.

She told him J.J. had left more than an hour earlier. Heat crawled up her neck, toward her ears. She asked him if he was sure J.J. didn't start working without punching in.

He said J.J. wasn't in the store, anywhere.

She hung up and went to the front door. She pulled it open. She saw his car out front. She walked across the porch and down the steps. She usually never went outside with curlers in her hair. But she was confused. She was feeling panicky. She went over to the car. She walked all the way around it. She even bent down and looked under it. She felt the hood. It was cold. He'd never even left.

Where the hell did he go?

She started cursing, but not loud enough for anyone to hear it. Not that she cared if they did. Between her first husband and her second one, the neighbors had lived through enough yelling and carrying on over the years to not be surprised.

She stood there, wondering what to do next. She marched back toward the house and went inside. She walked back to the phone on the wall in the kitchen and picked it up. She dialed a number she remembered by heart, even if she hadn't dialed it in so long that she couldn't remember the last time she had.

Twenty-five

BEFORE LESLIE COULD say anything else, the door flew open. Two jagged shadows rolled inside. The first moved like a brick wall that had come to life. I noticed a hole in his nose before I saw that his shoes seemed maybe three sizes too big. Behind him was Paul Verbania. I hadn't seen him since before my dad moved out, but I would have known him anywhere. Big head. No hair. Fleshy cheeks. Cigar dangling and bouncing.

Leslie pulled the cigarette from her mouth. She went over to Paul. She kissed him on the cheek.

I sighed. It was loud enough for me to hear it. I looked around to see if any of them had heard it, too.

"Look who it is," Paul said to me. "You don't look much like your old man. Consider yourself lucky."

I didn't know how to greet him. I extended my right hand. He took it. He turned his wrist, so that the spot where I was missing a finger was on top of the handshake.

"You still got that, huh?"

I didn't know what to say. Did he think it would grow back?

"Let's take a walk," he said to me. He kept going, so I followed. He told the other guy to stay out front. Then Paul asked me what I drank.

"I like Coke," I said.

He shook his head and asked Leslie to bring back two Iron Citys. He made a big show of bending toward her and saying, "Please."

I watched her while he did it. It seemed like she didn't want to look at him. I sort of felt like she was looking at me.

Paul turned around and kept going. The other guy pulled a chair from under a table and sat down. I saw from the corner of my eye that he turned a bag over and shook it. Stacks of cash fell out, folded in half and held together by rubber bands.

Paul led me to a back room. He sat down behind a big brown desk that was by far the nicest thing in his office, if that's what the room was.

"You like it?" he said.

I didn't know what the question was about. "What do I like?"

"This desk. You ever seen *The Godfather*?"

"It was sold out when we tried to go."

"Well, you should've kept trying. It's the best picture they ever made. It ain't all that realistic about some things, but it's the first time anybody tried to show what it really means to be a Sicilian in America. You know, they don't really want us here."

Again, I didn't know what he meant. "Who doesn't want us here?"

"The Americans. The English. Everybody and anybody who ain't Sicilian or Italian. We have to look out for ourselves. They got our people to come over here to do the stuff no one else wanted to do. Mining coal. Making steel."

"I won't work in the coal mines," I said, "or in the steel mills."

Paul struck a match and rolled the end of his cigar in the fire. He sucked on the back end and blew a white cloud over the top of the desk.

I held my breath until it faded away.

"Not a whole lot of choices around here for a young man. I heard you was in college."

"I was. I'm not anymore."

"What happened?"

"It wasn't for me."

"So what are you going to do?"

"I have a job at Foodland. Well, I did. I don't know if I still do. It's complicated."

"How complicated is it to bag groceries? Are you saying college isn't for you, but that is?"

"I need to make some money."

"There's plenty of other ways to make some money. You know, I got plenty of ways you can make some money."

"Well, I don't know how to put this. I don't think my parents want me doing that."

"Is it their life or is it yours? I don't want to start no family trouble, but you're the one who's got to decide what you're going to do. Nobody else."

"They want me to find a way out."

He sucked on the cigar so hard that the tip of it glowed like the sun. He blew the smoke right at me.

I held my breath again.

""Your way out of what? Your way out of who you are? Is that why you carry that English thing around?" He made a face. "*Jenkins.*"

I think I smiled when he said the name. "I was young when my dad left. My stepfather was different. He paid attention to me."

"Wait a minute. You're a man now, so you need to be spoken to like you're a man. Can I speak to you like you're a man?"

I think I nodded.

"*Jenkins* paid attention to you because he wanted to get inside your mother's skirt. Once he got his fill, how much attention did he pay to you? How much attention did he pay to her? Your dad left. *Jenkins* left. All you got is you."

"I've got my mom."

Leslie walked into the room. She had two bottles of Stroh's beer. She put them on the desk.

I tried hard not to look at her.

"I asked for Iron City," Paul said, "and I asked real nice."

"There's no Iron City," she said, "and you're welcome."

"Thank you," I blurted out, but she was already gone.

"So you got your mom," Paul said. "There ain't nothing wrong with that. But every man got his mom. And every man still got to make his own way. What you got to do is figure out how you're going to make your own way."

"So how do I do that?"

"You just do it. It just happens. But you're the one who does it. Nobody else."

I took a drink of the beer. It tasted bitter and stale. I tried not to show it. "My dad doesn't want me making my way the same way he made his way."

"Ask yourself this question. Do you think your dad listened to anybody else when your dad made his way?"

I took another drink. It was a little easier this time not to react to the taste. After I put the bottle back on the desk, Paul talked to me like I was a man for at least another half hour.

Twenty-six

I WAS AT the bar, still visiting with Jimmy Dacey. We were talking about whatever there was to talk about on a Thursday afternoon. The horse races were winding down for the day and soon the bets would be picking up on baseball. It was getting close to the end of the season.

The phone rang. I went over to pick it up. The voice on the other end was a woman. I knew right away which woman it was.

Maria sounded a little too close to hysterical. I tried to get her to calm down, not because I cared whether she was upset but because I couldn't understand nothing she said. She was saying something about J.J. getting snatched. I was confused. I thought she was saying someone came into the house and took him. I kept telling her to slow it down. She never really did, but I started to pick up more of what she was trying to say.

She said he was on his way to work but he never got in his car. I didn't know what to make of that. Were his friends mad at him about what happened at Bobby's? They should have been happy. If J.J. wasn't there, the other two would be taking a permanent nap under a few feet of topsoil right now.

I tried to think it through some more, but it was hard with Maria yammering away in my ear. I told her I'd figure it all out and call her back.

She was still yelling when I hung up the phone.

"I usually try not to eavesdrop," Jimmy said, "but I pretty much heard all of that conversation."

"I may need you to say it back to me, because I missed most of it," I said.

"I'll summarize it. She wants you to go find your son."

"I can't just drop everything I'm doing."

That's when he showed me those nice white teeth of his.

JIMMY DACEY

HOW DIFFICULT COULD it be? I practiced public accounting for decades. And I'd been hanging around this place every single day for six consecutive months. I could assume the captain's chair, at least for a little while. The man needed to go locate his son. I didn't mind assisting him, not in the least. I kind of liked the idea of doing it. Retired CPA turned temporary bookmaker. It was like something out of a film. Maybe they'd get Jimmy Stewart to play me. I smiled at that idea and got to work.

JOHNNY MESAGNE

I DIDN'T REALLY have a choice. I let Jimmy take over. I told him how to log the bets. He nodded and told me he'd take care of it. I knew it would be fine, unless Vinny decided to show up. Vinny wouldn't understand none of it. He wouldn't even try to. He was always looking for a reason to get pissed off, and me handing the keys to the bar over to one of my customers would have been more than enough to do the trick.

I thought about Vinny, and I thought about Paul. I thought about Paul's visit that morning. Then I knew exactly what had happened.

I thought about calling Paul's place, but it made more sense to just go there. Next I thought about calling Maria to tell her I'd figured it out, but I didn't want to get her hopes up in case I was wrong. Besides, if I told her Paul had sent for J.J., that would have been another thing to deal with. I'd have to deal with it at some point. I didn't want to deal with it then.

I walked back to my apartment, fast but not running. I got in my car. I drove to Paul's. It was almost three o'clock. I didn't know what I'd say when I got there. I mainly wanted to be sure that's where J.J. was. I wanted to be able to tell Maria he was safe. I guess I wanted to know he was safe, too. It was weird to feel that way about him. About anyone, really.

I hadn't been inside Paul's place in a long time. I tried to remember whether I'd been there since getting out. Usually, Vinny came to me to get the money.

I opened the door and there was Vinny, working on a count at a table near the back of the main room. He looked at me like he didn't recognize who I was.

"I'm looking for my kid," I said. "Is he here?"

"He was. He left."

"When did he leave?"

"I don't know. I wasn't taking notes."

"Where'd he go?"

"I told you I wasn't taking notes. Leslie gave him a ride."

"Leslie Fitzpatrick?"

"No, Leslie Nielsen."

I looked beyond Vinny, to the hall that led to Paul's office.

"Is he back there?"

"Yeah, but he don't want no visitors."

"I didn't say I wanted to visit him. Maybe I want to know what he was talking to my kid about."

"I think you know. I was sitting in the front seat today when he explained it to you."

I looked again at the hallway. I thought about going back there, Vinny or no Vinny. Then I thought about what Vinny would do to me if I tried.

"I don't get you," Vinny said. "You left that kid and his mom something like ten years ago. Far as I know you never looked back. Then you left this life six years ago. Far as I know you never looked back on that, either."

"So?"

"So what the fuck are you doing here? Why are you looking for your kid, and why are you coming around here? It don't make no sense. Paul decided to let you make book, and that's his business. If it were me—"

"It wasn't you, Vinny."

"If it were me, you don't get out until you're in the ground."

"Paul had his reasons to let me out," I said. "And Paul lets me earn, for Paul and for you and for me and for everyone else this thing supports."

Vinny went back to paying attention to the cash on the table in front of him.

"That was his decision. Like you say, he had his reasons. It's all weird to me. And it's even weirder now that the kid you don't have nothing to do with is coming around here and all of a sudden you give a shit."

"That's where you're wrong," I said. "I don't give a shit. The kid is grown. He's walking around with some other asshole's name. I went to Bobby's last night because Paul told me to. And I came out here looking for the kid because my ex-wife told me to."

Vinny looked up at me. He thought it was funny that I was caught in the middle of a mess I didn't make.

"Well, you came out looking, and you got your answer. Maybe next time you should know the kid's too old for you to go out looking. Especially since, like you said, he took some other asshole's name."

I turned around and left. I heard him saying something as I walked out. I was glad I couldn't tell what it was. It probably would have just pissed me off even more. I didn't want to be too pissed off when I did what I had to do next.

Twenty-seven

SEPTEMBER 20, 1973

LESLIE FITZPATRICK

AFTER I TOOK the two beers back to Paul's office, I waited out front for them to finish whatever they were talking about. I wanted to know, but I didn't want to know. I never asked questions about business. If I started doing it now, Paul would get suspicious, fast.

I thought about Maria. She didn't want J.J. getting mixed up with Paul. I'd told her I'd talk to Paul. Now that Paul was talking to J.J., it was too late for any of that.

Vinny sat at the table on the other side of the room, counting money. He didn't have anything to say to me. I didn't have anything to say to him. Like always, that was fine by me. Even sitting still, that guy could make the devil go hide under his bed.

I smoked a couple of cigarettes and watched the soap operas. After a while, I heard someone coming from the back. I turned around and looked at J.J. When did that boy become a full-grown man? And why couldn't he have looked more like his father? It would have been so much easier if he looked like his father.

I tried to act natural. I told Vinny that since Bobby wasn't back, I'd drive J.J. home. Vinny didn't think anything of it. Between the stacks of cash in front of him and the constant job of protecting Paul, he wasn't going to insist on driving J.J. home.

I looked at J.J. again.

"Are you ready?"

He seemed confused, like I was talking about something other than giving him a ride. I don't know. Maybe I was. Sometimes those impulses are hard to control. Why didn't he look more like his old man?

I told him my car was around the corner. He followed me. I could feel his eyes on me. Did I maybe throw in a little extra wiggle while I walked? Again, sometimes those impulses are hard to control.

J.J. JENKINS

I TRIED MY best not to stare at her as she walked in front of me. It wasn't easy. I kept telling myself, *She's my cousin.* And then another voice inside my head kept saying, *It's only by marriage.* And then some other voice kept reminding me that when Paul walked in she ran over and kissed him, and not like a niece kissing her uncle.

She turned around to say something. I dropped my eyes to the concrete.

"Are you OK with a girl driving you home?"

"Girl or boy, it doesn't matter to me," I said. I told myself how stupid that sounded as soon as the words came out of my mouth.

"Good," she said, "because some of you boys don't like it when girls drive."

She kept walking toward a small parking lot. I kept trying to keep my eyes away from those jeans that seemed like they were about to rip open. I looked up and saw an orange Volkswagen. She went to the door on the driver's side and unlocked it with a key from her purse. I started laughing.

"You drive one of these things?"

"Why do guys care so much about what people drive?" She ducked inside and reached across to unlock the other door.

"This is basically a hair dryer," I said as I got inside.

"Well, it's basically what I've got. So unless you want to walk home, you'll deal with it."

She put the car in gear and it chugged away.

"It's like this thing escaped from an amusement park," I said.

"Look, you made your point. You don't like my car. If being seen in it will ruin your reputation or something, you can duck your head."

"I'll stop it," I said. "I'm sorry. I just never thought I'd be caught dead in one of these."

"Well, you're not dead. And I never understood that expression anyway. Who gets caught dead anywhere? And if they're dead, why do they care?"

"That's deep. I'll never think of those words the same way again."

"You can think of me when you hear them," she said.

"I wouldn't be caught dead doing that."

LESLIE FITZPATRICK

HE MADE ME laugh. A real laugh. I didn't realize how badly I needed to laugh.

"I had lunch with your mom the other night," I said after I stopped laughing.

"Really? She didn't tell me that."

"She's worried about you."

"She's always worried about me."

"She's worried about you getting mixed up with Paul."

He got quiet after that one. I waited to see what he'd say.

J.J. JENKINS

I KNEW I shouldn't tell her what I'd talked to Paul about. I sat there trying to think of something to say.

"You got mixed up with Paul," I finally said.

"Well, that's different."

"How is it different? And isn't he married?"

She sighed, and then she didn't say anything for a little while.

"Plenty of men are married," she said. "That doesn't stop them."

"Stop them from what?"

The car stopped at a red light. She turned to face me. She was getting a little upset.

"Are you serious? Or are you just stupid?"

"So are you like his mistress or something?"

"That seems so sophisticated. I guess it sounds better than gumar."

"So he's married, but he sees you? And you're OK with that?"

"I feel like you're judging me," she said. "You've got a lot to learn, kid."

"I'm sorry. I don't understand this stuff. Do they all have mistresses?"

"I don't know. It's not like they put ads in the newspapers about it."

"But word gets around, doesn't it?"

"Not always," she said. "Sometimes people keep their mouths shut. Sometimes people are careful enough that nobody knows."

"You and Paul don't seem to be very careful."

LESLIE FITZPATRICK

I DIDN'T LIKE where this was going.

"We're careful enough," I said. "His wife doesn't know specifically, but she knows how it works. And it's not like anyone who works for him is going to tell her."

"Why wouldn't they?"

"Do I have to spell it out for you?"

He let that one go. He noticed we were getting closer to the street that led to the neighborhood where he and his mother lived.

"I'm hungry," he said. "I haven't eaten anything in a while. Pull into the Burger Chef over there. My treat."

"Aren't you worried about people wondering what the two of us are doing out together?"

"Why would I? You're my cousin."

"Step-cousin," I reminded him.

"Cousin is cousin. And there's nothing wrong with two cousins getting a burger."

That made me smile. Again, I didn't realize how badly I needed to smile. And then I realized that having someone who made me smile and laugh that way was about the last thing I needed right now.

Why couldn't he have looked more like his father?

Twenty-eight

SEPTEMBER 20, 1973

JOHNNY MESAGNE

I SHOVED THE front door to the house open. I didn't even think to knock first.

Maria was sitting on the couch, watching television and smoking a cigarette. She sprang up. I was lucky she never bought a gun.

"Maria," I said. "I need to see the boy."

"I tried to call you. He got home right after we talked."

"That's fine. I still need to see him."

"I know that look, John. I don't like that look."

"Calm down, Maria. Where is he?"

The kid came out of his bedroom. When he saw me, he tried to turn around and close the door.

"Hold on," I said. "You're coming with me."

"Where you taking him, John?"

"Stay out of this, Maria."

J.J. JENKINS

WHILE SHE WAS giving me the third degree after Leslie dropped me off, my mother didn't mention that she'd called him. It would have been nice to have known that. I could have at least been ready for round two.

I could already tell round two was going to be worse than round one.

"We need to go have a talk, Junior."

"We can talk right here," I said, shoulders stiffening. "We're talking right now. Put the last few days together, and this is the most we've talked in a long time."

"Your mother don't need to hear what we need to talk about."

My mother took that as her cue to leave. She grabbed her cigarettes and started for the bedroom.

My dad pointed a finger at her. "Sit yourself back down, Maria," he said. "Him and me is going for a ride."

She did what he said. After all the things they'd disagreed about over the years, they finally found something they agreed on.

He yanked the door open and said, "Let's go." When I didn't move right away his voice got louder. "Now," he said.

I decided to do what he said, even if I didn't want to.

My shoes were by the front door. I jammed my feet into them as fast as I could and started walking. My heels weren't fully inside. I didn't stop to try to fix them.

JOHNNY MESAGNE

I LIKED HOW it felt to give orders and have them obeyed. I didn't do that too much no more. Working alone in that bar was slow and quiet. I didn't have nobody working for me. I didn't have nobody to tell what to do. Not that I wanted to boss people around. It was just nice to know I could turn it on, like I did the night before when I told Bobby's guys what they needed to do about the one who got shot in South Wheeling. I could see in their faces they didn't really want to do what I said. They did it anyway.

I led the way to the car. That same car I been driving for ten years. I hadn't realized how long I had the thing until J.J. remembered it. I forgot I'd bought it just before I moved out. Where the hell had the time gone?

I got in. He did, too. Didn't hesitate at all. He didn't get smart with me again, either. If he was going to end up working for Paul, at least he knew how to be a good soldier.

I drove for a little while without saying nothing.

"What happened today?" I finally said.

"I was going to work. But Bobby came and got me. Paul wanted to see me."

"Why didn't Bobby bring you home?"

"He had something else to do."

J.J. JENKINS

I KNEW HE wouldn't like what I had to say about my meeting with Paul. He also wouldn't want to hear that Paul had a job for me to do, or that I'd told Paul I would do it. But if I tried to tell my father anything other than the truth, it would only make it harder. I waited for him to start asking those questions. I'd tell him whatever he wanted to hear.

"I ain't concerned about whatever you and Paul talked about," he said. It was like he could read my mind. Still, I felt glad I didn't have to tell him what was going on.

"I know you said you don't want me messing around with those guys," I said.

"You know where I stand," he said. "They know where I stand. I don't like it. I don't want it. But I ain't doing nothing about it."

"So what's this all about?"

He took his foot off the gas and turned to face me.

"This is about your ride home."

JOHNNY MESAGNE

"What about my ride home?" J.J. said, a little bit of attitude back in his voice.

"You know what I'm talking about," I said.

"She's my cousin, I'm not going to mess around with my cousin."

"First of all, she's your cousin by marriage. You know it, and I know it. We ain't really related to her. Second, and this is the important part. She's taken."

"You mean by Paul?" he said. "Paul's married. She's his mistress, right?"

That's when I knew that, no matter how smart the kid was, he was still too dumb for his own good.

"You think that matters?" I said. "If I got two dogs and someone messes with one of them, I'd still be pissed off, even though I got another one."

"But this isn't about dogs. He's got a wife. And he's got a mistress. It's two different things."

"Not to him it ain't. She's his property. If you mess with his property, you got a big problem."

"But I'm not messing with anybody's property," he said.

"I didn't say you were. I know Leslie. I know how she can be. You just need to steer clear."

J.J. JENKINS

I DIDN'T GET any of this. He says he doesn't care if I get involved with them, but he's worried about Leslie and me? Based on one car ride?

"I still don't understand why a guy with a wife would have any reason to—"

"It don't matter if you don't understand," he said. "What matters is you don't fuck around with her. Ever. Under no circumstances. Even if he's done with her five, seven years from now or whenever, you don't do it. There ain't too many rules in this life, but they're clear. You keep your mouth shut at all times, and you don't mess with nobody's woman, wife, mistress, mother, sister, whatever. That goes for the top guy to the bottom guy. But it especially goes for the top guy."

I didn't plan on messing around with her. Why would she want to mess around with me? She was older than me. A lot older than me. The whole thing seemed stupid.

"Am I clear on this?" he said.

I was getting a little frustrated with the whole conversation. He'd walked out of my life ten years earlier, and he barely came around after that. Who was he to tell me what to do?

"You know, for a guy who doesn't want anything to do with me, you sure seem to have a lot to do with me," I said.

"This is the end of it. I ain't stopping you from getting in that business. I ain't stopping you from messing with Leslie. I'm just telling you that messing with Leslie is the quickest way to end up getting out of that business, for good."

He didn't say anything else. I didn't, either. He turned the car around and took me back to the house. When he stopped, I got out and closed the door.

When I got back inside, my mother was standing there with her hands on her hips.

"So what was that all about?"

"Nothing," I said. "He just wanted to be sure I know where he stands on things."

"Well, he stands where I stand. I don't like any of it. You'd better get your ass over to Foodland and make things right."

"I'm not going back there," I said.

"You need a job."

"I got a different job."

She hurried to the kitchen and started speaking Italian. I didn't know what she was saying. I'm not even sure she did. When she switched back to English, I was surprised by what she said.

"You need to find your own place," she said. "I can't be worried sick every night about whether you're coming home. That part of my life ended ten years ago."

"Fine. I'll find my own place."

"When?"

"Soon enough," I said. "Until I do, I'll pay you rent. How does fifty dollars a week sound?"

"Where are you getting that kind of money?"

"I'll have it."

"I don't want his money," she said.

"Whose money?"

"Don't treat me like I'm stupid, son. I understand what's going on. I only wish you did."

I went to my room and slammed the door. If she wanted me out, fine, I'd leave. I was used to not being at home. Besides, I was too old to be living with my mother. I'd make some money. I'd find an apartment.

I sat down at that old metal desk. My wallet and car keys were on top of it. The stupid compass was lying there next to the keys.

I picked it up and twisted it around, just like I had in that exact same spot when he'd given it to me. The needle fluttered around inside, always pointing the same way. I thought about something Paul had said. I repeated his words out loud.

"There are lots of different directions a man can go. But he can only go in one of them. He's the one who has to pick it."

"What's that?" she said. It sounded like she was standing on the other side of the door. "Did you say something?"

"I was just talking to myself."

"Well, my grandma always said when you talk to yourself, you'll be sure to have someone listening to what you say."

She was trying to calm down. So was I. A lot had happened that day, and the night before.

I looked at the needle on the compass. It was pointed toward the front door to the house, same as it always had. It meant nothing, but right then it meant everything.

It was time for me to follow that needle. To do whatever I was supposed to do. Whether it was in my blood or whether it was what I wanted to do or some of both, it was time to start doing it.

Twenty-nine

LESLIE FITZPATRICK

I DECIDED NOT to go back to Paul's. I'd made my appearance for the day. If he wanted to take me to dinner, he'd call. On some Thursday nights he did, on some Thursday nights he didn't.

When I got home, I realized how tired I was. I changed my clothes and went to bed. Next thing I knew it was dark. I thought about getting up. I fell back to sleep before I could.

I slept until I heard the sound. I stayed there and waited to see if it would stop. Just when I thought it had, it started again. I got up slowly and reached for the bottom left door of the dresser.

JOHNNY MESAGNE

I WENT BACK to the bar after I finished with J.J. I felt bad about leaving Jimmy in charge for so long. I probably should have stopped somewhere to call him. But I knew where Vinny was, so I didn't have to worry about him showing up and seeing someone else running the place.

Then it occurred to me: what did Vinny think I did about the bar when I went to Paul's? He's lucky he's so mean, because he ain't all that smart.

Jimmy seemed fine when I got back. Happy, almost. I actually thought about hiring him to help me out. If things hadn't gotten so crazy, maybe I would have.

I closed up around eight and walked back to the apartment. I went inside and sat there drinking a beer, trying to figure out the best way to get in touch with her. It had been a long time. I thought about calling. That wouldn't be too good if Paul was there. I decided to just drive over to her house and see if she was alone. I went down the stairs, climbed back in the Oldsmobile, and made my way to Elm Grove.

I went up and down her street looking for that Cadillac. The nights Paul slept over, he actually made Vinny wait in the car for him. I guess Paul paid him good enough to deal with that.

The coast was clear. I parked on the street a few doors down from her house. I looked around to make sure no one was nosing through their curtains. I got out and walked toward the house and then to the back. I acted as natural as I could, walked as normal as possible. The houses was packed so close together that it was real easy to stand out.

I found what I thought I remembered was the window to her bedroom. The curtains was pulled shut. Over the glass there was a screen. I slid the screen up and tapped three times. I waited for a little while.

I tapped again. Still nothing.

I looked around to see if anyone was watching me. When I turned back, the wrong end of a .32 was sticking between the gap in the curtains.

LESLIE FITZPATRICK

I DID WHAT Paul always said to do. If anything happens at night, get the gun and point it at whatever it is. He never said how to know when to pull the trigger.

I stood there by that window, gun stuck through the curtains at whoever was outside knocking. *Should I shoot?*

I decided to wait until whoever it was broke the window. *But wouldn't that be too late?*

"Leslie. Put that thing down. It's me."

I knew the voice. I couldn't place it. I pushed the curtains aside and looked out the window.

I went to the back door, past the kitchen. I opened it and asked him exactly what the hell he was doing here, as quietly as I could.

"What the hell are you doing pointing a gun at me?" he said, not as quietly as he could.

"I didn't realize it was you."

"Maybe that explains why you didn't pull the trigger."

"Why are you here?"

"We need to talk."

I didn't want to let him in. Not after everything that happened. That part of my life was over for good. I didn't even want to think about it. But we couldn't keep going back and forth with him standing out there. Somebody would have noticed. There was a good chance somebody already had. I unlocked the screen door and walked away.

"I don't like this," I said after he came inside. I turned on the light over the stove. It wasn't as bright as the one over the table.

"The place don't look much different," he said.

"Is that an insult or a compliment?"

"It's just, you know, an observation." He pulled a pack of cigarettes from his pocket. He took one out and lit it. I reached over for one. I didn't wait for him to light it for me.

"I assume you didn't come to see if my place looked any different," I said.

"I came to ask for a favor."

I inhaled. I held the smoke in my lungs.

JOHNNY MESAGNE

SHE BLEW OUT the smoke nice and slow, like she always used to. It made a haze in front of those green eyes. I forgot how green they was. One of her eyebrows flickered a little bit.

"A favor, huh? One thing I've learned is favors get paid back with favors."

"Fine," I said. "I'll owe you. I know how that goes."

"First, I have to decide if I'll do you a favor. No one ever says what the favor is when they ask for one. That's usually pretty important to know."

"OK, I get it. I always said you should have gone to law school. And that's an insult, not a compliment."

She took another drag from the cigarette. "So what's the favor, Johnny Mesagne? What in the world is it that you need and that I have the power to do?"

Here we were. It was why I showed up out of the blue, picking at an identical scar we both tried to hide as best we could. I almost felt embarrassed to say it. But it was too late not to.

"I need you to promise me you won't mess around with my kid."

The cigarette fell out of her mouth. It hit the top of the table and made a black spot on the yellow Formica. She grabbed the cigarette and started rubbing the mark it left with her finger.

"Shit," she said. "Look what you made me do."

"Sorry," I said in a way that made it clear I wasn't. "It's just a table."

Those green eyes got narrow and mean. I remembered that look very well.

"It's my table. I don't have the money to go out and buy another one."

I didn't say nothing. She read the expression on my face the right way.

"You think I just ask him for any old thing and he gives it to me?" she said. "He doesn't want me living here in the first place. The last thing he'll do is buy me new furniture for a place where he doesn't want me living."

I didn't care one bit about her issues with Paul.

"Let's not lose track of the topic," I said.

LESLIE FITZPATRICK

I THOUGHT ABOUT telling him to get the hell out. But this thing about J.J. had me curious. Very curious.

"Why would you even think I'd be interested in your kid?" I said.

"If you're not, then it's the easiest favor you ever done."

I smiled at him, not a real smile but one that sent him a message.

"You're right. But it's a lot bigger favor if I am."

"What are you saying?"

"I'm just saying what I said." I looked back down at the spot on the table. I already knew there was no way to fix it. "Regardless of whether I am, you must think I am or you wouldn't be here. All I'm saying is, if I am, it's a lot bigger favor."

"Fine, let's assume you are. Let's assume it's a really big favor. I'm asking you to not mess around with him, and then I'll owe you a really big favor."

I puffed again on the cigarette. I made my eyes wide. I blew a cloud of smoke between us.

"I'll think about it," I said.

He stood up and headed for the door. "You thinking about it is what I'm worried about," he said.

Thirty

I USED A travel clock when I was at college, a little square case that popped open. I'd wind it up. I'd make sure the time was right. I'd set the alarm. I'd flip the switch. And then I'd shut it again. That ticking was too loud for me. The alarm would wake me up, even if the case was closed.

I'd been told to show up at Bobby's place on Monday morning, half past seven. I'd gotten through Friday and Saturday without any more issues with my mother. To get her off my case a little bit, I'd gone back to Foodland to basically beg for one more shot, even though I'd said I wouldn't. Mr. Gleason didn't ask me what happened on Thursday, and I didn't tell him. I just apologized. He gave me a couple of weekend shifts, because one of the other guys was sick. I showed up and worked hard, same as before. When I left on Sunday afternoon, I didn't really know whether I'd be back. I didn't want to be.

I set the alarm for half past six. I didn't tell my mother why I was leaving or where I was going. I didn't know where I was going. I just knew where I was starting.

I took a shower. Dried my hair with a towel. Shaved. Wore something casual, jeans and a pullover with a big collar. My hair covered the back of it. I grabbed the fake Rolex from the top of the desk and strapped it to my wrist. I only liked to wear it on special occasions. This wasn't really a special occasion. I just wanted to be sure I wasn't late.

I had that song in my head, "Live and Let Die." It has that part where an orchestra starts playing after Paul McCartney sings the words from the title. I liked that. I was in a pretty good mood. It was my first day on a new job. I didn't know any better.

I drove the Plymouth back to the same place where we'd taken Willie after he got shot. I parked in almost the same spot where I'd pulled that Camaro's wheel onto the curb. When I got out of the Plymouth, I saw Tony coming toward me on foot.

I asked if he was walking to work. He said he'd moved into an apartment not that far away. I remembered I'd need to find an apartment, too.

I checked the fake Rolex. It was ten minutes after seven.

"We're early," I said.

"Better early than late," Tony said, "especially after what happened on Wednesday night."

"How's Willie doing?"

"He'll be OK. He's out of commission for a little while. He lost a lot of blood. That doctor said he needed more, but it's not like we could take him to a hospital to get it. I'm surprised you're coming around, after everything that happened."

"The boss asked me to."

"Bobby? He seemed pretty pissed you was there."

"Not him. The other boss."

Tony's eyes widened. I didn't want him to think I was showing off. But I wanted to be straight with him. I didn't really know how else to explain why I was showing up there again, less than a week after things went to shit.

"You was good the other night," he said. "The way you talked to them. You wasn't scared. But you wasn't rude. It was good."

"It's hard not to be good when you tell the truth," I said.

"Someday we'll find out how good you are when you're not telling the truth."

I flinched a little when he said that. I kept walking without saying anything else. We got back to the store, Doggie Do-Rights. There was a grasshopper on the door frame. It flew away when I pressed the button.

I heard the dogs barking inside. Tommy eventually showed up and opened the door. He didn't say much, just turned around and walked to the back and expected us to follow.

When we got close to the cages, I looked at the dogs. There were five, like the other night. One was different. It was a German Shepherd. It was snarling more than barking.

The little one, Gnocchi, got on its hind legs and pressed its paws onto the cage. I bent over to pet the thing. It was little and it was ugly, so ugly it was sort of cute. It seemed to like me. I rubbed his snout.

A voice from the back room was calling for me. I pulled away from the cage and went through the doorway.

"Careful with them dogs," Bobby said to me. "You're already down a finger. Don't lose another."

There were two other guys sitting at the table, with Tommy. They all laughed.

Tony and I went toward the wall. We sat on the same stools they'd sent us to the last time we were there.

"I know we don't usually get started this early," Bobby said. "But we got a special assignment today. Phil, Rico, and the two new guys are doing it. You guys know Tony. And you sort of met J.J. the other night."

Phil and Rico didn't look too excited. I didn't expect them to be. One guy's mouth moved around a little. It made the long, thin hairs on his face sort of dance. I felt like he wanted to say something.

The other one, well, he just looked mad and mean. I got the feeling he always looked mad and mean. I remembered hearing about him. Rico. He used to be a boxer, I think. He got kicked out of the sport after he punched a referee who tried to get him to stop punching a guy he'd already knocked out.

Bobby said we'd all be working together. He told me to go over and shake hands with the rest of them. I was probably a little too eager. Phil gave me a limp wrist. Rico did the opposite. He squeezed my hand hard. I think I made a noise. When Rico let go, he gave me the finger.

"I said you'll be working together," Bobby told Rico.

"I don't like it," Rico said, right in front of me. "They made a fucking mess that we had to go clean up. This one wasn't even part of the crew. And now he is? Maybe I should make a fucking mess once in a while. Maybe I'd end up with Vinny's job."

"You don't have to like it," Bobby said to Rico. "You just have to do it. We been through this."

I didn't say a word, even though that asshole practically broke my hand. I took it. I didn't expect it to be easy, but I didn't expect them to treat me like shit. Paul wanted me there. I assumed that would count for something. I could tell right away it didn't.

I thought about offering to leave. But I knew what would come next. I'd end up back at Paul's. He'd want to know what happened, and I'd either come off as a rat for telling him how they acted or as a baby for not being able to handle my business. So I decided to just deal with it, and to wait for the right time to get them to maybe change their minds about me.

I didn't have a chance to think much more about it, because the next thing I knew Bobby was explaining what we'd be doing that day.

I wanted to get a taste of that life, and I was going to get it.

Thirty-one

LESLIE FITZPATRICK

I KNEW I wouldn't be able to fall back to sleep after Johnny left. I did the math. I'd already slept for at least seven hours. Now, I was wide awake. There was no point in even trying.

I wished I'd kept the rest of his cigarettes. I'd bought a pack from the machine at Paul's, but I smoked all of them while I was at his place. I didn't want to start buying them by the carton. Maybe I needed to. At least for now.

I went back to the drawer where Paul had left some cigars and took another one. It was that or nothing.

I cut off the end. I fired it up and sat at the table, thinking about the conversation with Johnny. Why would he come back here, after more than six years? Why in the middle of the night? And why did he think I would have any interest in, of all people, his own son?

I knew not to start asking Johnny questions. Questions like what his son said or did to make Johnny think he needed to ask me to stay away from him. Maybe J.J. said something to make Johnny think he was interested in me. It made me real curious.

How could it not? Sure, he was only twenty. But when you're starting to get a little older, there's nothing like thinking someone seven years younger is interested to make you feel like you're not getting older after all. I liked that feeling. Especially since I was determined to get a fresh start.

J.J. wasn't the right guy for that. I knew I should steer clear of him. He was Johnny's kid, for crying out loud. Why couldn't he look more like his father? I still never would have given it much thought if Johnny hadn't asked me to stay away. Why in the hell did he plant the seed?

I sat there, smoking that damn cigar and hoping the seed wouldn't do what seeds do. Sprout. Spread. Grow. No, I didn't need that. J.J. didn't need it, either. I needed to focus on getting away from Paul, not on finding someone else.

That was the right way to handle this. Johnny wanted a favor. After all this time, he was the last one I thought would be asking me for anything. It would have been easier to give it to him if he hadn't asked for it, if that makes any sense. Either way, I wished he hadn't.

I smoked more of the cigar than I had the time before. I hated to think I was getting used to them. I put it out in an ashtray. I took it to the sink and ran water over it. I threw it in the trash with the other one.

I went back to the table and sat there. I wished I had something to do. I decided I'd get a carton of cigarettes and a bottle or two of wine the next day. There would be more nights just like this until I finally got myself away from Paul.

I forced myself not to think about J.J. *Why did Johnny have to show up here tonight? Why did he have to plant that damn seed?*

I went through the house looking for something to read. My grandmother didn't have much of a library, and I hadn't exactly added to it. I found her bible, of all things. I picked it up and held it. There was so much in there. I flipped it open and started reading some of it. I skimmed through the first two chapters of Genesis. I got to the part about Adam and Eve. I read about the tree, and the serpent, and my goodness, how quickly it all turned nasty. Before I knew it, they'd pissed off God, had two kids, and one killed the other.

Was that really what happened when the world started? Do people actually believe that? None of it made any sense to me. Eat some fruit, get thrown out of the Garden of Eden, have a couple babies, and they grow up and start killing each other? Is all of this stuff really baked into who people are?

Maybe it is. It would explain plenty about the life I'd found myself stuck in the middle of. I cursed the younger version of me for ever getting caught up in this shit. First with Johnny. Then with Paul. Now maybe with Johnny's kid.

I read a little more from that bible before closing it. If I was looking for answers, I wasn't going to find them there. I wasn't going to find them anywhere.

That wasn't going to keep me from looking.

Thirty-two

J.J. JENKINS

BOBBY SENT US to Marion, Ohio. I'd never heard of the place. He said it was three hours away by car.

We took Phil's white Pontiac. Phil and Rico sat in the front, I sat in the back across from Tony.

Phil didn't talk very much. His jaw looked funny, like someone punched it really hard once and knocked it crooked. He did say Warren Harding was buried in Marion, Ohio.

I tried to act like I knew that. Tony shot me a look that said he didn't buy it.

Rico piped up and said the guy's name sounds like Warren Hard-on.

The job was simple, at least according to Bobby. A truckload of Stroh's beer, packed with nearly fifteen hundred cases, had left Detroit. It was heading for Huntington. The driver was going to exit Route 23 in Marion. He would stop at a gas station to take a leak. He would leave the keys in the truck. That's when Rico and I would climb into the truck, drive it away, and take it back to Wheeling. Phil and Tony would follow us home in the Pontiac, watching and

waiting and ready to help if help was needed. But Bobby said it probably wouldn't be.

Anyone who ever hears anyone say something like that knows
how it ends up going.

Bobby said the driver would get a quarter for each case of beer
in the truck. Paul would sell them for three bucks each to bars in
and around Wheeling. That was half of what they were paying to
the local Stroh's distributor. Bobby said that after the driver's cut of
three hundred and seventy-five dollars, Paul would make more than
four grand. Bobby didn't say how much of that any of us would get.

I didn't try to guess. I was still new to this. Paul had to work his
contacts in Detroit to line up the driver who would accidentally
leave his keys in the truck, go to the bathroom, and act surprised
the truck was gone. He'd have to report the truck as stolen, tell a
story to the cops that didn't make them suspicious, and probably
give a piece of his cut to whoever in Michigan had handed him such
a simple and clean score.

We rolled past the gas station ten minutes before the truck was
supposed to get there, at one o'clock. We couldn't park at the gas station. We didn't want anyone to see us or the car, even though Phil
had stolen an Ohio plate for it the night before. We found a spot up
the road. We pulled over and waited until the Stroh's truck pulled in.
That's when we'd start.

It worked, better than I thought it would. The truck arrived. We
drove to the gas station. Rico and I got out. We walked fast from the
Pontiac to the truck, without running. I kept my head down so no
one would get a good look at my face, just like Rico told me.

I climbed into the passenger side of the truck. Rico got in the
driver's side. I noticed tattoos all over his arms. His muscles weren't
big, but they stood out. Veins, too. They looked like rivers on a map,
from his wrists all the way up to his shoulders.

He turned the key, dropped the transmission into gear, and drove
away. "*Arrivederci*, motherfucker!" he yelled.

I looked back at the station, where nothing seemed to be out of the ordinary. "That was easy," I said. "That was too easy."

"The hard part was the setup. You don't just pick up a phone book and find a guy driving a truck full of beer who'll stop in the right spot and leave the keys and go take a piss long enough for a couple of guys to boost it. Our end of the job ain't no different than garbagemen."

"What do you mean?" I said.

"We pick up the trash in one place, and then we take the trash someplace else."

"Yeah, but garbagemen aren't stealing the trash."

"It ain't really stealing. A big company like Stroh's? They won't miss one truck full of beer. Besides, they got insurance. They'll get all their money back. Every penny. Maybe even more, after they fudge the paperwork on how much beer is really in here. And they will. You can bet on that."

"Well, sure," I said, "but then the insurance company is out the money."

"You ain't never dealt with no insurance companies, have you? They fuck everybody, all the time. They deserve to get fucked back once in a while."

I laughed at that. I didn't know what else to do.

"That shit ain't funny," Rico said. "That's real. They fuck us, and every once in a while we fuck back."

"I think I just learned more in the last minute than I did in all my time in college."

"Hey, that's an even bigger scam. All that money, for what? A piece of fucking paper too rough to even wipe your ass with."

"But the piece of paper gets you a job. That's what my mother always says. And those jobs can pay you pretty good money."

"You got a job. And it's going to pay you pretty good money. And you didn't need no piece of fucking paper to get it."

I left it at that. I checked the big mirror on the side of the truck.

The Pontiac was back there, where it was supposed to be. The truck had a radio in the middle of the dashboard. I turned the knob and clicked it on. "Live and Let Die" blasted out of the small speaker above the steering wheel.

"Change the channel," Rico said right away. "I hate that fucking song."

Thirty-three

SEPTEMBER 24, 1973

JOHNNY MESAGNE

I RINSED A few glasses. I had a decent crowd that day. Mondays during football season was usually pretty good because people either won money over the weekend and wanted to let it ride, or they was looking to chase their losses. I always knew who won and who lost because I made the books. As long as they kept coming back, I really didn't care why.

Jimmy Dacey sat across from me at the bar. Shirt and tie and jacket. Distinguished gentleman. A real endangered species. He was looking at me. I could always feel that from him. Not in a creepy way. Just watching. He could read people. I knew to never try to bullshit him.

"You're quiet today," he said.

"The Steelers put it to me yesterday. Can you believe it? They beat the Browns by twenty-seven points. I laid off as much as I could. If I push the line up too far someone will load up on the other team." I kept rinsing glasses.

He folded up a racing form he'd been reading. "How long have I been coming in here?" he said.

"It's got to be six months now."

"A little more than six months. Pretty much every day. So I've been here a lot. I've talked to you a lot. I've watched you a lot. You've got something more on your mind than taking a beating because Pittsburgh beat Cleveland by four touchdowns on Sunday."

"And you wonder why I don't like to play cards with you."

"I guess I shouldn't be revealing my secrets," he said, laughing a little bit. Then he looked around before leaning closer to me and getting real quiet. "I know about the other night," he said, "when you had to run out of here after you got a phone call. You haven't been the same since then. I've noticed it. I've felt it."

I leaned forward and whispered back to him. "Well," I said, "it's a long story."

"I've got time," he said, a little bit louder. "I may not have much time left, but I've got time."

I made sure no one else was listening before I kept going. "My kid's back in town. He got mixed up with some guys from Paul's crew."

JIMMY DACEY

I LOOKED AT him after he said it. I wondered why he'd be surprised that his son would do something he had once done. I didn't have a son of my own, but that seemed to be the way it worked. Not all the time, but often enough.

"Like father, like son," I said. I wasn't passing judgment on the situation. I was just stating facts.

"That's the problem," he said. "I don't want him getting involved with that stuff. And I don't want the headache of trying to keep him out of it. He's too old for me to tell him what to do. I wouldn't expect him to listen to me anyway. I ain't exactly been involved since Maria and I split up."

"How's she handling all of this?"

"She's worried. But if she wasn't worried about that, she'd be worried about something else. He's living with her, at least for now. But she knows she can't tell him what to do."

"You know, for someone who doesn't seem to want to be involved, you seem to be involved."

JOHNNY MESAGNE

WHY DID EVERYONE think I was involved? I was just doing what other people was telling me to do. I hadn't made no decisions on my own. I was trying to keep the peace. My own decision would have been to just keep moving.

"The kid's got to live his own life," I said to Jimmy. "He'll be twenty-one in a few months. Can you believe that? Besides, he took someone else's name. He can be someone else's problem."

Jimmy had a glass in front of him. It was almost empty. He drank a little more. When he put it back down, I scooped it up and filled it from the tap.

"On the house," I said, but with him it always was.

JIMMY DACEY

I DON'T KNOW why, but when Johnny said "house" it made me think of one of the poems I'd learned. I'd consumed just enough beer that day to launch into it.

"The house," I said. "The home. It stays as it was left, shaped to the comfort of the last to go, as if to win them back."

Johnny looked confused.

"Jimmy, you feeling OK?" he said.

"It's a poem by Philip Larkin. He wrote it when he visited his mother's house, after he'd grown up."

"What the hell does it mean?"

"I don't know. But you're in the process of figuring it out."

Johnny stood up straight. "What am I figuring out?"

"Where you fit in your son's life," I said. "Where you fit in your ex-wife's life. You've been focused on your own life ever since you moved out. The way it looks to me, that phone call you received the other night forced you to start focusing on your son's life. And on your ex-wife's life. Even if you don't want to."

"It's not my place. The kid's going to do what he's going to do. I can't force him to do nothing."

"But you can try to persuade him." I said, before taking a drink from the fresh glass of cold beer.

JOHNNY MESAGNE

I SHOOK MY head at that one.

"He knows where I stand. I just want to have—what's it called? A clean conscience. Yeah, a clean conscience. Whatever he does, he does. If he does something that gets him arrested or beat up or whatever, it's on him. Not me."

Jimmy was smiling at me. Then he frowned a little. Then he smiled again.

"You can say that," he said. "I'm not so sure you believe it."

"You better believe I believe it." I said that a little bit too loud. Some of the guys at the tables turned to look our way. "Look, I got enough to worry about without worrying about a grown man who decides he wants to do what his old man did. What's that saying? The apple falls off the tree?"

"The apple doesn't fall far from the tree," Jimmy said.

JIMMY DACEY

I TOOK ANOTHER drink of the beer. A long one. I put down the glass.

"So what do you want?" I said. "What do you, John Mesagne, want?"

"I guess I want my son to find another way."

"Have you told him that?"

"Not really. Not straight out like that."

"Well, you should tell him. And you should keep telling him. You won't get a clean conscience by washing your hands of the situation and walking away. You'll have a clean conscience only if you keep telling him over and over again what you think. If he still ignores you then, well, you've done everything you could."

Johnny poured himself a beer and drank almost all of it in one gulp.

"What if he don't listen?" he said.

"It doesn't matter if he doesn't listen. If you say it enough, he won't be able to ignore it. What matters is you need to keep saying it."

He filled his glass again and again drank almost all of it.

"I wish I would've talked to you about this the other day."

"Why do you say that?"

"It's another long story," Johnny said, finishing that beer. "And that's one neither of us got time for."

Thirty-four

RICO DROVE THE Stroh's truck back to Columbus on Route 23. That's where we picked up I-70, the road that went straight back to Wheeling. That's where they'd take the beer before doing whatever they planned to with the truck. That wasn't my concern. Maybe they'd sell it for parts. Maybe they'd crush it. Whatever they did, my job would be done.

I looked into the big mirror on the side of the door every once in a while. I wanted to make sure the Pontiac was still back there, just in case.

Just in case happened near Zanesville, about seventy-five miles from home. The truck started to lose power. It happened slowly at first, then it happened fast. The engine was dead.

Rico managed to glide the thing onto the first exit we saw, just outside town. He pulled the truck over to the side of the road, close to the bottom of the ramp.

I checked the mirror to make sure Phil and Tony followed. They stopped the Pontiac behind the truck. They didn't get out right away.

"What the fuck do we do now?" Rico said. "And why the fuck ain't those two coming to help?"

"Did you try to start it again?"

Rico turned the key a few times. He started speaking Italian. I recognized enough to get the idea. He switched back to English.

"It's fucking dead," he said.

I noticed Phil outside my door. Tony stood next to Phil. I turned the crank to open the window.

"What's going on?" Phil said.

"What took you so fucking long?" Rico said.

"We thought maybe one of you had to piss."

"No, but the fucking truck took a shit," Rico said.

"Should we check under the hood?" Phil said.

"I know how to drive it," Rico said. "I don't know how to fix it. Do you?"

Phil turned that crooked jaw of his toward Tony. "Do you?"

"I don't know nothing about trucks," Tony said. I could already see the sweat starting to roll over his mustache. "I didn't even know we was messing with a truck until this morning."

Well, this is great, I thought. *Four guys on the job, and three of them have no idea what to do next.* I pushed the door open and Phil stepped onto the running board.

"That driver reported this thing stolen by now," Phil said. "One cop car comes off the ramp up there, and we're fucked."

Rico was muttering in Italian again. I didn't expect many ideas from him. Tony stood there on the ground, sweat starting to wash crumbs from the hairs on his lip. It was up to me to think of something.

"We can't call a garage or a mechanic," I said. "And we can't drive all the way back to Wheeling and leave the truck here. We need to find a place in town where we can get another truck and put the beer in it."

"Get a truck big enough for all this beer?" Phil said. His crooked jaw wobbled even more when he talked fast. "Are you nuts? We ain't finding a truck big enough for all this fucking beer."

"Maybe we can rent a truck," I said. "Two or three of them, if we have to. Every town's got a U-Haul in it, right? I've seen them everywhere. We go find the closest U-Haul, we get another truck. We load up the beer, we drive it home, we unload it. Then we bring the truck back."

Phil looked at Rico.

"Well?" Phil said to him.

"We're fucked either way," Rico said. "We can either sit here and wait for it, or we can make ourselves think we're not fucked and try whatever it is he just said."

"I ain't interested in sitting here and waiting for it," Phil said. "So let's get in the car, let's go find the U-Haul, and let's see if they got a truck big enough to bring this beer back to Wheeling."

Tony and Phil started for the Pontiac. I climbed out and followed. Rico was behind me, still cursing in Italian and English, back and forth. We piled in the car and found the closest gas station. They sent me inside to ask the guy working there for directions to a U-Haul store, since it was my bright idea.

He rattled off the directions. I remembered them as best I could. I tried to guide Phil there without getting us lost. We eventually found it. They tried to send me inside alone again, but I told them it would be easier with a second person. Phil volunteered to go, which made sense, since all Rico could do was say "we're fucked" over and over again and Tony's mustache looked like a bathtub that was overflowing.

When we went inside, Phil stayed back. I knew that meant I should take the lead. I would have liked the opportunity to prove myself, if I wasn't scared shitless about everything that could go wrong. The guy behind the counter told me the biggest truck they had was twenty-six feet long. I guessed that we'd need two to get all the beer home. I hoped to God I was guessing right.

The clerk said he'd need somebody's driver's license. I started to pull out my wallet before Phil slapped a card on the counter. It was a white rectangle with stamped letters and numbers and no photo. He told me later he bought it when he was fourteen to get into bars. He also told me he had to read the license upside down to remember the name on it when it was time to fill out the paperwork for the truck. He signed his phony name, peeled off a couple twenty-dollar bills, and that was that.

Phil drove one of the trucks. I took the other. Rico and Tony followed in the Pontiac. We had to get back on I-70 toward Columbus, get off at the first exit past Zanesville, and then drive back to the spot where we'd left the Stroh's truck.

Rico pulled the Pontiac in front of it. We lined up the U-Hauls behind it. It would have been easier to move the beer if the trucks were back to back, but we decided that swinging one of the trucks around would attract too much attention.

We had to carry cases of beer from the back of the Stroh's truck to the back of the first U-Haul. It was going to take some effort and some time. Still, I started to get the feeling Rico wasn't quite so sure we were fucked, after all. I said we should fill the first truck and then Phil should drive it to Wheeling while we put the rest in the next one. I continued to silently pray that the two U-Haul trucks would be enough.

We didn't talk much about what would happen if the police showed up. We decided we'd try to get to the Pontiac and drive away before they figured out what was going on. If that didn't work, it would be every man for himself. Given the inability of the other three to even begin to come up with an idea for dealing with the broken-down truck, I liked my chances.

We got most of the beer into the first truck. I could tell the rest would easily fit in the second one. We closed it up and watched Phil drive away toward Wheeling. The rest of us worked even faster to get the job done. It was hot. We were sweating. But I was almost having fun.

After the rest of the beer was in the second truck, I asked Rico if he wanted to drive it.

"Be my guest," Rico said. "I'm done with these fucking trucks."

I opened the door and climbed up. Before getting in, I looked around one more time to make sure the coast was somehow still clear. It was.

I mouthed the words "holy shit" and got in.

Once I got the truck up to speed, I cranked the window all the way open. The breeze was strong. It dried my face, which by then was covered in dirt and dust. My arms were filthy, too.

But I was happy. The thing had gone sideways, and I'd fixed it. First day on the job, I was proving myself. I reached toward the dashboard and turned on the radio.

It was "Live and Let Die" again. I smiled. And I didn't change the channel.

Thirty-five

LESLIE FITZPATRICK

I FORCED MYSELF to get out of bed earlier than usual. I went to the kitchen and started a pot of coffee. I always made more than I could drink, mainly because I never wanted to run out. I checked the time. I picked up the phone to call Maria.

She answered after six rings. I could tell I woke her up. I apologized for doing it, but she said it was OK.

"J.J. left early," she said. "God knows where he was going. I came out to the couch to see if he'd say anything. Of course he didn't. I guess I fell back to sleep after he left."

"I was thinking maybe we could get some lunch," I said. "We haven't been to the Tea Room in so long."

"Sure," Maria said, with something in her voice. I couldn't tell what it was. Curiosity? Maybe I was being paranoid.

"Sure," she said again, and it was more convincing that time. "Let's go. Why don't you pick me up at eleven? We can beat the rush."

"OK. See you then."

I checked the clock. I had more than an hour and a half. I looked at the spot where Johnny had been sitting the other night. It really had been a long time since he'd sat there.

I poured a cup of coffee. Paul always kept a pack of Oreos in the cabinet. I took one. I twisted it apart and dropped the side without the cream into the mug. I sipped at the coffee while the cookie got soft and started to break apart. Once the pieces sank, I put the other half in the cup and kept drinking.

I just sat there. I forced myself not to think about anything. It was nice.

I went to the closet to find something to wear to the Stone & Thomas Tea Room. Maria said it reminded her of a place she'd visited once in New York City. There was something special about it, tucked in the middle of a department store that would be full of housewives happy to get out after a weekend of being stuck inside cooking and cleaning. I took a long shower and shaved all the spots I'd get with a razor at least every other day. I dried my hair and fixed it like always. I put on makeup before getting dressed in a pair of tan polyester pants and a white polyester blouse. I found a pair of brown shoes with low heels in my closet. I grabbed a large brown purse.

I saw the gun I'd pointed out the window the other night. I thought about sticking it in the purse. I decided not to. I picked up the keys to the Volkswagen from the nightstand. I went back to the kitchen. I opened the door to leave. I looked back at the clock. I had twenty-five minutes, more than enough time.

When I walked out the door, I bumped right into the center of Paul's chest.

"Where you going all dolled up?" he said. "I thought you was sick. I was coming to check on you."

I stepped back. "I am," I said. "I mean, I was. I'm better now."

He walked inside. I let him. I didn't really have a choice.

"You know, you got it all backward," he said. "People is supposed to get sick on Monday, not get better on Monday."

"I can't help it when I don't feel good."

"You been here all weekend?"

"I've known you long enough to know you already know the

answer." I dropped the purse onto the floor. "I stayed in all weekend. I had lady issues."

"Lady issues, huh? I ain't too good at math sometimes, but you just had lady issues a couple weeks ago."

"I can't control when I have lady issues," I said. I tried not to look right at him. I could feel him hovering over me.

He stuck his hand under my chin and lifted it. I could smell his cigars, mixed with shaving cream and English Leather. He got a fresh bottle of it from his wife every Christmas. He was just on the verge of being mad.

"I ain't too good at biology neither, but I thought lady issues happened every four weeks, not every two."

I made eye contact with him briefly before looking away.

"I don't know what it was. Maybe I'm pregnant."

He pushed my chin, not too hard but hard enough.

"Don't kid around about stuff like that. That wouldn't be good for me."

"It would be slightly worse for me." I felt a little bit of an edge in my voice. I wasn't sure that was a good idea, but I couldn't help it.

He was staring at me, studying me.

"So now that you're feeling better, where are you off to?"

"I'm having lunch with my cousin," I said. "And I'm supposed to pick her up in twenty minutes."

Paul reached inside his coat and pulled out a cigar. He started chewing on it.

"Well, you tell Maria I said hello. Are you coming by later, since you're up and around?"

"I'll be there. Probably by two."

He clamped his teeth down on the cigar and smiled, but not in a happy way.

"See you then," he said, turning his cheek and waiting for me to kiss him.

I held my breath and did it.

Thirty-six

SEPTEMBER 24, 1973

J.J. JENKINS

I PULLED THE U-Haul toward the garage, at the place where Bobby told us to go with the beer. The other truck was already there, the back of it open. Phil and a couple other guys were unloading the cases. I pulled as close as I could while still leaving them enough room to maneuver before I got out.

They stopped what they were doing. They actually started to clap for me.

"There he is," Phil said. "The guy who saved our asses."

A couple of the faces looked familiar. Most of the others didn't. Tommy whistled with a thumb and forefinger curled inside his lips. Bobby was there, too. He wasn't clapping, but he nodded at me and smiled, just a little bit.

"I told them the whole story," Phil said, that crooked jaw of his wobbling again. "I told them how you figured it all out, how everyone else didn't know what the fuck to do. But you knew. You knew, you son of a bitch."

Bobby stepped forward and put his hands out. Everyone else quieted down.

"OK," he said, "we're all proud of the new kid. Now, let's get the beer out of these trucks so they can bring them back. Who wants to follow Phil and J.J. and give them a ride home?"

Nearly all of them shot a hand in the air.

"Tommy," Bobby said, "you do it. And make sure you got a full tank of gas. We don't need no more unexpected shit happening today."

The trip back to Zanesville went smoothly, even though I was nervous the whole time. Phil and Tommy were in a good mood. They were talking and laughing. They treated me in a different way. It didn't make me any less nervous, but I liked how they were acting toward me.

I thought we'd go back to Doggie Do-Rights. Tommy drove to Paul's instead. We got out of Tommy's four-door Chevy.

Phil opened the back door for me. He made a big sweeping move with his free hand. "After you," he said.

I couldn't believe it. I followed them into Paul's.

The outer room was packed. I still saw her right away. Those green eyes, pulling me her way. I didn't try to fight it.

A hand clamped down on my shoulder before I could get to her. "How about this kid!"

It was Paul. He had a cigar in his mouth, and he was holding a bottle of beer. "Every job is easy until it ain't, and when it ain't it usually goes to shit. But not today."

I didn't know what to say. I'm pretty sure I thanked him.

"Get the kid a beer!" Paul pulled his hand away from me and started moving through the bodies. They all cleared a path for him.

I looked back at Leslie again. Those green eyes pulled me in like lasers.

"I heard you did good," she said. "I heard you did real good."

I looked around. She wasn't the only one watching me.

"I got lucky," I said.

"Bullshit," Phil said, grabbing my arm. "That wasn't luck. That was smart. That was smooth. We didn't know what the fuck to do once that truck broke down, but you did. We either would've had to leave the truck right there or risk getting collared. Ain't that right, Rico?"

I was surprised they were so loose and open about the fact that they weren't smart enough to figure out a problem that really wasn't all that hard. I guess it helps to be more than a little smart whenever everyone else around you seems to be more than a little stupid.

"We was fucked," Rico said. "Truck was dead. Totally dead. If J.J. don't come up with the idea to rent those trucks, it was all over. We was fucked."

I tried to take in the whole room, mainly to keep from turning back to those green eyes.

Someone dropped a quarter in the jukebox. Aerosmith's "Dream On" began to play. Someone shoved a bottle of beer into my hands. I took a long drink. It wasn't very cold, but it went down fast and it went to work right away. When I pulled it down, those green eyes were still there.

"Let's hear it for J.J.!" Phil yelled. "*Polizia vaffuncula!*"

They began chanting what he had said.

"*Polizia vaffuncula! Polizia vaffuncula!*"

I took another drink. I asked Phil what that meant.

"'Fuck the police,'" Phil said. He kept on yelling it. "*Polizia vaffuncula! Polizia vaffuncula!* That's the Sicilian way. We trust no one, especially not the government. Especially not the police."

I felt the green eyes getting closer. I finally allowed myself to meet them.

"I'm proud of you." She said it so only I could hear it.

"I really didn't do anything. This really isn't a big deal."

"It doesn't matter whether you think it is. They think it is. So let them."

She reached forward with her own bottle of beer and struck it against mine. The clink pierced through the rest of the noise.

I drank again, wishing those green eyes would stop watching me while wishing they never would.

Leslie raised her bottle toward her lips, slowly. I saw her lift the bottle up and let the beer flow across those lips and past them.

Thirty-seven

SEPTEMBER 25, 1973

JOHNNY MESAGNE

THINGS HAD STARTED to slow down. Only Jimmy Dacey and one other guy was still there. I'd been hearing bits and pieces about how J.J. saved the day with a beer truck they'd heisted north of Columbus. I tried to ignore it, mainly because the last thing I wanted to feel was proud of whatever he had done.

They was already selling the beer all through town. I kept hearing about how the truck broke down, how the crew froze up, and how J.J. came up with the idea that fixed everything. They rented U-Haul trucks. It wasn't rocket science, but most of the guys on that crew would have a hard time figuring out how to light a bottle rocket.

Right around five, the door flew open. In came Vinny. It was Tuesday, time to cough up the chunk of the action that would go up to Paul. Even though the Steelers had kicked the shit out of the Browns, we had a strong seven days. From horses to baseball to football, college and pro, we made more than three dimes. That's a good week.

I had the money ready. I shoved it in a brown envelope. Vinny would take it back to Paul's and count every last dollar. If he thought there was any mistakes, I'd hear about it. If he ever thought there was any skimming going on, he wouldn't say anything first.

"There he is," Vinny said to me when he walked in. "The father of the superstar."

"You want a beer?" I tried not to let what he said bother me.

"I'm taking it easy today. We drank plenty last night to celebrate what your boy did."

"Sounds like my boy did what anyone with half a brain would've done."

"Your boy got more than half a brain," Vinny said. He stood next to Jimmy, who gave Vinny a dirty look. Vinny either didn't notice or didn't care.

"I heard what happened." I handed the envelope to Vinny. "Seems like they got lucky to me."

Vinny took the envelope. He squeezed it twice, as if that meant anything. "Seems like you had a good week. But not as good a week as your kid had."

I looked away from him to the betting sheets for that night's action.

"My kid had a good day. One good day. Let's not make him into Lucky Luciano just yet."

"Sounds like somebody's a little jealous," Vinny said.

Now Jimmy was sticking his tongue out at him. I had to fight not to laugh.

"Jealous?" I said. "Of my own kid?"

"All I know is everybody's happy about what your kid did. Everybody but you, I think."

"It ain't my business. I don't see none of that beer showing up here for free or nothing. Shit, they ain't even tried to sell me none of it yet."

"They will," Vinny said. "They got a lot to move. Fifteen hundred cases. And it would've been no cases at all if your kid wasn't there."

"My kid can't help it they sent a bunch of dumbasses with him," I said. "Who wouldn't have known to go find other trucks when the truck they stole broke down?"

"You think we got geniuses in this outfit?" Vinny said, belching out a rare laugh. "Guys do what they're told to do. They ain't expected to

improvise. Your kid did. That makes him smarter than ninety percent of them."

"The way I remember it, I'd say he's smarter than a hundred percent of them, you included."

Now it was Jimmy who was fighting not to laugh.

"All I know is everybody's happy with your kid," Vinny said. "They
didn't know what to make of him. They thought he only got the job
because of who his dad is. Very first day, he proved himself."

I stood up straight and looked past the hole in Vinny's nose and
into those black, dead eyes.

"I was part of that for years," I said. "I know what the job takes. And
it takes a hell of a lot more than what my kid did yesterday."

"Well, now he'll get even more chances to show what he can do.
And you'll get even more chances to be jealous of him."

"You got any kids yet, Vinny?" I knew the answer, but I asked it
anyway. "Maybe someday you will. And maybe someday they'll grow
up. And maybe someday you'll get to see what it's like when you want
something more from your kids, but they're determined to end up
like their old man."

"I got no problem with my kids doing what I do."

"It's easy to say when you ain't got no kids. So why don't you just
get the fuck out of here, go find a gal you can get drunk enough to let
you knock her up, and come back in about twenty years and tell me
whether you want your kid doing this shit."

Jimmy had to cover his mouth after that one.

"This shit feeds plenty of people," Vinny said. "This shit raises
plenty of families. Are you ashamed of that, Johnny? Is that why you
got out? You too good for what we do? The way I see it, what you're
doing now ain't all that different. You just found a way to do it without getting your hands dirty. And you're damn lucky Paul decided to
let you."

"I didn't get lucky. My kid may have gotten lucky yesterday, but I
sure as shit didn't get lucky."

Vinny stood there for a little bit, just watching me.

"OK, Mesagne. We'll leave it at that. When I come back next week, I'll let you know what else your kid's been up to. Because he's getting shit done, and I can already tell it burns your asshole like hot peppers on the way out."

Thirty-eight

J.J. JENKINS

PAUL CAME OUT from the back, carrying a case of Stroh's beer. I assumed it was from the truck we stole.

"I usually hate to drink the profits," he called out to the room. "But tonight I'll make an exception."

He dropped the box on top of the bar. The bottles clanged against each other. He opened the lid and started tossing beers around. One guy had a bottle that went his way, but it hit the ground. It busted all over the floor.

"Goddammit, Pete!" Paul said. "Now go get a fucking mop and clean that up."

Maybe Pete could have caught it, but the throw didn't make Paul Verbania look like Joe Namath.

A bottle was coming at me. I reached up and snatched it, just it before it hit me in the nose.

"He's smart, he's quick, and he's coordinated!" Paul yelled.

"So you're coordinated?" Leslie said to me after the perfunctory laughter started to die down.

She'd been mingling a little bit. I hadn't noticed that she was back in my vicinity. We were standing near the pinball machine she'd been playing the first time I saw her there.

"I don't know about that," I said. "All I know is when something's coming for my face, I need to keep it from hitting me."

"Not all things that come at your face are bad."

"I guess not," I said. At least I think I said it. How could I remember exactly what I said after she said something like that? I remember the next thing I said, because it was so stupid.

"My mom's spaghetti, now that's something good I don't keep from hitting my face."

"Well, that's one thing," she said. "I mean, there are others."

LESLIE FITZPATRICK

I DIDN'T KNOW what I was saying. I couldn't help myself. Animal instincts. Law of the jungle, I suppose. My brain was trying to get me away from Paul, and something else inside me was trying to get me closer to J.J.

He was having such a hard time coming up with things to say to me. It was kind of cute.

He finally changed the subject. "So what do you do for a job?"

"I work here, and there," I said. "I do stuff Paul needs me to do."

"So you've got a job with benefits," he said.

I shook my head at him. What a shitty thing to say. But I could see he knew he was out of line.

"I just—I'm saying you work for him and he's, like, your boyfriend," he said.

"Boyfriend? I thought you were twenty, not twelve."

"Well, what is he, then?" He was trying hard to whisper.

"It's complicated." I looked down while I said it. "It's anything but permanent. I know he's not leaving her. And I know it's just a matter of time before I'm yesterday's news."

"I can't imagine you ever being yesterday's news."

J.J. JENKINS

WHAT A STUPID fucking thing to say. What a moron I was. Good, I thought. My dad wanted me not to mess with her. If I kept saying dumb shit like that, it wouldn't be a problem.

"What happened to your finger?" she said. Her question surprised me.

"I figured my mother told you."

"We talk about a lot, but we never talked about that."

"That's no surprise, I guess." I held up my right hand, showing off where my pinky had been. "No one in my family likes to talk about this very much."

I never really knew what to expect from her. I didn't expect what she said next.

"Well, I'm going to tell Paul I'm tired. And I'm going to go get my car. Fifteen minutes after I leave, I want you to walk out that door. Take a right, and go two blocks."

"And then what?"

"Then you can get inside that car you love so much."

I didn't ask the next *then what?*

LESLIE FITZPATRICK

I DID IT. I can't believe I did it, but I did. I walked over to Paul. I told him I was tired, and that I was going home. He nodded and listened. He didn't seem to care. I guess he didn't want to ruin his good mood over the truck thing working out.

I worked my way through the room, smiling and saying goodbye and whatever else I had to do so that I could leave. I didn't realize how hot it was in there until I walked outside. It felt like freedom, almost the same way it felt whenever I left that prison.

I tried not to think about what had happened just before I went through the door. I looked back. I saw J.J. watching me. I think I also saw Paul watching J.J. watching me.

J.J. JENKINS

I CHECKED THE fake Rolex over and over again. Fifteen minutes crept by. Tony asked me if they were keeping me from being somewhere better. I said I wanted to get home before my mother went to bed. Tony said I wouldn't have to worry about tucking my mother in much longer, that I'd have at least three months' worth of rent from today's score.

I listened and agreed, just to keep things moving. I tried to be less obvious about checking the watch. I guessed it had been fifteen minutes. I told Tony and the others I needed to go, that it had been a long day.

I turned around and looked for Paul. I didn't see him. I didn't know whether I was expected to personally tell him goodbye. I decided to just leave.

At first I didn't remember where she told me to go. Then it came back to me: *right turn, two blocks.* I saw that little orange fire hydrant on wheels. The engine was clunking and puttering. I walked to the passenger side window and tapped on the glass.

She smiled. Those green eyes seemed like they had a light behind them. She reached over to unlock the door.

I opened it. "This thing really does sound like an amusement park ride," I said.

"I'd hoped you'd gotten all of that out of your system the other night."

"I got more."

"Well, save some for next time," she said, and then she shifted into drive and pulled away.

Thirty-nine

SEPTEMBER 29, 1973

J.J. JENKINS

I KEPT A low profile for a couple days, staying close to the phone and keeping an eye out the window in case someone decided to show up with whatever my next job was. I didn't know whether I should go back to Bobby's and hang out. I wanted to go back to Paul's, but not because I was looking for more work to do.

Tony called on Wednesday night and said the beer was going like a cockroach on a stagecoach. I asked him what the hell that meant. Tony said it's Bobby's way of saying things are selling fast. It seemed easier to just say that, but it wasn't my place to tell them their sayings were dumb.

Tony said some of the salesmen from the legitimate beer distributors had started complaining about the sudden drop in demand. Once they heard the reason, the complaints stopped.

I knew the haul would be a good one. I remembered the numbers Bobby had talked about: nearly forty-one hundred bucks. I got a call on Thursday night to show up at his place the next day, and he gave me an envelope, like one you get from the bank. A strip of glue held it shut.

I asked him what it was. He didn't answer. I figured it out and felt dumb for asking.

I didn't open it until I got home. There was a stack of twenties inside. I counted them. Twenty-five in all. Five hundred dollars. I started doing the math. Two grand for the four of us, twenty-one hundred for Paul. Had the other guys gotten the same as I did? Maybe they got more. Maybe they got less. I wanted to know, but nothing good was going to come from trying to find out.

I decided then and there to always take whatever they gave me, and to ask no questions. That would be the best way to avoid trouble.

I wanted to know more about how it all worked. Money got passed up to Paul. Where did he send it? I figured he had people in Pittsburgh he needed to keep happy, and that nothing would keep them happier than getting a cut of whatever he was making.

The truck thing was easy, except when the truck broke down. Even then, we got it done. Maybe I had it wrong. Maybe it wasn't like the movies. Maybe they didn't beat people up, or worse. I could deal with stealing trucks. Like Rico said, those companies have insurance.

I sat on the couch. It was Friday night. My mother had gone out somewhere. For all I knew, she was having dinner with Leslie.

Leslie. The less I thought about her, the better off I'd be. If only it was that easy.

The phone on the kitchen wall rang. I got up and answered it.

"Nine tomorrow morning," someone said. I didn't ask who. "Same place."

I hung up the phone and looked at the clock. I went back to the living room and turned on the TV. *The Brady Bunch* was on. They were doing *Snow White and the Seven Dwarfs* to raise two hundred dollars so that they could buy a gift for a teacher who was retiring. Two hundred dollars. I fished that envelope out of my jeans and counted the twenties again. I peeled off ten and held them up to the TV. I smiled.

I showed up at Doggie Do-Rights on Saturday morning. Bobby let me in. There were only four dogs in the cages. I was able to say a quick hello to Gnocchi.

When I got to the back room, things felt different. It was just Bobby,

Rico, and me. Rico didn't move when I came in. He wasn't being rude, he just wasn't being anything.

"Where's everybody else?" I said.

"Nobody else," Bobby said. "Just you and Rico for this one. Sit down."

Rico still didn't move. I was too confused to be happy that I already had a seat at the main table. Bobby got right to it.

"You guys are taking a drive to Pittsburgh today. There's a guy up there been betting heavy with one of our bookies in Weirton. The guy's not paying. You're going to lean on him."

"What do you mean by that?" I said.

"You're going to tell him he's got one week to come up with the money, plus twenty percent," Bobby said. "Then Rico will give him a message."

"But the message is he's got a week to come up with the money," I said. "If I'm giving him the message, why's Rico telling him the same thing?"

Rico reacted by grinning. He looked down at a Styrofoam cup full of coffee. The steam rising from it mixed with the smoke from the cigarette in the ashtray he had next to him.

"No, kid," Bobby said. "Rico's giving him a different kind of message. Rico used to be a prizefighter. He still knows how to pack a pretty good punch."

I looked back at Rico. He put his fists up and smiled wide, showing a couple of cracked teeth and an upper lip that didn't stretch quite as wide on one side as it did on the other.

"So I talk, and Rico beats him up. Why do I need to be there for that?"

"It's safer with two," Bobby said. "It scares the guy more. He might try something if it's just Rico, if he don't figure Rico could rip him in half if he wanted. Besides, you never know what else could go wrong. You showed on Monday that if something goes wrong, you can maybe figure out how to make it go right."

I tried to stand up. I almost fell backward over the chair.

"I don't understand how me figuring out we needed to rent trucks to get that beer back from Ohio makes me some kind of mastermind. This is all new to me. I was in college not that long ago."

"Well," Bobby said, "you're getting a little faster education in your new line of work. It's like skipping a grade. Hey, Rico, you ever skip a grade?"

Rico was taking a drink of coffee. He turned his head and spit out a mouthful of it.

"Skip a grade?" he said. "I got held back so many times I was having wet dreams during the naps."

Bobby laughed. I didn't.

"This is still a lot different than driving away in a truck the driver lets us drive away in," I said.

"You're right," Bobby said, looking me in the eye. "It is. You showed you was a big boy on Monday. Now you get some big boy work. This is what you wanted to do, right? Now you're getting to do it."

"What would you say if I said I'm not sure I'm ready for something like this?"

"What would you say if I said Paul specifically told me to give this to you?" When I didn't say anything back to him, Bobby nodded. "Yeah, that's what I thought you'd say."

Forty

WILLIE HAD BEEN sleeping in his grandmother's basement for more than a week. It felt like more than a year. His shoulder hurt as much as it did the night it happened. He thought he needed a real doctor, but they kept telling him he couldn't go to a real doctor. That a real doctor would take one look at that hole in his shoulder and call the cops.

Willie was convinced that whoever came to the dog shop that night wasn't a real doctor, not even close.

His grandmother didn't know he'd gotten shot. He'd been hiding it from her the best he could. He wondered whether she had figured it out. If she had, she hadn't said anything about it. She was getting forgetful, but she knew enough to know nothing good would come from knowing the truth.

Willie sat there, stewing. He felt neglected and ignored. Hardly anyone had visited him. J.J. called one night to see how he was doing, but didn't say he'd come over. Tony had stopped by once. Bobby had been there, too, but he didn't stay for long. Willie figured Bobby felt like he had to show his face.

You take a bullet, but it really doesn't mean shit to anybody. On top of that, Willie told his boss at the record store that he fell down the steps and needed some time off. Willie didn't know how much longer he'd be able to pull that off before they found somebody to replace him.

Willie heard noises coming from the first floor. The door to the basement opened and someone came down the steps. He knew right away it was Tony. Willie was too happy to have company to be mad at him for not coming back sooner.

Tony got to the bottom and walked past the old wash kettle with a wringer on it. Willie's grandmother still used that damn thing. He kept telling her once he got enough money, he'd buy her a real washing machine. Every time he said it, she'd wave her hand and say in that Italian accent, "I no-a need-a nothing, Guglielmo. I no-a need-a nothing."

Tony flapped a hand in front of his nose."It still stinks down here."

"I'm used to it."

"Maybe it's you."

"All the more reason for me to get used to it."

Tony had a six-pack of beer. He was smoking a cigarette.

"You look like shit," Tony said.

"I figured you came to cheer me up. What the fuck would you say if you wasn't trying to cheer me up?"

"Don't worry about it. You always look like shit. So you must be getting back to normal."

"Nothing normal about this. My shoulder hurts. It hurts all the time."

"That doctor said it'll get better. Are you taking care of it like he told you?"

"What else do I have to do? The hole is getting better. But I can feel it in there."

"If you can get used to this smell, you can get used to that, too."

"I'd rather not."

"You know, you ain't the first guy to get shot and have the bullet still inside."

"Easy to say for someone who ain't never been shot."

"Bobby told me there's two kinds of guys in this business," Tony said. "Guys who been shot and guys who will be."

"That don't make my shoulder hurt no less."

Willie sat in an easy chair Tony had brought the last time he visited. Tony said it came from the place where they keep all the stuff they'd stolen but hadn't sold yet. Tony had said Bobby wanted Willie to have it. He liked it, but it didn't make his shoulder feel any better.

"I been sleeping in this thing every night," Willie said. "I can't get comfortable on the couch."

"You'll be up and around again before you know it," Tony said.

"I hope so. I can't take being cooped up. I can't make no money in here."

Tony pulled out an envelope from his jeans. He opened it and peeled away three bills.

"Here," he said. "You deserve this. If you hadn't been shot, you probably would've been on that job instead of our friend."

"Our friend." Willie spat on the cement floor after he said it. "We never should've got him that night. It's all my fault. That's why it all went wrong. We go up there with three guys, and that little prick gets spooked. So I get shot and now J.J. Jenkins is muscling in."

Tony opened a beer and handed it to Willie. He opened another one and took a drink. "You hear what he did?"

"Bobby told me when he was here. We could've figured that shit out. Who doesn't think when a fucking truck breaks down to go get another truck?"

"I didn't. I didn't really try. I got scared. Phil and Rico did, too. He didn't."

"Phil and Rico? Maybe Phil. Maybe. Rico is a dumbshit. And I know I can be a dumbshit. So if I'm a dumbshit and I think he's a dumbshit, that makes him a real dumbshit."

"He serves a purpose. He's a scary motherfucker. If something goes down, I want him around."

"Well, something went down with that truck and he pissed his pants."

"That made it easier for our friend to look good," Tony said.

"That's the problem. Our friend is looking too good. I bet he's getting bumped up over us. How much did they give him?"

"I don't know. I didn't ask. I got three hundred. I figure me and J.J. got the same, and Phil and Rico probably got more."

"I bet you every penny of that three hundred you got that J.J. got more than the rest of you." Willie forced himself out of the chair. The bullet felt like it was digging deeper and deeper into his shoulder, like the wriggling tip of a knife. "What the fuck was we thinking? We know who his dad is. We opened the door and pulled him through. Now he's in. And we're out."

"We ain't out. Far as I can tell, there's plenty of work to be done."

"Maybe we ain't out. But he's jumping the line. I guarantee it. We'll end up working for him. He should've been working for us."

"We're still working. Yeah, he got lucky. Maybe he gets bumped up too fast and he fucks up."

"Maybe he don't fuck up. Maybe he's a natural at this shit. And we're the ones who brung him in."

"You're thinking too much," Tony said, waving a hand at Willie. "Shouldn't we want our friend to be able to help us out?"

"Not if he's making money we should be making and getting jobs we should be getting. We was doing fine. Now he's in the way."

"I didn't know you was like this," Tony said.

"Well, I had some time to think lately. I got fucking shot. I hope that counts for something."

"I'm sure it will."

"Yeah, it will. And even then, you and me is both stuck on the ladder behind J.J. Jenkins."

"I don't really understand none of this, Willie. What are we supposed to do about it?"

"Nothing." Willie fell back into the chair. He winced when he landed. He put his head back and closed his eyes. "There ain't nothing we can do about it, at least not for now. But we ain't got to like it."

"It don't matter whether we like it," Tony said. "It matters that we do what they tell us to do."

"That's fine," Willie said. "But I'm telling you, before too long J.J. will be the one who's telling us what to do. I can feel it, same as I can feel this fucking bullet inside me."

Forty-one

SEPTEMBER 28, 1973

LESLIE FITZPATRICK

I THOUGHT ABOUT not going back to Paul's on Tuesday, the day after the thing with the beer truck. But I had to go through the motions, I kept telling myself. It was one thing for me to start being colder and more distant with Paul—and I was. It would be another thing for me to suddenly stop coming around. People would notice that, and then they'd start wondering. I didn't need anyone wondering about anything, other than Paul wondering why I suddenly wasn't interested in him that way.

He really was a different person in the bedroom. I never quite understood it. He was gentle, vulnerable even. And if he tried to start something and I wasn't in the mood or whatever, he backed off. He never pushed the issue. That's not what anyone would have expected from someone like him.

If I denied him enough, he'd start looking for someone else. Maybe I didn't know that, but I hoped it. I had to play along with everything else, and then just wait until he decided enough was enough, and if he had needs that I wasn't going to fulfill he'd get his fill somewhere else.

He wouldn't have any trouble meeting someone new. There was always someone as dumb as I was when I was twenty-one and Paul noticed me for the first time, when Johnny showed up at that stupid cookout with me on his arm.

This J.J. stuff wasn't making it any easier. I got caught up in the excitement after I heard what he did, and I drank just enough beer that night to do something stupid. Thank God we only kissed a little bit and nothing more. I wanted to do a lot more than that, but I knew to be careful. He was holding back, too—maybe because we were sort of related, or I was seven years older, or he knew I was with Paul. Probably some of each.

Being sort of related hadn't been an issue with Johnny. I doubted J.J. knew about that. I wondered whether Johnny would ever tell J.J. If that was the only way to keep us from getting together, maybe Johnny would.

I needed to avoid J.J., at least until I ended it with Paul. If Paul found out we even kissed, J.J. would go away and never come back. Why had I gotten involved with someone who did things like that?

Would he ever do something like that to me? However he was in the bedroom, he was different everywhere else. I'd seen it in his face, heard it in his voice. He never talked business around me, but I'd picked up enough to know what kind of business he did. I tried to play dumb, if only for the sake of my own conscience. But I knew who he was, what he was. I always had.

I knew where the money came from. I saw the things they kept in the warehouse. None of that stuff came from a store. I knew about the gambling. The prostitution. The drugs. Not a lot of drugs, but enough. I'd hear them joking about places that burned down. They'd say it turned into a Christmas tree. And I had a pretty good idea what it meant when I'd sometimes hear them talk about sending people to Ohio.

Did I need to worry about ending up in Ohio, if that meant what I thought it meant? What about J.J.? Was I too close to Paul to realize the danger? Was I dumb enough to think that if I was close enough to Paul, I wouldn't be in danger?

I went and found that gun, the one I stuck through the window at Johnny. I made sure it was loaded. I decided to take it wherever I went. I wouldn't be going to Ohio without a fight.

Forty-two

J.J. JENKINS

RICO TOLD ME I'd be driving to Pittsburgh. When I asked him what I'd be driving, he looked at me like I was stupid. That meant I'd be driving my own car, the Plymouth.

Before we left, he removed my West Virginia tag, stuck it in the trunk, and replaced it with a Pennsylvania plate.

I didn't ask Rico where he got it. I did point out to him after we got moving that the license plate in the back and the inspection sticker in the front came from two different states.

He said any cop smart enough to notice the difference deserved to arrest us.

When I heard the word "arrest," I almost wrecked the car.

Rico laughed and said getting arrested for driving a car with stolen Pennsylvania tags landed very low on the list of bad shit that could happen that day.

"Is that supposed to make me feel better?" I said.

The drive from Wheeling to Pittsburgh took about an hour. Halfway there, Rico flipped his chin toward an exit from Interstate 70. "There's a great whorehouse in Little Washington," he said. "Better than anything in Pittsburgh. Can you imagine that? Paul got nothing to do with that one. I tell him all the time he needs to figure out where they find the women and maybe try to hire them or something. Or just take the place over." Rico smiled as he said it, like he was proud of giving the boss business advice.

"How did you start working for him?" I said.

"When I used to box, Paul would come to the fights. So he knew who I was. And I got pretty good at stealing things. I guess they call it shoplifting. But I was never actually shopping. I went in to steal. Records was my specialty. I had this great pair of pants. I could cram thirty or thirty-five of them in there and then I'd walk out real funny, like some kind of duck. But nobody ever said shit to me. I hit every record store from Pittsburgh to Columbus, and then I'd start all over again. I sold them to Paul. Then he'd sell them to a guy who has this secondhand shop. Only none of them was secondhand, you know? They was all still in that plastic wrapper. So one day Paul told me somebody was late on a loan, real casual. Like we was talking about the weather. Then he asks if I'd go break the guy's arm."

"What did you do?"

"What do you think I did? Once you been in a ring against someone who fights back, grabbing someone who ain't a fighter and giving him a second elbow ain't hard to do."

"Are you going to break this guy's arm today?"

"Not unless he fucks around. Beating a guy up is easy. Punch him a few times hard in the stomach and he'll get the point. You ever been punched hard in the stomach?"

"When I was a kid, maybe six or seven years old."

"You get punched hard in the stomach by someone who knows how to punch, you ain't never forgetting how old you was. You'll remember the year, the month, the day, the hour, and the fucking minute."

Rico fell asleep not long after that. The back of his thick, square head pressed against the cushion. I glanced over and saw his mouth hanging open. A thick tongue was sticking over his lower lip. Even though he was breathing like a bulldog with asthma, he managed to stay asleep for the rest of the drive.

He woke up when the car rolled into the Fort Pitt Tunnel. "Take the Liberty Avenue exit," he said. He kept his eyes shut, even when the car came out of the tunnel and that great skyline was right there, smacking us in the face. "I'll tell you where to go."

I looked at the square green signs over each lane and found the one that pointed to the exit I was supposed to use.

Rico perked up, giving me directions that took us to a small parking lot, right off the street. No one was working there. The lot was maybe half empty. He told me to back into a spot away from the other cars. After I got the Plymouth in the right place, I saw him pull a set of brass knuckles from his pocket. He put them on and took them off again.

"Do you plan on using those?" I said.

"I brung them just in case."

He got out of the Plymouth and led the way down Liberty Avenue. It was a different world, that was for sure. Strip clubs, adult stores, peep shows. There were women who looked like prostitutes and men who were asking us if we wanted to spend time with some of the women. Rico ignored all of them.

I tried to stay focused on the back of Rico's shirt. It wasn't easy. I felt like Dorothy, but this sure as hell wasn't Oz.

"There it is," Rico said. He pointed to a sign that said "Lady Liberties." He bolted for the door and opened it. He started moving even faster once we got inside. I had to hustle to keep up with him.

It was dark. The air was hot and wet. It stank like something I'd never really smelled before.

Rico went over to talk to the bartender. He pointed in the direction of a man on the other side of the room. Rico dropped a crumpled up bill before walking away—a five, maybe a ten. He shot across the room to a guy who had long greasy hair that was gray and black. He had an eye patch, like a pirate. Rico bumped into four people on the way. They didn't complain, not after they got a look at Rico.

I was just close enough to Rico to hear what he said to the man.

"Are you Holloway?"

"Who wants to know?"

"Paul Verbania wants to know."

The man's body got stiff. He started looking around with his good eye.

"Don't waste your time," Rico said. "C'mon. Let's go for a walk." He snatched Holloway's arm.

Rico led him back through the bar, out the door, and down the street. I followed them. I could tell Rico was taking him to the parking lot.

Holloway was talking to Rico, but nothing made Rico slow down. If anything, he was pulling the guy harder toward whatever was going to happen near or on or in my car.

When he got to the lot, Rico let go of the guy. Then Rico gestured to me. It was time for me to do whatever I was supposed to do.

"Um, well, so look," I said. "You owe some money."

"I said I was going to pay it," Holloway said. He was practically yelling. "I'll pay it."

I looked at Rico. He seemed to be getting impatient. I turned back. "When will you pay it?"

"Soon. I'll pay it soon."

"You've got one week to pay it," I said. "Plus twenty percent."

"Twenty percent?"

Rico stepped forward and gave the guy an uppercut to the midsection. It lifted his feet off the ground. He fell down, bracing himself on his hands. He threw up all over his forearms.

I didn't know what to do after that. Rico seemed even more impatient with me.

"One week," I said. "Plus twenty percent."

Rico jerked the man back up to his feet, stepping backward and forward and unloading. Rico hit him as hard as he did the first time.

The man fell again, gasping and spitting. He puked again. "You broke my fucking ribs," he said, coughing after every word.

Rico was glaring at me. "I done my job," he said. "Now how's about you do yours?"

Something came over me. Maybe I was afraid Rico was going to hit me like that if I didn't do what he expected me to do.

My voice changed. I bent over and yelled at the guy on the ground. "Every fucking penny, plus twenty percent! Or it'll be a lot worse than broken fucking ribs!"

"OK, OK," he said, waving a hand that had vomit all over it. "They'll get it. All of it."

"Plus twenty fucking percent?" Man, I was on a roll.

His face fell into the puddle he'd made. He struggled to speak from the corner of his mouth. "Plus twenty fucking percent."

Rico motioned with his chin toward the car. I got in. He did, too.

I fumbled around with the keys.

"Just be calm," Rico said in a low voice. "Just start the car and drive."

I finally got the right key in the ignition. I pulled out of the lot and started back toward the tunnel out of town. I looked in the rearview mirror and saw the guy curled up in a ball.

"I think you killed him," I said.

"I didn't hit him as hard as I wanted to." He pushed in the lighter on the dashboard and put a cigarette in his mouth. "He'll live. At least until next Saturday."

I wondered for a second or two whether I would.

Forty-three

JOHNNY MESAGNE

ON SUNDAY AT the bar, I started hearing bits and pieces about the boy's trip to Pittsburgh. I know all about jobs like that. Paul only goes into that territory when he's chasing a debt, and he only does it after he gets the nod from the family that runs the town.

I tried to focus on my work, which was easy because there was a full day of football games. But I still caught a little here and a little there from the things the guys in the bar was saying. After a while, I asked Jimmy to keep his ears open. And he did. By the end of the day, I had a pretty good idea what happened the day before.

I decided not to do or say nothing until I slept on it. That night in my apartment, I kept hearing Jimmy's voice in my head, telling me to keep telling J.J. that I didn't want him in that world. When I woke up the next day, I knew what I needed to do.

I still had to work first. So I waited until after the Monday night game got started to walk back to my apartment and then drive to the house on Poplar. The Steelers kicked the shit out of the Oilers on Sunday, beating the number again. I took another bath. Bitched about it all day at the bar. It was a distraction. Still, even with that other issue, it would have been nice to make some of the money back from the Lions and Falcons on Monday night.

When I got to the house, I saw his car parked in front. I found a spot farther down the street. I sat there for a little bit thinking about what I was going to say. I finally got out and started toward the house.

J.J. JENKINS

I WAS SITTING near the TV, watching the football game. My mother was reading a paperback. She had a big tumbler of Riunite and 7-Up. She drank too much, but the more she drank, the less she asked questions I didn't feel like answering. Life would be a lot easier after I found my own place.

I heard someone coming up the steps. I waited. There was a knock on the door.

"Who the hell is that?" she said to me.

"I don't know. Why don't you go in your room and I'll take care of it?"

"Why would I do that?"

"Because there's a good chance it's for me."

"It could be for me, son. Remember, this is still my house."

"Please, just go in there. If it's for you, I'll come get you."

I was surprised that she did. Maybe it was another benefit of the wine.

After she closed the door to her bedroom, I went over and opened the front door to the house. That surprised me, too. I didn't know what to say.

"You inviting me in?" my father said.

"Are you coming inside? Or are you here to take me for another ride?"

"I just wanted to talk to you. Hopefully just you."

"She's in her room. She's reading a book."

"When did she start reading books?"

"When did you start caring what she did?"

"Fair enough. I hear the game. What's the score?"

"Seven to three, Lions."

"Hopefully they make the number. I got plenty of action on Atlanta because the Steelers beat Detroit so easy a couple of weeks ago."

I still didn't know what to say. He wanted something. I wanted to just get to it.

"Did you come to watch the game?" I said. I wasn't trying to sound like a smartass. I thought that would maybe get him to get to the point without me asking.

"I just wanted to talk a little. That's all. I been hearing things. Things I wish I wasn't hearing."

"Not everything you hear is true," I said, crossing my arms.

"I think what I'm hearing is true. Because I think someone wants me to know what's going on."

"I don't get it," I said.

"Look, Paul wants me to know what you're doing. So he has a way of making sure I know. I know all about the beer truck. I know what you did when the truck broke down. And I know what you did in Pittsburgh on Saturday."

"I didn't do anything in Pittsburgh on Saturday. I just talked."

"Yeah, you just talked. Rico did the rest."

"Rico did what Rico does. I didn't do any of it."

"You realize at some point they'll want you to do more than just talk. You get that, right?"

"Rico was a boxer. He's good at those things. They won't expect me to do that."

JOHNNY MESAGNE

I REMEMBERED BEING that young. I didn't remember being that dumb. Maybe I was. I probably was.

"Beating guys up ain't all they do," I said. "You get that, I'm sure. At some point, they'll want you to do things you don't have to be a boxer to do."

"Like what?"

"Use your imagination, son. Or just ask me about some of the shit I had to do. What the hell do you think you're signing up for, a glee club?"

"I don't understand why you care about what I'm doing. You said you wouldn't stop me from doing this."

"I'm not going to stop you. I can't stop you. But I can try to get you to understand how this goes. They're happy with what you're doing. So you'll get more stuff to do. Before you know it, you'll have to do something that deep down you don't want to do. By then, it'll be too late. And that will change you, for good. You know damn well what I'm talking about. It's just a matter of time."

"I'll deal with that when it happens."

I took a step closer so he'd get the point. He moved back from me a little bit. I was glad to see that.

"Do you really not know how this works?" I said. "You can't deal with it when it happens. Whenever Paul or Bobby or whoever tells you to do something, you do it. You can't say, 'No, thank you. What else you got?' You just do it."

J.J. JENKINS

I UNDERSTOOD WHAT he was saying. Maybe I knew deep down that he was right. Maybe I didn't want to admit it.

"I still don't know why you care," I said.

"I care because I only got so many chances before you're in too deep. It's happening faster than I thought it would. It may be happening just as fast as he wanted it to happen."

"He who?"

"You know he who," he said. "I don't know what he's trying to prove. I feel like this is his way of getting back at me for getting out six years ago. Part of me feels like he's been planning this the whole time."

"So wait, you think all of this is about Paul getting back at you, because you got out?"

"I don't know, but he seems to be getting a real kick out of rubbing it in my face. Six years after I got out, he's getting you in."

"I'm not in anything yet," I said.

"I guess I thought that once, too. Pretty soon, you'll figure out that what you think don't matter no more."

I was thinking about what to say next, but then he just turned around and walked away. "Tell your mother I said hello," he said. "And make sure you tell her I tried."

"Tried what?"

He didn't answer.

Forty-four

LESLIE FITZPATRICK

I MADE SURE I kept up appearances for the rest of the week. I went to his place. That pinball machine helped keep my mind occupied. I acted like everything was fine, normal. I had dinner with my mother on Wednesday night, same as always. I didn't tell her anything about what had happened, or what I was planning to do. She fished around a little bit. I said enough to make her think I wasn't hiding anything, even though I was hiding plenty.

Maybe she could tell. Maybe that's why she didn't push it. Maybe no matter how hard I was trying to keep her from knowing what was going on inside me, it showed. I hoped she was the only one who knew me well enough to figure that out.

Maria called on Thursday morning. We chatted for a while. I was nervous the whole time, waiting for her to mention J.J. and hoping I could talk about him without giving anything away. How would I explain to her that I was hopelessly attracted to her son? That the thought of being with him had become the one thing that was helping me put in motion an effort to get away from the most dangerous man around? I didn't want her to think less of me. I didn't want to get her in the middle of it, or to give her any reason to try to be.

She complained a few times about J.J. coming and going without telling her anything. I just listened and agreed with whatever she was saying. When she mentioned he would be getting his own place soon, my mind wandered about what would happen if he ever took me there. As long as he lived with his mother, the temptation wouldn't be as strong. The minute he moved out, well, I didn't want to think about that.

Nothing that happened the rest of that week changed my mind. Paul took me to dinner on Thursday night. I drank a little more wine than usual to keep myself calm. I couldn't tell whether he thought anything of it. He said something about spending the night. A little while later, I went to the bathroom and stayed there for a while. When I got back to the table, I told him I was sick and asked if he would take me home. He looked at me. I couldn't tell if he was suspicious. I was too focused on making him think I was actually sick.

I kept my hand on my stomach the whole way back to my house. He asked if I needed to go to the emergency room. I told him it wasn't that bad. He told me to call Vinny if I needed a ride to the hospital. I didn't know his phone number. I didn't ask for it. Maybe I should have. Maybe when I didn't, it made Paul wonder whether I was really sick.

I worried about that for the rest of the night. I should have asked for Vinny's number. I'd gotten cigarettes at the market and wine at the liquor store. I smoked and drank plenty of both until I finally felt tired enough to go to bed without thinking about it anymore.

Things were moving toward something. Something big. I didn't know what and I didn't know how. All I knew was I had to keep doing what I was doing. I'd made the decision, and I wasn't going to change my mind. That was the only thing I was sure about. No matter where all of this was leading, I needed to keep moving that way. I just needed to be more careful than I'd ever been, about everything I said and everything I did.

I can't lie. It was kind of exciting. After more than six years of being a small piece of someone else's life, I was starting to make my own path. Even if it all got out of control—and I had a feeling it was going to—I was the one who was calling the shots for myself.

Thank God J.J. didn't already have his own place, because I would have gotten in the Volkswagen and driven there. Whatever would have happened next would have been OK with me. Even if it would have caused everything to blow up. I felt like it was going to anyway. I might as well be happy until it did.

The phone rang early the next morning. Paul was checking on me. I could hear the traffic in the background of whatever payphone he was using. I told him I was feeling better, that I'd stop by the place later. When I hung up, I thought maybe he believed I'd really been sick. I also wondered whether he was checking to see if I was actually at home.

I'd had enough of these games. The sooner I could put all of this worrying and wondering behind me, the better off I would be. I kept telling myself to be patient. I knew I needed to be. I didn't know whether I could be. I just wanted all of this to be over, no matter what the ending would be. It wasn't smart, but I couldn't help how I felt.

Forty-five

J.J. JENKINS

I WOKE UP Tuesday morning thinking about what my father had said. It wasn't making me think much differently about what I was doing, but it made me a little leery about what could happen next. I decided not to sit around and wait.

I'd done two jobs. I was becoming one of the group, just as much as Tony and Willie. Maybe more.

I headed over to Bobby's. If no one was there, I'd go home. I stopped and bought a bag of burgers. If I had food, they'd be less likely to look at me like I shouldn't be there. It cost two dollars and thirty-five cents. I used to worry about that much money. Having a thick stack of twenties made it nice to not have to think about pinching pennies.

I parked on the street down from Doggie Do-Rights, walked to the door, and pressed the same buzzer I'd pressed three times before. *Practically a regular*, I told myself.

Tommy was coming toward the front. The dogs were barking again. He seemed irritated when he opened the door. Then he saw the bag I was holding.

"You brung food?" He snatched the sack and started walking away.

I assumed it was OK for me to follow him. There were three dogs in the cages. They barked and sniffed. Gnocchi started licking at the air.

"What's the deal with the little one?" I said.

"He always does that when he smells food."

"But why's he still here? Who owns him?"

"Some guy who went away a while back. Bobby keeps saying he's going to take him to the pound. I think Bobby likes him."

"What happens when the guy comes back?"

Tommy turned to me and raised his eyebrows. I figured out what he meant.

We walked into the back room. Phil and Rico were sitting at the table. They were playing Battleship, like a couple of kids.

"It's a miss, motherfucker!" Rico yelled. He pointed at Phil and laughed.

"F-seven," Rico said, making the next guess.

"Shit." Phil's crooked jaw wobbled. "Another hit. You sunk it."

"What I sink?" Rico said. It was the most excited I'd ever seen him. "What I sink?"

"Destroyer."

"Well, you got to say it. You don't just say, 'You sunk it.'"

"You should know it's the destroyer." Phil pulled out of the board a small plastic boat with red pegs in two of three holes and showed it to Rico. "You got three straight hits. If you sink something after three straight hits, it's got to be the destroyer."

"How do I know the destroyer got three hits in it?"

"You got a fucking destroyer right in front of you."

"Oh, yeah. I do. And you ain't hit it yet!"

Tommy told them I'd brought food. He tossed the bag of burgers toward Rico. He grabbed it out of the air.

"Thanks, kid," Rico said without looking my way. "See, he gets it," Rico said to Phil. "New guy should always bring burgers. You never brung burgers when you was new, Phil."

"We was new at the same time."

Rico took a huge bite and started talking as he chewed.

"That's true, but you still never brung no burgers."

"Is Bobby around?" I asked.

"Look at this," Rico said, forcing the rest of the burger into his mouth, "new guy thinks if he brings burgers, he can all of a sudden ask questions."

"I just wanted to give him a burger," I said.

"He said he had some shit to do," Phil said. He unwrapped a burger with his eyes glued to the field of boats and pegs in front of him.

"G-5," he said to Rico.

"G-miss." Rico opened another burger. "Hey kid, next time how's about some cheese on these?" He took another big bite. "B-3," he said around a full mouth.

Phil slammed the lid and stood up. "You're the luckiest sonofa-bitch I know."

Rico threw his arms into the air. "Battleship! Battleship! Good thing you didn't join the navy."

"Don't say that," Phil said. "We're lucky we didn't have to deal with that Vietnam shit. Those guys coming back from over there are fucked up, bad. That could've been us."

"Did you have low lottery numbers?" I said.

"Nope," Phil replied. "We both was supposed to go. And then the boss got us a letter from some doctor. He said we wasn't healthy enough to go. We didn't even have to go see the guy."

"I got a bad pancreas, I think," Rico said.

"Thank God I didn't have to worry about that," I said. "I was born a year too late."

"You would've been fine," Rico said. "You would've got a letter, too. Your old man would've asked for it and it would've happened."

"I guess so," I said.

"I know so," Rico said. "Why the hell does anyone want anything to do with that shit, anyway? I would've gone to Canada or back to the Old Country. Fucking Vietnam. They got no issue with me, I got no issue with them."

"You would've gone," Phil said. "License to blow people away, free food, and fifty-cent hookers. You would've gone in a second."

"Why do I need to go to Vietnam for free food and fifty-cent hookers when I can just go to your mother's house?" Rico said. He laughed as he said it, bits of burger flying out of his mouth.

The rest of us started laughing, too. We didn't notice Bobby walk in.

"What's so funny?" Bobby said. "I didn't hear no Jack Benny in here."

"I'm going to Phil's mom's house for a plate of stuffed shells and then she's getting her shell stuffed," Rico said, as we all kept laughing.

Bobby still didn't think it was funny. He came to the table and handed an envelope to Rico and an envelope to me.

"This is for that thing you did Saturday," he said. Then he gave an envelope to Phil. "This is for Friday night," Bobby said to him.

"Where's mine?" Tommy said.

"If you ever do something more around here than eat food, drink beer, and smoke cigarettes, maybe you'll get one," Bobby said.

"I do plenty!"

"I know you do. And you get your weekly pile. These guys are still, like, contractors. Paid per job. You know how it goes. We was both like them once."

I pinched the packet of bills, but I kept hearing the words "weekly pile." How big was the weekly pile? Whatever it was, getting paid by the job didn't seem to be a bad way to go. The new envelope was just as thick as the one I'd gotten before. I thanked Bobby, folded the envelope in half, and tucked it into the back pocket of my jeans.

"Why did we already get paid?" I said. "The guy had until Saturday to come up with the money."

"He paid every penny yesterday," Bobby said. "I guess four broken ribs will convince a guy to make good."

"I only broke four of his ribs?" Rico said. "I must be getting soft."

I was curious about something. "You never said how much the guy owed," I said to Bobby.

"You didn't need to know how much he owed," Bobby said. "But since it's all over, I'll say this. It was more than twenty dimes."

"Twenty thousand bucks?" Rico said.

"And that was before the twenty percent," Bobby said. "So you guys done good. Real good."

When I got home, I saw how well we'd done. In my bedroom with the door closed, I peeled the envelope open. This time, it wasn't twenties. It was hundreds. Like the last time, there were twenty-five of them.

My jaw dropped. I shook my head. I counted them twice. I counted them again. Twenty-five hundreds. Twenty-five hundred dollars. For what? Two hours in the car and a few minutes of tough talk?

My dad said they'd eventually want me to do more than talk. But if talking paid this much money, more than talking must pay a hell of a lot better. How much had been in Rico's envelope? I would never ask, but I would have loved to know.

I put the bills on the top of the desk, in a stack. I looked at it and fought off a smile. I looked at the compass. There was that needle, pointing toward the front door.

Forty-six

J.J. JENKINS

I WAS BACK in the chair at the desk Paul had gotten after watching *The Godfather*. He'd gone out to a payphone to make a call. I still didn't understand why he wouldn't just use the phone on the wall in the front room. I hope I'm never that paranoid.

Bobby had called the house and told me to be here at three o'clock. I wondered whether Leslie would be there. She wasn't. I didn't know whether to be disappointed or relieved.

When I arrived, Paul and Vinny were in the front room. Paul told me to go to the back and wait for him. So I did. I sat there, looking around the place. Other than the desk, it didn't look like the office of a guy who had the power to get someone to cough up twenty-four grand in just two days.

I saw a newspaper on the top of the desk. I was bored and didn't have anything else to do, so I pulled it toward me. It looked like he'd already flipped through it. I didn't think he'd care if I took a look.

The *Wheeling Intelligencer*. Wednesday, October 3, 1973. I used to deliver those papers when I was twelve, after my dad moved out. I had to get up a few hours earlier than usual. I'd pop open a stack of papers, roll them up, wrap them in rubber bands, and stick them in a cloth sack that was stained black on the inside from all the ink that rubbed off. Then I'd go door to door, sometimes on my bike and sometimes on foot, to get all of them delivered.

Today's paper had a headline about gas prices going up. Something about an oil embargo. I didn't know what any of that meant, but the article said gas could get even more expensive. It eventually might not be available at all.

I went to the sports section and found the final score from Monday night's game. It was Wednesday, but those games always ended too late to make the Tuesday morning paper. The Lions had trounced the Falcons, so Detroit had covered the spread. That was what my father had hoped would happen. I looked at the NFL standings, and then at the schedule for Sunday's games.

That's when Paul walked back in. "Thinking about joining your old man?" he said.

"Joining him?"

"You know, making book. You're looking at the scores."

"I pay a little attention to football," I said, folding up the paper. "I like it."

"Nothing wrong with that. It's good to know what's going on in the world. Sports, along with everything else." He was sitting at the desk. He opened a drawer, took out a cigar, and tapped the end of it on the main section of the newspaper. "I can't tell you how many ideas I got over the years from reading this. I read it every day. You should, too."

"I do," I said. "I mean, I will. Every day. My mom gets it at the house."

"You should be able to move out of there soon, too," Paul said. "I know what's in those envelopes you been getting."

"I need to find a place," I said. "I haven't really had time to look." That wasn't entirely the truth; I'd been putting it off.

Paul yelled for Vinny. I heard his shoes coming down the hallway from the outer room to the office.

"Go see that guy who has the apartments on 18th Street," Paul said. "Tell him I got someone who needs to rent a place."

"One bedroom or two?"

Paul looked at me.

"Just one," I said.

"Just one," Paul said to Vinny.

Vinny nodded and walked away. He seemed to have too big of a job to be asked to do something so basic. Maybe nothing Paul personally asked someone to do was ever really basic, since Paul was the one doing the asking.

"That seemed pretty easy. How do we know they'll have something?"

"He will," Paul said, grinning.

"How do you know?"

"After Vinny goes to see him, he will. You get how this works, right?"

"Well, I've seen how it works."

"No, no," Paul said. He coughed his way through a laugh. "Vinny won't have to lean on the guy. It's about respect."

"I just assumed it was about fear."

"Actually," Paul said, "there ain't much of a difference."

I nodded at him, feeling like I'd actually made an intelligent contribution to a conversation with the boss.

"I wanted to see you because I wanted you to know I been hearing good things about you," Paul said. "From everybody. They tell me you're smart for your age. I believe them."

"Thank you," I said. "I'm just trying to figure out how this all works."

"You're doing all right so far. Like I said, you're smart for your age. But you'll need to get smarter."

"I know. I'm paying attention to everything. I'm listening to the guys."

Paul pulled a desk drawer open and took out a lighter. He flicked it into a flame and dipped the end of his cigar into it.

"It's smart to pay attention," he said. "It's smart to listen. It's smart to know what to do. Some would say it's also smart to know what not to do."

I watched the end of the cigar. It glowed when Paul took a long draw. He blew out a cloud of smoke. It was so thick that, for a second or two, I couldn't see his face on the other side.

"I just do what I'm told," I said.

"That's good. That's how this works. Some things you don't need to be told. Some things you need to be smart enough to know without being told."

"I'm not sure I understand."

"There's rules about this life. If you're smart, you'll figure them out. If you need any help about that, maybe you should ask your old man."

Forty-seven

OCTOBER 3, 1973

J.J. JENKINS

As I was leaving, Vinny was walking back in. He said the place on 18th Street would have an open apartment in ten days. The rent was a hundred a month.

I'd already made enough to pay the rent for two years. How long would it be before I started looking for a more expensive place? I could have a house before I knew it, thanks to those envelopes.

I was feeling pretty good. I went home and told my mother I'd found an apartment. I should have known she'd start with the third degree. She couldn't believe I'd agreed to take it without even seeing it first. As if I was going to say anything to Vinny other than, "Thank you."

It wasn't worth explaining how I'd found the apartment or why I didn't want to do anything other than accept Paul's gesture. I hadn't even told her I'd met him. She would have flipped her lid if she'd known.

I went to the bedroom and closed the door. She was still ranting about how dumb it was to make that kind of commitment sight unseen. Deep down, maybe she didn't want me to move out.

She kept going. I lifted the mattress and pulled out the two envelopes of cash. I went to the desk and took out the money. I counted it again. I put it all in one stack and just looked at what I'd earned. For doing what? Hardly much of anything.

I held the compass again, so that the needle was pointing at the money—not a bad direction to be heading in.

"Smart for your age," I said. I liked the sound of that. I focused more on that part of what Paul said than the rest of it. I should have known what he was really saying. I still didn't agree that Leslie belonged to him.

He was married. I was stubborn. It was about to become a problem.

Forty-eight

OCTOBER 3, 1973

LESLIE FITZPATRICK

I STAYED HOME that day. I just couldn't go to his place. When he called me that morning from one of his payphones, I told him I wasn't feeling good. Later, I called my mother to tell her I wouldn't be able to make it for dinner that night, just in case Paul decided to have someone follow me around. I didn't feel much like going out anyway.

I watched TV, game shows and soap operas. I cleaned up the place. That was something I didn't do as much as I should have. I was content to be alone, especially since there weren't many people I felt like being around.

There was one person I wanted to be around, but I'd been doing my best to resist the urge.

J.J. JENKINS

I PUT THE money back in the envelopes and put the envelopes back under the mattress.

Going out to the garage, I filled the mower's tank with gas and cut the lawn. Front and back, I made the rows perfect. Then I got the long stick with the spikes on the end and cut a perfect edge where the concrete met the grass. I cleaned up all the loose pieces and put them in the trash bag where I'd dumped the thick green clumps from that big sack.

My mother looked out at me a few times. I acted like I didn't notice. I wanted to show her I could get things done without being asked or told. That I wasn't just some kid who waited to take orders. I laughed a little when I remembered those envelopes had come from doing just that.

She had lunch ready when I went inside. Two BLTs with extra bacon and a pitcher of lemonade. I didn't realize how hungry I was until I started eating.

I felt even better than before. I took a shower. I dried my hair with a towel. I found clean jeans and a blue T-shirt. I put on the fake Rolex. I told my mother I was going for a drive. She said to be careful. She always did.

LESLIE FITZPATRICK

I CLIMBED INTO bed in the middle of the afternoon to take a nap. It felt good to just be there. There were the usual neighborhood noises outside, doors opening and closing, kids playing, birds chirping. It was relaxing, in a way.

I fell asleep eventually. I don't think it was for very long. I heard a knock at the door. I assumed it was Paul.

It wasn't.

J.J. JENKINS

I DROVE OUT by her house, turned around, drove by again. Her little putt-putt was parked in the driveway. I smiled when I saw the orange paint and the bubble shape of it.

I parked a couple blocks away, just to make sure no one would see my car there. Paul's paranoia was rubbing off on me already.

Back at her house, I walked onto the front porch and knocked on the door. I waited.

LESLIE FITZPATRICK

"WHAT ARE YOU doing here?" I said after I opened the door.

"I wanted to visit my cousin."

"Have you lost your mind? I've got neighbors."

"And I have a cousin I wanted to visit. What's the big deal?"

I hurried him inside and shut the door.

"You don't just show up like this. I could have had company."

"I checked first," he said. Then he puffed out his chest. "I'm smart for my age."

"You're not that smart. And I'm not dressed for visitors."

"You look great."

"You can't just come here whenever you want. I don't know what I did to make you think that was something you should be doing."

"I do. After the other night—"

"The other night didn't happen. The other night can't happen."

J.J. JENKINS

"THE OTHER NIGHT did happen," I said. "You didn't act like you didn't want it to happen."

"Well, it's not happening again." Those green eyes were sending me a very different message. "You should go."

"I thought we could go for a ride or something," I said. "It's a nice day out. Let's go up to Oglebay Park."

"Look," she said, "this isn't high school. We can't just go out on a date. We can't go anywhere together."

"You said it yourself that first night you drove me home. We're cousins. Cousins spend time with cousins."

"This isn't smart, J.J. None of this is smart."

"I'm smart enough to keep my mouth shut. And I know you're smart enough to keep your mouth shut."

"Keeping our mouths shut isn't good enough. He's smart and he's jealous. He could show up at any time. It would be one thing if you weren't working for him. There are rules. Rules that apply to you now that you're working for him."

"I still don't get it. He's got a wife."

"That doesn't matter. If he had two cars, you wouldn't steal one of them."

"I heard something like that before. But I'm not stealing anything. Just borrowing."

"You're going to explain that to him?"

"He likes me. Besides, he won't know."

"He's already suspicious." She moved a little closer to me, those eyes still telling me something different than what her mouth was. "He's always suspicious."

"Well, I'm here. Visiting my cousin. So if he's going to be suspicious about that then he—"

LESLIE FITZPATRICK

I DON'T KNOW what came over me. Maybe I thought I was still asleep and it was all a dream. Whatever it was, I threw my arms around him.

I squeezed my hands against the muscles in his back. I pressed my pelvis into his and kissed him, harder than the time before.

His knees bent, and we tumbled to the floor. I took my feet out of my slippers. He kicked away his shoes. It kept going like that until neither of us had anything left to take off.

Forty-nine

JOHNNY MESAGNE

I LEFT THE bar a little earlier than usual. I had to give a few of the guys a little nudge. Jimmy got the hint without too much effort. He helped me get the others to realize I had somewhere to go. I actually thought about putting Jimmy in charge again, but I didn't want to press my luck on that one.

I should have done it anyway. It was Jimmy's questions about J.J. that made me decide to talk to him again, to not delay it. Jimmy said it was like the kid was in quicksand and I was the rope. It made sense. He also said some more of that poetry shit. It sounded good, but I didn't understand it. I never did. Does anyone? Or do they act like they do so people will think they're smart?

I drove to the house. Maria told me he'd left, smelling of the Hai Karate she'd bought him the Christmas before. She said he'd found an apartment. She complained that he'd agreed to it without seeing it. I didn't tell her Paul had probably lined it up for him, and that asking to go see it first wouldn't have gone over too good. I let her gripe, since that would keep her from asking me why I showed up to talk to him when I should have still been at the bar.

I managed to get away before she pieced all of that together. I had a pretty good feeling I knew where he went. Would he actually do something that stupid? I knew he would. No matter what I told him, he wasn't going to listen to me.

I hoped like hell I was wrong.

J.J. JENKINS

I'D DOZED OFF in her bed, at least I think I did. It wasn't for long, because the phone rang. She got up to answer it. I could tell pretty quickly it was Paul. I heard her say something about feeling better. I didn't know she was sick.

She came back and said they usually had dinner together on Thursday night, but he wanted to do it tonight. I was more relieved than jealous. I could quit worrying about him showing up, even though she was more worried about that than I was. And we did a lot more that afternoon than whatever was going to happen between them at dinner. I felt like I'd won, even though I wasn't sure what the contest really was. I laid back down and closed my eyes. I heard her getting herself ready. I fell asleep again.

JOHNNY MESAGNE

I DROVE PAST her house. The orange Volkswagen was parked in its normal spot. I didn't see J.J.'s car. I exhaled a little bit at that.

I took a left at the end of the block, drove down to the next inter-section, took another left. I was going to work my way back out to the main road. It was starting to get dark, but I saw a car that looked familiar. Too familiar.

J.J. JENKINS

SHE KEPT WAKING me up with sounds that were coming from the bathroom. It wasn't my place to tell her to be quiet. I could have just left. I should have just left. Why didn't I just leave?

JOHNNY MESAGNE

ONCE I REALIZED it was J.J.'s car on the other street, I drove back to her house. I tried to think what to do.

"Do I go in?" I said to myself. "Do I wait? Do I go in? What the fuck do I do?"

Before I could figure it out, I saw lights coming from the other direction. The bulbs in the front end told me it was a Cadillac.

I pressed the gas to block it. I hit the brakes and shifted the arm on the steering wheel to park. I jumped out. I could see the outlines of Vinny's head in the front, Paul's in the back.

As I got closer, the front window opened, next to Vinny.

"Johnny," Vinny said, "when the fuck did you turn into Evel Knievel?"

"Vinny!" I said it loud, turning my head toward the house. "Well, hello, Vinny!"

"Jesus Christ," he said. "I ain't going deaf."

"And it's Paul!" I said when the back window came down, still talking loud. Hopefully loud enough to be heard inside the house. "What are you doing here, Paul Verbania? And what do you know?"

"I know I think maybe you're too fucking drunk to be driving," Paul said. "What the fuck is into you? And why are you confused about what I'm doing here? What do you think I'm doing here? I think the real question is what the fuck are you doing here?"

"Well, Paul," I said loud again, before getting a little more quiet, "Maria made Leslie a pound cake. I was just dropping it off."

"Go get it," he said to me. "I'll take it in to her."

LESLIE FITZPATRICK

I WAS PUTTING on eyeliner. I stopped. It sounded like a voice was coming from outside.

"Did you hear that?" I called out to J.J. He didn't say anything. I heard it again.

I left the bathroom and went to the front door. I looked out one of the windows in the door without getting close enough to be seen from outside.

I couldn't believe what I saw.

J.J. JENKINS

JUST AS I was falling asleep again, she came running into the room telling me to get up and get dressed. I rolled around a little and got comfortable again.

"You have to go now," she said. "He's outside."

"Who's outside?"

She got up on the bed and started slapping my face, over and over again. "Paul. Paul. Paul. He's outside. And your dad is out there too."

"My dad?" I sprang up at that. I scrambled through the house, looking for my clothes.

"The kitchen," she said. Her words kept coming out in a sharp whisper. "Go out through the kitchen. Where'd you park?"

"A few streets over." I'd managed to find my underwear, T-shirt, and jeans. I was buttoning and zipping them up while looking for my socks and shoes.

"There's a fence out there," she said. "On the other side there's another backyard. Go out to the street in front of the house and find your way back to your car. Or walk home. Whatever, you just have to get out of here. Now!"

"OK," I said. She was all panicky. It was kind of funny. I knew not to laugh. "What about the neighbors?"

"Screw the neighbors! You have to go, now!"

JOHNNY MESAGNE

I SHRUGGED AT Paul. It seemed convincing to me. Maybe I could've been an actor.

"I already took the cake in to her," I said. "I was just leaving."

Paul had climbed out of the back seat. He was making his way to the door.

"There's plenty of empty spots out here," he said, waving his cigar around. "Why was you parked down the street?"

"Those spots was all full when I got here."

Paul put the cigar back in his mouth and titled his head a little bit.

"How long you been here?"

"Not long," I said. "I don't know. Maybe fifteen minutes."

Paul looked at the house. Then he looked back at me.

"She get any phone calls while you was in there?"

"Phone calls?" I said, hoping I was guessing right. "No, Paul, I don't remember no phone calls."

LESLIE FITZPATRICK

I CLOSED THE door behind J.J. I watched him climb the fence and run out of sight. I gathered up the clothes I'd been wearing and stuffed them in the hamper in the closet. I finished buttoning my blouse. I tucked it into my skirt. I waited.

He knocked on the door, hard. I walked over. I forced myself to smile, a real smile. At least I think it was.

"Paul," I said. "What are you doing here?"

"I suddenly been getting asked that question a lot today," he said. He walked inside and started looking around. He was sniffing, too, almost like a dog does.

"I thought we were meeting at the restaurant," I said.

"I decided to give you a ride, since I was on the way."

"Well, I'll be ready in a second. Put the TV on and have a seat. I'll be right out."

"I'm starving," he said as I started back to the bedroom. "I didn't have lunch. How about a piece of pound cake?"

"Sorry," I said. "There's no cake here. You left some Oreos in the kitchen cabinet, though."

Fifty

MY HEART POUNDED. A layer of sweat covered my body. I ran through the neighborhood until I found the Plymouth.

I finally saw it. I slowed down, tried to act natural. Like I was just another guy who lived on that street. I got in and drove away. I didn't look to see whether anyone was watching. Once the car started moving, I cranked the window open to get some fresh air. The wind felt good on my arm. The breeze felt good on my face. It was a close call, too close. But nothing makes you feel more alive than a close call.

I made my way out to the main road. I heard an engine behind me, roaring. I looked in the rearview mirror. Another car was up against my rear bumper. I flinched, thinking it was going to ram me.

I pressed down on the gas. It gave me some distance from the other car. Just enough to realize what the other car was. Oldsmobile. Holiday Red.

I yelled a few cuss words. I saw a pizza shop up ahead on the right. I turned into the parking lot and pulled into an empty space. The Oldsmobile swung in next to me.

JOHNNY MESAGNE

I GOT OUT of the car and went straight for him. I think he was waiting for me to get inside the Plymouth, across from him. Nope. I reached right through the window where he was sitting and pulled him out.

He yelled as he got yanked from the car headfirst. Once his legs was free, I whipped him around and let go. He slammed into my car and fell down.

J.J. got back to his feet fast. I was impressed. But instead of coming at me, he braced for more. When I didn't go after him, he ran a hand over his face and checked it for blood. Then he looked at his arms and legs, probably to see if anything was broken.

"What are you doing?" he said to me.

"No," I said. "What are you doing? And who was you doing it with?"

J.J. JENKINS

I SAW SOMEONE walk out of the pizza shop, with two white, flat boxes. He saw us, he heard us. He turned around and went back inside.

But I knew the rough stuff was over. He was just getting my attention. It worked. He walked up to me, until our noses were practically touching.

"I know where you was," he said.

I started to say something. He stopped me.

"Now ain't the time to talk. Now's the time to save your stupid ass."

Fifty-one

OCTOBER 3, 1973

J.J. JENKINS

I'D HEARD THEM say the Wednesday poker game usually starts right after five o'clock. When I got to Doggie Do-Rights and pressed the buzzer, I looked at the fake Rolex. It was fifteen after eight.

Tommy came trudging through the shop to let me in. I was starting to wonder whether his only real function was to answer the door. He seemed disappointed I didn't have a bag of food. I made a mental note to do it the next time. If I made it to the next time.

I followed Tommy past the dogs. I bent over to pet Gnocchi. He sniffed my hand and yapped. I walked through the door.

"What, no burgers?" Rico said to me. Tommy sat back down at the table. Bobby and Phil were there, too. They had piles of red, white, and blue chips in front of them. Two ashtrays overflowed with butts. Beer bottles popped up like dandelions all around the edges. A pot of chips was in the middle of the table, right under a bare light bulb that was buzzing.

"I forgot to stop," I said to Rico.

They were in the middle of a hand. They picked up where they left off when Tommy came to get me.

I knew the first part would be easy. I hung around while they played. I asked if anyone needed a beer from the fridge. They said they were fine for now. I volunteered to go get more cigarettes. They said they had plenty.

I went over to the wall on the far side of the room. A clock with the Marsh Wheeling Stogies logo in the middle threw off a white glow. It said it was twenty after eight.

I grabbed a stool and started to sit near the place where I sat that first night with Tony, while Willie was in the back waiting for the doctor. I shoved the stool hard against the wall. When it hit, I kicked the cord from the outlet. The face of the clock went dark.

"What the fuck is with the racket?" Bobby said. "And you better not break that fucking clock."

I fumbled with the plug, trying to get it back in the holes. I acted like I couldn't do it.

"I can't get it back on," I said.

"Goddammit," Bobby said. "You know, maybe you're getting a little too comfortable around here."

"I'll fix it," I said. "I can fix it."

"Sure," Rico said as he fiddled with his chips. "College Boy'll fix it. Hey, College Boy, maybe you can go rent another clock at the U-Haul store."

They laughed at that, which was fine by me. It kept them from realizing what I was up to. I pulled the clock off the wall and pretended to inspect the back of it. As my eyes scanned the case, my right hand found the dial that moved the minute hand. I twisted it, flipped it around to check the front, and then twisted it a little more.

I put the clock back on the wall. I stuck the plug back in the outlet.

"There," I said. "Good as new."

"You got lucky this time," Bobby said. He didn't look up from his hand to see the time on the clock.

Yep, that part was easy. The next part wouldn't be. And it would take plenty of luck, in more ways than one.

Fifty-two

LESLIE FITZPATRICK

I FINISHED GETTING ready. I was nervous. The more I tried to calm myself down, the more nervous I got. Paul was out there, looking around. Did J.J. get both of his socks? Were my panties on the ground somewhere?

I tried to focus on what I was doing, not on whatever he was doing. I listened, but I didn't hear anything. Then I thought I did. I wasn't sure what it was.

I thought about that gun. It was in my purse. But where was my purse? In the kitchen? The living room? Could I get to it if I needed it? And would I really know what to do with it if I had to?

That would have made for one hell of a headline in the newspaper. *Prominent local businessman killed in his girlfriend's house.* Better than him killing me. Of course, that wouldn't have made a headline.

I quit thinking about all of it long enough to get dressed. I checked myself in the mirror. Nothing about the reflection gave away what I'd been doing. Yes, my makeup wasn't as crisp as usual; it was hard to do it right with shaky hands. But even that didn't cry out that I'd been rolling around in bed with Paul's newest employee.

I found the right pair of shoes in the closet. I put them on and walked out to the living room. Paul was standing there. He was holding the trash can from the kitchen. I hadn't emptied it in a while.

"You want to explain this?" he said.

"Um, it's the garbage?"

"Do you know what's in the garbage?"

My pulse instantly raced. I tried to keep a straight face. A bead of sweat was already forming at the top of my forehead.

"Garbage?" I said.

He threw it down. Some of the trash spilled out. Then he held up his other hand.

"You've had someone here," he said, "and he's been smoking my cigars."

I instantly felt more relieved than I should have.

"I smoked those," I said.

"You? You smoke cigars?"

"I didn't have any cigarettes. That was all I could find."

"Two cigars?"

"I didn't have cigarettes twice."

"Women ain't supposed to smoke cigars."

"How are they any different than cigarettes?"

"You know you don't inhale these, right?"

"Yeah, I know. My stepfather smokes them, too."

"You could have just said he was here and smoked them."

"I could have, but that wouldn't have been the truth. The truth was that I smoked them."

He picked up the trash can and dropped the cigar butts back into them.

"So you're telling me I can always count on you to tell me the truth?"

"Paul," I said, "why would I lie to you about anything?"

He gave me a weird look before he took the trash can back to the kitchen. He didn't clean up the stuff that had spilled out.

Fifty-three

I MADE SURE the clock was working and that it was an hour behind the actual time. I walked toward the poker game. Phil shot me a look, pulling his cards together and wiggling his crooked jaw around.

"What did I do?" I asked.

"Now that you and Rico done a job together, I don't know what kind of hand signals you two come up with."

"Here's a hand signal." Rico gave Phil the finger.

"I'm just watching," I said. "I've never played poker before."

It was a lie. And it worked.

"We should deal you in," Bobby said. "No time like now to learn."

"I don't have any money."

"Bullshit," Bobby said. "I filled your envelopes. Both of them."

"It's not with me. Plus, I need that money."

"We all need the money we got," Tommy said. He had a mouthful of potato chips. "That don't stop us from playing cards with it."

"I'm just getting started," I said. I fiddled with the fake Rolex while I talked. "I need to save."

That worked, too.

"What's that watch worth?" Rico said.

"I don't know," I said. "You know, it's not an actual Rolex."

"A fake Rolex is still nicer than a real Timex," Phil said.

"I'd rather have a real Timex than this," I said.

They kept playing. Bobby won the hand with two queens and two sevens. Rico had two queens and an ace. Bobby had to explain to Rico why Bobby's hand was better. Rico swore in Italian as he took the cards for shuffling and dealing.

"Why don't you put that Rolex in the pot?" Bobby said to me. "One hand."

"I wouldn't have anything else to bet."

Tommy took off his watch and slid it to the center of the table.

"One hand," he said. "My watch and your watch. No other bets. Winner gets both."

"This was a gift," I said. "I can't lose it."

"Maybe you won't," Rico said. He put his own watch in the pot. "Maybe you'll win two more watches."

Bobby put his watch in. Phil did, too. Four watches, waiting for mine. It was going just like I needed it to.

"I can't," I said.

"You was just saying you'd rather have a real Timex than a fake Rolex," Phil said. "There's four real Timex watches, right here."

I pretended to think about it. I looked at the watch. I opened the clasp, took it off, and put it with the others.

"I'm in."

"Get a stool and take a corner," Bobby said.

"This is getting good," Rico said. He slapped the deck onto the table. Tommy wiped the crumbs from his hands and cut the cards. Rico picked up the bottom half of the deck, dropped it on top, and started dealing. One card to each of us, five times.

I waited to look at my cards until I had all of them. I opened the hand slowly, with the bottom pressed against my chest. I had the three of clubs, seven of diamonds, ten of clubs, queen of hearts, eight of clubs. I put them together again and made my eyes dart around the table.

"J.J. ain't got shit," Rico said.

"Is anything wild?" I said.

"This ain't grade school poker," Bobby said. "You make a hand or you don't. How many cards you want?"

I looked at my hand again.

"Looks like he wants five," Bobby said.

"Make it seven," Tommy said, mouth again full of potato chips.

"Actually, I need two."

Bobby stopped laughing. He checked his own hand again. I had to decide whether to try to draw a straight or a flush. I'd lied about never playing poker, but I hadn't played enough to know whether I had a better chance at getting a nine plus a jack or a six, or two more clubs.

I picked two cards out of the five. I set them aside. Rico put two new cards on the table in front of me.

Tommy also wanted two cards. Phil took three. Bobby asked for one. Rico said he'd take four.

"Looks like Rico is the one who ain't got shit," Phil said. Rico said something to him in Italian.

After everyone had their new cards, I picked up mine. I added them to the three I kept and spread the hand apart.

Tommy slapped his cards against the table.

"Three kings, boys. Looks like I'll have the time of my life tonight."

Phil cursed. He threw two tens, an eight, and two nines near the watches.

"Almost had a fucking full house," he said.

Bobby went next. He put four cards on the table.

"I had the three, four, five, six," he said. "I needed a two or a seven for the straight." He threw the two of hearts on top of the rest of the cards. "And I got it. I bet you never dropped a deuce like this one, Tommy."

Rico said something else in Italian and threw down an ace of spades with nothing else to go with it.

"Well, kid," Bobby said. "Time to show me what you ain't got, and to take one last look at that Rolex of yours. Until you see it on my wrist every day."

I looked at the cards again. I waited a little bit. I spread the cards open and placed them on the table, face up.

"I got five clubs. Is five clubs anything?"

Fifty-four

LESLIE FITZPATRICK

PAUL DIDN'T SAY much on the way to the restaurant. He didn't say much while we ate. I didn't say much, either.

He watched me, though. I could feel it. He would spin the cigar left and right in his mouth. He knew not to light it while we ate. But he just kept chewing on it.

His private room in the back of the restaurant was barely big enough for the table where we sat. It was always a little cold, too. The vent in the ceiling pointed right at Paul.

I ordered veal. Paul got his same New York strip, medium rare. He let it sit there while he watched me eat.

"Your steak will get cold," I said, chewing with the left side of my mouth. "You'll have to send it back to the kitchen."

"It'll be fine," he said. "You see, this steak will wait for me to eat it. That's one of the benefits of being at the top of the food chain."

"The food chain? We're talking about cows. It doesn't take much to be higher on the food chain than a cow."

"When you're on the top of the food chain, it don't matter. You're higher than everything."

I took a drink of wine. "Are you feeling OK tonight?" I said.

He picked up his steak knife and looked at the jagged blade.

"You tell me how I'm feeling tonight."

"How should I know how you're feeling?" I said, cutting another piece of meat. I pressed my fork into it and put it in the right side of my mouth.

"You don't know, because you don't pay attention. I pay attention. To everything." He stabbed the knife into the steak. The handle was pointing straight up. He smiled at me, not in a nice way.

"Aren't you going to cut it?" I said.

"The steak will wait for me to cut it."

I took another drink of wine, longer than I should have. When I put the glass down, the waiter showed up and filled it from the bottle near the edge of the table. He noticed the knife sticking up from the steak. He started to say something. Before any words came out, he closed his mouth and left.

"Did I do something?" I said to Paul after the waiter was gone.

"You tell me." He stared at that knife.

"I don't know what you mean," I said, before drinking more wine.

"You'll figure it out. You're smart for your age."

He took out the knife and sawed the steak in half. He put the cigar on the lip of an ashtray. Then he slammed the knife flat on the table, close to me. He kept his hand over it. A drop of blood landed on the white cloth. I watched the stain spread.

He kept one hand on the knife and picked up half of the steak. He took a big bite. He chewed it with his mouth open.

"Now this is good," he said. A red trickle started down from the corner of his mouth. "It's good to ask for something and get what you asked for."

I reached for the wine glass. I nearly knocked it over. I grabbed it tight and lifted it. I watched Paul while I took another drink. I looked at that hand on the knife.

He finished half of the steak and started on the other half. The waiter stayed away until the steak was gone. He put a fresh napkin next to Paul's empty plate.

He wiped his face and hands. He belched. He stood up. I made sure the knife was still on the table before I got up to follow him. He walked down the short hallway to the door. The Cadillac was sitting out there. I heard Vinny start the engine.

Paul got in his usual spot. I opened the door behind Vinny and sat. I tried to focus on my plan. I knew what I was maybe going to have to do with him. It made me feel queasy. I actually thought about shooting him after he fell asleep. Maybe before. If I was going to shoot him, it would be better to do it before anything else happened. The wine was giving me those ideas. It kind of made me want to drink more wine.

Neither of us said anything until the car pulled up to the house. I didn't know whether I could actually do it. Maybe with enough wine I could.

"Are you coming in?" I asked once the car stopped.

"Not tonight," he said. "You already had enough company today, I think."

I froze. Then I tried to act normal. I looked at him. He was smiling the same way he did after he stabbed that knife into the steak.

"Sleep tight," he said. I got out of the car and went in the house.

AFTER SHE WAS gone, Vinny glanced in the rearview mirror. He never understood why Paul was messing with that girl. He ran the whole region. He controlled territory across the river in Ohio. Pittsburgh let him have a few of the towns in Pennsylvania. He had no rivals, no enemies. Nobody fucked with him. He was making a shitload of money. Vinny knew, because he counted all of it. Every last penny.

Paul had no worries, as far as Vinny could tell. The local cops were taken care of, all of them. The feds would leave them alone as long as they didn't mess with civilians. They could have had a field day with the things the Verbania crew did. They also didn't get paid enough by Uncle Sam to have their cars blow up or their kids go missing.

Paul had it made, in Vinny's estimation. And Vinny feared it was going to be something like this that brought him down.

Vinny couldn't tell Paul. He wouldn't listen. He'd say it wasn't Vinny's place. But wasn't it? At times being a good number two meant keeping number one from fucking things up for himself and everybody else. Vinny had decided a while ago to try to nudge Paul away from her, at the right time. Maybe the right time was coming. In Vinny's eyes, there was always something about her that was unpredictable. He had a feeling she was starting to get old enough to figure out she could cause problems. She wasn't dangerous yet. Soon, she could be.

Vinny wasn't sure. He told himself he worried too much. He just didn't want to see a guy who had everything in his life under control piss it all away because he got too attached to a woman who wasn't even his wife. If Paul was going to cheat, why not get around more? Why just mess with one? It didn't make sense to Vinny. It never had. It never would. But he knew if he didn't make the right move at the right time, it could end up being a big problem for Paul. Which would make it a big problem for Vinny.

He pulled the car away before she got inside her house.

"We need eyes on her all the time," Paul said. "Something's going on."

"You want I should talk to her?" Vinny said. Vinny knew what Paul would say, because Paul knew Vinny meant more than just talking.

"Not yet. I want to figure this out on my own. And I guarantee you that I will figure it out."

"What's to figure out?"

"Something is to figure out. Something is going on."

"But so what if it is?" Vinny said.

"Do I need to remind you who I am, what I do? That if my girlfriend is out fucking around on me and word gets out, I look weak?"

"There's no one out there to look weak to."

"There could be. If I get soft, that's when someone starts thinking they can try something. Next thing you know, I'm the one who's in Ohio."

"Just cut her loose then," Vinny said. "Is any broad worth the headache?"

"It's too late for that. Something's going on, and I need to figure it out. I need to take care of it. Then maybe I can cut her loose."

"So how do we figure it out?"

"I don't know where it ends," Paul said, "but I absolutely know where it starts."

Fifty-five

J.J. JENKINS

"THE KID GOT a fucking flush!"

Rico said it three or four times before flipping back to Italian.

I picked up the five watches with my hands. I checked the clock on the wall again.

"I can't believe it's already half past seven," I said. "I need to be somewhere." I said the time out loud again before I left.

I started through the shop. The dogs barked at me, four of them this time. I made a little whistle at Gnocchi. I liked that little dog. I could hear them still complaining in the back room about what had happened. It made me smile a little bit.

At the front door, I pressed those watches against my stomach and pulled up the bottom of my shirt, carrying them like they were in a pouch so I'd have a free hand. I went outside and pulled my car keys from the front pocket of my jeans. I opened the door to the Plymouth and dropped the watches onto the front seat.

I looked at the watches and smiled again.

When I got back home, my father's car was parked out front, the engine idling. I drove past it and stopped in the first spot down the street I could find. I walked back to the Oldsmobile.

JOHNNY MESAGNE

IT WAS GOOD he come back at all, but that didn't mean he was in the clear. Not hardly. If he didn't leave there with a clear alibi in place, he was still in danger. I guessed I was, too. I was a little surprised I thought about him before I thought about me. Jimmy made me think that way. I hadn't decided whether to be happy about it.

When he got closer to the car, I looked at his wrists. My stomach flipped a little.

"You ain't got a watch on," I said when he got to the window. "I knew it wouldn't work."

"You said it was our only move."

"I should have thought of something better."

Then the kid smiled. "You didn't need to. It worked."

"Where's your watch then?"

"In the car with the rest of them. It went just like you said it would. I acted like I broke the clock. I set it back an hour. I started messing with my watch. The next thing I knew they were dealing me in for a pot that had five watches."

"So you won the hand?"

"I started two cards short of a straight or a flush. I needed a nine and then a jack or a six."

"Always go for the flush in that spot."

"I did. I pulled two clubs. Dropped my hand last. Bobby had a six-high straight. Then I asked them if all clubs is anything good, like I didn't know I won. They shit their pants."

"When did you leave?"

"Right after that. The clock said it was seven thirty. I made sure I said what time it was. Twice."

"So unless one of those idiots figures it out—which they won't— Bobby will say you was there until seven thirty. You'll be in the clear. At least for now."

J.J. JENKINS

WE WERE BOTH happy talking about how I changed the time on the clock and got their watches away from them. Things turned fast when he started talking about why I needed to do any of that.

"This is just the beginning," he said to me. "Paul's suspicious, and he's smarter than the both of us combined. We have to assume he'll think it was one of us."

"Why would he think it was you?"

His face twisted up for a second or two. I hadn't been around him enough the past ten years to know what that meant.

"Well, I was outside the house," he said. "And I was acting weird. I had to act weird to make sure one of you heard what was about to happen."

"Why won't he just make Leslie tell him?"

"She's not really in the life. It would look bad if he leaned on her."

"To who?"

"To him. To anyone. I don't know. I just know there are lines he won't cross. Plus, he's been with her a long time. He probably wouldn't want to do anything to her."

I cringed when I heard the words, thinking of the guy we left on the ground in Pittsburgh with a collection of broken ribs.

A gust of wind blew past me. I got a whiff of her scent from the top of my T-shirt.

"If he won't make her tell him, then maybe he won't figure it out," I said.

JOHNNY MESAGNE

I WAS GETTING sucked into this thing for one reason and one reason only. As I sat there talking to him about it, I started to get pissed off.

"I was as clear as I could be with you," I said. "I told you it was do-not-touch and you touched anyway."

"I didn't think it was a big deal. He's like twenty years older than her, and he's got a wife. How does a married guy have full rights to his mistress?"

"Because of who the guy is. Ain't you figured that part out by now? He's the boss. We don't mess with nothing that belongs to the boss."

"I still don't understand any of this."

"You don't have to understand it. It's hands off. I told you. It would be different if I hadn't told you. There's plenty of birds in the sea, or whatever. Find one that ain't already been claimed by no one in the crew, especially no one higher up than you. And don't think about doing something really stupid like running away with her. He'll make it his main job in life to track you down and turn you into a pile of prosciutto."

He flinched when I said that. I'm glad he did. He finally needed to realize what he was dealing with.

"So what do I do?" he said.

"You do the one thing that everyone on earth is good at. Nothing. Not one fucking thing."

"What about Leslie?"

"What about her? Stay away from her. Isn't she like ten years older than you?"

"Seven."

"That's still seven too many. And even if the two of you was born on the same fucking day at the same fucking minute of the same fucking hour in the same fucking hospital, the biggest problem here is that she's Paul's property. Do not touch. It's like Adam and Eve and that apple."

"You know," he said, "they ate the apple."

"So did you. I'm just trying to make sure this time around that the man that runs the garden don't find out about it."

Fifty-six

OCTOBER 4, 1973

J.J. JENKINS

THE PHONE RANG the next morning at ten o'clock. I rolled out of bed and ran in to get it before my mother could. I had a feeling it was work, and I was right.

I knew from the voice it was Bobby. He said to be at the usual place at eight o'clock, sharp. Before I could ask any questions, he hung up.

I stayed inside the house that morning, thinking about what had happened. I counted the money again. More than once. I fiddled with the compass. I opened the drawer to the desk and looked at the four new watches. I found a brown paper bag in the kitchen to put them in. I tried not to think about whether they wanted me there for a new job or for something about Leslie. Did I need a gun? I'd never had that thought before, not once in my life. Not that it would do me any good in the back room at Bobby's. If something was going to happen, I would need something bigger than a pistol.

I kept in my room as much as I could. I didn't want any questions or lectures from my mother. I didn't want her to see how nervous I was getting. It got worse as the day went on. I managed to eat with little conversation a steak she'd scorched under the broiler. I thanked her, got the bag of watches, and left.

I stopped for more burgers, with cheese on them this time. I ate one on the way to town, thinking it would calm my nerves. It didn't. After I parked, I felt like throwing up all over the concrete.

I didn't have to ring the bell this time. Tommy was standing at the door waiting for me. I gave him the bag of burgers. His face lit up. I took that as a good sign. It would have been hard for him to get excited about free burgers if they were about to turn me into dead meat.

The dogs barked, same as always. I said hello to Gnocchi, same as always. I held my breath before going into the back room. I was still surprised by what I saw.

Bobby, Phil, and Rico were sitting at the table. Tommy joined them. Tony and Willie stood against the wall, staring at me. They didn't look happy to see me.

"The gang's all here," I said. I put the bag of watches on the table. "I felt bad about last night. I wanted to give you these back."

Bobby nodded at the gesture before catching himself. His face turned hard.

"You better give us those watches back," he said. "My clock is still fucked up. It was like an hour slow when I got in here today."

They each claimed their watches, except for Tommy. He was focused on divvying up the cheeseburgers.

I went over to the wall with Tony and Willie. They didn't move for me. I walked past them. It made me the farthest one from the table. I was pretty sure at that point that nothing bad was going to happen, at least not for now.

Bobby lit a cigarette and took a long drag. He looked around the room before blowing out the smoke.

"Paul thinks there'll be a problem with gasoline," he said. "Something about the Middle East and an oil embargo or whatever. He says gas will get expensive first, then it'll get more expensive, and then it'll be gone. I don't get it, but it ain't my job to get it."

"So what are we going to do," Rico said through a thick jaw filled with beef and cheese, "steal a gas station?"

"Sort of, I guess. Paul already owns a gas station. In Warwood. And he's got a truck that can fill the pumps."

"Where do we come in?" Phil said. His crooked jaw slid around, like it did whenever he was thinking about something.

"We're going to fill the trucks," Bobby said.

"With what?" Rico said. "Are we going to go shooting guns into the ground like the Beverly Hillbillies and hope we hit oil?"

"We don't need to do that," Bobby said. "There's already plenty of gas. It's everywhere."

"Everywhere?" Rico said, putting his hands out and looking up. "Is it going to start raining gasoline around here or something?"

Bobby turned around and picked up a piece of garden hose from the floor behind him. He held it up.

"Every car has gas in it," he said. "And every night, we'll hit them, one by one."

Rico grabbed the hose. He looked into one end of it.

"How do we do that? Climb under the car and shoot a hole in the tank? The fucking thing'll blow up, won't it?"

"We'll siphon it," Phil said, grabbing the hose away from Rico. "My dad did that once. My uncle's car was out of gas, and my dad siphoned a can of it from his own tank. He got a mouth full of gas and was spitting it out for like an hour, but it's pretty easy to get gas out of a car this way."

"They got a bunch of gas cans at the station Paul owns," Bobby said. "You put the empties in your car, you find a quiet spot, you fill up the cans. Them cans hold a gallon each. Once the gas is flowing, you move the hose from one can to the next. When all your cans is full, you bring them back and empty them into the truck. Then you go back out again."

Phil pulled a notebook from his pocket. He started writing on one of the pages with a small pencil he kept jammed into the spiral at the top.

"Gas is like forty cents a gallon now, right?" he said. "For every five cans, that's two bucks."

"Paul thinks the price will go up," Bobby said. "And that once it runs out altogether, we can name the price."

"It just seems like a lot of work for not much money," Phil said.

"It's easy money," Bobby said, "because nobody will know it's happening. Will it take some time to fill the cans and take them back and empty them and go again? Yeah. Will we stink like gas when we're done every night? Sure. But that's the plan."

"Who's going to be stealing the gas?" Phil said.

"All of you," Bobby said. "I'll stay at the station and supervise. We'll do it from eleven o'clock until four in the morning."

Phil kept scribbling in the notebook.

"OK," he said, "if he can sell it for eighty cents a gallon, and if we can fit twenty cans in our cars, that's sixteen bucks a load. And if it takes a half hour to find a couple cars and steal twenty cans—"

"That's thirty-two bucks an hour," Bobby said. "What's minimum wage?"

"I was getting a dollar sixty an hour at Foodland," I said.

"So if we get half of the money, that's like ten times what College Boy was making to bag corn flakes and shithouse paper," Rico said.

"When do we start?" Phil said.

"We'll run it Sunday night to Thursday night until further notice," Bobby said. "Those are the quietest nights of the week. Friday and Saturday, who knows when someone'll be leaving a house or getting home late? It'll be good money. Best of all, it'll be free money."

"Who'll keep track of how much we each bring in?" Phil said.

"That's a good question," Bobby said. He started looking around at everyone in the room, flopping the hose while he spoke. "You're all going to get notebooks like Phil's here, and you're all going keep track of the gallons you get. And you're all going to be operating on the honor system."

When he said the words "honor system," the end of the hose was pointing directly at me. I felt my face turn red. I hoped it was too dark in there for anyone to notice.

Fifty-seven

AFTER BOBBY CALLED everyone and told them to report to Doggie Do-Rights at eight that night, the buzzer went off in the front room. Tommy went out to see who it was. Bobby listened closely. It sounded like Vinny. And it sounded like Vinny wasn't alone.

The dogs barked. Bobby heard Vinny tell them to shut up. Paul muttered something like, "These fucking dogs." Bobby didn't know why they were there so early in the day, or at all. Paul never visited. If he wanted to see Bobby, Paul sent for him.

Bobby looked up when they came in. He nodded, trying to act as if it was normal for them to just show up like that.

Paul pulled the cigar out of his mouth and sniffed. "It smells like shit in here," he said.

"I don't smell it," Bobby said.

"Our course not. Your nose is used to smelling shit."

"I guess so," Bobby said. He didn't know what else to say. He wanted to ask what the hell this was all about. He figured Paul would get to it. Saying "it smells like shit in here" was as much small talk as he ever made.

"Did you guys play poker last night?" Paul said.

"Every Wednesday."

"So the answer is yes?"

"Yeah, we played poker."

"Who was here?"

"The usuals. Me, Tommy, Phil, Rico."

"Was the new kid here?"

"He came by."

"When?"

Bobby looked at Tommy. Tommy shrugged.

"I ain't asking the fat man," Paul said. "I'm asking you. When was he here?"

"I don't know when he got here. He left at half past seven."

"How long was he here?"

Bobby started to look at Tommy again, but stopped himself.

"Not long. Half hour, tops."

Bobby didn't tell Paul about losing their watches to the kid in poker. It wasn't something Bobby felt like bragging about.

Paul looked at Vinny after Bobby was finished. Vinny nodded.

"Thanks," Paul said.

"Is there something I need to know about?"

"When there's something you need to know about, you'll be told about it."

Bobby just sat there. He waited for them to go. He hoped they would.

Paul turned around. Vinny opened the door.

"You need a window back here," Paul said as he walked out. "Or get a candle. Maybe a bunch of them."

Bobby kept sitting there, even though Paul had already walked out.

PAUL AND VINNY got back in the Cadillac. Paul farted when he sat down. Vinny was as used to that smell as Bobby was to the stink in his back room.

"Well?" Paul said.

"The kid has an alibi, if that's what you were looking for."

"Something still don't add up."

"Why did you think it was him?"

"I got my reasons," Paul said.

"Well, it wasn't him. What's next?"

"I don't know. I'll figure it out."

"Johnny was there, not the kid," Vinny said.

"Johnny wouldn't mess around with her. And she wouldn't mess around with Johnny. Not after everything that happened."

"Why do you think she'd mess around with anyone?" Vinny said. He wouldn't have put it past her. He just wanted to get an idea of what Paul was thinking.

"It's been six years," Paul said. "She knows I ain't leaving my wife. I could see her thinking about making a change."

"She's smart enough to know how that would go for her."

"Sometimes I wonder how smart she is," Paul said.

"She ain't dumb enough to mess with someone from the crew. And the kid can't be dumb enough to mess with her. She's like ten years older than him."

"That don't matter when you're twenty. You remember being twenty. I know I do. You got one thing on your mind."

"But we just found out the kid is clean," Vinny said.

"I guess that leaves Johnny."

"He was acting strange. Maybe he was covering for someone else."

"Who else would it be? Cashews? Jerry? She wouldn't want to fuck with either of those two."

"Do you want to go see Johnny?"

"No," Paul said. "I want you to bring him in. I'll give him a chance to come clean. One chance."

Fifty-eight

IT WAS THURSDAY night. The last few regulars was leaving. One of them opened the door to walk out. And in walked Vinny.

I had no idea he was coming. I never knew when he was coming, except on Tuesdays to get the money. I never did much to make him feel welcome. He never did much to make me feel like he wanted to be. I put up with him, he put up with me. That's pretty much how it had always been.

He had a brown jacket on. Had his hands deep in the pockets, almost like they was stuck in there. He didn't say nothing. He just looked at me.

I waited for him to talk. He kept looking at me.

I finally said, "What's going on?"

"I think you know."

I didn't pay him much mind. I'd been working on closing the place up. I got back to it. If he wanted to tell me, he would.

So I emptied a few ashtrays and washed a few glasses and swept up some tip seals plus whatever else was on the floor. Vinny just stood there with his hands still in his pockets, watching everything I did.

I was almost done shutting the place down. I started turning off the lights.

"So, tell me, what's going on?" I said.

"Like I said, you know."

Lights off, I headed for the door. He followed me. I pulled the door shut and locked it with the key. I saw the Cadillac in the spot right in front of the bar. Vinny opened the passenger side. He walked around and got inside. I knew what that meant, what I was supposed to do.

I got in and pulled the door shut. He drove away. The wheels rolling under me. I knew we was going to Paul's.

Once we got there, I waited for Vinny to lead the way in. I tried to read Vinny's face, but there was no use. *If they was planning to do something to me, they wouldn't have brought me here*, I told myself. I tried not to think about the possibility that they'd bring me here before doing something to me.

Either way, I had no choice. The boss had sent for me. When the boss sends for you, you go, no matter what.

Vinny led me to the back room. Paul sat behind that desk, the one he thought was the same as Brando's in *The Godfather*. I didn't think it was the same, but he thought it was. And that was all that mattered. He smoked a cigar. A cloud of smoke filled the room.

"Sit down," he said.

"You need me to stay?" Vinny said. His hands was buried back inside the pockets of that jacket.

"Wait out there," Paul said, eyeballing me. "I'll let you know if I need anything."

Vinny left. I heard his clown shoes flapping down the hallway. I sat down. Paul puffed on that cigar and blew the smoke right at me.

"I'll get right to it," he said, as if he ever did things any different. "I know you lied to me. And you know I don't like being lied to."

"I'm sorry," I said. Since I told him a couple of lies while I was in front of Leslie's house, I didn't know which one he knew about. I had to fish around for more. I decided to get right to it, too.

"What did I lie about?"

"Don't be cute, Mesagne. You know and I know you didn't take her no pound cake."

I tried not to react. If that was the only lie, maybe I'd survive this.

"I know. I don't know why I said that. Now that J.J.'s back in town, I been over to Maria's house a few times. I feel like maybe there could maybe be something with her again. I wanted to talk to Leslie about that."

Paul sat forward. The tip of the cigar glowed and he sucked on the other end.

"Why didn't you tell me this in the first place?" he said.

"I don't know. I should have. I guess I was, I don't know, embarrassed or something. Especially with Vinny there. He always wants to bust my balls about something. It was stupid. I'm sorry."

Paul blew out more smoke.

"That still don't explain all of it. You was trying to let her know I was outside. I ain't no moron. It was almost like it was her and someone else inside and you was giving them a signal."

"I know," I said. "That was dumb, too. I guess I wanted her to know you was coming, and that you knew I'd just been there. You know how she is. She gets nervous. She gets confused. I didn't want her to freak out."

"But there was nothing to freak out about. You went to talk to her about Maria. That's a fair explanation. One you should've given me then and there."

"I didn't," I said, standing up. "I don't know what else to tell you. Look, you won this thing six years ago. I didn't say shit about it. I just walked away. So now I'm getting grilled when I had every right to be upset back then?"

"Back then was back then."

"But back then still matters. I didn't say nothing about nothing. I didn't make no stink."

"I also let you out."

"That was the least you could do. I held up my end. I never caused no trouble. I didn't break no rules. Why would you think I'm up to something now, after all this time? After all that happened back then?"

Paul added another cloud of smoke to the haze that kept getting thicker.

"I don't know. I just do. Something's going on. And I'll figure out what it is. But I'm willing to say after thinking it over and talking to you man to man, I don't think you messed around with her. Which as you know, would have been bad."

"So what does that mean?"

"It means you're in the clear. At least until I figure out what the hell is going on. Or if I find out you ever lied to me again."

Fifty-nine

J.J. JENKINS

I SHOWED UP early Sunday night at the gas station in Warwood. It had a Mobil sign in front. The light inside it was off. I went to the small building behind the bank of pumps. The truck was in the back. That was the thing we were going to fill with gasoline we stole from other cars.

Bobby saw me coming. He showed me the room with the empty cans. They were all red. There must have been a least a hundred in there.

I drove the Plymouth near the room with the cans. Fifteen of them fit in the trunk. I took five more and put them on an old bed sheet I'd covered the back seat with. Bobby gave me a long piece of green hose. I left before any of the others showed up. The sooner I got started, the sooner I would be done for the night.

Bobby told me not to start too close by, to fan out in order to reduce suspicion—especially if that Mobil station ended up being the only place around with gasoline.

I drove about a mile away. I took a right turn from the main road and went deep into the neighborhood. At a spot that seemed quiet and far enough out of the way, I parked next to a house that was dark, inside and out. A car was parked across the street, with the flap to its gas tank facing the road. I started taking empty cans out of my car.

I moved as fast as I could without making much noise. I opened the trunk quietly and took out ten cans. I pushed the lid down, but didn't close it. I carried the cans across the street, two at a time, and put them next to the car in five rows of two each.

I pulled open the cover to the gas tank, unscrewed the cap, and stuck the hose deep inside. I kept my right hand close to the opening to the tank. I pinched the hose, hard. I blew as much air out of my lungs as I could before putting my mouth on the hose. The taste of the rubber filled my mouth. I sucked in the air from the tank.

As soon as I felt the gas coming, I jerked my lips away and stuck the hose in the first can. The sound of gasoline hitting metal came out of the can. As the gas got close to the top, I pulled out the hose. I moved it to the second can. Some gasoline spilled. There was no way around that. But within just a few seconds, I heard the gas filling up the second can.

I kept going, one after another until all ten cans were full. I held up the hose, but the gas kept coming. I pulled it out. None of it got on my clothes, somehow.

I carried the cans back to the trunk, two at a time again. I screwed the lids on each of them before putting them back in the trunk. I pushed the lid down until I felt it click shut. I walked back over to the other car and screwed the gas cap back in place. I folded the flap shut and went back to the Plymouth. I pulled away, starting the search for another car I could use to fill the other ten cans.

After all twenty cans were full, I went back to the station. Bobby showed me how to climb the ladder and pour the gasoline into the hole at the top. It actually took more time to do that than it did to steal the gas. Still, in less than an hour after I'd started, I'd made the first full deposit of twenty gallons of gas into that truck.

Bobby seemed happy with me. I went back out with the twenty empties. I filled them again, emptied them again. I did it five times in all before he told me to call it a night. I crossed paths once with Rico and twice with Tony. I didn't see Willie or Phil on the first night. As far as I could tell, it was going smoothly for the rest of them, too. All in all, it had been even easier than Bobby had explained.

We all did it again on Monday night, Tuesday night, and Wednesday night. Each time, I poured a hundred gallons of gas into the truck.

Then came Thursday night. I showed up at the gas station and drove past the unlit Mobil sign. I took the Plymouth to the back, got twenty empty cans, and started all over again. Maybe it was too easy. Maybe it was too simple. Maybe I wasn't being as careful as I needed to be.

I went back to a spot kind of close to where I'd gotten the first ten gallons, on Sunday night. I found a car. I lined up the cans next to a Buick and started siphoning again.

The sixth one was filling up. I saw a car coming. The headlights seemed bright. I turned my face away, like Bobby had said to do. I waited for the car to pass by. It didn't. It stopped. I noticed the outline of dome lights on top of the roof just before they started to flash, one blue and one red.

I heard a voice order me to freeze. I threw my hands in the air. Gas kept coming out of that hose. It got all over me.

Sixty

JOHNNY MESAGNE

I WAS LUCKY Maria and Leslie got along so good. After I sent J.J. to Bobby's on that crazy poker scheme that somehow worked, I went straight to see Maria. I told her exactly what had happened. I told her exactly what she needed to do.

She didn't hesitate or argue or do anything other than go along. I told her to call Leslie the next morning and invite her to lunch. I told Maria where to take Leslie. I told Maria what she needed to say. Maria promised me she'd do all of that. I didn't tell her that if J.J. wasn't able to pull off our plan to make them think J.J. was at Bobby's when he was actually at Leslie's, it wouldn't matter.

Maria wasn't thrilled with J.J. or Leslie, but the situation was too important for worrying about that stuff. I didn't have to tell her the stakes.

OCTOBER 4, 1973

MARIA AND LESLIE met for lunch at a little place across the Ohio River, in Bellaire. They both smoked their way through a hamburger and fries. They talked about what had happened the night before. Leslie started to get a little emotional. Maria urged her to hold it together. Leslie apologized over and over again. Maria eventually had to get firm with her. She had no choice. She didn't want anyone to notice them.

Johnny had gone looking for J.J., Maria told Leslie, and found J.J.'s car a few streets away from Leslie's house. Maria told Leslie that Johnny was figuring out what to do when Vinny and Paul pulled up. That Johnny tried to make noise so Leslie and J.J. would know Paul was there. That Johnny had told a stupid-ass lie about taking her a pound cake.

Maria told Leslie what Johnny would say to Paul, if Johnny ended up getting a chance to replace his first lie with a better one. Leslie listened to everything Maria said. Maria had Leslie repeat the story back to her, twice.

LESLIE FITZPATRICK

MARIA GOT REAL quiet. She looked right in my eyes. She talked real slow.

"You realize what will happen if he ever finds out about yesterday," she said. "And you realize yesterday has to be the end of it. You're the adult. You're older than him. A lot older than him. You have to avoid him, ignore him, not see him, not think of him. You have to have absolutely nothing to do with him."

She was right. I kept saying I was sorry. We smoked so many cigarettes that we ran out. She went to the machine by the front door to buy another pack.

We came up with a system for keeping in touch, in case Paul was bugging my phone. If Maria called and said, "How are you?" and I said, "I'm fine," that meant there were no issues or problems or reasons for concern. If I said, "I'm doing OK," that meant there was an issue we needed to discuss in person.

MARIA CALLED LESLIE every day after the day they met for lunch in Bellaire. Every day, Leslie said she was fine. Maria doubted she actually was.

Maria also had been keeping an eye on J.J. She didn't say anything to suggest she knew about him and Leslie. Johnny told Maria to assume the house would be bugged. Maria told Johnny it didn't matter, that she would have had a hard time talking to her son about whatever he was doing with her uncle's stepdaughter.

That weekend, J.J. started leaving the house at night, and coming home late. He didn't say where he was going or what he was doing. Nothing else seemed unusual. He didn't seem upset about anything. Maria assumed Johnny had told J.J. to stay away from Leslie for good. Maria didn't see or hear anything to make her think he wasn't listening.

One week after Johnny had shown up to tell Maria what was going on, Johnny came to the house. It was late. J.J. was gone. Johnny stood in the doorway and gave Maria a piece of paper. A message was written on it. She looked down to read it. She could barely make out his handwriting. That wasn't anything new.

Met with him. Every thing is OK, I told him what I told you to tell her. All is good for now so long as we keep them a part can you keep them a part? If you can then nod after you read this and then burn it in the sink after I leave.

Maria nodded. She smiled, a little bit. Johnny smiled back before turning around and leaving.

Maria picked a lighter up from the kitchen table and carried the note to the sink. She lit the paper on fire, holding a corner until most of it had burned up. Small pieces broke away and turned black. She dropped the rest of it into the sink. She turned on the water before what was left could scorch the white porcelain.

A week had gone by. To Maria, it felt like it was over. It felt like it was finished. She didn't know at the time that was just wishful thinking.

VINNY HAD BEEN watching Johnny's apartment every night since he had taken him to Paul's. Johnny usually went there after closing up the bar and didn't leave. Vinny stayed each night until two in the morning. Paul still expected Vinny to pick him up in the mornings, at the usual time. He paid Vinny well enough to sometimes not sleep very much.

On Wednesday night, Vinny's patience paid off. Not long before eleven o'clock, Johnny walked outside and got in the car and left. Vinny had an old Dodge from Paul's lot. He remained real still so that Johnny wouldn't notice someone sitting inside.

Vinny waited to pull away, so that Johnny wouldn't notice he was being tailed. Vinny had a hunch where Johnny was going. He pulled onto Poplar Avenue. Vinny knew the kid wasn't there; they were running the gasoline scam. Johnny was going to see his ex-wife for some reason.

He parked down the block and grabbed a pair of binoculars. Johnny went to the door. He talked to her for a little bit. He left. He got in his car and drove away. Vinny waited for a little bit and then followed Johnny back to his apartment. He stayed there again until two o'clock.

Sixty-one

OCTOBER 11, 1973

J.J. JENKINS

IT STUNK IN the back of the cruiser. The gas that got on my clothes plus someone's puke plus whatever someone used to clean it up came together into something I'd never smelled before. The cops in the front seat acted like they'd never smelled anything like it, either. They laughed back and forth about how they had all the evidence they needed to prove I was stealing gas because I was wearing it.

I didn't think it was funny, obviously. Nothing would have made me laugh during that ride to the station. I'd never been arrested. I'd never even been pulled over. Handcuffs were digging into the skin of my wrists, squeezing the tendons inside. My shoulder ached from where one of the cops, the smaller one, had jerked my arms behind my back while I was face down in a puddle of gas.

I tried to get comfortable. I couldn't. Not with my hands locked behind my back like that. I leaned into a corner of the seat and wished we would get there already.

The car pulled up to the station, in one of the reserved spots near the door. I looked at the building. I was about to find out what it meant to be booked and processed and whatever else they did when they brought someone in.

"Let's go," the smaller cop said to me. He pushed the butt end of a nightstick into my left kidney. It's hard to move with your hands caught behind your back; you really do learn something new every day. It didn't help that my shoulder was throbbing, or that the stink of gas was still rushing up to my nose from my shirt. At least I didn't have to keep smelling the vomit mixed with whatever was supposed to take away the smell of the vomit.

Things moved quickly after they took me inside. I was charged with petit larceny and conspiracy to commit grand larceny, whatever that meant. They took my fingerprints, then my mugshot. I traded my clothes soaked in gas for a gray one-piece uniform. Before I could put it on, I was searched in a way I'd never been searched before and never want to be searched again. Once that was over, it was a relief to be shoved into a cell.

One other man was there. He had long hair and a scraggly beard. He had that back-and-forth wobble of someone who was drunk.

I sat at the end of a bench attached to the far wall, as far away as I could get from the other guy. I worked my arm around, trying to loosen up my shoulder. I avoided looking at him. He was determined to talk to me.

"You're a little young to be in here," he said. "Did you ditch school or something?"

I ignored him. I kept working on my arm. I stared straight ahead. I could tell he was watching me. I glanced his way. His bushy eyebrows were equal parts gray and black. He was working them around while he thought about what to say next. They looked like a couple of caterpillars trying to decide whether to mate or fight.

"First time?" he said.

I finally looked straight at him. He was smiling. Most of his teeth were gone. Of the three I saw, one was mostly white, one was crooked and yellow. Another was dead and gray with a thin gold strip around the edges.

"Well, it's either your first and your last or your first of more than a few. I can't tell which one you'll be. Seriously, what did you do?"

"I'm not talking," I said.

"You just did," he said. He started laughing, like what he said was the funniest thing he ever heard in his life. "I bet you did something bad. Real bad. But of course you didn't do nothing. Nobody ever did nothing. I still bet that whatever you didn't do was bad. Real bad."

"I didn't do anything. And that's all I have to say."

I leaned my head back. I closed my eyes. I waited. I couldn't see a clock, but I could hear *tick . . . tick . . . tick* echo through the cell I was in and the other empty cells near it.

I opened my eyes.

"Don't they give us a phone call?" I said.

"I thought you was done talking."

"I always heard you get a phone call," I said. "I think you get two."

"It's only one," my cellmate said, "but I ain't got no one to call. You can have mine." He laughed again, so hard that he started coughing and hacking.

Out of nowhere, the small cop was back. He looked taller without his hat on.

"Well," he said, "we were going to have a nice little chat about why you were stealing so much gas in the middle of the street, but it looks like you've got some important friends. So I guess I got my answer."

"What do you mean?"

"I mean you're out. You made bail. Your boss or whoever he is showed up with the cash."

"Paul?"

"Verbania?" His face flashed something that seemed almost like panic before it went back to normal. "God, not him. Bobby Marroni is here. Let's go."

He pushed the door to the cell open. I stood up. The other guy tried to get up, too.

"Virgil, sit your wrinkled ass back down," the cop said.

I followed him, passing by the guy whose name I assumed was Virgil, unless that was the nickname they'd given him. It was obvious he was a regular.

Even in his condition, he must have noticed I was missing a finger. He said something about me getting arrested for taking a four-finger discount. He started laughing and coughing and hacking again as the cop led me out of the jail.

He took me back to a counter near the door that led to the main room of the station. He picked up a clipboard and started rattling off everything they'd collected from me.

"Blue jeans that stink of gas . . . T-shirt that stinks of gas . . . socks that stink of gas . . . tennis shoes that stink of gas . . . wallet with thirty-seven dollars inside . . . one quarter . . . two pennies . . . a Rolex, probably hot or fake or both . . . and a pocket watch, probably hot or fake or both. You got two watches?"

"This one's a compass," I said.

"Compass? Well, it sure led you to the wrong place tonight."

I changed out of the gray jumpsuit. I handed it back to him and got dressed in my gas-soaked clothes. He held the thing I'd been wearing up to his nose.

"Now this stinks of gas, too," he said.

"Were you hoping to not have to wash it?"

"You think it got washed before we gave it to you?" He tossed the jumpsuit onto a table and pushed that door open. He waited for me to walk through it.

When I did, I saw Bobby there. He looked more pissed than I'd ever seen him. I already missed being in that cell.

Sixty-two

EVERY MORNING, VINNY would ease himself into his own car, a Ford Galaxy. He hand-picked it from a car carrier Jerry Pasquale's crew had hijacked a year or so before. Vinny would drive it to Paul's house. He'd park it out front and march toward the Cadillac in the driveway next to the house.

Vinny would check the Cadillac for any bombs. He'd get in. He'd hold his breath. He'd turn the key and start it. Just as Paul demanded. Vinny assumed Paul knew if the Cadillac ever exploded, it would take out half of his house. That would have been the least of Vinny's problems.

Sally always met Vinny at the door. She always had coffee ready, too. She never asked questions, talking mainly about the weather or something like that. Vinny kept his answers short. He was respectful. He'd even make himself smile a little bit, when he was supposed to. He knew how to handle himself around her. If he didn't, he wouldn't have been Paul's driver.

Not many bosses have their top guy double as their driver. But the thing in West Virginia didn't quite follow the rulebook of the Five Families. Vinny reported to Paul. Bobby, Jerry Pasquale, and Cashews Ciccone reported to Vinny. Bobby, Jerry, and Cashews had their own crews. Bobby had Phil, Rico, and Tommy. Bobby had been breaking in Tony and Willie before J.J. had ended up falling in Paul's lap. At that point, Paul had twenty-three soldiers, not counting the bookies, the loan sharks, the people who ran the whorehouses, and the ones who handled the drugs. It was mostly pot. They pushed a little coke and heroin, too. They were careful about that. Too much of that shit would bring attention they didn't need.

The gambling, the loans, the whorehouses, and the drugs kept a nice flow of cash coming. The rest of it came from stealing. They stole whatever they could, however they could steal it. Trucks were easy, chock-full of goods they could fence. They'd steal cars, too. Sell them whole or chop them up.

The crews also supplied the muscle. If people didn't pay up or if they caused any trouble, they took care of it. They did whatever had to be done. Sent messages whenever they had to be sent. Sometimes they'd light up a bar or a house or whatever. Sometimes, they'd break a few bones. Sometimes, they'd send someone to Ohio. Every once in a while, they'd hit someone out in the open, but that was only when a specific message needed to be sent. It was risky; they didn't do it too often. When it needed to be done, Vinny was usually the one who'd work with Paul to figure out who would do it and how it would be done. Sometimes, it would be planned out carefully. Other times, it happened fast. Paul made those decisions. He'd usually run it by Vinny, but it was always Paul's call.

They ran all of Wheeling and the other towns in the sliver of West Virginia that shot up like a middle finger to the rest of the country. They had business in Ohio and Pennsylvania, too. Paul knew how to keep the people in Pittsburgh and Youngstown happy, so they didn't mind giving him room to operate across both borders. He had connections in Cleveland, too. It was a good thing. It was running smoothly. No one was stupid or brave or big enough to infringe on Paul's turf. Whenever they tried, Paul and company shut it down, fast enough and hard enough to make sure anybody else who was getting any ideas would look for other ideas instead.

It helped that no one really paid much attention to what was happening in West Virginia. The rest of the world thought they were backward, dumb, inbred, redneck. Paul didn't mind it. It kept other wiseguys from getting wise to what he had.

Wheeling was anything but backward, dumb, inbred, or redneck. It wasn't much different from any of the places around Pittsburgh. It looked the same, it felt the same. It was the same. If Mason and Dixon had made it to the Ohio River like they were supposed to, Wheeling would have been just another overgrown pimple oozing coal and cranking steel in Southwestern Pennsylvania.

They had all the right politicians in their pocket. They bought them when they could. When they couldn't, they'd find a way to make a mess that only they could clean up. Sometimes it took a little time, but they had it under control. City cops, county cops, state cops, judges, whatever. Prosecutors were important, too, since they decided who did and didn't get charged with crimes. They had to be a little more careful with the feds, and they were. Some lines they didn't cross. That's why Paul was always so careful about how far they went with drugs.

It took plenty of money, but when most of the income was never reported to the feds it was easier to pay people off. Paul basically viewed the bribes as the taxes he didn't pay. If they let him operate without interference, he didn't mind it. If he got any interference, he dealt with it. It wasn't revenge. It was just part of doing business.

Sometimes, it was revenge. Vinny never liked that. He thought revenge got in the way of business. And it was revenge that was getting in the way of business, ever since the day Vinny and Paul ran into Johnny in the street outside Leslie's house. The sooner Vinny could get Paul to forget about all of it, the sooner they could focus on business again.

Vinny sat there thinking about that while Sally was talking about whatever she was talking about. He listened enough to know when to nod or smile, but he wasn't really paying attention. He heard Paul coming down the steps. Vinny heard him shout "I'm leaving" to Sally and "let's go" to Vinny.

He knew Paul wanted to hear if anything had happened the night before. Vinny wished he would have been able to tell Paul that Johnny went home and stayed home, same as he had every other night since he started sitting outside Johnny's apartment.

Vinny thanked Sally. She picked up the mug he'd been drinking from. It wasn't great coffee, but it was better than anything else Vinny was getting for free. Besides, it would have been rude for him to not drink some of it.

He hurried to catch up with Paul, clown shoes flopping through shag carpeting in the hallway that led to the front door. By the time Vinny got outside, Paul was already in the back seat of the Cadillac. The engine purred. It was a lot nicer than Vinny's Ford, but he didn't need a flashy car, not when he spent most of his time driving Paul's.

Vinny looked at the house as he backed the Cadillac out of the driveway. Who would have dreamed someone like Paul lived there? It all looked so normal. If anyone knew how much cash was hidden inside the floorboards, the walls, the attic, and the basement. They'd buried three trash bags full of hundreds in the backyard, under dirt covered by plants and bushes and weeds. It would have been easier to get that money than it would have been to rob any bank around. Not that anyone would be dumb enough to try to steal from Paul, even if they knew the cash was down there.

"What's the word?" Paul said.

"I think Johnny's using Maria," Vinny said. "To coordinate with her. To pass messages. He stopped by his old house last night after eleven. He stood at the door and talked to her for maybe five minutes."

"Where was the kid?"

"He was out stealing gas. They been doing it all week. That truck's almost full. We need to store it somewhere else until we need it. And we need to find another truck."

"I got a line on two more. I wanted to see how this would work before we get Jerry involved. Maybe we get Cashews's people in on it, too."

"Do we trust Cashews's people to not fuck it up?"

"If his people would fuck up something simple like this," Paul said, "Cashews may need to get himself some new people."

Vinny looked in the rearview mirror at Paul. He had a piece of toilet paper stuck to a spot where he'd cut himself shaving.

"So what do we do about this other thing?" Vinny said.

"I don't want to lean on her. We been over that. She's already scared shitless. If she goes off the deep end, then I've got to worry about her going to Sally."

"You think Leslie'd say something to your wife?"

"Desperate people do stupid shit. Besides, she ain't too much fun to be around when she's afraid of her own shadow."

"Maybe it's time for a clean break."

"We been over that, too," Paul said.

"You want to talk to Mesagne again?"

"I still don't think Johnny's messing around with her. If he was, he wouldn't use his ex-wife to cover his tracks. He'd just run."

"So what do you think he's doing?"

"If I was a betting man, which of course I am, I'd say Johnny is protecting someone."

"Who?"

"I'd say there's only one person Mesagne would try to protect. And that would explain why he's working with that someone's mother."

"The kid?" Vinny's eyes widened as Paul said it. "I thought he was clean."

"I thought so, too. I need real proof before I make a move. He has potential. It would be a fucking waste if it was him. I think I need to get him a little rattled. That's when people make mistakes."

"What are you thinking?"

"They're making another run tonight with the gas, right? Talk to that lieutenant we took care of after he beat up the kid in Steubenville. You know the one I'm talking about?"

"Yeah. Bishop. I got his direct line at the station."

"I have a project for him. And don't say nothing about it to nobody. Especially not to Bobby."

That was when Vinny knew Paul wasn't going to leave it alone. That was when Vinny knew they'd only ever get back to business if Paul got the answers he was looking for. Whatever they were. And if that meant the kid ended up in Ohio, so be it. Vinny just wanted it all to be over with.

Sixty-three

OCTOBER 12, 1973

IT WAS BAD enough that the kid got himself arrested, Bobby thought.
It was even worse that Bobby got blamed for it. As if he'd told the
kid to get arrested. What was Bobby supposed to do? Hold the kid's
hand? Bobby told him to be safe. Bobby told him not to do anything
stupid. Bobby did his job. The kid didn't do his, or he wouldn't have
got himself pinched.

J.J. came walking out of the jail with a look on his face like he was
confused, or something. That made Bobby even more upset. As he saw
it, there wasn't anything to be confused about. J.J. got himself arrested,
and Bobby got himself blamed for it. So, yeah, Bobby was pissed.

Bobby turned away and walked out of the station once he saw J.J.
He assumed J.J. would follow him. If he didn't, good, Bobby thought.
He didn't want to deal with J.J. *He fucked up. He's young. He's brand
new.* And Bobby hadn't been the one who brought the kid on. Bobby
didn't want him. Bobby told them he didn't want him.

"Wait up," J.J. said.

Bobby just kept going. He'd walked to the jail from the dog shop.
It was close enough. And Bobby was mad enough that he needed to
burn some of that anger off with a little exercise.

"Where did you park?" J.J. said.

Bobby kept on going. "I parked back at the place. It ain't that far. If I can walk, you can walk. You're young. You got fresh legs."

"I can tell you're upset," J.J. said.

"You're a real genius. If you'd been that smart earlier, we wouldn't be in this mess."

"I did what you told me to do. I went out and got gasoline."

"I didn't tell you to get arrested."

"I didn't plan on that part."

"Well, Paul is going to be pissed. For all I know, he's going to pull us off the job. I can't say I'd blame him."

"Hold on," J.J. said. He stopped walking. Bobby did, too. "Do you think I was out there banging on the cans? I was quiet. I was careful. Just like every other night. A cop car just showed up. What was I supposed to do?"

"You was supposed to not get hauled in," Bobby said, and started walking again.

"I'll try to remember that next time."

Bobby turned around and swooped in on J.J., meeting him face to face. "Now ain't the time to be a smartass," he said. "This is a big fucking deal."

Bobby turned back around and kept going toward the dog shop.

"Am I missing something? Am I the first guy who works for Paul to get arrested?"

"It don't happen too often," Bobby said. "Paul pays a lot to make sure of that."

"Apparently he doesn't pay enough," J.J. said. "Otherwise, I wouldn't have been."

J.J. had a point, but Bobby didn't want to admit it.

"He pays enough that you got out of there fast," Bobby said. "But there's still a mess to clean up. You ever been in trouble before?"

"Never." J.J. was catching up with Bobby.

Bobby wasn't trying to let J.J. gain ground. J.J. was just faster than Bobby. He wished he was that young again.

"What did you say to them?" Bobby said.

"Nothing. They didn't even know my car was across the street."

"Well, I figure you'll plead guilty to something. You'll pay a fine and get put on probation or whatever."

"So I'll have a record?"

"Big deal. It's like a scar. Only it's on paper, not your face."

"I still don't know what happened," J.J. said, now next to Bobby. "It wasn't like the cops were just cruising around. It's like they knew exactly where I would be. Do you think someone saw me?"

"I can find out if they was responding to a call. If they wasn't, maybe it don't make sense. But that don't change that it happened."

They were getting close to Doggie Do-Rights.

"So what's next?" J.J. said.

"I need to go see Paul in the morning," Bobby said. "After I heard about it, I had Tommy drive me straight from Warwood."

"How did you know?"

"Vinny has a police radio. I guess sometimes he just sits there and listens to it."

"Don't you think he already told Paul?"

"Vinny told me I have to tell him. Vinny don't like to be the one to give him bad news when he's not the one who done it."

Bobby unlocked the door. The dogs started barking. Bobby and J.J. walked to the back room.

"It's late," Bobby said. "You can walk home in the morning."

"Walk home? I live like five miles from here."

"You'll have to call someone for a ride, then. Or maybe you can just hitchhike."

"Can't you give me a ride?"

"I can, but I ain't. Besides, you stink like gas. I don't need that in my car."

"What am I supposed to do?"

"Find a place to lay down."

"Do you have a cot?"

"I got a floor."

J.J. JENKINS

AND JUST LIKE that, he left. I heard him stop and talk to the dogs on his way out. He was making goofy sounds at them, like he was a different person. A normal person.

How could he just leave me here? On top of everything else, I was hungry. I checked the fridge. It had beer and only beer. I looked in the cabinets near the sink behind the table where they always sat. I found a can of peanuts. It was half empty. They tasted stale. I didn't care.

The salt made me thirsty. I got a beer. An opener hung from a string tied to a magnet on the side of the refrigerator. I drained it in four gulps. I got another. I finished it and got one more.

Halfway through the third beer, I was starting to feel a little better. The smell of gas coming from my clothes didn't seem as bad. I was either getting used to it or getting a little drunk. I looked at that clock on the wall. It was fifteen after four. I looked at the phone on the wall next to the clock. I knew her number. I'd looked it up in the phone book and memorized it. I thought about calling her.

I watched the minute hand spin around a couple times. I kept thinking about calling her. What would she say? Was she alone? It was early Friday morning. She said something about Paul staying over on Thursday nights. She also said she'd been trying to make it so he wouldn't stay on any night. That was before the shit hit the fan. I hadn't talked to her in a week. I wanted to.

I drank that beer too fast. It was making me think about doing something really stupid. I keep looking at the clock, then at the phone, then at the clock. Then at the phone.

When the clock got to twenty after four, I stood up. I walked to the phone. I picked up the receiver and pressed it against the side of my face. I started dialing her number.

Sixty-four

OCTOBER 11, 1973

Paul sat behind his desk. Vinny stood by the door. He had money to count, and Paul was keeping him from doing it. But if the boss wanted to talk and Vinny didn't want to listen, the boss would find someone else to do the listening.

Paul had the newspaper. He was reading an article out loud. It was about the Vice President resigning. Spiro Agnew. What a name. Vinny thought it sounded made up. Then again, the best names always sound made up.

Agnew had pleaded no contest to tax evasion because he got ten thousand dollars in kickbacks from an engineering firm in Maryland. That was the guy's biggest mistake: never take dirty money from a company that pretends to be clean.

Paul said something about Agnew being the first Vice President to get indicted since Aaron Burr, for killing Alexander Hamilton. Vinny figured maybe those guys weren't much different than them, after all. Vinny wondered if he was in the wrong line of work.

Paul started talking again about whatever was going on with gasoline, a shortage. Embargo. Vinny didn't really understand any of it. Paul thought they would make ten grand from selling the gas Bobby's crew had been stealing. But the scam ended up having another purpose. They were going to get the kid arrested. Paul thought that would get him rattled enough to do something dumb, and that would make it easier for them to figure out whether he was the one messing with Leslie. Vinny didn't understand that, either. He just wanted to be done with all of it.

Paul asked Vinny if everything was ready to go, whether he'd called Lieutenant Bishop to set it up. Vinny told Paul it was all squared away.

"They're going to watch for him when he gets started," Vinny said. "They'll tail him. They'll catch him with the cans out. One of the cops knows what's going on. His partner won't be wise to it."

"How much is this going to cost?"

"No charge. Bishop is still very grateful."

"He should be," Paul said. "We saved that guy's ass."

Vinny thought about what to say next. He didn't need any trouble. But this distraction was also something he didn't need.

"Are you sure this is the right move?" Vinny said. "Getting one of our own guys hauled in?"

"He won't slip up unless we knock him off balance. He ain't never been arrested. It's going to shake him up. Maybe enough that he'll go see her. Or call her."

"I ain't sure getting arrested will get him to mess around with her if his old man told him to stay away," Vinny said.

Paul folded up the newspaper and slid it across the top of the desk.

"Then maybe we've got to shake him up a little bit more."

Paul was always thinking five steps ahead. Usually, Vinny knew where he was going. This time, he didn't.

"What you got in mind?"

"I got something. But let's see if this one works first. Is her place wired yet?"

"We got the phone line covered."

"That's it?" Paul said.

"She's been home too much. Whenever the guy's ready to put the bugs in, she's there. Whenever she's not there, I can't get ahold of the guy."

"Get them in there. If he shows up, we need to hear it."

"If he calls, we will."

"If that place ain't bugged, you need to stop sitting outside Mesagne's place and start sitting outside hers. If he's getting pinched tonight, we need eyes on her place after he gets out."

Paul didn't say it like he was asking. Which told Vinny he was looking at another night of maybe five hours of sleep, if he was lucky.

Yeah, Vinny thought, *this fucking thing has to end.*

Sixty-five

OCTOBER 12, 1973

J.J. JENKINS

I HAD DIALED the first six numbers. I stuck my finger in the circle with the last one. It was a seven. I spun it clockwise and stopped at the metal lip. I held it there, staring at the *DEF* in black letters over the number three.

I hung up. I took my finger out of the dial. It was almost twenty-five minutes after four.

There was no way I'd be able to sleep in there. No way. If I was going to have to walk home later, I might as well walk home now.

I went out into the shop. I bent over to see the little dog, Gnocchi. He seemed happy to see me. The other dogs barked, too. I didn't pay attention to the rest of them.

After a minute or two, I left through the front door. I pushed the button in the knob to lock it. I started making my way to the house, to my bed.

I wasn't sure how long of a walk it would be. It was more than five miles, easily. Maybe it was seven. I got home at fifteen after six. I peeled off my clothes that still smelled like gas and landed on the mattress. I was out before I realized it.

My mother woke me up, making noise in the kitchen. It turned out she was grilling ham and cheese sandwiches. I didn't complain. I woke up starving. I went to the table in my underwear. She started to say something, but she didn't.

I ate three sandwiches. She started making a fourth.

"Are you still moving to that apartment tomorrow?" she said.

"If tomorrow is Saturday, yes," I said. "Tomorrow."

"What are you doing for furniture?"

"It's furnished."

"Oh. You didn't tell me it was furnished. I guess that makes the rent not so bad. Of course, if you'd actually seen the place first. Or the furniture."

"It'll be fine. And if it isn't, I'll find another place."

"I thought you had to sign a lease."

"I think I do, but I can probably get out as fast as I got in."

"I do not want to know," she said.

"You've probably spent plenty of time in your life not wanting to know about things."

"With your father, I never wanted to know. Which worked out because he never wanted to tell." She put a cigarette out and got a fresh one. "Is there anything you want me to know?"

"You truly don't want to know," I said, standing up from the table.

"The thing is," she said, "I think maybe I do. We can talk about anything. But maybe out on the porch."

I didn't know what to say to that. I was standing there in only my underwear. "This isn't a conversation to have right now."

"Why isn't it? I'm your mother. If there's something going on, I can help you."

"I'm twenty. I'll figure it out. Besides, I've been getting plenty of fatherly advice on things."

"Really?"

"I know. That was how I felt. The guy leaves ten years ago. I hardly see him or hear from him. Now, he's everywhere."

"He feels bad about what he did."

"He should feel bad. I was only ten. He gave me that stupid compass and then he was gone. He said we'd spend time together on weekends. But I hardly ever saw him. That's why I didn't fight it when Frank wanted to adopt me. I assumed only kids without parents got adopted. But if my dad wasn't going to act like he was my dad, I guess I needed another one."

"Frank ended up being just as bad. Maybe worse."

"He changed after you married him. You didn't know he'd do that. It lasted longer than it should have."

"Why did you keep his name?"

"Why did you?"

"I guess I did because you did. I didn't want you to be alone with that name."

"I just never thought about it. I was sixteen. My name was who I was. I was worried about other things by then."

"And you're worried about other things now."

"Everybody's always worried about something. I'm not that old, but I'm old enough to know that."

"It's one thing to worry about paying the light bill. Some people got bigger things to worry about."

"We've all got something to worry about. And if we didn't have something to worry about, we'd be worried we didn't have anything to be worried about."

She stood up and grabbed my forearm. I didn't expect that.

"I worry about you. All the time. You know that, right?"

"I know you do. I'll be fine."

"You don't know that," she said. She let go of me. She looked like she was getting ready to cry.

"Nobody really knows whether they'll be fine," I said. "We tell ourselves we'll be fine. Isn't that really how it works? We worry on the surface, but deep down we think we'll be fine?"

"So why worry about anything?"

"I don't know. Maybe we worry so we can tell ourselves after we're done worrying that we'll be fine. If we didn't worry, we'd be asking for something bad to happen."

"That doesn't make much sense. Plenty of people worry, and bad things still happen to them."

"Right, but they don't think bad things will happen to them. They still think they'll be fine."

She took out another cigarette and lit it.

"So are you worried?"

"Yes," I said. "A little."

"Do you think you'll be fine?"

"I suppose I do."

"Will you be fine?"

I laughed a little bit. I started to walk away.

"J.J. Stop. Answer me. Will you be fine?"

"Do you want me to say what you want to hear, or do you want the truth?"

"I want the truth."

"The truth is, right now, I don't really know."

She didn't say anything else. I walked out of the kitchen. In my bedroom, I started getting ready to move to my new place.

Sixty-six

OCTOBER 12, 1973

J.J. JENKINS

I PACKED UP most of the things I'd taken to college. I'd make more than one trip if I needed to. It would be easy, since I wasn't leaving town.

I stopped and wondered whether I'd ever be leaving town again. If I did, where would I go?

Before I could go anywhere, I needed my car. I walked to the closest bus stop. A quarter and a dime got me to town, and another quarter got me to Warwood. I made my way to where I'd left the Plymouth. I took it home, with five empty gas cans in the trunk and five more in the back seat. I never found out what happened to the ten cans that were in the street.

The phone started ringing just as I walked inside. "Doggie Do-Rights. Eight o'clock." I tried to ask whether that was morning or night, but the line went dead before I could get the question out.

I assumed I was supposed to be there that night. I got there early and pressed on the buzzer.

This time, it was Bobby instead of Tommy who greeted me. Without saying anything, Bobby led me to the back room. Gnocchi was up on his hind legs, barking at us. Barking at me. I bent over to pet him. I made it quick so Bobby wouldn't notice. He still seemed mad.

Only Rico was at the table, waiting for us. He had an empty beer bottle lying flat to his left and a full one standing up to his right. I could see the small beads of condensation on the one that still had beer in it. He had a cigarette tight in his mouth. It wasn't lit.

Bobby sat down. He told me to do the same. I sat where Tommy usually did. The cushion was flatter than the cushion on the other chairs.

"I talked to Paul about the other night," Bobby said. "He was pissed. He has a lawyer lined up to handle it all. You'll plead guilty to some bullshit like disturbing the peace, you'll be on probation for a little while. That should be the end of it."

"When do we start back with the gasoline?" I said.

"We're taking a little break from that. Not long. Just a few days, I think."

"Good," I said. "I've got too many shirts that stink like gas, even after I wash them."

Rico laughed when I said it. The sound was low. It almost rumbled out of him.

"There's worse things you can stink of than gas," he said.

"Anyway," Bobby said, "Paul thinks it's time for you to make your bones."

"I thought I've been making my bones."

Rico laughed again, in that same deep, gurgling way. Bobby shook his head.

"You don't understand," he said. "There's only one way to make your bones."

"To make your bones," Rico said, "you've got to, you know, make some bones."

"Wait a minute," I said. "I thought that would be later on."

"This ain't college," Bobby said. "Here, graduation comes whenever the boss says it comes."

"You already seen what it's like," Rico said. "What we did to that asshole with the eye patch in Pittsburgh. This is basically the same thing."

"When we left Pittsburgh, the guy was still alive."

"Sometimes when we're done," Bobby said, "they're alive. Sometimes when we're done, they ain't. Like the first night you ever came here."

"But that wasn't planned," I said. "That was an accident."

"Accidents happen," Bobby said. "Sometimes accidents happen on purpose. There's an accident that needs to happen on purpose in Canton."

"In Canton?" I said. "Ohio?"

"The woman who runs one of Paul's whorehouses lives there," Bobby said. "She works for two weeks, then goes back to a town where no one knows what she does. She stays there for a week, then she does it all over again. She's been skimming. She got warned about it before. She did it again."

"How many times did she get warned?" I said.

"Once," Bobby said. "She's lucky she got that."

"You give people one warning, they always think they get more," Rico said.

"She ain't getting another one," Bobby said. "Paul wants you and Rico to go take care of it."

I tried to stay calm. I could feel my hands starting to tremble. I kept them under the table.

"So we're going up to Canton, and that's it?" I said. "She's gone? Just like that?"

"It ain't quite that simple," Bobby said. "But it ain't some badass who'll fight back. Besides, like Rico said, she probably thinks she's getting another warning. She won't expect nothing because she'll think Rico wouldn't be showing up to paint her house with some young kid she ain't never seen before."

"If it's that simple, why doesn't Rico just do it himself?" I said.

"We been over this," Bobby said. "I don't make the orders. I just pass them out. The order is you and Rico."

"What do we do after it's done?" I said. "Do we have to take her, the body, somewhere?"

"Not on this one," Bobby said. "This one isn't one that disappears. This is one that gets found. This is one that sends a message to anyone else who thinks about fucking around with Paul's money. Sometimes, that's the way it needs to happen. It keeps us from having to do it to someone else who thinks they're smarter than Paul."

"Too many fucking people think they're smarter than Paul," Rico said. "And that's kept me pretty busy over the past few years."

"When is this supposed to happen?" I said, trying to ignore what Rico had just said.

"It's not when it's supposed to happen," Bobby said. "It's when it will happen. It will happen two days from now, on Sunday."

I looked at Rico. His face was hard and set. He still hadn't lit the cigarette that was sticking out of his mouth.

"Can I talk to Paul about this?" I said.

They both laughed at me.

"Kid, sometimes you're really smart," Bobby said. "And sometimes you got cat shit for brains. Paul won't talk to you about this. He needs layers. He needs buffers. If I let you talk to him about this, it'll be my ass."

I turned to Rico.

"You're OK with this? Doing that to some woman you don't know?"

Rico's mouth moved a little bit, like he was thinking about something that there really wasn't any reason to think about.

"I know her," he said. "Nice gal. Made me a pie once. Apple. It was good. But this is the job, kid."

"We're clear then?" Bobby said. "Meet here Sunday at three. We'll have a car you can use to go up there. I'll have all the information for you then."

Bobby stared at me for a few seconds. He looked at Rico. Then he looked back at me.

"So we're clear on everything?" Bobby said.

Rico slapped his hands on the table. It made me flinch. He stood up.

"I'm clear," Rico said. "Now, Phil and me are going up to Little Washington to get laid. Hey, kid, it's that place I was telling you about. You want to come with us?"

"I'll see you on Sunday," I said. I had no interest in ever going to a place like that. After the order we'd gotten, I just wanted to go home and get in bed.

My stomach started churning. I followed Rico out. After he got in his car and left, I threw up all over the sidewalk, right next to the Plymouth.

Sixty-seven

LESLIE FITZPATRICK

I'D BEEN WITH him for six years, even though I really wasn't with him. He had a wife. He had me. I knew the situation when it all started. One day later, one week later, one month later, one year later, it became whatever it was.

There was no future in it. It was a trade-off. I got money, security, a sense of power or at least of being close to it. He got companionship, and more. Lately, he'd been getting a lot less of either. I didn't know whether it would get him to move on. But I wanted it to, and it was the only plan I had.

What was I to him, really? A trophy? But who saw it? The people who worked for him? His friends? Did he even have friends? Everyone he knew was part of the bigger plan. They either worked for him or he paid them off to do whatever he wanted. I'd never really thought of it before, but I don't think he actually had any friends. Other than his wife. Other than me. But I don't think he ever thought of me as a friend. I never thought of him that way.

Really, what was I trying to prove? He wasn't very much to look at. He was going bald and getting fat. His mouth stunk like cigars. And if it wasn't for the cigars, he'd probably have bad breath. His teeth were stained yellow from coffee and tobacco. They were crooked on top. He was getting jowls. He looked a lot older than he was.

But I knew what I was getting myself into. Yes, I was a lot younger when it started. But I was old enough to know. I accepted it. For better or worse. Four words I was never going to say in front of a priest. Not with Paul. Maybe not with anyone.

What did I really get from him? A little time, a little attention, a decent amount of money. There was no commitment, at least not from his side. He expected me to not see anyone else, even as he went home to his wife most nights. What was I thinking?

And now here I was. Twenty-seven years old. Stuck in a thing that would last only until he decided to end it. Wasting the best years of my life with someone who would never let me have kids. He knocked me up that one time. I never told him about it. I handled it. I knew what he'd say. I didn't want to hear him say it. So I just took care of it. I still thought about it, every day.

I'd only ever stop thinking about the baby I could have had when I actually had one. Would I actually have one? It would never happen with him. I knew that. That was why I needed to move on. But I still needed him to make that decision. I was trying to push him that way. It wasn't easy. Not at all. Especially not after that day with J.J. His mother told me to stay away from him. And I did, as best I could. I knew what would happen to him if Paul figured it out. It didn't make me feel any different.

That letter I got from my father had helped me come to terms with everything. It let me know, with words that wouldn't be obvious to whoever at the prison reads those letters, that someone else was there the day a robbery had gone bad and a bystander had gotten killed and two of my father's co-workers, or whatever they were, had been shot dead by police and multiple life sentences had been handed out.

Someone else had made a quick escape, taking the only car the group had brought and leaving the others behind. Someone else had made it clear to the ones who were there that they'd take the fall,

keeping to themselves that someone else had been there. This someone else had made it clear that, if they didn't, action would be taken
against their family members, including any and all children, no matter their ages. The letter made it clear to me that this someone else
was Paul Verbania.

That was the thing that finally made me want to leave Paul. J.J. was
the one who made it all come to life. He was too young to be the right
one for me, but he was the right one to pry me away from Paul. J.J. was
the right one to help me get myself ready for the right one, whoever
the right one might be.

Paul hadn't been showing up as much. That was good. I tried to act
like everything was normal when I saw him. It wasn't. I didn't want it
to be. But I needed Paul to be the one who decided to end it. He had
to do it, or it would never happen.

It was a Friday night, nine days after J.J. had visited. Paul showed
up. I didn't know he was coming. I heard the Cadillac pull up to the
house. I waited for him to knock on the door. I opened it, doing my
best to act like everything was normal, even though it wasn't.

"Hello," I said, without much feeling in it.

"Hello to you," he said. He came inside and started walking around,
looking for something that wasn't there. J.J. hadn't been back since
he ran out the back door and climbed the fence.

"I didn't know you were coming," I said.

"I just wanted to stop by and say hello."

"That's it? Hello?"

"I guess I wanted to see you."

"Well, you see me. What else do you want to do to me?"

He spun to face me. He was already mad. It was like he was looking for a reason to be.

"What does that mean?" he said.

"You haven't been around much at all lately," I said, trying to put
it all on him. "When you're here, you're constantly watching me. It's
like you're trying to figure out how to open a safe."

"Safes can be cracked."

"Please," I said. "I've never been very hard to crack."

"Something's different. We both know it."

"If anything's different, it's because this thing is all it's ever going to be. It's been that way since the beginning."

"You knew it since the beginning." He started walking around the room, still looking for something. "You never had a problem with it."

"I was only twenty-one. I didn't care where it was going because where anything was going was the last thing on my mind. It's different now."

"So you agree. Something's different."

"I'm twenty-seven. Everyone I went to school with has a kid. Most of them have more than one."

"You don't want a kid. You can't take care of a kid. Remember the dog I got you? How long did that thing last? A week?"

"That dog shit all over the place."

"Babies shit all over the place, too."

"Is that why you and Sally never had one?" I said.

The moment his wife's name came out of my mouth, he came at me. He put his left hand on my throat. I gasped.

"You been smart enough to not mention her for six fucking years. Don't get stupid on yourself now." He let me go and turned away. "Besides, she wanted kids. I didn't."

"How does any man not want kids?" I said. "It's not like you're the one who has to inflate like a balloon for nine months and then squeeze a bowling ball out of your ass."

He wandered toward the kitchen, still searching. He got quiet.

"I don't want nobody paying for my sins. I don't want nobody ending up like me. And I don't want my kids becoming orphans."

"A gangster with a heart," I said. "Who would have ever guessed it? That heart is so big you've deprived your children of even existing."

He stopped. He looked back at me.

"It's my choice. I know it ain't really the Italian way, but it's my way."

"Well, God told Adam and Eve to be fruitful and multiply."

"That's the last of his orders I need to worry about."

"I still don't get it. When you're gone, what will you leave behind?"

"Nothing. That's the legacy I want."

"Plenty of people would say that's the legacy you deserve."

He looked at me after I said that. He smiled, but he wasn't happy. He knew who he was. He knew that I knew it. He was surprised I'd say it out loud.

"I know a thing or two about people getting what they deserve," he said. And then he walked out the door and slammed it behind him.

Sixty-eight

OCTOBER 13–14, 1973

J.J. JENKINS

I MOVED MY things to the apartment on Saturday. It was one day after I found out about the next job, and one day before doing it. I tried my best not to think about what was going to happen on Sunday.

I filled the trunk of the Plymouth with clothes and shoes and record albums. I put a small stereo with a turntable and that thin, floppy arm in the back seat. My mother had given me some knick-knacks from the basement. They were in a cardboard box that said "Hawaiian Punch" on each side. She said the things would help give the place some character. I didn't argue with her, even if I never planned to put that stuff out anywhere. She gave me some old sheets for the bed, along with a container full of chocolate chip cookies. She placed on top of the Tupperware a loaf of banana bread wrapped in tin foil.

The apartment had a small bedroom, a smaller kitchen, a decent-sized living room, and a bathroom roughly the size of a closet. The closet was not nearly the size of a normal closet. It was on the top floor of a two-story building. There were four units, as best I could tell. The main door opened to a pair of brick steps. One of the bricks was missing. The concrete sidewalk at the bottom had a thick and ragged crack, deep enough to trip someone. I made a mental note to not let that someone be me.

I carried my things upstairs, one box and suitcase after another. I tried not to think as I did it. If I had, I would have been thinking that, with each step, I was getting closer to Sunday's trip to Canton.

Sunday came anyway, as much as I didn't want it to. I made the short walk to Doggie Do-Rights. It allowed me to show up right on time. I usually was early. Today, I didn't want to be there a second before I was supposed to arrive. I put my finger into the buzzer at three o'clock sharp. Before I knew what was happening, Bobby ripped open the door and pulled me inside.

"Slight change of plans," he said. "Tony's going."

"So I don't have to go?" I said, allowing myself to feel relieved, if only for a few seconds.

Bobby shook his head at me, like I should have known the answer already.

"Tony's going, too. It's a three-man job now. I know you're going to ask why, and you know what I'm going to say."

"But the job's still the same?"

"Yeah. Only now when Rico shows up with two other guys, maybe she's a little more leery, you know?"

"So why send three?"

"I said you was going to ask me that, and I said you know what I'm going to say."

I probably shouldn't have said what I said next. At the moment, I didn't care.

"When you get these orders, do you ever ask whether it's a good idea? Whether there's a better way?"

He laughed at me, pretty much like I knew he would.

"You really do got a lot to learn, kid. Only Vinny can get away with that. I seen it. Me and Jerry and Cashews, we just do what we're told when we're told how we're told. And I been told to send Tony with you and Rico. It don't matter whether you like it or I like it or anybody likes it."

I didn't know why he was being so candid with me. It wasn't putting my mind at ease. He didn't like the idea of sending three. Why should I? Was this some sort of a test? Or were these guys really not very bright?

I didn't have a chance to figure it out, not that day. It was time to go. They sent us in a black Pinto. It had a small back seat. As the new guy, I knew where I'd be sitting for the entire trip, especially with Rico telling Tony to drive. I wished he'd told me to drive. Then again, maybe I would have steered that little piece of shit right off the Fort Henry Bridge and into the river.

"What's this broad's name, anyway?" Tony said after the car crossed into Ohio.

"I don't want to know," I replied, cramped in the back seat and already feeling nauseous.

Rico turned around and gave me a dirty look.

"You think not knowing her name will make her any less dead?"

"I'd just rather not know."

"Too bad," he said. "Her name's Linda Palinda."

"That ain't her fucking name," Tony said. "It can't be."

"I think her first name's something different," Rico said. "But with a last name like Palinda, people will call you Linda."

"Unless you're a guy," I said.

"That's the first thing I'd call a guy named Palinda," Rico said with a snort.

I got quiet for a few seconds. Then I thought of something.

"Will Mr. Linda Palinda be home?" I asked.

"See," Rico said, "you're already calling him that."

"I hadn't thought about a husband," Tony said. "What if he gets in the way?"

"He's supposed to be working tonight," Rico said.

"What if he isn't?" I said. I wasn't looking for a reason to worry. I was looking for a reason to cancel the plans.

"I got a description of his car and the license plate number," Rico said. "We'll know if he's there."

"What if he is?" I said.

"If he's there," Rico said, "we'll call it off."

"Maybe we'll get lucky and he'll be there," I said without thinking.

Rico turned around again, giving me a dirtier look than the one he gave me before. "Lucky? If by lucky you mean we waste four fucking hours driving up there and back and then we have to do it again tomorrow or the next day or whenever, then I guess that's lucky. But it sure as shit don't sound lucky to me. We got better things to do than drive back and forth to Canton twice."

Tony nodded at that. It was obvious he was trying to kiss Rico's ass, and to make me look bad.

"You're right," Tony said. "We've got to do it anyway. Might as well do it now."

I kept quiet after that, mainly because I was pissed at Tony. Then I got curious again.

"How are we supposed to do it? Are we going to shoot her or something? Won't that be loud?"

Rico had leaned back against the headrest. His eyes were closed.

"You seen what I did to that guy in Pittsburgh, right?"

"So you'll punch her to death?"

"No," Rico said. "But I can handle her with my hands. No guns. No noise. Quick and clean and easy, at least as quick and clean and easy as this stuff ever goes. You won't even get no blood on your shirt."

I looked down at what I was wearing. It was dark blue with thin white horizontal stripes.

"For that shirt," Tony said, "a little blood would be an improvement."

Rico laughed. After that, things got quiet and stayed quiet for a long time. I knew there was no way to get them to turn around and go home. I was hoping for something that would make it not happen. Flat tire. Tornado. Nuclear war. Anything.

Usually long drives feel like they take forever. This one went by way too fast. As we got closer to Canton, Rico pulled out a sheet of paper. It had directions written on it to 37 Winfield Way, the home of Linda Palinda and Mr. Linda Palinda.

"How can she be married and working in a whorehouse?" I said.

"I don't think she turns tricks no more," Rico said. "Maybe she does. Alls I know for sure is she runs the place."

"But how can she do something like that and be married?" I said.

"Lots of married people screw other people," Rico said. "If you can get paid for it, even better."

Rico started spouting off directions to Tony. "Turn here" and "not there, here" and "shit we missed it, turn around."

Eventually, Tony found Winfield Way. We started searching for house numbers. At first, they were in the eighties. The numbers were going down, even to the left and odd to the right. Once we got through the forties, Tony pulled the Pinto toward the curb. He parked it in front of an empty lot next to 37.

"It would be better if we parked right in front," Rico said.

"Unless you plan to move the car that's already there, this is the best I can do," Tony said.

"Maybe that's the husband's car," I said, pointing at a silver Dodge Dart parked at the curb in front of 37 Winfield. "Check and see."

Rico reached into the pockets of his trousers. He fished around for a piece of paper that had the make, model, and license number of Mr. Linda Palinda's vehicle. Rico checked his pants for it again.

"Fuck," he said, turning his pockets inside out. "I can't find it."

For an instant, it was the best I'd felt all day. I had a feeling it wouldn't last.

Sixty-nine

JOHNNY MESAGNE

SUNDAY HAD BEEN a good day. The Steelers lost. Cincinnati beat them by twelve points. I won plenty. That meant Paul won plenty, too. Yeah, it was a good day.

The four o'clock games had started. There was a decent crowd in the bar. The Cowboys and Rams were playing in Los Angeles. I had the game on the fourteen-inch TV that was hanging from the ceiling to the left of the front door.

As I was watching the game, I noticed Vinny walk in. There went my good mood.

I didn't pay no attention to him. I could sense him moving toward me. I was standing behind the bar. He was across from me, next to Jimmy. I had a feeling Jimmy was making another face at Vinny.

"Business good today?" Vinny said, as if he didn't know the Pittsburgh score.

I looked over the top of my reading glasses.

"So far," I said. "The Steelers finally took their dick out of my ear. I'm a little loaded up on Minnesota, though. Hopefully the 49ers can cover."

Vinny nodded at that, and then he just kept standing there.

"It's a few days early to be making a collection," I said.

"I was just passing by. Wanted to see how things was going. I figured it was good that Pittsburgh lost one."

"Yeah, it's good," I said, because of course it was and he knew damn well it was. "It's very good."

"You seen your kid lately?"

I didn't know where he was going with that, but I figured I wasn't going to like it too much.

"Been a few days." I said to him. "Why?"

"I thought maybe he'd tell you."

"Tell me what?"

"Hey, how about giving me a cold beer?" Vinny said.

I probably seemed a little irritated, but I did what he asked. I grabbed a glass and filled it under one of the taps. I tried to read his face. As usual, he gave nothing away. I slapped the beer onto the bar. It made a loud clap.

"Here's your cold beer. Now, what's my kid supposed to tell me?"

He picked it up and took a drink. He slammed the glass back down, same way I had.

"You really don't know, do you?" he said.

I went back to looking at the betting slips for the late games.

"You got your free beer," I said. "I'll see you when you come back for Paul's money."

Vinny leaned forward. His words came out in a whisper, but even though the place was pretty much full, I still heard him.

"Your kid is making his bones," Vinny said.

My eyes sprang up.

"That's right. He got sent to Canton today with two other guys."

"Canton? What the fuck is in Canton?"

"Linda Palinda's in Canton."

"Linda Palinda? From that place in South Wheeling?"

"She lives in Canton when she ain't working here," Vinny said. He took another drink. "She's been messing with what don't belong to her."

I looked at the front door and then back at Vinny.

"Paul's sitting outside in the car, ain't he?"

"Don't matter where Paul is. What matters is your kid's on his way to Canton right now."

I looked at the door again. I looked back at Vinny. I looked at the crowd of people around him.

Then I looked at Jimmy. He knew me good enough to know what I was thinking. He dug his hand in his pocket and then reached toward me with his car keys, keeping them tight in his palm so Vinny couldn't see them. Jimmy slipped them to me when Vinny wasn't watching. Once I had them in my hand, I pulled off my glasses. I dropped the betting slips and the pencil I was holding. I started for the door. I knew I could get there faster than Vinny, since nobody else was behind the bar.

I beat Vinny outside. I started looking for the Cadillac. Another car was parked in front of the bar, where Vinny usually stopped. I ran to the left, toward the parking lot.

I saw the Cadillac there. I ran to it. I opened the back door on the passenger side and got in. I could see Vinny hustling to catch up in those big ass clown shoes of his.

"What the fuck is this?" Paul said.

"You already sent J.J. to paint somebody's house?"

"Get the fuck out of here," Paul said. He could see Vinny closing in. "Get this fucking guy out of here!" Paul yelled to him.

"I want you to call it off!" I said.

Vinny reached in, grabbed me by the top of my pants, and tried to yank me out of the car.

"Call it off!"

"How am I going do that?" Paul said, in a voice that was all innocent. "He's already on his way." Then he got real mean. "Now get the fuck out of my car."

Vinny pulled again, hard. I went flying out of the Cadillac. I saw Jimmy's car across the way. I got inside and started the engine. I put it in reverse. It jerked backward. I almost hit Vinny. I wouldn't have cared if I did. I popped that car into drive and floored it.

"I ALWAYS KNEW Mesagne had a screw loose," Vinny said to Paul as the sound of the squealing tires subsided. "I never knew how loose it was."

Paul was laughing. But then he got mad again.

"You know," he said to Vinny, "you're supposed to be the one who protects me from shit like this."

"Where do you think he's going?" Vinny said.

"I don't know and I don't care. But I know this. If he's going to Canton, he'll be too fucking late."

Seventy

OCTOBER 14, 1973

J.J. JENKINS

IT WAS MY chance to try to talk them into calling it off, at least for now.

"Let's go find a payphone and call Bobby," I said to Rico. "We need to be sure that's not the husband's car."

"How are we supposed to find a payphone?" Tony said.

"They're everywhere," I said. "There was a gas station like a half mile back there. It'll have a phone somewhere."

Rico didn't want to hear any of it. He slammed his hand hard onto the dashboard.

"You guys don't get it," he said. "We're already here. If we leave and then drive to a gas station and walk inside and make a call and come back here, the chances of someone seeing us and remembering us and describing us goes up. Way up. So we just go in and do what we have to do. If he's in there, I'll handle him, too."

Rico opened the door and put his right foot into the street.

"I'm going. If you guys don't want to come with me, we can deal with that when we get back to Wheeling."

Tony opened his door, too. He popped the seat for me. I didn't want to go, but what was I going to do? I had no choice. I climbed out. My knees were stiff after being stuck in the back seat for so long.

Rico walked toward the front door of the house, like he was supposed to be there. Like it was all normal. Like he wasn't there to kill whoever was inside. Whether it was one person or two or twenty.

The house was yellow. The siding was dirty. A gutter had come loose in one corner. It looked like the grass hadn't been cut in a while.

The air felt cool, not cold. It was cloudy, dreary. My stomach swished around while I walked. My heart started pounding. I put my hands in the front pockets of my jeans and tried to act natural. Nothing was natural about any of this.

Rico looked back at us. He jerked his head, letting us know he wanted us to hurry up. He walked up to the porch. He pulled back the screen and banged his knuckles on the door, three times.

JOHNNY MESAGNE

I KNEW I'D never make it to Canton in time. I drove Jimmy's car to my apartment. It was faster than walking or running. Every second counted, if I was going to keep this thing from happening.

I left Jimmy's car running. Who was going to steal it? If anyone did, I'd buy him another one.

Once I got inside, I picked up the phone and dialed zero. I asked the operator how to get a phone number in Canton. She connected me to someone in the Cleveland area code. So I asked that operator for Linda Palinda's number.

She didn't have a listing for Linda Palinda. That made sense, since the number would be in her husband's name. The operator said there was eight Palindas in the area code. I asked for any Palindas in Canton. She sighed real loud and said it don't work that way. She has all the Palindas in the area code, without the cities. I said I'd take whatever she could give me.

She rattled off numbers. I found a pencil and started writing them on a piece of newspaper that was on the table in the kitchen. The tip wasn't sharp. The numbers come out blurry. I hoped I'd be able to read them when it was time to start dialing.

J.J. JENKINS

A SHORT WOMAN came to the door. She was skinny. She looked frail. Her hair was straight and black. She had a line of silver roots down the part in the middle of her head. I didn't know what a whorehouse madam was supposed to look like, but this lady sure didn't look like one. She was like anyone else who would have been living in that neighborhood. She reminded me a little of my mother. Something in her face, I think.

"Rico?" she said. She was surprised. I tried to figure out if she looked nervous. I couldn't tell. She looked at Tony, then at me. She smiled at me, I think.

"Hi, Linda," Rico said. "We was in the area and wanted to stop by. You busy?"

"Not at all. Jimmy's at work. I'm just watching TV."

I exhaled a little too loudly. Rico and the woman both looked at me.

"Sorry," I said. "I think I had some bad fish earlier."

"Did you guys want to come in?" Linda said, directing the question to Rico.

"That'd be swell," Rico said. He stepped inside and turned back and shot me a look.

JOHNNY MESAGNE

I HAD A list of numbers along the blank edge of the newspaper. I wrote too fast. I had to squint a little to make all of them out. I looked at my watch. It was twenty after five.

I dialed the first number. The line clicked. Then came that far off sound of a long-distance call ringing.

"Hello?" It was a man's voice.

"Yeah, I'm looking for Linda Palinda. Does she live there?"

"Nope." He hung up before I could ask if he knew her or whatever. I thought about calling back. I decided to maybe do it if I didn't get nowhere with the other numbers.

I tried the next one. This time, it was a woman who answered. She said she wasn't Linda Palinda in Canton and she didn't know no Linda Palinda in Canton, but her ex-husband had a cousin in Canton and maybe his wife's name was Linda. She said she'd have to call her ex-husband to see if he knew the number. I decided it just made more sense to move on to the next one on the list.

J.J. JENKINS

RICO INTRODUCED US to Linda. I was a little surprised he gave our real names, but what did it matter?

She told the three of us to have a seat. I went to an easy chair. It probably was the spot where her husband watched TV. Tony took another chair. It looked like something a guest would use. He technically was one, so I guess it made sense. Rico plopped onto a couch near the entrance to the kitchen.

Linda stayed standing. She asked if we wanted her to make some coffee. Rico once again said that'd be swell. What was it with Rico and "swell" all of a sudden? I'd never heard him say it once, and now he says it twice in like a minute. Maybe, deep down, he was feeling a little nervous, too. Maybe no matter how many times a person does something like this, it never gets much easier.

"Honey, if you ain't feeling good, the bathroom's upstairs," she said to me. "You know, from the fish."

At first I didn't know what she was talking about. I probably looked surprised. "Oh, thanks," I said. "I feel better now. But thanks."

She smiled at the three of us and left the room. I could see her in the kitchen. I also could see Rico watch her leave.

Once she was out of the room, Rico pushed himself up. From where I was sitting, I could see Linda at the sink. Her back was turned to Rico. He began walking toward her, slowly. A feeling like panic rose inside me.

JOHNNY MESAGNE

I MADE IT through six of the Palinda numbers. No luck. For two of them, no one answered. I waited twelve full rings on each one before hanging up.

I looked at that paper again. Only two numbers was left. I decided to try the last one first.

Someone picked up during the second ring. But no one said nothing. It sounded like maybe somebody put a hand over the phone. I could hear sounds in the background, but they was muffled. It sounded maybe like someone was banging on something. I said "hello" a couple times, but still nobody said nothing. The line went dead, then the dial tone come back on.

I dialed that number again.

J.J. JENKINS

LINDA STAYED AT the sink. She was getting the pot ready for a fresh batch of coffee. I could hear the noise from the sink. The water pressure sounded high. It made it easier for Rico to sneak up behind her.

He was maybe three feet away when the phone on the wall rang.

She turned around to answer it. When she saw Rico there, she dropped the coffee pot onto the linoleum. It shattered. Glass exploded into the air. The way the pieces flew reminded me of a firework going off.

Rico snatched her by the neck with his right hand. I jumped up, but I stayed where I was. The phone started to ring again. He pulled the receiver off the wall and whacked her over the head with it, at least five times. She was knocked out.

In one motion, he swung the phone back onto the hook and then clamped his hands onto each side of her head. It looked like he was holding a grapefruit with a wig on top of it. Then he snapped her neck. I heard it crack. I threw up on the floor. He dropped her body onto all the pieces of glass.

Tony ran into the kitchen, for some reason.

"What did you do?" Tony said.

"What do you think I did?" Rico's nostrils were flaring. He was sweating. His eyes were crazy. A lot crazier than usual.

"She's dead?" Tony said.

"She's dead." Then the phone started to ring again. Tony flinched.

"Don't answer it," Rico said. "Let's go."

Tony looked at the body on the floor.

"What if she ain't dead?"

"She's dead," Rico said.

The phone rang again. Tony started looking around that kitchen. He saw a butcher's block with all of the knife handles sticking out of it. He grabbed one and turned around. For a second I thought he was going to stab Rico, or at least try to. The phone rang again. I felt myself hoping a little bit that Tony really would stab Rico.

Next thing I knew, Tony stuck that blade deep into Linda Palinda's chest. Blood squirted out, all the way to the ceiling. Somehow, it didn't get on either of them.

"What the fuck are you doing?" Rico said. The phone rang again.

"Making sure she's dead."

He grabbed Tony by the back of the shirt and threw him out of the kitchen. The phone rang again. Tony nearly fell onto the floor in the living room, near the spot where I'd puked. The knife went flying. It almost hit Rico as it went by his face. The phone rang again.

"Don't go running out of here," he said to us. "We'll walk. We're calm. We're easy. We get in the car and we go, like nothing happened."

Rico led the way. The phone rang again.

"Like this," Rico said, and he really did look like a guy who was walking through a grocery store looking for potatoes or tomatoes, not like a hitman who had just killed someone. He swung the front door open, and then he pushed the screen out. As we walked out, the phone rang again.

JOHNNY MESAGNE

I TRIED THE last one. A man answered. He said Linda Palinda didn't live there, but that his brother in Canton had a wife named Linda.

"Do you know his phone number?" I said.

"I don't know if I should just give it to anyone who calls up," the man said to me. "What's this all about?"

"I just need to talk to her. It's kind of important."

I could hear the man talking to somebody else. I couldn't make out what they was saying.

"Fine," the man said to me. "I guess it's OK. You ready?"

I grabbed the pencil and started writing. When I was done, I looked at the full list of numbers.

"Hello?" the man said to me. "Did you get that?"

I stared at the paper. I hung up the phone without saying anything else. I could hear him still talking as the receiver hit the cradle. I kept staring at that paper. I knew it was too late.

Seventy-one

OCTOBER 14, 1973

J.J. JENKINS

I JUST WANTED to get back home. But Rico said he was hungry. We knew not to resist him. He would have said he did all the work, so he should get to decide whether to pull off and eat.

We stopped in Cambridge, close to where Interstates 77 and 70 meet. There was a diner not far from the exit. The place smelled like new tires; I couldn't tell why. Rico ordered fried chicken. The sounds he made when he cracked the wings with the same hands he used to snap Linda Palinda's neck made me feel queasy all over again.

I didn't order anything. Tony got a plate of fries. I knew he did it so that Rico wouldn't be the only one at the table with food. Tony hardly ate any of them. Rico helped himself to the rest, pouring ketchup all over them. I tried not to look at the plate. I sat there with my mouth shut, waiting to leave. I eventually asked for a ginger ale. It didn't help.

I kept watching Rico. Something came over him when it was time to kill Linda Palinda. He was slowly coming back. I never wanted to see him make that change again. I figured it was just a matter of time before I did. Would I make the same change, whenever I got the order to do something more than just show up and watch?

When we finally got back to Bobby's place, Rico said he wanted to have a few beers and unwind. Tony said he'd join Rico. I just wanted to get away from them. I said I was tired, that I wanted to go to sleep. They were probably glad I left. I was about as much fun that night as a kidney stone.

The fun was just starting for me, even if I didn't know it. As I walked back to my new apartment, I didn't notice the car that was parked out front.

I went inside the building and up the steps. I had my head down. I stopped when I saw two shoes in front of me. I looked up, and there he was. The expression on his face answered any questions I would have asked him.

JOHNNY MESAGNE

I LOOKED AT the kid. He already seemed different. That's how it worked when you saw that happen to someone.

"I tried to keep you out of this, son," I said.

"I didn't know it would move so fast," he said.

I stood up on the step. "Let's go inside. You can show me your new place."

J.J. JENKINS

I TOOK OUT my keys and unlocked the door. It was brown. It had been touched up in spots with paint that didn't match the rest of it. I walked in. He followed me. Once he was inside, he started strolling around.

"Not bad," he said. It wasn't great, either. Empty, bare walls. Thin, rough carpet that hadn't been replaced in at least ten years, maybe twenty. Chairs and tables and a couch that looked like they'd been there since the building had been built, maybe seventy years earlier. A thin stained-glass window lined the side wall of the main room.

I felt sick again. I slipped into the bathroom and threw up, two or three times. I didn't have anything left to unload, but that didn't stop my body from trying.

"You ain't the first one to puke his guts up after something like that," he said to me.

"I can still hear the sound of it happening."

JOHNNY MESAGNE

I DIDN'T WANT to tell him the truth, that he'd never stop hearing the sound of it happening. Ever. I asked instead if his mother has been to the new place.

"Not yet," J.J. said. "She was going to come today, but I had to work."

"I know everything about your work today," I said. "I tried to stop it."

"How?"

"It don't matter. Obviously, it didn't work."

J.J. raised his hands. I saw that missing finger of his.

"I didn't do it," he said. "Rico did."

"Tell that one to a jury."

"I can't imagine ever being the one to actually do it."

"Tell that one to Paul," I said. "You know it's just a matter of time before the order is that you're the one painting the house."

"Well, maybe this isn't for me then."

"Maybe it's too late for that. Once you're in, you're in. Once you do a job like that, they can't let you out, because then they have to worry you'll turn rat."

"They let you out."

"I was what they call a special circumstance."

"Well, isn't this a special circumstance?" J.J. said. "I mean, I'm your kid. That should count for something."

"It's too complicated."

"It wasn't too complicated for you."

J.J. JENKINS

HE STARTED WALKING around the apartment. I could tell he was thinking of something.

"Remember," he said, "I still work for him. So I ain't really out."

"What if I work with you? That way, they don't have to worry about me, just like they don't have to worry about you."

"Is that really the life you want? Hanging around a bar and taking bets, pouring beers and smoking cigarettes all day?"

"It beats bagging groceries at Foodland."

"But you can be more than that, son. You can be better than that."

"Not if I can't get out."

He kept roaming around, looking at whatever. Thinking of whatever. He stopped. He stared at the stained-glass window. It showed the sun rising over a purple mountain.

"I got an idea," he said.

I waited for him to tell me what it was. I hoped I would like it.

Seventy-two

OCTOBER 15, 1973

J.J. JENKINS

I WAS EXHAUSTED in every way I could be, but I couldn't sleep. I hadn't set up the phone in my apartment. At least that kept me from being tempted to call her.

I still had a car. It was a few minutes after two o'clock. For more than an hour, I'd been staring at the stain on the ceiling from where the roof had leaked. I finally said, "Fuck it," and stood up.

I got dressed. I left the apartment as quietly as I could. I hadn't met any of my neighbors yet. I didn't want it to happen right after I woke up their families in the middle of the night. The steps creaked under my feet, but I couldn't do anything about that. I made it out the front door and headed for the Plymouth.

I drove back toward her house. There was a gas station not far from where she lived, right off the main road. I pulled in and parked. I walked to a phone booth. I pushed the door and stepped inside. I dropped a dime in the slot and dialed her number. I took my chances on Paul possibly being there.

The phone rang five times. Her voice was groggy when she answered.

"Hello?"

"Are you up?" I was whispering with a deep voice, for some reason.

"It's two-thirty," she said. "Who is this?"

"You know who it is."

"You can't come here."

"Are you up?"

"Do not come here," she said. She was now awake, and she seemed upset. "Where are you?"

I told her. She told me to get in the car and wait. She said she'd be there in fifteen minutes.

LESLIE FITZPATRICK

IT FELT LIKE I was still asleep. Like it was all a dream. Had he really called me? Thank God I was alone.

I pushed myself out of bed. It really had happened. I told him I'd meet him. I needed to go there before he showed up. I felt like everyone in the neighborhood had been looking through their windows at me. I don't know which one of them Paul had paid off. Maybe all of them.

I got myself dressed and left. I didn't really like the idea of starting the car that late. J.J. liked to joke about the engine, but that engine was just small enough to not wake anyone up.

J.J. JENKINS

I WAITED IN the Plymouth until I saw the headlights coming. The outline of the orange Beetle was unmistakable. As the car pulled in, I finally started to forget about what had happened in Canton.

I jumped out of my car and ran toward hers. I grabbed the handle on the passenger door while the Volkswagen was still moving. I yanked it open and threw myself inside. I kissed her. The engine was still running. I could tell she was surprised, but that ended fast. She gave in, grabbing the back of my head with one hand and wrapping the other around my chest.

"I missed you," I said.

She broke away from me. "We can't do this. You know what will happen."

"I don't care. Besides, I'm trying to get out."

"So what if you get out? You think that'll make it OK for me to two-time Paul?"

I laughed when she said that.

"You're right. You can't two-time the two-timer."

LESLIE FITZPATRICK

I PUSHED HIM away and crossed my arms.

"I should have stayed home," I said.

"If you didn't come here, I was coming there."

"You come to my house, and we're both dead. I think they have my neighbors watching me. Every time I look out the window now, I see eyes from other houses."

"Is there somewhere we can go?"

"You mean right now or for good?"

"I was thinking right now, but I sort of like the idea of going somewhere for good," he said.

"We'd have to go overseas. Anywhere in the country, he'd find us."

"Baloney. Who does he think he is, Al Capone?"

"You don't know him like I do," I said. "You get him pissed off enough about something, and he won't stop."

"So we leave the country."

"Sure. Fine. What languages do you speak?"

"They speak English in England, right? I can barely understand them on TV, but it's still English."

"OK, J.J. Let's just pack our suitcases and get all the money that we don't have and go to a place where we don't know anyone and have no jobs and no idea how to get jobs."

"It's funny. When the people from England sing songs on the radio, they sound just like us. But then when they talk, they sound like they're from another planet."

"Are you listening to me at all?" Leslie said. "Do you seriously think we can just run off to London?"

J.J. JENKINS

I WAS LISTENING to her. Was she listening to me? Maybe this was the right way to handle it. Take off. Disappear. Put all of this behind us. Start over, somewhere. It didn't have to be another country. Once we got far enough away, he'd give up trying to chase us.

"Let's figure it out later," I said to her. "What if we drive to my place and then I'll bring you back here after?"

"After what?"

"C'mon, Leslie. We're way past questions like that."

"We need to be smart," she said. "I only came here because there's no way you can come to my house. And if we leave one of our cars here for two or three hours, God knows who will see it."

"We can park your car somewhere else. We can hide it."

"Listen to yourself," she said. "We can sneak around like that for a while, but then we'll get too comfortable and make one false move and that's it, for you and for me."

"We can always be careful."

"It's easy to say it now. Eventually, one of us will let our guard down. It's better this way. At least until I can get him to end it with me."

"Well, when will that be?"

"I don't know. I'm trying."

"You need to try harder."

"Do you think this is easy for me?"

I could tell she was getting mad. I had an idea. I blurted it out.

"We're worried about him doing something to us. What if we do something to him?"

"Who do you think *you* are, Al Capone?"

"It would solve our problem."

LESLIE FITZPATRICK

How was I letting myself get mixed up with this stupid kid? He wanted to go after Paul? Good Lord.

"It would solve our problem because we'd both be dead," I said. "Vinny's with him everywhere he goes. So you'd have to be able to deal with them both. Trust me, J.J., you're not ready to deal with either one of them."

J.J. JENKINS

I couldn't argue with her about that, not after what I'd seen in Canton.

"So what do we do?" I said.

"Not a thing."

"You don't mean that."

"I mean it, J.J. What did you think would happen between us? I'm twenty-seven. You're twenty."

"I'll be twenty-one soon."

"And I'll be twenty-eight soon. Do you really want to be with someone seven years older than you?"

"I don't know why that matters."

"You can say that now, but it just doesn't make sense for anything but a fling. You don't want a wife that much older than you."

"How do you know what I want?"

"Well, maybe I don't want a husband that much younger than me. Did you ever think of that?"

"I still don't think any of that matters. I know how I feel when I'm with you. I think I know how you feel when you're with me."

"Unfortunately," she said, "life isn't that simple."

I sat there for a while, half stewing and half thinking.

"So what do we do?" I said.

"You get in your car and go home. Then I'm going to go home. Tomorrow, you'll start looking for someone who's closer to twenty than me. Maybe I'll get a chance at some point to start looking for someone who's closer to twenty-seven than you."

I sighed. I shook my head. What a shitty fucking day this had been.

Seventy-three

OCTOBER 15, 1973

JOHNNY MESAGNE

I PARKED OUTSIDE Paul's place on Monday morning. I was going to sit there for as long as it took for that Cadillac to show up. He was going to hear me out, no matter what.

Vinny pulled up just after nine. He stopped right by the front door. I got out of the Oldsmobile and walked toward the other car.

I could tell Vinny was surprised. He pushed the door open and jumped up. I didn't know he could move that fast, especially with those clown shoes. He stepped to keep me from getting to the back door.

"Well, if it ain't Mario Fucking Andretti," Vinny said.

"I want to talk to Paul."

"Maybe he don't want to talk to you."

"I need to talk to him." I tried to move around Vinny to catch Paul's eye.

"You need to calm down," Vinny said. "That stunt you pulled was not smart, Mesagne. Ditching me in the bar and jumping in the back seat with Paul? Peeling out and attracting all that attention? You're lucky things turned out the way they did."

"I'm guess I'm luckier than Linda Palinda," I said.

"Well, for now."

"Can't I just talk to Paul for a little bit? I only need five minutes. We had a good day yesterday. The 49ers covered. It was our best haul of the season."

"I should tell you to fuck off just to make a point. Get back in your car. You can sit there and wait. If Paul wants to talk to you, I'll come get you."

"What if he doesn't?"

"Then I guess you may be sitting there a while."

I went to the Oldsmobile. I waited. The sun rose up. My stomach started to growl. I had to piss. My feet were cramping. I got out and stretched. I checked my watch again. I'd been there for a couple hours. I got back in and rested my head against the window. I closed my eyes. Maybe I fell asleep, maybe I didn't. Next thing I knew, Vinny was banging on the glass.

"Let's go," he said. "You got five minutes. Clock starts now."

I got out of the car. I followed Vinny inside. He led me back to the office.

Paul was behind that desk of his, and Vinny stood off to the side. Paul nodded toward the empty chair. I sat in it.

"So you know what happened yesterday," Paul said. It didn't come out like a question.

"I do."

"That's the job. You know that as good as anyone."

"He's too young to be pulled in that deep."

"I think he's about the same age as you was when you got started."

"It was different then," I said.

"How was it different? Making your bones is what it's always been."

"We did it because we had to do it. He didn't need to do it. You didn't need him there."

"That's up to me," Paul said. "It's one of the best things about being in charge."

I looked at Vinny. He was there in case I made a move. I could tell he was hoping I'd be dumb enough to try.

"I want you to let him out," I said to Paul.

They both started laughing at me.

"You realize what you're asking for?" Paul said.

"I do. I should. I asked for it before."

That's when Paul stopped laughing.

"It was different then. Way different."

"Do you really think letting me out squared us?" I said. "After what you done?"

He looked at Vinny before looking back at me.

"You seemed to think so when I done it," Paul said.

"I didn't have no other choice. So now I'm asking you. Think back to what happened then, and ask yourself if it was fair to just let me out."

"If I done that with every deal I ever made, it's all I'd be doing. We done a deal. That deal was done. Six years ago. So forget about that. You want to ask me to let him out, you've got to come up with something better than a case of buyer's remorse from 1967."

"Maybe I can," I said.

Paul looked at Vinny again. They made faces at each other, like they thought what I said was interesting. Paul turned back to me.

"I'm listening," he said.

Seventy-four

OCTOBER 15, 1973

ONCE JOHNNY GOT back in his car, Vinny opened the door to let Paul out of the Cadillac. They went inside Paul's place. Vinny knew it was too early for Paul to be dealing with Johnny. But Vinny felt like it made sense for Paul to hear Johnny out. Vinny thought maybe it would help solve this other problem, one way or the other.

"What the fuck did he want?" Paul said to Vinny, after they were inside.

"He wants to talk to you. He says he only needs five minutes."

"Fuck him. He gets zero minutes."

"It's only five minutes," Vinny said. He flipped the light switches on. "He had a good day yesterday."

"It wasn't a good day when he decided to bum rush me." Paul said. He had a newspaper tucked under his arm. "I still don't understand how he gave you the slip."

"I told you he was behind the bar. He had a straight shot out the door. I had to weave through a bunch of guys."

"You should've thought about all that before you ever walked in."

"Well, I told him to wait out there," Vinny said. "If you decide to talk to him, I'll go get him."

"Let him sit there and rot."

Vinny had a paper bag in his hand containing the cassette that their people who were listening to Leslie's phone had made. Vinny had a tape player in there, too. He held up the brown sack.

"I got this thing. Looks like there was a couple of calls last night."

"Bring it back. Let's listen to it now."

They went to the office. Vinny put the bag on the desk. He opened it and took out the cassette player. The rectangular device felt thick and solid in his hands. There was a row of buttons at the bottom. There was a lid over the spot where the tape snapped in place. It said PANASONIC in big letters.

Vinny pulled out a tape with 10-14-73 written in black ink on the label above the two little wheels that turn to move the tape through the player. He pressed the eject button, and the lid opened. He slipped the tape inside, pressed rewind. It took about five seconds to get back to the start. After it did, Vinny pressed play.

The first call came from Leslie's mother. They talked and talked and talked and said not a damn thing. The second call came from Maria. She sounded half-drunk; she usually did. She kept asking Leslie over and over if she was OK and if she needed to talk about anything. She said something about going back to Stone & Thomas for lunch. *Who eats lunch inside a department store?* Vinny thought.

Then came the call that got their attention. They both leaned closer as it started, like they knew it was going to be something good before they heard any of it. It was Leslie and some guy. They couldn't tell who it was. He was whispering.

Hello? . . . Are you up? . . . It's two-thirty. Who is this? . . . You know who it is . . . You can't come here . . . Are you up? . . . Do not come here. Where are you? . . . The Texaco station, right when you get into Elm Grove . . . Get in your car. I'll come there. Give me fifteen minutes.

"That's our guy," Vinny said.

Paul told Vinny to play it again. He hit the rewind button for a second or two, then pressed play. It started just as that call was beginning.

"Who is that?" Paul said.

"It's our guy."

"I know it's our guy. But who is it?"

"He's talking too soft," Vinny said. "I wish he would've said his name."

"Well, that would make it easier to figure out who it is," Paul said, rolling his eyes.

"So what do we do with this?" Vinny said. "Do we find someone who can like figure out people's voices?"

"Play it again," Paul said.

They listened to it a third time.

"It's our guy," Paul said. "Now we just have to figure out who our guy is."

"I hate to say it," Vinny said. "But it may be time to lean on her. I can do it if you want."

"If anyone's going to talk to her about this," Paul said, "it'll be me." He pushed the eject button and removed the tape. He picked it up, staring at it. "I really wanted to figure this out without going after her. But we finally got a smoking gun. We just don't know who pulled the trigger."

"Then the next step is to find that out."

"I guess that's what I need to try to do," Paul said. He stuck the tape in the front pocket of his trousers.

Seventy-five

PAUL WAS WILLING to listen to my idea. That caught me off guard. I asked if I could piss first. I had to go, but I also wanted some time to get my head right, to make sure it all come out the way I wanted it to.

"You ain't old enough to have prostate troubles," Paul said.

"I been sitting out in my car for three hours."

Paul waved his hand at me. Vinny smiled, almost like he knew I was rattled a little bit. I walked down the hall to the bathroom. Same stained sink, same cracked urinal, same smelly toilet. I pissed in the bowl. Flushed it with my foot. I washed my hands. I saw myself in the mirror.

It'd been more than six years since I been in that same spot. I looked thinner. Maybe by twenty pounds. I had a few stray gray hairs deep in my eyebrows. I had a lot more over my ears. And there was more gray than I thought on top of my head. That bare light bulb shining down on top of my head didn't help hide none of it.

I was getting wrinkles under my eyes. I could see cords starting in my neck. I was getting old. I wondered how many truly good years I had left. I wondered whether I'd get to find out.

When I got back to the office, Paul was reading a newspaper. I noticed a tape recorder on the desk for the first time. I thought that was a little strange.

"If you took a shit," he said, "I hope you flushed twice."

"I said all I had to do was piss."

He closed the newspaper and pushed it away.

"So you've got me in suspense. What's your idea?"

"A trade."

"A trade? Like in baseball?" he laughed and turned to Vinny, who didn't react.

"I suppose you could say that," I said, smiling at Paul before turning serious. "Here it is. J.J. gets out. I get back in."

From the corner of my eye, I noticed Vinny go stiff.

"Bull-fucking-shit," Paul said.

"I mean it. I can still keep making book too, or you can find someone else. Whatever. Either way, I'll get back in."

It looked like Vinny wanted to say something. He didn't.

"Nobody's ever gotten back in after getting out," Paul said.

"Who ever got out other than me?" I said.

Paul sucked hard on his cigar. The end of it looked bright enough to cut through fog.

"I need to think about this," he said. "I need to talk to some people. Tell me this. Why? Was you thinking about getting back in, and this just gives you a way to bring it up?"

"Once I got out, I never thought twice about coming back. You may not believe that, and if you don't there ain't nothing I can say to make you. I'm just trying to come up with a way to get my kid out."

"So you don't want to do it, but you'll do it if it means getting your kid out?"

"That's my offer."

"What about five years from now, when you've had enough and you want out again?"

"I doubt anyone's getting out twice."

Paul sat back in his chair. His eyes got real narrow.

"So the kid wants out just because he saw what happened yesterday?"

"What other reason does he need?" I said. "He's twenty. He wasn't ready for it. It's that simple."

"I wasn't going to let him out. No way. But I sure as hell didn't expect this. Would you start your own crew, or what? I already got three guys."

"I'll do whatever you want. You want to knock me all the way down to the ground floor, I'll do it. I'll even take the kid's spot."

"Bobby used to work for you. I don't know how he'd feel about you working for him."

I looked at Vinny real quick. He seemed pissed. I liked that.

"He'll feel however you tell him to feel," I said to Paul. "Ain't that how it works?"

"You know how it works. I'll give you that." He looked at Vinny again and still got no reaction.

"Give me two days to kick it around," Paul said. "I want to see if any of the other bosses ever done something like this. I need to talk to Vinny, talk to Bobby. I probably should talk to Jerry and Cashews, too, because this will affect them." Paul took out his cigar and pointed the end that was in his mouth at me. "Until then, you say nothing to nobody. Especially not to your kid."

"Whatever you say," I said. "You're the boss."

I looked at Vinny again. I ain't no lip reader, but it wasn't hard to make out the two words he mouthed at me when Paul wasn't looking.

Seventy-six

OCTOBER 15, 1973

VINNY COULDN'T BELIEVE Johnny had offered to get back in. Vinny also couldn't believe Paul was thinking about letting Johnny do it.

The problem with the kid was going to end at some point. Vinny knew that. He just wanted it to go away before it distracted Paul enough to screw up the business. If Johnny got back in, that was a different issue, mainly for Vinny.

It was delicate. Paul needed good soldiers, people he could rely on. They needed to do what they were told. They also needed to know their place. Paul didn't have to worry about anyone on the outside. The real threats were going to come from the inside, if they came from anywhere.

Vinny wondered whether he was being a little selfish. Would Johnny be dumb enough to make a run at Paul? Would Johnny be dumb enough to make a run at Vinny? Maybe, Vinny thought, Johnny would be smart enough to pull it off.

Is that selfish? Vinny thought. Or is it protecting what he's got? Aren't they the same? Why does one sound bad and the other sound good?

Bad or good, Vinny didn't want Johnny back on the crew. Johnny was fine where he was. He wanted out, he got out. He needed to stay out. Vinny hoped he could push Paul that way without it being obvious. Vinny didn't need Paul thinking Johnny was any concern of Vinny's. Paul would find a way to use that against Vinny; he'd seen Paul do that with plenty of other guys.

Before Paul would figure out what to do about Johnny, Paul wanted to deal with the other thing. He had the tape in his pocket. Vinny knew what Paul wanted to do with it. Vinny hoped it would help Paul get the answer he was looking for, so that they could finally get all of it behind them. Maybe if it really was the kid, Vinny thought, they wouldn't have to worry about J.J. getting out. Or Johnny getting back in.

Vinny wasn't rooting one way or the other for J.J. to be the one who was messing with Leslie. But if it was J.J., and if J.J. ended up in Ohio, the other problem never would become one. So, yeah, Vinny hoped it *was* the kid. And it would be easier to help make Paul think it was J.J. than it would be to get Paul to not bring Johnny back.

Vinny drove Paul to Leslie's house in Elm Grove. He didn't call first. He said he wanted to catch her cold. That orange car of hers was under the carport. Vinny never knew why Paul bought her an orange car. Orange attracted way too much attention.

Paul got out of the back seat of the Cadillac. He had the sack with the tape recorder in it. He knocked on the door.

Vinny saw it swing open. He watched Paul walk inside.

LESLIE FITZPATRICK

I ALMOST DIDN'T answer the door. But there weren't many people it could have been. And whoever it was knew I was home, because my car was out there.

I looked through the window on the door. It was Paul. I tried to keep a normal expression on my face. I opened the door and stepped back. I think I managed to smile. He walked in without looking at me.

"It's two o'clock," he said. "You sick again?"

"I guess I slept in. I was up late."

"I know," he said. He had a bag. He started opening it.

"I'm not really hungry."

"It ain't food," he said. "I need you to hear something."

He had a tape player. I didn't know where this was going, but I had a feeling it wasn't going anywhere good. He put it on the table in the dining room. It landed hard and took a nick out of the finish. Any other time, I would have complained about that.

He dug a hand deep in his pocket. He pulled out a tape. He looked at it. He flipped it over. He pressed a button on the player. The lid popped up. He stuck the tape inside. The bad feeling I had was getting worse.

He pressed another button. The tape spun. He pressed another button and stepped back, like he'd just lit a cherry bomb.

I heard voices. I recognized my mother's. The other one didn't sound like me, but I knew from the words it was. The bastard had tapped my phone.

I was too nervous to be mad. I tried not to react. I tried to stay still. I tried to put on a look like I didn't care. *Maybe I should act like I'm mad*, I thought. I was too scared to think straight. I looked right at the tape player so he couldn't read my eyes.

The call from my mother ended. I could feel him staring at me. It felt like needles all over my face.

The second call started. It was Maria. I knew what the next call would be. That was why he was here. I tried to focus my thoughts on a plan. I couldn't.

Then it started.

Hello? . . . Are you up?

I stayed still when I heard J.J.'s voice, even if it really didn't sound like him.

It's two-thirty. Who is this?

You know who it is.

I tried to keep my eyes on the tape player. Paul was keeping his eyes on me. That feeling of needles turned to heat. I was mad at what he'd done, but being mad wasn't going to make this go any better.

You can't come here.

Are you up?

Do not come here. Where are you?

The Texaco station, right when you get into Elm Grove.

Get back in your car. I'll come there. Give me fifteen minutes.

Paul pressed another button and the tape stopped.

"Did you go?" he said.

"Nothing happened."

"Nothing happened this time. But it happened before, didn't it? It happened here. That day Mesagne was outside yelling and screaming. He was here."

I crossed my arms. I was still mad. I was having a hard time controlling it.

"I don't know what you're talking about," I said.

"Sure you don't," he said. "You know me enough to know I'm plenty of things. Stupid ain't one of them. You know exactly what I'm talking about. You're cheating on me. That's bad news for you. And worse news for him."

I still didn't have a plan. I decided to buy time until I came up with one. If I came up with one.

"I've got friends," I said. "You've got friends. Just because I've got friends doesn't mean I'm fucking them."

"You got quite a mouth on you," he said. He looked like he wanted to laugh at me.

"Sorry if you've never heard talk like that before."

"I heard plenty of it. I just don't expect to hear it from a woman."

"Well, it's the seventies. Women's liberation. Equal rights. If boys can talk like that, the girls can, too."

He took a step closer to me. I watched his hands. He put them in his pockets. I wondered what else he had in there.

"And if the boys can fuck around," he said, "the girls can, too. Right?"

"I'm not," I said. "That phone call doesn't prove anything, other than you tapped my phone."

He ignored what I was accusing him of. He was too busy doing the accusing.

"Regardless. Humor me. Who's your friend?"

I kept getting madder. It finally started to take over.

"Why? So you can whack him?"

His lips smiled but the rest of his face was dead serious. He started talking slowly.

"I'm just curious. If I got competition for your affections, I deserve to know who it is."

That was when I got too mad to hold any of it back.

"Bullshit!" I said. His head jerked a little bit. "I know how you deal with competition! You kill it!"

He stepped toward me. But he stayed calm. That scared me even more.

"I don't know where you're getting all these crazy ideas, Leslie. Do I get a little jealous? Who doesn't? I just want to know where I stand. I want to know what I'm up against."

"What does it matter? I've been up against your wife for six years."

He stopped smiling. His right hand came flying out of his pocket. He grabbed my arm. He squeezed it. Hard.

"I told you never to mention her."

"Well, if I can't talk about your wife, then there ain't no reason for us to talk about any friends I might have."

He squeezed even tighter.

"Who is it?"

"You're hurting me," I said.

He squeezed even tighter, and then he twisted my arm.

"If I decide to hurt you, it'll hurt a lot more than this."

I tried to ignore the pain.

"I'm not stupid. I know who you are. I know what you do to people."

He bent over and put his face right across from mine. I smelled his breath. It stunk.

"If you was still in school and this was a test, you'd be failing it. Bad."

And then came the closest thing I had to a plan, even if it was probably too late for one.

"If this is a test, then I've got a question for you. Who was the youngest person you ever rubbed out?"

That's when he laughed, right in my face. Little bits of his spit landed near my mouth.

"Rubbed out? You been watching too many Jimmy Cagney movies."

I held firm. What else could I do?

"Answer the question," I said.

"It's a stupid fucking question."

"Is it still a stupid question if I tell you I'm pregnant?"

He let go. His eyes scanned my face. I think he was trying to figure out if I was bluffing.

"This is a hell of a time to tell me that."

"I just found out on Friday."

He stepped back.

"When did you plan to tell me this?"

"I'm telling you right now."

He kept looking at me. Then, out of nowhere, he picked up the tape player. He held it for a second. I actually thought he was going to hit me with it. But he put it back in the bag. He closed it up. He turned around and walked to the front door.

"Where are you going?"

He turned back before he left.

"I'm going to talk to your doctor."

"You don't know who my doctor is."

"Sure I don't," he said.

Seventy-seven

OCTOBER 15, 1973

VINNY SAT IN the car, not knowing what to expect. He didn't hear any yelling or screaming. That didn't mean he wouldn't have to deal with whatever mess Paul might have left inside the house.

Paul carried the bag with the tape player in it. Vinny didn't make eye contact with him. He'd learn whatever he needed to know after Paul got back inside the Cadillac.

Paul opened the back door and climbed into his normal seat. He pulled the door shut, slamming it.

"Drive," Paul barked.

Vinny didn't say anything at first, waiting for Paul to talk. Vinny's curiosity eventually took over. He decided it wouldn't hurt to ask an obvious question.

"Did she tell you who it was?" Vinny said.

"Just fucking drive."

"Where am I driving to?"

"Take me back to the place," Paul said. "We need to find the tape from the day she called the doctor's office. You remember that one?"

"Last Tuesday, I think. Why?"

"We may need to go talk to that doctor."

Vinny knew right away that "we" meant him.

"When we get there, go see Mesagne," Paul said. "Tell him to come back. I think I got an answer for him."

"You do? Already? I thought you had people to talk to."

"Part of being the boss is getting to change your mind."

Vinny drove back to Paul's. They went to the office. Vinny got the tapes from a cigar box on a shelf in the closet. He brought it out to his desk, went through it. Vinny found the one labeled 10-9-73. He took the tape player out of the bag, and he replaced the tape that was inside it with the other one. He pressed play.

She had called Dr. Ronald McCoy's office. She asked for an appointment. She said she was having a lady issue. The woman who answered told her to be there on Friday at eleven.

"You know that guy?" Paul said. "McCoy?"

"I don't, but all these doctors and lawyers around here like to bet. I guarantee you he puts money with one of our guys."

"Go find out. No phone calls. Go see them one by one until you figure out where he's placing action. That'll make it easier to get him to cooperate."

Vinny didn't know what Paul was getting at with any of this.

"Is Leslie sick or something?"

"Something like that. Maybe. I don't know. That's what I'm trying to find out. Go get Mesagne. He can be the first one we ask about Doc McCoy."

"You OK to stay here if I go?"

"Lock the door. But I'm fine. I got a gun or two back here. I think I remember how to use them."

Vinny got in the Cadillac and went to get Johnny. Johnny seemed surprised and confused, but he didn't ask any questions.

Vinny didn't say anything on the way back. Johnny didn't say anything, either.

They went back to the office. Johnny sat in the same spot where he'd been earlier in the day. Vinny stood in his usual place. Johnny looked nervous. That made Vinny feel a little better.

Paul just stared at Johnny, fucking with him. That made Vinny feel a little better, too.

JOHNNY MESAGNE

"THAT WAS A fast two days," I said to Paul.

"I made my decision. Why should I wait?"

I just nodded. I looked over at Vinny. He wasn't showing anything.

"I'll let you back in," Paul said.

My jaw wanted to drop. I tried not to let it.

"Really?"

"Don't get too excited," Paul said. "I'm letting you back in. But I ain't letting the kid out. Not yet. I want to see how this works before doing that."

"So wait, I'm joining a crew with my kid? We're both going to be soldiers working for Bobby?"

"I'm putting you with Cashews," Paul said. "You'll still make book. But you'll have other stuff to do. Like I said, I want to see how it works."

"But that wasn't the deal," I said.

"It's the deal now," Paul said. "If you want it, fine. If you don't, no skin off my ass."

I looked at Vinny. That fucker who always has a stone face was suddenly all smiles.

"Can we talk man to man?" I said to Paul. "Just you and me."

Paul looked at Vinny. The smile went away fast. He shook his head.

"It'll be fine," Paul said. "Take a walk down the hall. We're all friends here. If Johnny was going to make a move, he wouldn't do it like this."

Vinny looked at me. He pointed his finger.

"You better not fuck around, Mesagne."

"I just want to talk to him, not to you."

Paul waited for Vinny's clown shoes to carry him out of the room.

"You want to talk," Paul said. "Start talking."

I leaned forward and talked quietly.

"I understand why you want to take your time. But I really want to get the kid out. Not later, now."

"I know you do. If everything goes like it should, he'll be out."

"When do you think it will be?"

"Whenever I think it's time. Could be a week. Could be a month."

"Could be a year," I said.

"Could be, I guess. I don't know. You know, it was a pretty big deal for me to let you out six years ago. That don't happen."

"I understand. But what happened before, that also don't happen. Or at least it ain't supposed to happen. Not under the rules that was told to me."

"You shouldn't have been messing around with her in the first place. She's related to you."

"By marriage," I said. "You know about that, right?"

"I know, I know. I hear it from her. I don't need to hear it from you, too. You mean to tell me you didn't have a piece on the side when you was married to Maria?"

"Nothing regular like that."

"Then you wasn't married long enough. Look, I know what happened was fucked up. That's why I let you out. It's also why I ain't never told no one the real reason."

"I haven't told no one, neither," Johnny said. "But some of these guys are smart enough to figure it out."

"You think too much of these guys. They're just smart enough to do what they're told. I ain't looking for much more than that. You was an exception there, too."

"If I didn't know no better, Paul, I'd think you just called me smart."

"You're smarter than most. And you ain't a bad negotiator. But there's one thing I have to know before I can accept your offer."

"What's that?"

"Whether your kid's the one that's been fucking Leslie, because there's a chance you're going to be a grandpa."

"You're paranoid."

"Maybe I was, but now I got reason to be. I got her on tape, talking to someone on the phone. I still don't know who it is, but I plan to find out."

"It ain't my kid."

"If it ain't your kid, why do you want him out?"

"I never wanted him in. I should have told you that at first. I had my chance. I blew it. That thing in Canton fucked him up. It's too late for me to change it. But I can try to keep him from having to do it again."

"He didn't do nothing. He was just there."

"That was enough. He'll never put that behind him. I just want him to not be there for another one. And I want to make sure he's never the one doing it."

"You also want to make sure it's never done to him."

"Why would it be, Paul? The kid ain't done nothing. He's a kid. He's my kid. Why can't we just turn the clock back a couple weeks and act like none of this ever happened?"

"A lot of people would still be here if they could turn the clock back on whatever they did that made them gone," Paul said.

I wasn't getting nowhere with him. I didn't want to push my luck. He was letting me back in. Hopefully he'd let J.J. out. Hopefully J.J. wasn't the one who called Leslie. Hopefully if he was, Paul would never figure that out.

My only other choice was to make a move on Paul. I wasn't wired to think that way. I wish I had been.

Seventy-eight

As VINNY DROVE Johnny back to his place, Johnny said Doctor McCoy wasn't one of his customers. Johnny said he wished he was. McCoy was the right kind of gambler. He liked doing it, not being very good at it didn't stop him from doing it, and he had the money to cover his losses.

Johnny said Doctor McCoy placed all of his bets with Freddie O'Shea. McCoy started using O'Shea because McCoy thought he was Irish.

After Vinny dropped Johnny off, Vinny drove to O'Shea's bar in Benwood. It was time to find out just how active McCoy's betting habits were.

JOHNNY MESAGNE

AFTER VINNY TOOK me back to the bar, I focused on getting through the rest of the day. Once I was done, I closed up and walked straight to J.J.'s apartment. I didn't worry about whether nobody was tailing me or watching me. I probably should have. I didn't even think about it. I wanted to talk to him as quick as I could.

He didn't know I was coming. He didn't have a phone yet. I probably wouldn't have called him anyway. I climbed the steps to his door and started knocking hard and fast.

"I'm coming, I'm coming," I heard him say. "Hang on a second."

I didn't stop. I kept banging until that door opened up.

J.J. JENKINS

HE HAD A weird look on his face. Whatever it was, it was pretty important.

"We really need to talk," he said.

JOHNNY MESAGNE

HE LOOKED SCARED. That was good. He needed to be scared. I sure as hell was.

"Have you broken it off with her?" I said after I got inside and closed the door.

"No," he said. "She broke it off with me."

"What did she say?"

"She told me to start looking for someone closer to my own age."

"Not bad advice," I said. "It also ain't bad advice to start looking for someone who ain't sleeping with the boss."

"We've been through this over and over. I don't like it. Maybe I was still going to do what I wanted to do. But if she doesn't want it, I'm not going to force it."

"Who knows what she's eventually going to want?"

"What do you mean? She told me what she wants."

"She ain't told you everything," I said. I sat down. I told J.J. he should, too.

"Whatever this is," he said, "I don't like it."

I decided to get on with it.

"I think she might be pregnant," I said.

VINNY PARKED THE Cadillac outside Freddie O'Shea's place on 6th and Main St. The Dolphins would be playing the Browns that night, and O'Shea had a decent crowd in his bar.

Things got quiet once Vinny walked in. And it wasn't because he was the only white man in the building. Vinny liked that people were afraid of him. That was half the battle. More than half, actually.

A path opened for Vinny as bodies moved out of the way. He walked back to where O'Shea was sitting. He was at a table playing Yahtzee for fifty-cent pieces.

O'Shea stopped when he saw Vinny coming. The other three guys playing with him fell silent and stared at him.

"We need to talk," Vinny said. "Two minutes. Tops."

O'Shea jumped up. He told two of the other guys to keep their eyes on the third one. He took Vinny to a storage room in the back. It was full of stuff he'd bought from Paul to sell to whoever wanted it.

"Good thing the Steelers finally lost yesterday," O'Shea said.

Vinny didn't waste any time. "Ronald McCoy. He's a doctor. Does he bet with you?"

"Yeah. All the time. Of all the problems I got, Doc McCoy sure ain't one of them."

"How much does he bet in a month?"

"I'd have to check the paperwork to be sure, but it's got to be at least a thousand. I'd say he usually loses at least seven-fifty of it."

"Thanks," Vinny said. He turned to leave.

"That's it?" O'Shea said. "I wish every meeting I had with you went so easy."

J.J. JENKINS

I WAS TRYING to process what he'd just told me.

"Did you hear what I said?"

"Yeah," I said. "Leslie may be pregnant. I guess the first question is whether it's mine or someone else's?"

"You mean yours or Paul's? Unless Leslie has been even busier than we know."

"You shouldn't talk about her like that," I said.

"I know her better than you realize. I know her better than you do."

"I'm not so sure about that."

"Maybe you should ask her. If she ever talks to you again."

"If she's pregnant with my kid," I said, "she'd better talk to me."

"It's not safe to talk to her now. Paul is still suspicious. If he ever puts two and two together, we got a lot bigger problem than Leslie being pregnant."

"So what do I do?" I said. "He'll be watching her even closer than before."

"I think he's got her phone tapped, too. So I wouldn't call her."

"Well, then there's nothing I can do but sit and wait for her to show up someday with a kid that has nine fingers."

My father jumped up from the chair.

"I got it!"

"You got what?"

"I think I know how to get you two in a place where you can talk."

Seventy-nine

BOBBY HAD TOLD Tony and Willie to come to the dog shop on Tuesday morning at nine. Bobby was glad to see them walking toward the entrance fifteen minutes early. He needed to know they would do exactly what they were told to do, with no mistakes or misunderstandings. Especially since he was preparing to give them something very important to do.

Bobby didn't know why it was important. But Paul had given the order. That automatically made it important. Bobby needed to show Paul that Bobby's people would listen.

Bobby had told Tommy to take the morning off, and not to ask why. Paul had told Bobby that only Tony and Willie should know about the job. Bobby checked to see if anyone was watching when he pulled the door open to let them in.

"Looks like we're the first ones," Tony said.

Bobby led them to the back, dogs barking again. The room on the other side of the door was dark, except for the light from the Marsh Wheeling Stogies clock on the wall.

"You're the only ones," Bobby said once they were all inside.

Tony turned to look at Willie, then Tony looked back at Bobby.

"What's this?" Tony said. "We get a job for ourselves?"

Bobby motioned for them to sit at the main table. They seemed proud of this development. Bobby took his usual chair. He spoke quietly and slowly. He wanted them to recognize how sensitive the subject was.

"We need to talk about J.J.," Bobby said. "And what we say don't never leave this room. Got it?"

They looked at each other. They looked back at Bobby. They nodded at the same time.

"Do you know if he's seeing anyone?" Bobby said.

They looked at each other again. They both opened their mouths at the same time. Tony was the first one to talk.

"We ain't really been around him much lately," Tony said. "Ever since that night Willie got shot and J.J. started getting work ahead of us, it's just been different."

"He acts like he's better than us," Willie said.

"Irregardless," Bobby said, "does he have a girlfriend? Or maybe somebody he's messing around with?"

They both shrugged.

"I don't know," Tony said.

"OK," Bobby said. "I'll be more clear. Have you heard or noticed anything about him and Leslie?"

"Paul's Leslie?" Willie said. "Who'd be dumb enough to go near her?"

Tony started rubbing his mustache. Little bits of food fell out of it.

"You know, that night we got back from Zanesville with the beer truck, I was picking up on something between those two," Tony said.

"What did you see?" Bobby asked.

"They was chummy," Tony said. "Flirty. Like I thought if she wadn't already Paul's, maybe something would happen with them. But then I remembered she's like a lot older than us."

"She's almost thirty," Willie said, his eyes bulging. "That's old."

"Did you notice anything else?" Bobby said to Tony.

"No, but I wasn't really looking for nothing. I never thought J.J. would mess around with Paul's woman. Is that what happened?"

"Again, none of this leaves here. Maybe he is. Maybe he ain't. If you guys can find out one way or the other, that'd be helpful."

"Why don't you just ask him?" Willie said.

"It ain't like he'll admit it," Tony said to Willie.

Bobby was relieved that they both weren't morons.

"He absolutely ain't admitting it to me or to no one else in charge," Bobby said. "Maybe he'll let it slip to one of you. He won't think you're trying to find out."

"If we ain't trying to find out," Willie said, "why are we asking him?"

Bobby rolled his eyes from Willie to Tony.

"I think they want us to poke around, without straight-out asking him," Tony said to Willie.

"Just see what you can find out," Bobby said.

"When do you need to know?" Tony said.

"As you soon as you can find out. There's some shit going on I don't really understand, but what I do understand is that people are trying to figure this out, and you two are the ones who know him better than the rest of us."

"Is he in trouble?" Willie said.

"Just let me know what you find out. Whether he's in trouble is something somebody else will have to figure out."

Bobby thought they seemed kind of happy when they heard J.J. might be in trouble. He wasn't surprised. J.J. had cut the line in front of them. If J.J. ended up out of the picture, they'd be right back where they had been. This prompted Bobby to be as clear as he could be.

"I don't want no exaggerations," Bobby said. "I just want to know what you find out. We can't be wrong about this."

Bobby believed they got the point. But he still thought they seemed to like the idea that J.J. could be in trouble.

Eighty

OCTOBER 16, 1973

VINNY STOOD ALONG Market Street. He checked his watch. It was exactly eight o'clock. He leaned against a building, pretending to read a newspaper. His lips were on a cigarette and his eyes were on the entrance to the Laconia Building. Doctor McCoy would be easy to spot: tall, with a thick head of red hair.

Five minutes later, McCoy was in view. Vinny folded up his newspaper and stuffed it in a trash can as he crossed the street. Vinny could see that McCoy was a big man in town, waving at people in their cars and speaking to everyone on the street. For a crook like Vinny who operated in the shadows, it was weird to see a crook who maneuvered in broad daylight.

McCoy stopped dead in his tracks when he saw Vinny coming. Vinny wasn't surprised. He knew how he looked. He knew what it did to people, whether they knew him or not. Vinny was someone you knew right away or prayed you didn't.

"Morning, Doc," Vinny said.

McCoy nodded and waited for Vinny to continue.

"Got a minute?"

"Inside," McCoy said, flipping his chin toward the building. He led the way. Vinny followed McCoy through the main door and across the lobby. He stopped about twenty feet past the elevators.

"I'm sorry, but do I know you?" McCoy said.

"No, but you may know my boss. His name is Paul Verbania."

McCoy took off his glasses and wiped them with a handkerchief. It had his initials on it.

"Fancy," Vinny said.

"Excuse me?"

"That's fancy. To have your initials on your hanky."

McCoy shoved the handkerchief into his pocket.

"It was a gift from my wife."

"It's good to have a wife," Vinny said.

"Yes," McCoy said. "It is."

"So do you know my boss?"

"I know the name."

"You should. You do plenty of business with one of his bookies."

McCoy put his glasses back on.

"I beg your pardon, but I have never failed to pay him. Not a single time, not a single penny."

"It ain't about that. You got a patient. Leslie Fitzpatrick. She's a friend of Paul's."

"This is highly irregular, sir."

"Well, Doc, placing a grand or so a month in illegal bets is highly irregular, too. So let's consider ourselves even in the highly irregular department."

McCoy leaned forward and watched the bodies coming through the main door. People were moving toward the elevators. Vinny could tell McCoy was nervous that somebody would see him talking to Vinny.

"What do you want from me?" McCoy said.

"I need to know something. Is she pregnant?"

"That's confidential information."

"I understand that," Vinny said, the words churning slowly through his mouth. "But is she pregnant?"

McCoy glanced at the front door again before looking back at Vinny.

"I know she's not married. Are you her boyfriend?"

"You're getting warm."

"Paul Verbania?"

"You're getting a lot warmer."

"I could get in real trouble for this."

"You could get in real trouble for gambling, too. It would be awful to see an article in the paper about a local doctor placing a grand a month in illegal bets. Especially when there's plenty of other doctors people could go to in this town."

McCoy stared at Vinny, who could tell McCoy was looking at the chunk of Vinny's nose that had been cut out. McCoy wanted to ask Vinny about it. McCoy should have been glad he didn't.

"OK," McCoy said. "Yes. She is."

"Do you know if it's Paul's?"

"Yes, if he's the only one she's had relations with. Does she have more than one partner?"

"Possibly. Maybe."

"Well, unless the other guy is anything other than white, there won't be any way to know whose it is."

"One more question," Vinny said. "How far along is she?"

"I'd have to check the chart. But I don't think she's very far along. A month at most."

Vinny stuck out his hand. McCoy hesitated before shaking it.

"Thanks, Doc," Vinny said. "You been a real help."

Eighty-one

OCTOBER 16, 1973

J.J. JENKINS

I STILL HADN'T set up the phone in my apartment. I needed to get that done. The calls to be wherever and whenever I needed to be could come at any time. It wasn't good enough to pop into Doggie Do-Rights a couple of times each day to see if they had any new work for me.

Before I could get around to getting a phone, I had to figure out how to see Leslie. My father said he'd come by on Tuesday afternoon to talk more about the plan for getting us in the same place. When the knock on the door came, I assumed it was him.

It wasn't. Tony and Willie were crowding the entrance. They each had a six-pack of beer. Tony had Schlitz, and Willie had Iron City.

"We brung you a housewarming gift," Tony said. He walked right in without me inviting them. He grabbed a bottle of beer and tossed it to me.

"Nothing says warm house like warm beer," I said.

"Shit," Tony said, "these ones ain't cold. Put them in your fridge. Willie got the cold ones."

"I do?" Willie said.

Tony reached for a beer from the container Willie was holding with his good arm. Tony wrapped a hand around one of the bottles.

"These ain't cold neither," Tony said. "Guess we need to go out and find some cold ones. How about it, J.J.?"

"I'm sort of waiting for someone."

"Oh really?" Willie said it slowly, drawing out the second word.

"It's not like that," I said.

"Why ain't it?" Tony said. "Ever since I got my own place, I need to put a revolving door on the bedroom."

"We're not all that blessed, Casanova." I headed for the kitchen with two six-packs of not-cold beer.

"Don't sell yourself short," Willie said from behind me. "Sure, Tony's the ladies' man. But you ain't so bad yourself. You got—what's that word, Tony?"

"Charisma," Tony said. "J.J.'s got charisma. Talks good. Knows what to say, when to say it, how to say it. The kind of thing the girls don't always notice, but the ladies love."

"Now that you got your own place," Willie said, "the ladies will be even more impressed. You know, the older ladies?"

I closed the refrigerator. When I turned back around, it felt like I caught the tail end of Tony giving Willie a dirty look.

"I've been too busy to chase skirts," I said.

"Sometimes the skirts chase you," Willie said.

"I guess," I said. "You know, if it's all the same, maybe we can get together later on."

"How about tonight?" Tony said. He was wandering around the main room, checking out the apartment.

"I'm thinking later on in the week," I said. "I have some things going on."

"Well, we got things going on, too," Willie said. It seemed like he was being defensive.

"I guess we all have things going on," I said.

Tony stood at the window, looking down at the street below.

"Willie's just a little sensitive," Tony said. "He thinks you're getting too big for your friends."

"Too big for my friends?" I said. "What's that supposed to mean?"

"It means that we brung you around," Willie said, "and now you're getting all sorts of work, and we ain't getting shit."

"Bring me around?" I said. "You took me to what was supposed to be some basic thing you guys were doing. Willie, you got shot. Tony killed a guy. That's how I got brought around. Besides, Tony's getting work. He just had a job the other day. Remember that one, Tony? Didn't we have some fun up in Canton, Tony?"

Tony turned, palms up. "I ain't trying to start no trouble. I'm just explaining why Willie's a little agitated."

"We're all a little agitated," I said. "It comes with the work."

Tony inched closer to me, studying my face. "You seem a little extra agitated. You could use a night out."

"Later this week," I said. I was trying to keep tabs on both of them. Something was making me leery. "We'll go out and have a good time."

"We can find us a gal or two," Willie said. "If you ain't already got one that's speaking for you, that is."

"I already told you I don't," I said. "Why are you two so interested in my love life all of a sudden?"

"Well," Tony said, "sometimes you hear things."

My back got stiff at that one.

"Like what? What are you hearing?"

Willie opened his mouth. Tony waved him off. He leaned toward me and whispered.

"There's some talk going around about you and Leslie," Tony said.

"Who's talking about that?" I said, not whispering back at Tony.

"It's just around," Tony said. "If I was you, I'd want to know. She's Paul's girl, after all. If he finds out, that wouldn't be good."

"Finds out what?" I said to him. "What's there to find out?"

"You tell me," Tony said. "I seen you that night after we knocked off the truck. You was using some of that charisma on her."

"It looks like I need to be clear on this, my good friends," I said.

"There's nothing going on between me and Leslie. And you should tell that to whoever sent you here to ask me about it."

"Whoa, hey," Willie said. He was trying to act insulted. He wasn't doing a very good job of it. "What kind of shit is this? We come to bring you some cold beer, well, it wasn't cold, but we brung you some beer and we make a gesture when you're acting like you're better than us, and this is what we get? Accusations?"

"I didn't start with the accusations," I said.

Tony stepped forward. He tried to put his hands on my shoulders. I stepped back from him.

"I'm sorry," Tony said. "We didn't mean nothing. We're your friends, your *gumbadi*. We'll be your friends even when you're one of the bosses and we're still taking the orders."

"Look, I have enough trouble without rumors about me and Leslie. If you guys hear any more talk like that, let me know. And make sure you say nothing's going on."

"Sure thing," Willie said. "Anyone asks, we'll tell them nothing's going on. But if anything's going on, you know you can trust us, right?"

"Sure," I said. "I trust you."

As soon as they were outside the apartment, I pushed the door shut and twisted the lock above the knob as hard as I could.

Eighty-two

MY DAD TOLD me to go through the service door and take the steps up to the fifth floor. I was supposed to meet the doctor early, before any of his employees showed up for work. I didn't think I was late. As soon as I saw him, he complained that I was. I said I was sorry.

Then he started into something about making a few harmless bets and getting caught up in Italian dramatics. He said *Eye*-talian. It always pissed my mother off when someone said it that way. He kept going on about sneaking someone into his place of business and coming up with a scheme for keeping his staff from knowing about it and letting an examination room be used for a visit of some sort, potentially conjugal.

I kept apologizing. I told him it wasn't my idea. I told him I didn't want to impose. I told him I appreciated the opportunity. I told him the visit would be short. I told him I wasn't entirely sure what conjugal meant, but that all we'd be doing was talking.

I'd been sitting alone in the room for nearly three hours. I'd get up, walk around, sit down. There was nothing to do. Nothing to read. There was an eye chart with a giant E on top and all the other letters below it, each row smaller than the one above it. There was a poster that showed the digestive system, all the way from the entrance to the exit.

The doctor told me that, if anyone came in, I was supposed to say I was his gardener and I'd injured my hand, which was making it hard to work. But no one had come in.

The door finally swung inside, just after ten o'clock. The doctor came in first. Leslie followed him. The doctor didn't say a word. He didn't even look at either of us. He just walked back out and closed the door.

LESLIE FITZPATRICK

I COULDN'T BELIEVE what I was seeing.

"I'm supposed to have an appointment with the doctor," I said to him. "What the hell are you doing here?"

"I'm the appointment. It was the only way we could talk. My dad thinks your phone is tapped."

"I know it's tapped. I feel like they're following me everywhere I go. They probably know I'm here."

"You've got a reason to be here. They don't know I'm here."

"Wait," I said. "How did you know I have a reason to be here?"

He looked away from me.

"I know what's going on," he said.

"Looks like good news travels fast."

"It doesn't matter how I know. I just know. I want you to know I know because I want you to have it. I want to help you take care of it."

J.J. JENKINS

TEARS FILLED HER eyes right away.

"You don't know if it's yours," she said.

I stepped toward her. I put my arms around her waist. I leaned down to look in her eyes.

"It's mine," I said. "I know it is. He wouldn't be trying so hard to find out who you've been seeing if it was his."

I hugged her. I pulled her body toward mine. She started crying. She buried her head in my shoulder. Pieces of her hair were tickling my neck.

"They said I've been pregnant less than a month," she said. "It's been at least two months since the last time with him."

"Does he know how long you've been pregnant?"

"I don't think so."

"So I'll be a father."

"I can't keep it, J.J. He won't want me to keep it, even if he doesn't think it's his."

"Who cares what he wants? It's not up to him."

She pulled herself away from me.

"He showed up at my house the other day with a tape of when you called me on Sunday night. He couldn't tell it was you, but he knew it was me. If I didn't tell him I was pregnant then, I don't know what he would have done to me."

"We need to figure something out," I said. "You need to have that baby."

"I need to do a lot of other things, too."

"Let's just get out of here. Leave all this behind."

LESLIE FITZPATRICK

I LIKED THE sound of it and hated the sound of it, both at the same time. But I knew that leaving would be a huge mistake.

"Snap out of that nonsense," I said to him. "We'd never be safe. No matter where we go."

"We'd be a hell of a lot safer than we are now. We'd have a chance.

It's a big world. He's got like twenty guys who work for him. Most of them are dumbasses."

"You can go," I said. "If he ever figures out this baby isn't his, you should already be gone. Eventually, he'll piece everything together."

"Tell me this," he said, "and tell me the truth. If it was just you and me and none of these other issues and you got pregnant, would you keep the baby?"

I felt more tears gathering when he said it.

"I don't know," I said.

"I do. So you're going to keep it. We're going to keep it. And if it means we have to get out of here for good, we're getting out of here for good."

J.J. JENKINS

THAT'S WHEN I told her about the plan my father and I had come up with for a fresh start. I told her to have a suitcase packed and ready. I told her that the time to go could come without much notice. I told her that she'd have to answer then and there whether she would come with me.

She listened to everything I said. She didn't say yes, but she also didn't say no. She got herself together after I finished talking. She left the room without asking me how I'd gotten there and how I'd be getting out.

After she was gone, I waited. Just like the doctor told me to do. About ten minutes later, he came back. He pretended to examine my hand. He led me out of the office. He was saying loudly that my wrist should be fine and that I'd be back to taking care of the lawn and the shrubs and the trees in no time at all.

I walked out through the waiting room. I went down the steps at the back entrance to the building. I walked straight back to my apartment. No one saw me.

SHELLY MATTHEWS HAD been working for Doctor McCoy for nearly fourteen years. She did her job. She kept to herself. She caused no problems in the office, for anyone.

She felt guilty about what she had done. But her husband said she had to do it. That it was extremely important. He emphasized the word *extremely*. She didn't know what would happen if she didn't do what he told her to do. She didn't want to find out.

She told herself she wasn't really doing anything wrong. It wasn't like it was a crime. At least, she didn't think it was. Her husband had given her a special phone number to call. He told her that whenever Leslie Fitzpatrick had an appointment, she was supposed to call that number right away. She was supposed to tell whoever answered the phone everything she had seen.

Shelly went to the break room. Doctor McCoy had put a phone there in case someone called the office while the girls were eating lunch. Shelly dialed the number. She told the person who answered that she had seen Doctor McCoy take Leslie to one of the rooms, without saying any names, like she'd been told. Just "him and "her."

She said it didn't look like he was actually in there with her for very long. Shelly said that, when she left, it looked like maybe she'd been crying.

Shelly was asked whether she saw anything after that. She said that he went back into the same room after she had left. That he had come out with another patient. Shelly said she didn't notice him go in. She said he was young. She said she heard him say the other guy was his gardener. She heard him say something about the gardener injuring one of his hands. She said she looked at the patient's hands. She said it looked like something was wrong with one of his fingers.

Eighty-three

OCTOBER 18, 1973

THE CALL CAME to the phone in the front room of Paul's place. He didn't like using the phone there for business. Vinny told Paul they didn't have any other choice. They couldn't sit in the car next to a payphone all day, every day, waiting for it to ring.

They'd gotten lucky. They knew a guy whose wife worked for Doctor McCoy. The guy knew to do what he was told. He knew the value of a favor. He also knew saying yes would be a lot better for him and his family than saying no.

Vinny answered the phone. He talked to her. After the call ended, he went back to the office. He told Paul what she had said. It wasn't verbatim, but it was close enough. The whole time, Paul sat there, chewing on a cigar and listening.

"So what do we think?" Vinny said.

"She said he injured a finger or was missing a finger?" Paul said.

"Injured a finger."

"That may not be enough," Paul said. "Do we lean on her, or do we lean on him?"

"What about both?" Vinny said.

"The problem with the rough stuff is they'll tell you whatever you want to hear in order to get you to stop. If I attach your nuts to a car battery long enough, you'd confess to killing Lincoln."

"I never killed Lincoln," Vinny said. "Kennedy, yes. Lincoln, no."

"We ain't getting any real answers that way. How real does the answer need to be? What's the test? What's the thing they do in court?"

"Beyond a reasonable doubt," Vinny said. "I still owe reasonable doubt a few rounds of drinks."

"Right," Paul said. "Beyond a reasonable doubt. How strong do we need to feel about it? Is it OK to think we know it's the kid, even if we ain't completely sure? Even if we never could be completely sure?"

Vinny realized this was his chance to put it all behind them. To get Paul focused on business again, and to keep Johnny out. Vinny asked himself if he felt bad, and told himself the days of feeling bad about what he did had ended a long time ago.

"You're the judge and the jury and the hangman," Vinny said. "So if you think it's enough, it's enough."

"Is it enough, though? What do we know at this point?"

"Well, we know—or at least we think—someone was in her house the night Johnny met us in the street."

"No, I know someone was in there that night. We also know the kid was at Bobby's then."

"We think he was," Vinny said. "We know someone called her the other night, and she went to meet him. We just can't make the voice."

"I wish we could make that fucking voice."

"We know she's about a month pregnant. Which I guess means it could be yours or whoever's."

"Right. The baby could be mine, or it could be his," Paul said. "Whoever he is."

"Should we bring the kid in and see what he says?"

"If we do that, we've got to be ready to finish the job. Otherwise, there's a good chance he runs. I don't want to chase him all across the country."

"We got the reach."

"But what do we say when people start wondering why we're tracking down some kid who ain't never done shit?" Paul said. "The more people know why we want him gone, the worse it makes me look."

Vinny was close to getting Paul to agree to just end it now. Vinny simply had to say the right thing, and maybe Paul would get there on his own.

"So because you don't want people to know what he did, we give him a pass?" Vinny said.

Paul looked at Vinny. "Maybe I'm thinking the opposite. Maybe the only way to contain this is to take care of it, now."

Vinny didn't respond right away. He wanted Paul to be sure. He wanted Paul to think it was his decision and that Vinny didn't have anything to do with it.

"So this one ends up in Ohio?" Vinny eventually asked Paul.

"No message needs to be sent on something like this. It just needs to be over and done and gone."

"Who do we give it to?"

"He did that thing in Canton with Rico and that new kid, right? We'll say they're doing another job like that in Cadiz. The kid will think it's all normal. Rico and the new kid can handle it right at the place. Dig the hole. Put him in it. Case closed."

"Can we trust this other kid?"

"From what I hear from Bobby, it sounds like him and his friend, the one that got shot, would like to have the other one out of the way. Besides, if he does anything to show he can't be trusted, there's plenty of open land in Ohio. He can have the spot right next to his friend."

Vinny kept quiet after that. It was Paul's decision. Paul needed to think that. He didn't need to think Vinny cared about it, one way or the other. Then Vinny decided it was time to keep talking.

"When does this happen?" he said.

"Work with Bobby to come up with a story about who they're taking care of. Then get Rico and the kid in there so Bobby can explain it. Then have Bobby meet with all three of them and give the assignment. What's today?"

"Thursday."

"See Bobby tonight. Have him meet with the other two on Friday night, and then do it all on Saturday afternoon."

"Saturday afternoon it is," Vinny said. He was feeling pretty good about how it all had happened, because it meant it was all going to be over, soon. Vinny still threw in a little extra to make it look like it was all Paul's idea. "You're sure about all of this?"

"I'm as sure as I'll ever be."

"Is that sure enough?" Vinny knew he was taking a chance when he said it, but he also knew Paul well enough to know he was past the point of no return.

"I ain't completely sure it is, but it's time to put this behind us," Paul said.

That was the best news Vinny had gotten in weeks. The kid goes away. Johnny doesn't get back in. Life goes back to normal.

As long as Rico and the kid take care of their end. There wasn't any reason why they shouldn't. Two of them against a guy who didn't know what was coming. That should be the easiest part of solving their problem.

Eighty-four

JOHNNY MESAGNE

I NEEDED TO talk it all through with J.J., but things was getting too hot for that. Vinny started coming by every day, more than once. Just popping in, looking around, and leaving. When I'd walk from my apartment to the bar, I felt like I was being watched. When I'd walk from the bar back to my apartment, I'd feel it again. There was no safe place to meet J.J., not in Wheeling.

Maybe I was worrying too much. But I'd rather worry too much than not worry enough.

It wasn't like we could meet in one of the other towns around Wheeling. I had to figure Paul had eyes everyplace. Whenever he really wanted to, he did. Hell, I wasn't even sure how to get word to J.J. about where to meet.

It just kind of come to me on Friday morning. I was behind the bar. Jimmy Dacey was sitting there, sipping on a beer and not worrying about no one telling him it was too early to be sipping on a beer, even though it probably was.

"You want to do me a favor?" I said.

"Sure," he said, without even asking what it was. I probably shouldn't have put him in that spot.

I sent him to J.J.'s apartment. I knew no one would follow him, even if someone was following me. I hoped that whoever was watching J.J. wouldn't make Jimmy. Vinny would have been the only one to know Jimmy to see him. I figured it was someone from one of the other crews watching J.J.'s place, if anybody was.

I told Jimmy what to tell J.J.: where to meet me, what he needed to do to spot a tail, and then how to shake it. I figured we was driving far enough away that nobody would track him that far. I knew how to get away from somebody following me before they figured out I was leaving town. I wasn't worried about two different tails thinking me and J.J. was heading for the same place.

When Jimmy got back, he said J.J. was surprised when Jimmy said where we was meeting. But J.J. told Jimmy he'd be there.

I got to the diner at about seven o'clock. Yeah, I drove all the way to Columbus. It was the only place I felt safe about seeing him. J.J. was supposed to get there at half past seven. I waited for a booth to free up back near the door to the kitchen, so I could sit there and watch the rest of the place. I ordered a beer and some onion rings while I waited. I watched everybody who come in. I figured after about fifteen minutes that we'd be OK talking there.

I drank the beer. I drank another. I switched to cigarettes after the onion rings was gone. I told the waitress we'd order more food after my boy showed up. She asked how old he was. She smiled at me and said I looked too young to have a kid that old. I kind of wished for a second or two that I wasn't going back to Wheeling that night. Then again, they work for tips.

He was late. I tried not to worry too much about that. He was going to a new place for the first time. He'd have to find a place to park. He'd have to figure out where he was going. I asked the waitress for a cup of coffee. I smoked a couple more cigarettes. It was close to eight when he finally come through the door. I was relieved. I saw him looking around. I waved real quick. He saw me and come back to the booth and sat down on the other side.

"I was starting to think you wasn't showing up," I said.

"I told your friend I'd be here."

I didn't want to lecture him about being late. I was just glad he made it.

"I guess I'm just nervous," I said.

"I'd say you're nervous. This is a long way from home for us to meet."

"We need to be extra careful," I said.

"I know. I didn't know it before, but I do now. Besides, you're not the one who might be wearing cement shoes at the bottom of the river."

"Well, if they find out what we're up to, we'll both be sleeping on either side of the same fish."

"Why are you sticking your neck out?" he said. "I appreciate it and all, but why are you doing it, especially when I made this mess on my own?"

I finished the cup of coffee in one drink.

"I got plenty of shit to make up for. This may not get me all the way there, but it's a start."

J.J. JENKINS

HE HAD A pack of cigarettes on the table. I never really smoked much, but I thought maybe it would calm me down a little bit. From the minute that old man had told me my father wanted to meet me two hours away from home, I hadn't felt right. Things were moving toward something big. The best outcome for me at this point would be driving away and starting a new life somewhere else. And the worst outcome was I wouldn't get a chance to.

A waitress came over. I could tell he had already been charming her. We ordered some dinner. She brought more coffee for both of us. He wanted to let me eat before telling me whatever he'd brought me there to tell me.

The food helped. I calmed down. I didn't realize how hungry I was until I started eating. I ate too fast, like I always did. He went slow. He watched me. I waited for him to be ready to say whatever it was he needed to say.

When my food was gone, he started talking.

JOHNNY MESAGNE

I TOLD HIM exactly where he'd be going. I told him I knew people there, that I'd set it all up. The time difference made it easier. Thursday night after I got back from the bar, I told the old lady downstairs from me that my phone was on the fritz. I asked if I could make some calls from hers. I gave her a hundred bucks. She didn't know what to say other than thank you. She sat in the other room with the TV turned up so loud that she didn't hear nothing I was saying.

I had to call in a bunch of favors to make it work. I probably owed a few more after I was done. I was fine with that. It was the only way to get him out of town, the only way to give him a decent chance. I got a place lined up for him, big enough for Leslie and the baby, if she decided to go. I had a job ready for him, too. I told him everything. I had names and numbers on a piece of paper for him. He just sat there and listened. I think he was amazed I done it all. I was a little amazed, too.

Then we talked about Maria. I told him if Leslie went, Maria should go, too. I hadn't said nothing to her about it, but I wouldn't have to tell her to go. I wouldn't even have to ask. Once I told her why I was doing it, she'd insist. I didn't know how he'd feel about his mother living with Leslie and him. He didn't say nothing about it, so I figured he was OK with it.

I told him he should be ready to go on Sunday morning. With college football games going on and guys maybe hung over from Saturday night, he'd be long gone before anybody noticed. He'd gas up the Plymouth. He'd go to Leslie's. He'd tell her it was time to go. And either she would or she wouldn't. If she said yes, they'd pick up Maria and take off. Was it a perfect plan? No. But it was the best one I could come up with.

J.J. JENKINS

I SAT THERE listening to everything he said. I was trying to process all of it. There were some flaws in it, some calculated risks. But as it all settled in, I knew it was the only way out.

"This is all happening really fast," I said.

"If it don't happen fast, it might not happen at all," he said. "Truth be told, it might not be a bad idea for you to just keep going right now."

"But she's not with me."

"She might not be with you on Sunday, either."

"I have to take that chance."

"I just hope you get to."

"What does that mean?"

"I think you know," Johnny said. "Before we get to Sunday morning, we need to get through Saturday."

"Why don't I just leave tomorrow morning?"

"Because I got one more move I might make. If it works, there's a chance maybe you don't have to go at all."

I perked up when he said it. I didn't expect to hear that, not after he spelled out exactly what needed to happen. I tried to get him to tell me what he was talking about, but he wouldn't.

The waitress brought the bill. He put two twenties on the table as we got up to leave. I'd never known him to be so generous. Then again, I guess I hadn't really known him very well at all.

JOHNNY MESAGNE

I LOOKED AROUND the place before we walked out. I was sure we was fine. And we was. At least for right then.

Out on the sidewalk, he kept asking me how there was a way he might not have to go. I told him not to worry about it. If it came to that, it would all make sense. I just told him to be ready to go on Sunday morning at eight o'clock, unless he heard otherwise.

Like I told him, the plan wasn't perfect. The thing I was thinking about doing could make it closer to perfect. At least I had a couple hours in the car on the way home to figure that part of it out.

The other thing I knew was that, no matter what your plan is, plenty of shit can happen to change it.

Eighty-five

BOBBY SAT DOWN at the table in the back room of Doggie Do-Rights. Rico sat to one side of Bobby, Tony to the other. Bobby lit a cigarette. He took a long drag and blew out the smoke. Rico knew Bobby well enough to expect to hear something important. Tony had no idea what he was about to find out. Bobby didn't know if Tony was up to it. But Tony would have no choice. Bobby had no choice, either.

It was a big deal. It involved one of their own. That didn't occur very often. Bobby still wasn't sure why it was happening. But it wasn't for Bobby to ask questions. He had a job to do. He just needed to do it.

Bobby told them they'd be back there the next day, and that J.J. would be with them. Bobby said he'd be giving them the address of a guy in Cadiz who needed to go away for good. The guy's name was Pete Pucillo. They called him Pierogie. Bobby said he'd tell them the guy had been to one of Paul's whorehouses, and that he'd beaten up one of the girls who worked there. That she had to go to the hospital for a week. That they'd gotten the nod from Pierogie's people in Cleveland to make a move. That when the guy left his place, they'd grab him and take care of him.

Bobby told them they were really going there to take care of J.J. They'd put him in the place in Cadiz where guys often go away. Tony

347

would pretend to be lost while looking for Pierogie's house. Rico would pretend to get mad at Tony. Rico and Tony would act like they were arguing. They'd end up fighting. They'd wrestle outside the car. When J.J. came out to try to break it up, Rico would shoot J.J. They'd dig a hole in the place where they'd dug plenty of holes over the years. And that would be that. They'd never talk about it again to no one, no matter what.

They didn't ask Bobby any questions. Rico knew the drill. Tony was simply speechless.

Bobby kept looking at Tony, who just sat there, nodding.

Bobby told them people would start asking about J.J. They needed to act like they didn't know anything about where J.J. was. They were supposed to pretend to be as confused as everybody else. Gradually, they'd put out the word that maybe J.J. had just moved away.

Bobby told them, mainly so Tony would understand, that before too long people would just quit asking, and everything would be normal again. Bobby said, again for Tony's benefit, that they should never get into any talk about why J.J. would have left. Maybe he went back to college. Maybe he just wanted to go live somewhere else. They didn't know. Nobody knew. Bobby also made sure Rico and Tony knew that if anybody started saying that it possibly had something to do with Leslie, they should say it was bullshit and change the subject.

Bobby could count on Rico, but he'd have to keep an eye on Tony. Bobby hoped Tony was smart enough to know that, if he didn't do what he'd been told to do, he'd end up in the exact same place as his friend.

Eighty-six

J.J. JENKINS

WHEN I GOT back from Columbus, I pushed the door in. There was something on the floor. It was a piece of paper, folded over twice. I picked it up and opened it.

Four oklok tomaro. And get your fuckn fone hookd up!

That was all I needed, a job on Saturday. One day before I was leaving for good.

I spent the rest of the night wondering what I'd be asked to do on Saturday at four *oklok*. I kept thinking about it while packing my things for the trip.

I had one suitcase. I put everything into two piles. Things I would take, things I would leave. I went through everything I had. I filled the suitcase. I left clothes for the next day. I'd just wear the same stuff on Sunday.

Hopefully, Leslie would be able to get her things in one suitcase. If my mother decided to join us, three suitcases would probably fit in the trunk. We could put one in the backseat, if we had to.

I thought about where we'd be going. Or maybe where I'd be going alone. I'd never been there before. I'd never even heard of the town.

Yes, life was about to change in a very significant and permanent way. Unless whatever my father was talking about ended up happening.

He was taking a real risk for me. I knew that. I appreciated it. I thought of the compass he'd given me. I'd treated it like a joke for ten years. I was feeling differently about it.

I started looking for it. I couldn't remember where I'd last seen it. I checked the pockets of the suitcase. I emptied it out and looked through everything I'd packed.

It wasn't there. I needed to find it before I left. I decided to go back to the house and look for it on Saturday night, after whatever it was they were going to tell me to do.

But before I went to Doggie Do-Rights on Saturday afternoon, I needed to let my father know about my new assignment.

Eighty-seven

OCTOBER 20, 1973

J.J. JENKINS

I SET THE travel alarm for six o'clock Saturday morning. When it went off, I had that feeling of not knowing where I was, of not realizing what was going on. Some days, that's a pretty nice feeling.

I needed to tell my father about the meeting. I wanted to call his apartment. They had a payphone on the wall outside Neely's Market. He'd said something about phones being tapped. I'd have to be careful with what I said and how I said it.

I counted out the change I had in my jeans. Two quarters, five dimes, two nickels, four pennies. I threw the pennies onto the carpet and put the rest of the coins back in the front pocket.

It was cold outside. There was a light rain, pretty much a mist. I looked around to make sure no one was watching me.

I made the walk to Neely's. A phone book hung from a rusty chain, below the payphone. I looked for *J Mesagne*. Nothing there. I dropped a dime in the slot and called the operator. She said that if there was a John Mesagne in Wheeling, he either had an unlisted number or he didn't have a phone.

The rain was coming down a little harder. I checked behind me, to be sure no one was looking my way. I put another dime in the slot and dialed.

My mother answered after seven rings. I apologized for waking her up. She snapped out of it when she realized it was me. I asked her if she had the phone number for his apartment.

"Why do you need to call him?" she said.

"I just need to ask him something."

"At six-thirty in the morning? Something's going on, J.J. I want to know what's going on."

"Nothing's going on. I just have to ask him something."

"You tell me what it is," she said, "and I'll call him and get the answer for you."

"I'm not doing that. Please, give me the number. If I don't get it, I'll just drive over there and knock on the door."

"He won't like you waking him up before nine."

"Then isn't it better if I do it by phone?"

She didn't have an answer for that. She told me the number. She said it again to make sure I had it right. I thanked her, and I told her I'd see her tomorrow. She wanted to know what was going on tomorrow. I said, "Nothing, I'm just going to come see you." I hung up before I said something else I shouldn't say.

I put in another dime. I dialed the number. I let it keep going past eight rings. After twelve, I heard someone pick it up. His voice was gravelly.

"It's me," I said. I tried to make my voice sound different, deeper.

"Who's me?"

"Me. The guy from last night."

"Don't say no more," he said. "Give me the number where you are."

I looked at the dial. I told him. I hung up and waited.

I assumed he'd be calling back. I stood there in the rain, waiting. About ten minutes later, the phone rang. I grabbed it.

"Hello?"

"This line is safe," he said. "What's going on?"

"There's a meeting today."

"Where?"

"The dog shop."

"When?"

"Four."

"What for?"

"Don't know."

"Could be something. Could be nothing. Could be anything."

"That really narrows it down," I said.

"Smartass."

"What should I do?"

"Are you packed?"

"I packed last night. Should we move everything up a day?"

"Well, I haven't talked to your mother yet."

"She can come later, if Leslie goes."

"I think you need to see what it is. If it's nothing, you stick to the plan."

"What if it's something?"

"If it's something," Johnny said, "I'll figure something out."

"That's easy for you to say. You're not the one who may end up on the wrong side of something."

"I think I know what we need to do here. Do you trust me?"

"Let's see. Guy who walked out the door when I was ten and never looked back. Sure, I trust him."

"I'd like to think I've done a few things lately to change that."

"I'll give you that one," I said. "But it will probably take a little more than a few things to make up for what happened."

"Well," he said, "that's what I'm trying to do. To do it, I need you to trust me on this one thing."

I decided to trust him, and to resist a very strong and sudden urge to just pack up my car and leave.

Eighty-eight

OCTOBER 20, 1973

J.J. JENKINS

YEP, I SHOULD have just left.

I suppose they thought we did a good job in Canton. Six days later, we were heading to Cadiz to take care of someone else. This one was going to be buried, apparently wherever they planted their bodies. I realized I'd literally know where the bodies were buried. I didn't want to.

Tony drove again. Rico rode shotgun again. I was stuck in the back, again. This time, the car was an AMC Gremlin. It wasn't quite orange and it wasn't quite yellow and it wasn't quite big enough to carry the three of us.

"We need a nickname," Tony said. "Two jobs in less than a week. Same three guys. Maybe we keep doing it over and over again."

"One was enough for me," I said, fighting to get comfortable in the car.

"What should our nickname be?" Tony asked Rico.

"Just drive the car," Rico said.

"That ain't very catchy," Tony said.

"What?" Rico said.

"Look, I'm just trying to make some conversation," Tony said. He seemed nervous, and that he was dealing with his nerves by talking.

"Sometimes," Rico said, "the best conversation's no conversation."

He put the back of his head against the top of the seat and closed his eyes. Tony looked at me in the rearview mirror.

"This one'll be a little different from the last one," Tony said.

Rico's eyes shot open.

"What the fuck did I just say?"

"What? I thought you said you didn't want to talk to me. I didn't know you didn't want me talking to J.J."

"Let's just stop talking," Rico said. "This ain't that long of a drive. I need my energy, because I got a feeling I'll be doing all the work again. Unless you plan on doing something more than stabbing the guy after he's already dead."

The words made me shiver. I pulled my knees up to my chin. They were almost there anyway. I looked out the window, at the trees. The leaves were coming down. They'd be bare until spring. I tried not to wonder where I would be then.

We got closer to Cadiz. I kept telling myself I should have just left. With or without Leslie, I should have just left. I wasn't paying attention to the road signs. I didn't notice the exit Tony took. Same as in Canton, Rico had the directions. Cadiz. I'd never been there before. I'd probably never be back again. I just hoped I'd be anywhere after today.

Rico kept telling Tony where to go.

"Go right here . . . Take a left up there . . . Get in the other lane."

It looked like we'd made it through downtown. We were getting close to a place called the Harrison County Fairgrounds.

"Where does this guy live?" I said.

"I think we're getting close," Rico said.

There were fewer and fewer houses. Eventually, there were none. My hands were starting to shake a little bit.

"I thought the guy lived in a neighborhood," I said.

"He does," Rico said. "I think someone got us lost."

"I just did what you told me to do," Tony said.

A sign said we were entering Sally Buffalo Park.

"If you did what I told you to do," Rico said, "we'd be at the guy's house right now."

"J.J.'s my witness," Tony said. "You tell me turn left, I turn left. You tell me turn right, I turn right. J.J., didn't I do everything he told me to do?"

"It doesn't matter," I said. "If we're lost, we're lost. Let's just turn around."

"Hey," Rico said to Tony. "Remember when you was trying to think of a nickname? I got one for you. How about dipshit?"

Tony told Rico to go fuck himself. Then Rico hauled off and punched Tony in the side of the head. Tony jerked the steering wheel to the left. The car spun around and stopped.

"Get out," Rico said to Tony.

"What?" Tony said.

"You heard me. Get the fuck out of the car. Now."

I waited for both of them to get out. I thought about climbing into the driver's seat and taking off once they were both gone. I should have.

Eighty-nine

JOHNNY MESAGNE

I COULDN'T REMEMBER the last time Maria was in my car. It had to be just before I moved out. So it was more than ten years ago, right after I bought the thing.

She packed fast once I told her what was happening. She didn't think twice about it. She was going with J.J. and Leslie, if Leslie actually went. We'd find out soon enough.

"I still don't understand why we have to go right now," she said.

"You still may not be going anywhere," I said. "It all depends on whether Leslie is willing to go."

"So J.J. is just going to go by himself, if she doesn't go?"

"Leslie is having our grandchild. You need to be wherever she is."

"We're just going to show up at her house and tell her she's packing up to leave for Arizona for good, out of the blue on a Saturday afternoon?"

I checked the rearview mirror to make sure no one was tailing me.

"She knows it may be happening," I said. "But I'm pretty sure she's expecting the news to come from J.J., not from his parents."

"This is fucking insane," she said.

"You don't have to go," I said. "You could've just told me you don't want to go."

"I can't let her go all that way by herself. Especially if she's pregnant."

"Then you made your choice. We'll find out what choice she makes."

I stopped the Oldsmobile in the street, in front of Leslie's house. Her Volkswagen was under the carport. I got out with the engine still running.

"You're just going to leave the car like this?" Maria said.

"I won't be long. She knows to have her stuff ready, if she's going."

I walked toward the house. I had no idea what she was going to do. I looked around to see if anyone was watching. I didn't see nothing.

I stepped up onto the porch and opened the screen. The door behind it flew open. She marched right past me, lugging a suitcase.

"Pull that door shut, will you?" she said.

I just looked at her, surprised she was ready to go so fast.

"Are we going or not?" she said.

She started walking to the Oldsmobile before I could say anything. She opened the back door and stuffed her suitcase inside. Then she turned to look at me, hands on her hips.

"You came to get me, right? I don't know where J.J. is. I'm guessing Maria will tell me, if she knows."

I didn't know what to say. I just nodded at her.

She put her hands in one of the pockets of her jeans. She pulled out a set of keys and threw them to me, underhanded.

"Here," she said. "We'll take your car. You just got yourself a free Volkswagen."

I caught the keys with my left hand.

"Maria knows where we're going?" Leslie said.

I nodded again. She got into the front seat and shut the door. The next thing I knew, they was gone.

It was just me and that orange piece of shit. I got in. I started it up. It chugged like a train with a clogged stack. I figured out how to get it in reverse. I backed down the driveway. I pushed that stick on the floor into gear. I pulled away.

Before the car started rolling, I checked my watch. I had three hours.

Ninety

J.J. JENKINS

"I DON'T WANT to get out of the car," Tony said. He held the steering wheel with both hands. One was at eleven o'clock and the other was at one. He had his elbows pressed against the bottom of it.

Rico had exploded out of the passenger side. He left the door wide open. He ran around the front of the Gremlin. After the spinout, the car was facing the direction we'd come from. Rico's feet were slipping in the dirt as he tried to get to Tony.

Once Rico made it to the other side of the car, he yanked the door open. He put a hand on Tony's neck and ripped him out of the car. Rico pulled so hard that he tumbled backward onto the ground. Tony fell toward Rico. Rico lifted with his feet and pushed up, sending Tony through the air. I couldn't tell whether I was watching the circus or studio wrestling.

Tony's back slammed against the ground. Rico rolled over and jumped up. He stood over Tony.

"What the fuck is wrong with you?" Rico said. I could see his spit flying everywhere.

Tony got up fast. He hit Rico with a tackle like you'd see on a football field. They were on the ground rolling around. Tony was cussing in English, and Rico was swearing in Italian. Rico got the upper hand. Tony's hands were covering his face. Rico was punching with each hand, hitting Tony's arms.

"J.J.," Tony said, "help me."

I looked for a weapon. There was a shovel in the trunk. I thought again about getting into the front seat and driving away. Why didn't I just do that?

I didn't know what to do. I popped the seat on the passenger's side and got out of the Gremlin. Rico and Tony kept fighting on the grass. Tony was holding his own, somehow. I went to the back of the car. I'd need the keys to open the trunk and get the shovel. But what was I going to do with it? Hit Rico in the face?

Tony had gotten pinned under Rico's kneecaps. I saw Rico reach into the back of his jeans. He pulled out a gun. He pointed it at Tony's forehead. Tony threw his hands between the gun and his head.

"Rico!" I shouted. "Wait!"

Rico kept pointing the gun at Tony. They both were breathing heavily. Sweat from Rico's nose dripped onto Tony's palms.

"Don't do it," Tony said. "Don't do it."

"Rico, we're on the same team here," I said. "We need to work this out."

Rico turned to look at me. The gun was still pointed at Tony.

"Sorry, kid," Rico said.

"Sorry?" I said. "Sorry about what?"

That's when Rico swung his arms toward me. The barrel of the gun went from pointing at Tony to pointing at me. I closed my eyes. I heard a loud bang.

Ninety-one

LESLIE FITZPATRICK

IT TOOK A little while to get my bearings behind the wheel of Johnny's car. It was so much bigger and stronger than mine. Maria just watched me as I tried to figure it all out.

She told me to take I-70, heading west. We went through the tunnel. We went over the bridge. We crossed Wheeling Island. Soon, we were in Ohio.

That's when I asked her where we were going.

"Arizona," Maria said.

"Arizona?"

I couldn't believe it. I shouldn't have been surprised. We were going far away. That was about as far away as we could go.

"Johnny knows people out there," Maria said. "J.J. will be set up with some work. They're getting us a place. Johnny will help pay for everything, too."

"Just like that," I said. "All those years in one place and we're gone. Just like that."

"I don't mind," Maria said. "J.J. is really all I got. With a new family member on the way, I wouldn't want to be on the other side of the country from him. Or her."

"I know how weird this all is," I said. "I didn't plan for it to happen."

"It's OK. It's not like we're really related. I like to say we're related because it always made us more than friends. Now we'll be even more than that."

"Well, we will be that."

Maria got quiet for a little bit.

"I could use a cigarette," she said. "I probably shouldn't."

"You can just roll down the window and blow the smoke out."

"No. I seen enough on TV about it. You don't need any of that stuff around you while you're expecting."

"We'll be in the car for a long time. Arizona is practically California."

"We're not driving to Arizona," she said. "Johnny got us plane tickets. We're flying out of Indianapolis tomorrow."

"What are we doing with the car?"

"I don't know. Leaving it. Johnny said he'll take care of everything. He had this thing forever. Maybe he'll never pick it up."

"Do you know where J.J. is? I thought he'd be the one to come get me."

"Johnny wouldn't say much to me about that. I know he doesn't want me to worry. I got the impression that Johnny and J.J. have something to take care of before J.J. can meet us. He probably will be driving out there, so we may have to stay in a hotel for a couple days."

I turned to look at her.

"What if he doesn't show up?"

"We'll worry about that when it happens. For now, let's try to think happy thoughts. Happy thoughts about new beginnings."

After Maria said it, she opened her purse. She pulled out a pack of cigarettes. She took one out, lit it, and rolled the window open just enough so that the smoke could be sucked out for good.

The sight of it reminded me that I had a letter in my purse. I needed to mail it to my father—but I'd do it in Indianapolis, before we went to the airport. If I sent it from Arizona, someone at the prison might see it and tell Paul where I was.

Ninety-two

OCTOBER 20, 1973

J.J. JENKINS

My entire body flinched at the sound of the gunshot. I closed my eyes and ducked my head. I raised my hands, the same way Tony had. Then I heard a scream. It was high pitched. It was loud. I'd never heard anything like it.

I opened my eyes. I pressed my hands over my head and my face and my chest, trying to figure out where I'd been shot. I hadn't been.

I looked back at Rico and Tony. Tony was trying to get away from Rico. Rico was still on his knees, over Tony.

There was a dark spot just above Rico's left eye. A red circle. That's when I realized that he had been shot. That he was dead.

Tony was the one who was screaming. He kept on screaming as he tried to get away from Rico, or whatever was left of him. I didn't understand why Rico's body wasn't falling over. He was there on his knees, dead and not moving. I'd never seen anything like it. I hope I never see anything like it again. Lifeless face. Eyes open. Body not moving. A corpse propped up like a statue. Blood and brains were sprayed all over the side of the Gremlin. I probably would have gotten sick if I hadn't been so confused about what had just happened.

I turned around. My father was standing there, holding a gun. He was walking toward us. He was pointing it at Tony. I heard a thump. Rico's body finally had fallen backward.

Tony was still screaming. But he was also trying to say something. None of it made any sense. He looked at my father, looked at the gun. Tony finally started crying.

"It wasn't my idea," Tony said. "It wasn't my idea. I just did what I was told. What was I supposed to do? J.J., what was I supposed to do?"

Tony had managed to push himself away from Rico's legs. Tony just sat there on the grass. He wasn't trying to get away. He knew he couldn't.

I turned back to my father. He kept moving toward us. He kept the gun pointed at Tony. He looked at Rico to make sure he was dead. I didn't know much right then. One thing I knew for sure was that Rico was dead.

"J.J.," Tony said to me. "We go back a long ways. We're friends. I had to do it. I'm sorry."

"Quiet," my father said to Tony. "Who gave you the order?"

"Bobby," Tony said. He seemed relieved after he said it. "It was Bobby."

"When did you know?"

"Yesterday," Tony said to my father. Tony suddenly didn't seem quite as relieved.

"When?"

"I don't know when," Tony said. He was getting closer to crying again. "Maybe seven o'clock."

"So you knew about this for almost a full day, and you didn't try to figure out a way to let your friend know what was happening, so he could maybe run away?"

Tony looked at me. He looked back at my father. He looked at me again. He started looking around for anyone to save him from what was about to happen.

"They would've known!" Tony said. He was yelling. "They would've known and I would've been whacked for it!"

My father put a finger over his mouth. Tony got as quiet as he could get.

"Here's what happened," my father said to him. "You made a bet. You thought it was a good bet. A safe bet. Maybe it was. But sometimes even the safest bet blows up in your face."

I shouted, "No!"

It was too late. I heard another loud bang.

Ninety-three

OCTOBER 20, 1973

J.J. JENKINS

I LUNGED AT my father. I pushed his arm, the one holding the gun that was smoking from the hole at the end of the barrel.

"What did you do?"

"They brought you out here to kill you."

I looked at the two bodies next to the Gremlin.

"That could be you," he said. "If I didn't tail you here, it would be."

"You followed us?"

"You think I just happened to stop by?"

"How did they not see you?"

"It helped that I didn't have my car." He pointed away from where he stood. The orange Beetle was sitting there, at the side of the road.

"Leslie's car?" I said. "Why do you have Leslie's car?"

"Because she's got my car. Leslie and your mother are on their way to Arizona."

I looked back at the two bodies.

"Don't feel bad," he said. "It was you or them. They knew what they signed up for."

"How did they not see you behind them?"

"Well, they wasn't real smart. Once I knew who was in the car and once I figured the car was going to Cadiz, I knew they'd bring you here."

"This is the place you were talking about at Bobby's that night?"

"This is it, and it's about to have two more bodies in it."

"So what," I said, "we're burying them?"

"We can't just leave them here." He looked at the Gremlin. "I'd bet good money there's a shovel in there."

"It's in the trunk."

"Well, we need to get to work."

We did. I helped him put the bodies in the front seat of the Gremlin. Rico first, then Tony on top of him. I threw up twice while we did it. After the bodies had been moved, there was a bunch of blood and pink clumps on the ground outside the Gremlin.

"What do we do about that?" I said, pointing to the mess in the grass.

"Nothing," he said. "If anyone notices, the last thing they'll think is two guys got shot here."

He got in the Gremlin. He drove it deeper into Sally Buffalo Park. He went to a spot where the field ended and a forest began. I walked alongside the car as it crept toward wherever he was going. I kept looking around. No one else was out there. It was starting to get dark. The moon was out. It would soon be the only light we'd have. He went into the woods as far as he could before the Gremlin would get stuck.

"We'll have to carry them the rest of the way," he said. "You get the legs."

I didn't want to do it, but what could I do? We had to get rid of them before we could leave. I knew that. We dropped Tony in a spot where they both could be buried. Then we got Rico and brought him to the same place.

My father sent me back to the Gremlin to get the shovel. We took turns digging until the hole was long enough, wide enough, deep enough.

He rolled them both into it. I threw up again. He started shoveling dirt from the pile onto the bodies. We took turns doing that, too. I started crying hard.

"Hey," he said, "I told you we did what we had to do. You'd be in that hole right now, not them. You get that, right?"

"I do." Why did I think this was something I should be doing?

"It's my fault," he said. "You knew what I did but you didn't really know what I did. Now you do. Now you move on from it, from me."

"You make it sound easier than it will be," I said. "I can't move on from what I've seen."

We kept putting dirt on the grave until the bodies were covered. He told me to drive the Beetle back to Wheeling. He took the Gremlin, blood all over the outside and whatever had seeped out from the bodies in the passenger seat.

He told me to park the Beetle in the alley between 17th and 18th Street, by the building where I lived. He said he'd get rid of it the next day. He had a plan for getting the Oldsmobile back from Indianapolis by Tuesday. He said he told my mother to leave the keys hidden inside and the door unlocked.

By Tuesday, I'd be a lot closer to Arizona. Maybe I'd already be there. I didn't know how long it would take. I needed to get away from Wheeling as fast as I could.

I knew I could never go back.

I didn't want to.

Ninety-four

BOBBY WAS AT Paul's, sitting in the chair on the other side of *The Godfather* desk. Paul wasn't happy. Bobby wasn't, either.

"This ain't no good," Bobby said, over and over again.

Paul looked at him. He started shaking his head. "I know it ain't no good," Paul said. "It ain't no good I had to leave my house on a Saturday night and come here and figure out what the hell your guys done."

"It ain't like them," Bobby said, directing his words to both Paul and Vinny, who was standing in his usual spot and saying his usual nothing. "I'm scared."

"Scared about what?" Paul said. "Rico's our best guy when it comes to that kind of stuff, by far. That kid couldn't handle Rico, not in a million years. There's no way he could handle Rico and the other one."

"Tony," Bobby said. "His name's Tony."

"Whatever," Paul said. "Knowing Rico, they went straight to a whorehouse after they was done."

"They always check in after a job like this. Especially this one. How many times have we done this to one of our own?"

"Maybe we need to do it more often than we do," Paul said. He looked at Vinny after he said it.

Bobby fumbled with his combover. "I did exactly what Vinny told me to do," he said. "We had a plan. It was a good plan. It was easy. Like you said, Rico's our best guy for this."

"So why the fuck did you drag me in here?"

"Because I know something happened."

"So why don't you drive out to the place and look around?"

"That's what you want me to do?" Bobby said.

"Here's what I want," Paul said. "I want this job done. If it's done, it's done. If it ain't done, that's a different issue."

"I guess I need to go to Cadiz then."

"You need to do whatever you need to do to get me an answer. But I don't want to hear nothing until tomorrow morning. Now, can I go home? My wife is already pissed off at me. The sooner I get home, the better the chance I actually sleep inside the house tonight."

Ninety-five

JOHNNY MESAGNE

AFTER J.J. TOLD me about his meeting at four o'clock, I knew I had to change things up. I had time to do everything I needed to do, but not as much as I would have liked.

The college football games was starting at noon. I needed to get to the bar and take the bets. But then I needed to get down to the real work. I had to go get Maria. I had to see if she'd go to Arizona. Then I had to see if Leslie would go, too. Then I had to get them on their way.

I went back to Mrs. DiPasquale's apartment to make more calls. I gave her another hundred bucks. She was starting to get a little leery about everything. She probably figured she was too old to get whacked, if it came to that. Maybe she was.

I called the guy in Baltimore who could line up plane tickets, fast. He still owed me a favor for something I handled before I got out of the life. He said he'd thought I forgot about it. He knew it was time to make good.

I wanted to get them far enough away from here before they flew, so I picked Indianapolis. He said he'd book the tickets. I had to trust him. I had to believe he knew there would be consequences if I couldn't. I told him I'd mail a check on Monday for the plane fare. I told him I'd throw in an extra thirty percent for his trouble. He laughed and said that was maybe too much, but he didn't tell me not to do it.

I got to the bar at ten. The place started to fill up. The phone was ringing with bets for the games. I focused as best I could on doing the job, same as always. Jimmy showed up by eleven. He would be the key to making everything work.

I asked Jimmy to take over. I told him I would be gone from right after noon until maybe two. There was something I had to do. No, I couldn't tell him what I was doing.

He agreed to help. He knew how to take the bets, how to keep the records. I mean, the guy had been an accountant. He said he'd swallow the evidence and wash it down with a beer if the cops showed up. I laughed when he said that. I told him that cops showing up to bust a gambling joint that had been working out in the open for years was the least of my concerns that day.

I left at five after twelve. I went to the house. Maria was expecting me; I'd called her from Mrs. DiPasquale's after lining up the plane tickets. I told Maria I'd be stopping by at half past twelve, maybe a little earlier. I told her she needed to be ready to hear something pretty big. I told her she needed to be ready to make an even bigger decision. She made some joke about maybe I was going to ask her to marry me again. I didn't say nothing when she said that. That probably let her know something serious was going on.

I pulled up to the house at twenty-six minutes after twelve. She was standing inside the door, waiting for me. I walked inside and got to the point. She started crying after I told her that J.J. was in real danger, and that he had to leave town right away. I told her about Arizona. She agreed to go with him. I told her it only made sense if Leslie went, too. I told her, no matter what, she needed to be wherever Leslie was, since Leslie was going to be having our grandchild. Maria kept right on crying when I told her that.

Maria packed faster than she ever packed in her life. We left to get

Leslie at a quarter to one. By the top of the hour, Leslie and Maria was on their way to Indianapolis, in my car.

I still had plenty of work to do. I went back to the bar. I handled the action on the late afternoon games. I asked Jimmy to take over again. I needed to go by Bobby's place and figure out what was going on. I told Jimmy maybe I would be back in less than an hour. I told him maybe I wouldn't be back at all. I told him if I wasn't back by six o'clock he should lock up and go home. If I got back before eleven, I would go to Jimmy's house to get the keys. If I didn't make it by then, we'd meet at the bar the next morning. I had to hope Vinny wouldn't come sniffing around while I was gone.

Jimmy, God love him, asked for only one thing from me. He wanted the full story on whatever I was doing and why I was doing it. I told him I'd tell him the whole thing the next day. I owed him at least that much.

It was getting close to four when I parked Leslie's car in a spot that put me close enough to see what was happening but hopefully far enough away from being seen. I wished that damn car wasn't orange. It stood out like a sore fucking thumb.

I saw J.J. going toward the door at Bobby's. J.J. went inside pretty quick.

I looked at the passenger seat. There was the gun I brung. I picked it up and held it. I didn't want to have to use it, but I would if I needed to. I hadn't shot it in a long time. I hoped it still worked.

I waited and watched. Maybe a half-hour later, Rico, J.J., and one of the others walked out of the dog shop. They got into an ugly little car on the other side of the street. They pulled away. I followed them, close enough to see where they was going. I counted on them not being smart enough to check to see if they was being tailed.

I figured out what was going to happen when they started to drive toward Cadiz. I was glad I came, even if it meant I'd need to use that gun. If it meant saving my kid, I would've used my bare hands if I had to.

On the way back from Cadiz, I stopped at a car wash to clean up that piece of shit they drove there. I scrubbed the outside and sprayed the inside, in the spot where the bodies had been. I wanted it to be ready for the drive to Arizona. I hoped the thing could make it that far.

I took it back to J.J.'s apartment. I parked it a couple blocks away, where it wouldn't be noticed. I walked to J.J.'s. He was still shook up. I told him he needed to snap out of it, for his own good. We swapped car keys.

On the way there, I kept checking to see if anyone was watching me. No one was around. Why would they be? They thought Rico and the other one had taken care of J.J. in Ohio. As far as the rest of them knew, it was over.

I threw the kid a curveball. I told him he should leave by midnight. I told him the head start would help, since they wouldn't figure out what had really happened until the next morning.

I also told him not to take the Plymouth, that he should just leave it parked on the street. Maybe they would think he was in town if his car was still there. I also told him to keep the lights in his apartment off, since Bobby's place was just down the street.

I told J.J. I'd stop back just before midnight, right before he left. J.J. said I didn't need to do that, since it had been such a long day and I was probably tired. I told him I needed to be sure he got started on the trip to Arizona.

He said the Volkswagen was in the alley, right where I told him to put it. I told him again I'd take care of it the next day, that I'd just walk back to my apartment for now.

That was the only lie I told him. After I left his apartment, I doubled back to the alley. I started the Volkswagen and drove away. J.J. didn't need to know what I was going to do next.

Ninety-six

JOHNNY MESAGNE

IT WAS HALF past eight by then. I drove to Jimmy's. I never been to his place before, but I knew where he lived. He had a nice little house in Fulton, near the bottom of the big hill that led to downtown. I parked on the street and went to his door. Jimmy opened it right away, even before I could knock. He seemed excited, I guess, by everything that had been going on. If he knew what was really going on, he wouldn't have been so excited.

He held out the keys to the bar.

"You look like you've had quite the day," he said.

"Is it that obvious?"

"I can tell you've been through the wringer. I'll look forward to hearing the whole story in the morning."

"The story's still not over," I said. "But it should be soon. You'll get every detail tomorrow."

"It's about your son, isn't it?" he said.

"It is, but that's all you're getting for now."

"Whatever you're doing, if you're doing it for the good of your son, you're doing a good thing. Just remember that."

I think I smiled. I can't really remember.

Ninety-seven

OCTOBER 20, 1973

JOHNNY MESAGNE

AFTER I LEFT Jimmy's, I got back in that Volkswagen. I sat there for a long time. I held the the keys to the car in one hand. I held the keys to the bar in the other. I finally put the keys to the bar in my pocket. I started the car. I turned it around and started driving to a place I hadn't been in years.

PAUL WAS MAD his Saturday night had been disrupted. Vinny agreed with Paul. There was no way Rico and the other one hadn't managed to take care of the kid. No way at all.

Then again, Bobby was as scared as Vinny had ever seen him. Vinny couldn't just ignore that.

Vinny followed Paul down the hallway and into the main room, with Bobby trailing Vinny. Paul moved as fast as he could to get to the car and get home. Vinny slowed down and turned to Bobby.

"Go back to your place," Vinny said, whispering in Bobby's ear. "I'll take him home and I'll meet you there. We'll figure out what we need to do. Call Tommy and Phil and tell them to be ready to go. Don't tell them what for. We can send them to Cadiz to check things out, if we need to."

Bobby still seemed scared. Paul didn't notice anything. He was far too focused on getting home to his wife.

JOHNNY MESAGNE

I PULLED ONTO Paul's street. Everything about his place was normal. Normal house, normal yard, normal driveway, normal garage, normal neighborhood. Normal neighbors who knew Paul's life wasn't exactly normal. I figured they treated him like they treated their other neighbors. No one ever wants to get too close to a gangster, but no one ever complains about knowing one. You never know when it could come in handy.

I figured he'd be home. His wife had always insisted they spend Saturday nights together. She was smart enough to know he had someone on the side, but she was still his wife.

The Cadillac was parked in the driveway. I parked the Volkswagen behind it. I got out. I walked up onto the porch and rang the bell. I could see someone moving through the blur of the peephole in the door. It swung open.

"John Mesagne," Sally said. She acted happy I was there. I knew her good enough to know she wasn't. She turned around. "Paul," she said. "Guess who's here? It's your friend John Mesagne."

She gave me another smile. It was fake. I didn't care. I just needed to say to him what I needed to say.

"It's so good to see you," she said before walking away. "How's Maria doing?"

"Maria's good, far as I know," I said. And that really was the truth, as far as I knew. "How've you been?"

"Just great. Just wonderful. Absolutely wonderful. Well, here's Paul. Please do take as much time with him as you need."

Paul's face looked normal until Sally was gone. Then it got all mean and red.

"What the fuck are you doing here? You come to my house? You better be drunk or high or both."

"Nice to see you, too," I said.

"Fuck that," he said. He looked over his shoulder to make sure she was gone. "Why the fuck are you here?"

That's when I told him my story. My story about what had happened in Ohio. My story about what had happened with Leslie. But none of it was true. I said all of it to buy J.J. some time.

Paul listened to me. When I was done, he said I was full of shit. That my story made no sense. That six years after Leslie left me for Paul, there was no way she'd cheat on Paul with me. So I stepped back and pointed to Leslie's car, parked right behind the Cadillac. I held up the keys to it.

Then I turned around and left. I told him to tell Sally I said to have a good night.

Ninety-eight

VINNY MET BOBBY at Doggie Do-Rights after Vinny took Paul back to his house. They were trying to figure out what to do about Ohio. Bobby thought his only choice was to send his guys there to see what was going on.

The phone rang while they were talking it all through. Bobby answered. His eyes bulged. It was Paul, calling from his own house. Paul was looking for Vinny. Bobby told Paul that Vinny was sitting right over here.

Bobby knew Paul didn't like talking on the phone anywhere, especially not from his own house. But Bobby also had never heard Paul sound that way before. Paul was so mad that Bobby almost didn't recognize Paul's voice.

He gave Bobby an order. Bobby still couldn't believe Paul was saying those things on a phone line. Bobby didn't say anything back to Paul. Bobby just listened. He eventually told Paul they'd do what he wanted them to do.

"And do it right fucking now!" Paul yelled the words, even though Bobby had already said they'd do it.

Bobby hung up the phone.

Vinny was just looking at Bobby. He'd heard the other end of the call. He stood up from the table.

"Well," Vinny said, "so much for sending two of your guys to Cadiz."

Ninety-nine

OCTOBER 20, 1973

J.J. JENKINS

I PARKED THE orange Beetle in the alley, right where my father told me to put it. I went back to my apartment. I finished packing. I checked for the compass again. I still couldn't find it.

I ate some ham and cheese from the fridge. I drank two of the beers Tony and Willie had brought me. I thought of Tony. My knees gave out. No matter what he and Rico were planning to do to me, Tony had been my friend.

I heard someone coming up the steps. I got myself together. It was my father, with the keys to the Gremlin. He actually wanted me to drive that thing to Arizona. And he wanted me to leave at midnight, not in the morning.

I didn't like it, but he made sense. It was time to go. It wasn't like I was going to sleep very much that night, anyway. I might as well start putting permanent distance between myself and Wheeling.

Paul's people thought I was dead. Every minute they thought that was true was another minute for me to get farther away. I agreed to leave by twelve o'clock, sharp.

My father told me to keep the lights off. He'd be back just before midnight. I told him he didn't need to come back. He said he was coming back, anyway.

I looked for that damn compass again. It pissed me off that I couldn't find it. It had to be back at the house. I didn't really have time to go there looking for it. Besides, my father wouldn't want me to. But it wasn't like he was going to know about it.

I found that little alarm clock. I cranked it up and set the bell for half past ten. I crawled onto the couch. Those two hours went by in a flash. I woke up, snapping out of a fog. I got the keys to the Gremlin, and I left for the house on Poplar Avenue.

I parked in front just before eleven. I walked inside. I flipped on the lights and started looking around. Since my mother had left so fast, I found a box and filled it with things she might want—some pots and pans she always used, some of her favorite utensils. I found a smaller box for some little decorations I knew she liked. I grabbed some old photos from the bedroom, ones she had in frames.

Then I started searching for that damn compass.

I checked the top of the desk. I checked the drawer of the desk. I checked the drawer of my dresser. I checked the thin strip of floor space around my bed. I looked under the bed. I checked the closet. I did it all again. I was getting hot and sweaty.

I finally ripped the mattress from the box spring. And there it was, right where I'd kept the envelopes of cash before I moved to my own apartment. I didn't remember putting it there. Maybe I had, I don't know. I wondered for a second whether my mother had put it there. But that would make no sense. Too bad I couldn't ask her. I hoped that I soon would be able to.

I picked up the compass. I held it. I spun it around. I looked at the needle, pointing right through the door that led from my bedroom and then out the door that led from the house. I put the compass in my hand and squeezed it.

I stood there, thinking. I thought about when he'd given it to me. I thought about everything he'd done back then. I thought about everything he was doing now.

I changed my mind about something. I went to the kitchen to find a piece of paper and a pen.

One hundred

JOHNNY MESAGNE

I DROVE BACK to my apartment after telling all those lies to Paul. I sat on the floor. I smoked a cigarette. I stared at the wall. It really needed to be painted. I didn't bother to hide the Beetle outside, because Paul knew I had it.

The phone started ringing. I pushed myself up and went to it. I held my hand over the receiver and let it ring a couple more times. I didn't really want to answer it. I figured I should.

"We're in Indianapolis," Maria said. "We're staying at a Holiday Inn near town. I left so fast today, I didn't get much cash."

"How much do you have?"

"A couple hundred dollars. There's a shoebox under my bed with more. Can you go get it and give it to J.J. before he leaves?"

"How much more?"

"At least eight thousand."

"Eight thousand? Where did you get eight thousand dollars?"

"Little by little. Look, I had to protect myself. I had to protect our son. It'll come in handy out here."

I looked at my watch. It was almost eleven.

"He's leaving in the morning," I said, lying to her so she wouldn't worry any more than she already was. "I'll get it before he goes."

"Just go get it now," she said. "You always put things off until the last minute. Who knows what'll happen by the time it's morning?"

I stopped to think about what she said. She didn't know how right she was.

"How's Leslie?" I said.

"She's Leslie. But she's not Leslie. All of this has changed her. In a good way, I think. At least I hope. I don't know yet, really."

After we hung up, I left the apartment. I started up the Beetle for the drive to the house on Poplar Avenue.

I didn't check to see if I was being tailed. I suppose I was too worn out to care.

One hundred one

OCTOBER 20, 1973

JOHNNY MESAGNE

I GOT TO the house on Poplar Avenue at about thirty minutes to twelve. I still had a key to the front door. I used it to get in. A few lights was on. It all felt different to me. Stuff was missing. Stuff I didn't remember Maria taking when she got herself packed that afternoon.

I wondered what would happen to the place if she never come back. Maybe I'd move in. Maybe I'd sell it.

I went to our old room to get the money. There it was, under the bed just like she said. I took off the lid. It was full of cash. I counted all of it. Eight thousand, two hundred, and twenty-seven dollars. I thought about keeping everything above the eight dimes. But I just put it in two big wads and stuffed them in my front pockets. I'd give it all to the kid to take with him.

The house still felt weird to me. I walked around for a little bit. I could almost hear our voices from dinners and holidays and happy times. Not that there was too many happy times. But there was some.

It felt so different, but still the same. It was empty and it was full. Full of those memories from a different time. A different life is what it really was. Might as well have been a different person.

I walked around some more. I decided I'd sell the place. I could never live here again, not without them.

I turned on the light in J.J.'s room. I hadn't stood right in that spot since the night I left, the night I'd found that old compass and made up some bullshit story about it being something that was passed down from father to son and so on. I looked down at the desk. There was a piece of paper, folded in half. It had "Dad" written on it.

I picked it up. I read it. I read it again. I just shook my head and tried not to cry.

I folded up that paper. I stuck it in one of my pockets. I reached down and picked up the compass. I looked at it. The needle was pointing to the front door. I squeezed it in my hand and walked that way.

One hundred two

THE NOTE IN John Mesagne's pocket was written on a piece of paper that wasn't stained by any of his blood. It was retrieved by police who had arrived in response to the highly unusual occasion of a man being gunned down in a suburban neighborhood in a small West Virginia town. The note was tweezered into a bag separate from the one that would hold more than eight thousand dollars in cash, until after the case was closed as unsolved and the money was returned to his estate for processing along with the rest of the property to be distributed on behalf of a man who had died without a will.

His closest relatives, a son and an ex-wife, had left the jurisdiction without notice or information as to their whereabouts. He had no living siblings. As a result, a niece in North Carolina received an unexpected surprise nineteen months later, in the form of a certified check from the Circuit Court of Ohio County, West Virginia. It paid her the money that was in his pockets on the night he was killed. She'd eventually get another check for the net proceeds from the sale of the house on Poplar Avenue, since the house had at all times been listed in his name.

She also received an envelope with a letter explaining that the enclosed piece of paper was found in the deceased's pocket. On one side, it said *Dad*. On the other side, it said this:

You gave me the compass when you left home. Now that I'm leaving home, I'm giving it back to you. I appreciate what you've done for me. I know I should have listened to you from the start. I finally did. That should count for something, right? I know what would have happened if you hadn't shown up today. I hope I will be the same way when I'm a father. I hope when it matters most, I can do for my children what you did for me.

The note was signed *J.J. Mesagne.*

One hundred three

OCTOBER 21, 1973

JIMMY DACEY

I GOT TO Johnny's bar just before nine o'clock on Sunday morning. The lights inside weren't on. I tried to twist the knob. As I expected, it wouldn't turn.

I knocked on the door. I waited a little while before knocking again.

I stepped back. I looked around for any sign of Johnny. He'd promised to tell me what had happened the day before. I was ready to hear all of it.

I adjusted the knot in my tie. I pulled back the cuff of my sleeve to check my watch. It was fifteen minutes after nine.

Soon, one of the other regulars showed up. He said hello to me. He tried the door. I didn't stop him from finding out for himself that it was locked.

"Where's he at?" the man said to me. I shrugged. He muttered something about a bet he wanted to make before the football games started later that day. He said he didn't want to have to bet with someone else because he was up more than a hundred from the college games the day before and he wanted to let it ride on the Steelers giving seven to the Jets.

I shrugged again. The man grumbled away, saying he'd come back later.

OCTOBER 21, 1973

J.J. MESAGNE

I GOT BACK to the apartment at half past eleven. I put the suitcase in the Gremlin and went back upstairs to wait for my father.

At twelve o'clock, there was no sign of him. At ten after, I cursed that I didn't have a phone. I grabbed some coins and went back to the payphone outside Neely's Market. I was surprised I still remembered the number, after everything that had happened that day.

I dropped the dime. I dialed. I let it ring over and over again. I hung up. The coin fell. I placed it into the slot again. I dialed again. Still no answer. I hung up and walked away. I left the coin in the slot.

I headed back to my apartment. On the way, I decided to make a quick stop.

OCTOBER 21, 1973

JIMMY DACEY

I WAITED IN that same spot. The hands on my watch moved past ten o'clock and began to creep toward eleven. I could hear the phone inside ringing from time to time, usually two or three calls in a row. Several more of the regulars showed up. They asked where Johnny was. Some of them got mad at me because Johnny wasn't there. I wanted to say to them, "How is it my fault?" I didn't. I was too nervous that he wasn't coming at all.

OCTOBER 21, 1973

J.J. MESAGNE

I PULLED OFF my T-shirt and wrapped it around my right fist. I punched one of the panes in the broad lattice of the front door to

Doggie Do-Rights. Glass shattered. The dogs started to bark, loud. I reached in and flipped the lock.

I went inside. No lights were on, but I could see well enough from the glow of the street lamps through the windows. I put my T-shirt back on as I walked. I got to the cages. There were five dogs. I bent down to see Gnocchi.

"Want to go for a ride?" I said.

OCTOBER 21, 1973

JIMMY DACEY

EVENTUALLY, ONE OF the local police officers—one of the many who never came around, who never gave Johnny a hard time about anything because they were all appropriately taken care of—walked down from the station and whispered something to me. Then he turned around and headed back the way he came.

I sighed deeply. I pulled back the cuff of my shirt. I checked the watch one more time. I looked around, searching for any proof that what I'd just been told possibly was a mistake.

The stream of regulars had subsided. Word apparently was getting around about what had happened. Just before noon, I started back toward my car.

My mind raced. I tried to think of my poems. Of anything other than what had happened. Different verses sprang into my brain. One of them finally stuck. As I walked, I recited it.

"Luck is not chance. It's toil. Fortune's expensive smile is earned. The father of mine is that old-fashioned coin we spurned."

ACKNOWLEDGEMENTS

MY DAD WAS a gambler. Once he realized the house always wins, he became a bookie.

In Wheeling, West Virginia, no bookie worked on his own. My dad was connected to the local mob. The boss was Paul Hankish. In 1964, Hankish's car exploded. The blast was supposed to kill him. Instead, it merely blew off both of his legs. Which of course caused him to be known from that point forward by the subtle and nuanced nickname of "No Legs."

As far as I ever knew, my dad was a bookie and only a bookie. But I once found a clip with a couple bullets missing in one of his jackets. I showed it to my mom, who took it, looked at it, tucked it into the pocket of her housecoat, and never breathed a word of it to anyone.

I didn't know much about what the Hankish crew did at the time. I've learned more about it since then, based on articles and other public information. (No Omertà was violated in the writing of this book.)

I got the inspiration for *Father of Mine* in a dream I had the night I turned 55. I thought about it the next day and, the day after that, I sat down and started writing. I finished the first draft within two months, and I spent many hours after that editing, revising, and eventually rewriting most of the book. I then read it and revised it again and again and again and eventually realized the process had to end at some point. It finally has ended. For better or worse.

Along the way, several people helped me find the right path and get there. My agent, David Black, had great ideas for improving the story. I resisted at first, before realizing he was right. The book was and is better than it would have been, thanks to his help.

When I decided to bypass the traditional publishing model, Drew Magary helped me understand that the process of going it alone isn't nearly as complicated as it seems. With the platform we've built at ProFootballTalk.com over the past 20-plus years, it made sense to cut out the middleman, drop the price point, and go straight to the consumer.

Clair Lamb did an excellent job of editing and revising the manuscript. When I was looking for someone to give it one final proofreading before sending it to print, Ron Vaccaro of NBC Sports volunteered to do it. I knew that, if there were any lingering typos or errors, he would spot them. (And he did.)

My nephew, Anthony Zych, crafted the cover. That was an unexpectedly rewarding part of the process, trading ideas and concepts while shaping the cover into something we both thought was pleasing to the eye and meaningful to the story, in multiple ways. Anthony is a very talented artist, as the cover confirms. My dad, who had a very close relationship with Anthony and died when Anthony was only ten years old, would be very proud of him.

Ultimately, thanks to you for reading the book. Assuming that you actually read the book and didn't just buy it so that you could read the acknowledgements. Now that you have, give the book a try.

Printed in Great Britain
by Amazon

54687070R00225